Fantasy Titles by

M L CHAMBERS

Creatures that Breathe

Never Lovelier

Destroy Our Delights

Kendry the Vicious

M L CHAMBERS

# DESTROY OUR DELIGHTS

A VENGEANCE AND VOWS NOVEL

# Content Warning

Please be advised, this book contains mature themes. For a complete list of content warnings, visit m-l-chambers.com.

A special note on gender. In this novel, 'female' and 'male' are used to reference a *creature*'s gender. However, this is for ease of separating *creatures* from mortals and is a representation of gender expression, not sex assigned at birth. It also reflects the character's viewpoints on the separation of creatures and mortals. Notoriously, the Greeks and their gods were inclusive with regard to gender identity and expression as well as sexual orientation, and the same is true within these pages.

*Cover Design by Moonpress* | *www.moonpress.co*

"We are perpetually laboring to **destroy our delights**, our composure, our devotion to superior power. Of all the animals on earth we least know what is good for us."

Homer, *The Iliad*

## Atlas

### THE PATH CONTINUES

Time continues to circle.

Same as the Titans failed their children, the Olympians, so did the Olympians fail their children, the mortals.

Mortals have cast aside the Gods that breathed them to life, and creatures, distant descendants of the Divine, those imbued with the immortal blood, ichor, live in hiding.

Restless.

Seething.

Fighting amongst themselves for scraps of power.

Chaining the weak.

Killing the outcasts.

My family included.

We were broken, disappearing, creatures going extinct, power draining, until Hope came.

King Kadmos, Vein of Elpis, the Unifier, Dawn's Blade, the Crusader, the Last of his Blood, Final in the Line of Hope, forged unity through strength. The Great King banished ancient blood rites, eviscerated old prejudices, and pushed for mortals and creatures to co-exist in peace.

Those in power never want change.

Adversaries, Gods, immortals, and beasts alike fought the King.

To defend Kadmos's virtuous charge, he recruited the most skilled warriors to be his sword, and a motley crew of mortals and creatures became the heroic Kingsguard. So effective was the Kingsguard that when Kadmos married, he formed the Queensguard for his wife, Queen Vinia, Protectress of Creatures, She of the Mortal Realm, the Hope of Hope.

The members of both guards were gifted extreme power to force change and launch hope. It was working.

Until thirty-eight years ago, the Kingsguard failed.

Kadmos's assassination ended the war and the charge for change. The Kingsguard, for their failure, was cursed. Branded with marks on their necks, they fell from grace, hated by both sides of the war, and became the Blackguard.

Mercenaries bound by tragedy, cursed by Hope.

We live in the fringe, in your backyard, searching, scrambling for our cure: the death of Kadmos's killer. Every year that passes without our revenge, our curse worsens. It's marks have spread to our wrists, our ankles. Soon it will kill us.

Hunted by the Queensguard, hated by creatures, we are forgotten by the Gods.

Our only lead to avenge Kadmos is that of a Divine sigil branded into the flesh of a creature we freed from captivity. She vows no connection to the Great King, but only those of his Divine blood can impart his sigil.

This, and the Queensguard's attempt to hide all evidence of her existence must mean Kadmos was betrayed by someone within his own palace. Determining the origin of her sigil steer us to who among the King's inner circle plotted against him.

For Hope, we now leave the path of vengeance to Drake.

# Drake

IT WAS A SELF-DESTRUCTIVE ENDEAVOR BORN OF HUBRIS AND INSECURITY

*Philadelphia, 1923*

I'm staring down the barrel of a gun over nine stolen dollars, and all I see is Ma's face.

When these black-suited goons knock on our door, she'll answer with flour-dusted hands, her scream piercing the neighborhood quiet before she collapses. I picture her kneeling there on our worn floorboards, apron bunched against her face, white powder puffing into the air with each sob.

Kathleen and Brigid, they'll do what older sisters do—harden their chins and fetch Father Donnelly from Seventh Street to light a votive. But little Eileen? Christ, she's barely ten. She'll cry until her face matches her copper hair, eyes swelling shut just like when they found Da face-down in that drainage ditch after he bet the house on a lame horse.

Ma used to pinch my cheek and call me 'your father's son' like it was something to be proud of. That stopped cold the day she found the bookies' notes and empty liquor bottles hidden behind the coats. After that, Da would stagger home with empty pockets, blaming her for every sideways glance from the neighbors. "Should've never married Irish," he'd mutter into his collar, as if his own mother hadn't stepped off the same damn boat.

I was only six when Eileen was born, but I still see Da's face twisting at the sight of those copper curls on her tiny head.

Da wouldn't hear of me having a proper name like Seamus or Patrick—said it'd mark me too Irish for decent work. So I doubled down, thickened my brogue until it dripped like Irish whiskey from my tongue. Made his entire face pucker red.

The neighborhood boys didn't take kindly to it. But while they bloodied my nose, their wallets lay unguarded. A split lip was a fair trade for the coins I'd lift—enough for penny candy, the occasional wager, and eventually, a seat at the bar where men nodded at me like I belonged.

I liked that feeling. The high.

Turns out, I take after Da a little too well.

Each breath burns like I've swallowed broken glass, my lungs still heaving from the chase. My Sunday trousers tear against the concrete where they've shoved me down, kneecaps throbbing against cold stone.

Beside me, a gray-haired fella who should've known better weeps worse than a sinner at Mass. On his left, another's teeth chatter like dice in a cup, ratty clothes soaked as if he's been dunked in the Schuylkill.

The tall, lanky goon who snatched me looms over my bent form, nostrils flared, breath sharp with onions and cheap rye. "Cosgrave's the pickpocket. Stole from our feckin' pocket. Cost me a bloody eye."

His partner's eyes are bright. "Kid's got sand. Didn't piss himself running." Like he's impressed. Like we're swapping legends over a round at Haggerty's, not splitting open our kneecaps on gravel.

They're Murphy's men. Dressed in fine charcoal suits only they wear, matching hats, cufflinks of light silver palms. Every week another lad disappears off my street only to show up a month later, eight pounds heavier with a black eye and a charcoal suit.

Murphy's boys like to say the wool's sharp enough to make you bleed. Whole street's convinced they're tailored from human skin, dyed with gunpowder.

I believe it, now, kneeling here, counting my last breaths.

My neck cracks as I lift my gaze to the pistols poking free from their sleeves. "You'll make a mess if you do it here," I say. "Neighbors'll know. Cops'll come sniffing. Italians hang close—maybe they don't like bodies near 'em"

The one with the gap-tooth sighs, rolling his wrist with the weight of the piece. "No cops gonna bust into our dealings. They owe us for cleaning up the filth, ain't that right, Conor?"

Conor's long nose wrinkles. "We got the coppers in our pocket, and them Italians are scared of us, not the other way round."

"Murphy's scared," I say.

Otherwise, his gambling dens would be all over this city.

The gun digs into my cheek. "Murphy will paint that on your tombstone, Cosgrave."

"Nah, he'll carve it on your sister's pretty back," Conor muses, anticipating, like he's already sampling them on his tongue.

"Murphy ain't got the time," says Gap-Tooth. "But we'll put them to work paying off your debts. All night, every night. Ain't a man on this block doesn't want up their skirts."

My stomach drops, twists, and fills with cement slush. "Leave them alone—"

The pistol whips my forehead. Pain slices at my temple, shakes my teeth.

Conor shakes out his hand. "I wager Murphy gets the redhead, but the other two?" A smirk. "They'd be busy. Debt's gotta be paid. Flesh or blood. Or both."

His gun tilts under my chin, cold pressed to the bone.

There's a hot, meaty taste in my mouth. For a second I imagine his bullet tearing up through palate and tongue, blowing out the back of my skull. The noise it would make. The mess. Bits of me glistening on shoes worth more than our whole apartment, slicking the fucking sidewalk.

They want me to cry. Want whimpering, begging, sobbing. I wonder if I can manage it, just for show.

Can't.

I glare into the Gap-Tooth's grin, blood in the cracks of my teeth. "You won't touch them. I won't fucking let you."

"What are you gonna do?" Conor taunts.

"I'll kill you!"

They laugh. I'm a big amusement. Course I am—they're holding guns, wearing hats. They have the power, not me.

"Start with Cosgrave," Conor says. "I'm sick of his mouth." A pause. "Go on then."

"Me?" Gap-Tooth frowns. "I got the snotty gambler not last week."

"Yeah, 'cause it's your job. Handle it."

"Matilda just washed my suit nice. We've got a date."

"Tilly's gonna get washing again, then, yeah?"

Gap-Tooth's knuckles shake, rolling nerves under beefy skin. He hesitates with his aim. Doesn't have the stomach for it.

I do.

"Let me do it." My pulse is rabbit-wild, but my voice stays steady. "I'll shoot 'em for you. Easy. Cleaner that way."

Conor snorts. "You? A fucking rat? You'd shoot your own?"

"It's them or me. I want to leave my sisters out of this, and I don't care about dirtying my clothes."

Conor's got denial on his face, but Gap-Tooth's hand drops. "You ever held a gun?"

No.

Never wanted to. Never hit someone harder than a slap

over the skull. I show my teeth. "Just tell me where you want them."

They weigh it. Brains scraping two thoughts together.

Then Gap-Tooth hands me his gun, grip warm and sweaty from his palm. It's not as heavy as I guessed. Smaller too. Like a toy I could lose in an afternoon. Nothing that could kill.

I grip it tight. My breath goes citric—acid-bright. Scorched steel under my tongue, rust and rage and a crisp back-alley static.

I could shoot them.

Two shots, I walk away.

But I'd have to raze the entire block to keep it from Murphy's ears.

It'd be worse then. Personal. Not just a thief—a killer. A murderer. Conor lends me a hand up, cufflinks shining silver. He wouldn't have time to duck. We're too close for shit aim to matter. Any shot would kill him.

I take his hand and rise.

The gun's just an extension of my hand now. Heavy as guilt. Familiar as lying to priests.

Gap-Tooth shoves the first mark forward. The old man, snot-and-tears kind of weeping, fear rolling off him like the black clouds that puff out of the steel mills. "Get on with it then, Cosgrave. Quick." He grins, tongue worrying at his teeth. "Prove you ain't soft. Or we do your sisters next. Right here where they can watch you decompose."

I picture our neighbor Nanette dragging her bedsheets over on wash day and telling Ma, "Did ya not hear? Drake, the city's best mistake. The boy put a bullet in two sorry souls. All 'cause he didna want to pay back his thievin'."

Better gossip than a grave.

Better these two than my sisters.

I grip the pistol, slick with other men's deaths. Conor's

gaze skips to the dirty snow blocking the street drain. He doesn't want to watch.

"You ever killed a man, Cosgrave?" Gap-Tooth asks. He doesn't look away, makes the hair on my arms lift, thinking about why. What else he's seen. Or done.

"Does it matter?" I thumb the hammer back.

It takes me four hours to drag their deadweight through back alleys to Schuylkill, where I stuff rocks into limp pockets and dump them. The river swallows them without complaint.

My stomach empties itself again and again until there's nothing left but clear, frothy bile, and then I retch for another hour.

I try to wash my hands in the bank, water like ice, but I'm shaking too hard. Red sticks to my fingernails.

When I deliver their full wallets to Conor, he's not alone. The man is older, taller, cleaner cut. His suit whispers money instead of shouting it. But I'd recognize him in nothing but his shorts and a bag over his head just from his stance. Legs spread, leaning back, hands loose. Arrogant. Colin Murphy. He studies me with eyes that see profit in broken things. "You're a survivor. Just like me."

He offers me a job.

"One you'll take well to or die trying," he says.

I accept with a numb nod.

Ma's waiting when I stumble through our door for supper. She cups my face, narrow thumbs gentle on my temples. "Neighbor's been talking. Sherry's cousin saw you with those Murphy loons." Steam rises from the pot behind her, a thin broth that'll have to stretch between four bowls. "People ought to mind their business." She turns, using her skirt to take the soup off the stove.

She pretends not to see the mud on my knees. I tug my sleeves down over the fleck of blood.

"Don't worry about me, Ma. I'm grown." My voice is steadier than it has any right to be. "Nobody's going to give us trouble anymore, and I'm out of it, I promise." I clear my throat. "In fact, I got myself an … apprenticeship."

Her mouth tightens, flat and pale as linen drying on the line, but her gaze doesn't waver. "Doing what, exactly?"

She knows. She always does. The way a priest knows when absolution's a lie.

I want to tell her I've been blessed by the Virgin herself, hired to shine shoes. Sweep floors.

But Eileen's green eyes appear dinner-plate wide from the hallway. Brigid's shadow curves around the door in question marks, arms folded, jaw already braced for a fight. Kathleen's arms cross in knots, elbows sharp as a butcher's edge.

I keep it simple.

"I'm taking out the trash. Cleaning. Stuff like that." I sink into the chair. "It'll be good. I'll be good at it."

Conor's parting words echo through my head: "It gets easier."

Ma doles out supper with a hush. We eat to the tinny sound of Mr. Doyle's radio filtering through the ceiling. When I finish scrubbing the last plate, Ma's hand catches my wrist, grip still strong despite everything. "Whatever mess you've stepped into," she whispers, "do not track it through this house, Drake."

"I'll never let it touch you." I mean it with everything in me.

Still, I'm an orphan by the next winter.

Lowering Brigid and Kathleen into the cold ground in the following fall. When spring comes, Eileen's gone too—vanished before I can beg her to save herself from what follows me like a shadow.

1

# Theia

## THE DARKNESS BEHIND HIM FELT HUNGRY

*Present Day*

Exhibit D that Rod is a Bad Person worthy of spontaneous hemorrhaging: the obscene chrome sticker on his flat-brimmed hat. It catches the over-white kitchen light and glints directly at my eyes, like a miniature disco ball of awfulness.

That's what he is—a party favor left over from a lesser God's trash heap. He smirks at me, all teeth, fingers still hovering where he'd just attempted to massage my neck, as if he's considering whether to try again or call me a prude.

Combine this anthropological discovery with the skull-encrusted vape pen in his jeans pocket, his habit of calling the bartenders 'Champ' as if they were his interchangeable children, and how he's soaked himself so densely in musk body spray, it might qualify as chemical warfare, I don't believe any of the three realms would miss him if he suddenly were to …

Instantly lose all blood flow.

Misplace his throat.

Become a desiccated corpse.

I twist my fingers in the soft hem of my dress. Am I being too harsh?

Optimism's hard-wired in my bones. It's what I survive on.

The little pilot light of hope that never goes out, no matter how many creeps try to blow on it.

If we were in a mortal dorm, crushed by used Econ textbooks and the tangy sour funk of takeout wings, this might all be acceptable. Reasonable even.

I might even find the way he scrambles to find a clean cup for me in his cabinets … endearing.

Except Rod's pushing forty.

And the longer he searches—barely glancing in his dishwasher, halfheartedly rummaging through the junk drawer—the more I become certain that he's stalling.

Exhibit E Rod deserves to die: he put something in my drink.

An oblong tablet that fizzed and tasted like a slurry of old Girl Scout cookies, rotting apples, and sour almond. It's supposed to make my bones light, the world syrupy, and slam me into deep, unshakeable sleep.

I've taken this one before, in a dose thirty times the size. Under sterile conditions after trials of Zolpidem, Temazepam, Triazolam, Lemborexant, and Cyclobenzaprine.

Not to brag, but if it's got an X, Y, or Z in the name, it's been injected straight into my veins in lethal quantities.

If drugs worked on me, I'd be strapped to a table somewhere with a tube down my throat and a clipboard-wielding crowd commenting on my choice of toenail polish. Sea salt green.

Once, after an I.V. of Propofol, I told the techs opposite the glass that my butt was going numb. I swear on Hestia's hearth, they almost high-fived. Decades of trials, and here it was: the first sign of a vulnerability.

For all of six seconds, I was their favorite pinned bug.

They waited for my butt to enter pins-and-needles white noise mania before a trembling lab coat slid open the slot and stuck his wrist in my cell, believing I'd been dosed into oblivion. I don't remember the color of his skin, but the veins in his palm were lovely. Fat and blue.

What happened next was beyond my control.

One minute I'd been wiggling my ankle to cajole blood to venture north. The next, bright, luscious red splattered the monitors, the needle in my arm was bereft of its tube, and warmth, pure radiant warmth, stroked my skin.

The sun.

Gods of Olympus, I'd missed it. Hungered for it. I remember standing there motionless, bare feet on concrete, paper-thin medical gown clinging to my back with my chin lifted to the sky. I remember the sound of my skin as it began to sizzle.

Rod, which I am increasingly convinced is not even short for Rodney, but for something heinous like "Rodimus Prime" or "Hot Rod," slides himself back into my orbit.

"You okay, babe?" he asks, hat tipped on his head like a sail. The block lettering on the front reads 'Spitters are Quitters'.

Almost forgot. Exhibit F: Rod forgot my name.

I nod instead of asking if he's made his living off a viral mugshot. If he hawks gas station t-shirts with nonsensical catchphrases only drunk people find funny. If mortals spot him on the street and point, "You're *that* guy. The guy who punted a cantaloupe at the cop car," and he shoots them finger guns back, saying, "Hell yeah. Feed the pigs."

It's a wonder of modern democracy and mortal fortitude that Rods still lurk in the wild. That the species survives, thrives, and gathers enough loose couch coins to buy beer and hats with stickers so new they squeak when you rub them.

Yet they proliferate.

I'm the last of my kind. So maybe I'm the one in the wrong.

Maybe I've been locked up too long and Rod is Today's Average Mortal™. It's entirely possible that men have gone from suit-wearing gentlemen to dudes in bedazzled jeans who are convinced they *need* to start a podcast.

"I like a girl who's thick," Rod says, circling around the counter, stare as hopeful as a vulture.

Most observations of me have been either: clinical—five foot, brown eyes, brown hair, brown skin (the trifecta); or hypercritical—freak, horror, monster. It's nice to swing outside the norm. I glance down at myself. The dress is crushed velvet, daffodil yellow and lovingly cups the wide curve of my hips. I do look thick. I smile, lightly tugging my hem. "What else do you like?"

"Can I be honest?" His tongue's out for a second. "I like a girl who's a little wild. You know what I mean?" He leans in close, hand landing on my waist, thumb pressing into the curve of my hip. "I like a girl who doesn't play hard to get. Or, you know ... plays hard. You look like you want to get wild tonight."

His cologne's gone from chemical weapon to wading through a smog drain in Thessaloniki. Still, I ask, "I do?"

He tugs me closer. "You still feeling okay, baby? You want to sit down?"

That's the answer then.

Guess this is what passes for predatory in Pawtucket, Georgia after midnight. Impatiently waiting for the roofies to hit.

Rod's breathing thickens. He skims his fingers down my skirt, meeting mine at the hem. Holding hands? No. He bats my hand away, fondles my bare thigh.

His face hovers, pink and sweaty, and he chokes out another line—some variant of "You're crazy sexy, you know that?"

It's time.

I've given Rod every chance.

The first roofie might have been a slip-up. He thought I'd

dropped it and returned it to me, mistook it for a flavor enhancer, missed his own drink for mine.

The second pill squished between his fingers and dusted into my soda water? Maybe he's a budding chemist, wondering how powder and carbonization interact.

The third roofie? Dumped into the tap water of my dirty cup? Come on. It's as if he wants to be a husk.

Our uneven reflection in his patio door is no great tableau. Rod clinging to me, tongue resting on his lower lip as he gropes my hip, all flop sweat and expectation. Me, a little too pale, a little too stiff, frown not sitting right on my lips.

He doesn't notice. Why would he? Rod's the kind of guy who thinks boundaries are for traffic cones and referees, not females.

My best friend Nat would have turned Rod into a cautionary tale in time for the evening news. *Local idiot found choking on his own genitalia.*

Picturing her revolted expression at Rod's greasy thumb lifting my skirt brings a slight smile to my cheeks.

Nat doesn't hesitate.

Not at all. As one of the Furies, fierce defenders of the Underworld, Hades's own Divine killers, she knows how to shred a man into fun-size pieces.

"Think of it as preventative care," Nat likes to say, iron whip wrapped lovingly around her wrist. "Predators thin the herd. We thin the predators."

But Nat's not here.

Which is great. So great.

She's living her best life. Fated to a Demigod who worships her, carrying what will be the realm's most beautiful baby and tracking down an assassin like a supernatural bounty hunter. Her wildest dream. Her no-way-can-that-ever-happen-to-me. Except it did.

And I am too happy for her to steal her away from that dream because killer instincts skipped me.

Which leaves me and Rod.

"Hey," I say. Shape my mouth into a smile. "You're ... sweet, but I'm not really in the mood. I've never actually done this before. Not on my own, I mean, and I thought I could. I *was* in the mood, but now ..." Merciful Gods in Olympus, I was *so* in the mood. I stare at the shadows off his patio, tearing away to pat Rod's shoulder. "I'm sorry. I think it's better if I go. It's not you. It's me."

"You're shitting me," he says. "You wait until now to change your mind?"

"It's more like performance anxiety."

"You think I got time for this?"

His face cracks open with spit and rage. Nothing elegant about it. The hand on my waist bunches, bruising, and the next second it's in my hair. A fistful at the roots, yanking my head back.

I taste static. Ozone crackle. Heat. My gums wake with a throb, ugly and anxious, strobing red. The dim lighting becomes a razor, forcing a squint. I try to stay soft. Mortal. But the edges go sharp. My ears pop.

The quick pound of Rod's heartbeat teases me, as fast as a Cyclops in the presence of Zeus.

Buried under my candy-shell of optimism, the killer uncoils. It sucks the air out of my throat. Spreads. Blooms up my spine.

Rod's hand in my hair burns. I swallow back the pain, stay in control.

If I don't, it's not a body they'd find, it'd be a massacre. The crime scene photos would be big red blurs. *Local Blood-bath! Suspect Demonic Psychopath. More at ten!*

My stomach lurches.

No. That's not me.

Rod's yelling. Profanities, threats. Hateful face bloated red.

A hand wrenches onto my shoulder, thumb carving a print into my throat, vanishing the air from my lungs. He thrashes me, gripping my hair so tightly my eyes water. "You fucking whore. You think you tell me what to do? I—"

The front door detonates.

No knock. No creaking hinge. No warning. Just raw violence and him. Drake, black-clad, shadow-eyed, filling the hallway like a storm banked over a raging ocean.

Rod freezes.

He's a mortal, nothing but slick red blood pulsing through his veins. To him, *Blackguard* is some metal band, *Kadmos* sounds like an all-natural Greek yogurt, and the *Butcher of Boston* is a Netflix documentary he scrolled past. He thinks torturers only exist in John Wick movies.

Other than breaking and not quite entering, Rod has no rational reason to fear Drake Cosgrave.

But something cold and primordial shrinks the room. Even Rod, built out of pork rinds and bottom-shelf triple-sec, catches the vibe.

Black hair hanging messy around his eyes, Drake Cosgrave drags the entire night behind him as he enters the paltry apartment. His mouth is set in a firm, unamused line and my heart squeezes in his presence, ignoring the angry tension in his shoulders, the storm front of his eyes, how he absorbs the flickering horror of Rod's kitchen and makes it holy.

He's here. He came.

Rod's hand tightens painfully. "Who the fuck are you?"

Classic. I guess the "Are you the pizza guy" line was still loading.

Drake's gaze skips, lazy, from Rod's greedy grip on my hair to the awkward hitch of my dress and my limp hands at my sides.

His whole body suggests motion, but he stands quiet, watchful.

Drake's tone is the same bland resonance as a telemarketer on hour thirty. "Haven't we talked about this, Theia?"

"I'm going by 'babe' right now." My voice is thin from lack of air.

"It doesn't suit."

"That's just because you're not used to it yet."

"It's not."

"You haven't really tried it out."

"And I won't," he says, keeping that wrecking-ball inertia, shouldering inside, heavy boots smacking the tile, not an ounce of hesitation.

Rod angles himself behind me. "You need to get out of my house, man."

Drake ignores him. Opens Rod's cabinets. Closes them.

"Why are you alone?" he asks as he attends to the drawers.

"Trying to find inner peace," I manage despite Rod's clamp on my hair, baring my throat, bowing my back.

Drake nods, rifling through a drawer of lighters, bread ties, and plastic sporks. "Were the rules I set out too complicated for you?"

"No, I—"

"You're not supposed to leave the compound without supervision."

Rod's hand twitches. "If you don't get the fuck out in two seconds, I'm calling the cops. Last warning, pal."

"Pal?" I echo. *So I guess everyone gets a nickname.*

Finally, Drake turns to Rod. "How many did you give her?"

He's found what he was looking for: a plastic baggie of pills. White, tiny. Not baby aspirin. He holds them up between two gloved fingers. "This is the last time I'll ask politely. How many?"

Rod sputters, lets go of me, stumbles back against the Formica counter. "What the fuck, man? You can't just break in here and start snooping around my shit. You crazy?"

Light green eyes glide to me. An arch forms in his dark brow.

"Only three," I tell Drake, as if it might spare Rod.

Composed, methodical, Drake shuffles two, three, four, *five* pills into a plastic cup, pours lukewarm tap water over them. Adds two more for good measure, and slides the pasty concoction across the countertop. "She's smaller than you," he says, voice flat as rebar. "That ought to be fair, then. Drink."

Rod's lip quivers. The chrome sticker hat turns on its orbit, signaling full terror. "I didn't give her anything. She's lying, and fucking crazy. I've never seen those before in my life."

My jaw drops in offense.

Meanwhile, Drake unspools a smile. It's carnivorous, violent, a thing that doesn't belong in kitchens or with witnesses. It says: drink or die.

My stomach flutters.

My date gags as he chokes the drug cocktail down, face leaking. The aftertaste must be miserable. I step aside as he staggers toward the couch, body already betraying him.

"I so easily forget how fragile mortals are," I say, watching Rod crumple into the cushions. "All in all, not my worst first date."

A low noise in Drake's throat.

"No one even died."

A brow raise. As if to say: *yet.*

"Say your goodbyes. We're leaving." A verdict, not an option.

"No," I whine. "*Please*, I want to stay here and leaf through the Playboy by his toilet."

"You think this is funny?"

I shrug. "More poetic, I guess. Drugging the drugger."

"Theia."

"Like fishing for a fish that feeds off fish."

"Are you still going?"

"A besting doll of fishes, if you will."

"Besting?" He shakes his head as if suddenly remembering the saying. "By coming here tonight, you have undermined every ounce of effort made to keep you safe. Every attempt to protect you." Drake's breathing is so even, so measured, it's worse than shouting. "You're reckless, irresponsible, and self-indulgent. Running off without telling anyone."

He acts like I'm not wearing bruises down my neck. Like being fondled by a man with a vape pen collection is all part of the itinerary.

I don't correct him.

Don't explain that this is all necessary for survival. That self-indulgence is actually binge-watching *Below Deck* and eating a chocolate swirl sheet cake in one sitting. That I don't *want* to do this, to *be* this. I can't help it.

But one honest word about what's happening inside me, what I am, and the freedom vanishes. Poof. Gone. Cartoon Scooby-Doo exit. My new protectors will exchange worried glances over my head, and then escort me back to padded walls with observation windows.

For my own good, of course.

I firm my chin to keep it from wobbling. "I needed air."

"You ever pull something like this again, I'll sew your shadow to the floor."

"Pretty sure my shadow's not the issue here." I nod at where Rod's drooling onto his own thumb.

The killer part of me—the angry patient, scalpel-curious part, grown in glass cages and weekly 'vital checks'—wonders how many pills it takes to strip a man's ego from his spine and hang it from the ceiling fan.

That's not me though.

I fling my hair over my shoulder. "Just so we're clear," I say, "Zeke was my designated escort tonight. I would not dare to break your precious protocol."

"The request was that you remain within visible line of sight of a *responsible* member of the Guard."

He means the Blackguard, but can't say it. Even the name

is a punishment—a cruel twist on what they once were: Kingsguard, sworn to King Kadmos, the God of Hope's last heir, the true Vein of Elpis. Drake and his brethren sacrificed mortality to bridge the three realms, join mortals and immortals in peace, only to watch their king's throat tear open beneath an assassin's blade. The Gods, ever vengeful, cursed them to an eternity of hunting the assassin, never to rest until vengeance is complete.

If that wasn't bad enough, creatures—the Gods' Divine offspring—ripped apart the Kingsguard's reputations, transforming them from heroes into villains. Protectors became terrorists. The damned who left the realms to burn.

The Blackguard rescued me, protected me. Not with a cup of warm milk and fuzzy blanket, but with loaded guns and possessed shadows.

"Zeke has foresight," I remind Drake, overcoming the urge to shudder at his tone. "He'd know if something bad was going to happen."

Gloved hands flex. "He didn't see me coming."

*And I'm the biggest bad there is*, his eyes say.

Twin streaks of heat score my cheeks. "I wouldn't dream of calling your interruption bad."

"Everyone else would."

I tilt my head at him. "Well, you did drug half the party."

His lips barely move. A ghost of a scoff. But when he speaks, his words cut clean as an Argos's talon. "I thought it was a date."

Something electric dances along my vertebrae. "Drake, if I didn't know better, I'd think you were jealous."

"I don't get jealous."

He says it like jealousy is beneath him. An evolutionary dead end. Like the last guy who accused Drake Cosgrave of wanting anything was found pickled in a jar behind the deli counter and sold as a warning.

I try not to smile. "Not even a smidge?" I hold a finger

and thumb close together, light barely visible between them. "Not even, like, one molecule of regret?"

He doesn't dignify it with an answer. Eyes cut to Rod, slack-jawed and spasming on the couch. "Have Rune run a background check before your next date. You've got terrible taste."

Something in my chest pinches. Disappointment, I think. That he's really not jealous. Not at all.

It burns, raw and citrus up my sinuses, that not-at-all. I want to scoop out the disappointment and drop it in the trash next to Rod's chewed-up napkin and the bloodless dreams of everything I'm supposed to want.

"Let's go," he says finally, eyes sweeping from the unconscious body straight to the exit.

I might as well be paint on the wall.

Outside, streetlights buzz like hummingbirds, shuddering against the dark. Spring in the Deep South never gets cold, but I shiver at the breeze, unaccustomed to air flowing over me willy-nilly.

Drake waits for me on the sidewalk, silhouette as stark and unyielding as a gravestone marker.

The car's idling at the curb. Zeke's behind the wheel, knees spread, picking at his teeth with the corner of a maxed-out Dunkin' Donuts rewards card, his sheet-white mohawk defying gravity. His eyes snap up, gleaming, wolf-bright. "You get what you needed, babe?"

I literally cannot stop my smile.

The Blackguard can be so dark. Sinister. Candles flickering ominously and veiny bat wings, and calls coming from inside the house. They wear leather jackets unironically and have no less than ten weapons on their person at any time.

The curse put on them—the one that tortures them any moment they aren't fighting to avenge their dead king—has really put a damper on their outlook. It's a lot to be around. Heavy.

But when Zeke grins at me, it's like a cold soda exploding in my mouth. Cherry-bright laughter, pulse and sparkle, the promise of a getaway car always running.

Nat says he's certifiably insane.

I think he's fun.

I lean through the open window, inhaling the faint scent of Mary Jane and raspberry syrup. Have to blink to adjust because his blue eyes are that bright.

"I had unexpected company," I tell him, ramming a thumb at a hovering Drake. "But the night wasn't a total disaster."

I breathed fresh air, wore a pretty dress. Successfully passed for a creature with control.

Zeke grins. "Did I call it, or did I call it?"

"You promised me a cosmic shift in my fundamental reality."

His frown is genuine. "Did you not get it?"

"I got roofied."

"Good stuff?"

"Terrible aftertaste."

He considers this. Asks, "Moldy pennies or more like dusty nickels?"

So much hope in that question. Like maybe one day date rape drugs will surprise me. Maybe next time the artisanal roofies will taste like coconut, or ripe peach, or something more fun than old currency and basement dank.

"Neither. Like if you licked a subway pole and chased it with almond milk."

"Ooh!" Zeke sparks with glee. "How's your head? Your stomach?"

"That's enough," Drake snaps. "Get in the car."

No please. No warning. He rips the door open and gestures for me to shuttle in, and I do. One: because his voice is vibrating with edge, true edge, the kind you only get after years of snapping necks and taping up the loose ends. And two: it was very gentlemanly of him to open my door.

Zeke whistles low. "Someone's in a mood."

"Apartment six needs cleaning," Drake says, flipping a wallet open. "Gregory Hasten. If he wakes up—*when* he wakes up—I want him to break into a cold sweat at the mention of breath mints."

"Now that's poetry." Zeke's grin stretches wide.

Drake plucks the joint from between Zeke's fingers, crushing the ember between gloved fingertips. "And no blood sigils this time. Or pentagrams."

"Please," Zeke scoffs. "Like I'd waste a summoning on a night when the moon's half-assed and I'm out of mugwort."

A moment later he's gone, car door slamming behind him, unlaced combat boots crunching gravel as he disappears into the building.

Perhaps he's a smidge crazy.

I picture some poor jogger spotting those twin blades crossed over his back, mistaking them for some cosplay prop. I open my mouth to question Drake about the wisdom of letting a centuries-old immortal roam free with deadly weapons, but the ice in those green eyes freezes the words in my throat.

He only ever looks at me like that.

As if my very existence is an infection he can't cure, a splinter wedged too deep to extract.

As if I'm his true curse.

Above him, the streetlight coughs and sputters out.

"Are you hungry?" I ask, my voice small in the darkness. "I could be talked into a sweet treat. Or maybe pizza. Deep dish only. Peelers choice. Though there's not that many places open at this hour. Maybe burritos or—"

Drake drops into the driver's seat and slams the door. Hard.

The optimism that has kept me alive and sane for the last hundred years shrinks.

Exhaustion washes over me.

I don't know how long I can do this.

How many days I can look up at him with my brightest smile, with an invitation, with a new dress and fresh lip-gloss and have him look straight past me.

I've wanted a soulmate since I learned the word. My guiding star, my sense of being, my purpose was finding him.

Here he is.

And he hates me.

## 2

# Theia

## HE BELIEVED LIFE WAS CRUEL AND HE EXPECTED CRUELTY

I've never had a real job—not surprising when you're abducted regularly and spend your developmental years shuffling between monitored cells. Frankly, my skill set is basically nonexistent. Doesn't mean I don't dream.

If I could have my pick, a résumé that couldn't be rejected, references utterly besotted with me, I'd be a waitress at a diner that never closes. The kind with tacky laminated menus and bottomless burned coffee.

Just like this one.

When I tell Drake this, he's horrified.

"Do you have any idea how many creatures I've killed in an IHOP?" he asks.

"Two?"

"More."

"Three?"

"More than that."

"*Four*?" I'm aghast.

He rubs his temple.

We chose a booth—obviously—and each have a mug of coffee in front of us, steaming and untouched, courtesy of the extremely exhausted Mai, whose favorite pancake is the *Spectacular Berry Surprise!* according to the button pinned to her apron.

I can't remember how we ended up here, facing each other, butts stuck to squeaky beige vinyl. One minute I'm being hauled home like a teenager past curfew and the next, Drake's pulling off the highway and parking in a customer-only spot.

"Cinnamon bun addiction?" I'd asked, admiring his stubborn cheekbones in the blue open sign glow.

Drake turned off the car. "You're hungry."

I was forming the world's best denial: 'hunger? never heard of her,' when my stomach growled. Drake opened my door for me, sighed deeply at the no Wi-Fi and no cash signs, and here we are.

First date?

Between us sits a tabletop placard with cartoon fangs, advertising a tower of reddish pancakes. *Dracula's Delight.* A promotion running all October.

We're cresting summer now.

I start a mental countdown clock, taking in the lights that can't decide if they want to stay on, the aqua floor tiles polished thin by a million shuffling feet.

Drake looks completely wrong against the backdrop of cheerful menus with their sunny yellow borders and dancing pats of butter wearing tiny top hats. His gun forms a telltale bump beneath his jacket, those black gloves hug his hands like a second skin, and that tattoo—the mark of his curse—peeks out above his shirt collar. Black enough to swallow light. He's all hard edges and deliberate stillness, the kind of person who makes a corner booth look like a tactical position.

Mai passes by, hairnet askew, and I tell her somewhat wobbly, "I'd love that fantastic Dracula special and your most delicious cheesecake slice. Drake's going to have ...?"

"Nothing. And please bring me the bill with the food. Thank you."

That punctures any hope of us putting two straws in a vanilla milkshake.

"Don't be a waitress," Drake says once Mai's out of earshot. "For the love of the Gods, don't."

"Why not?"

"The hours drain you. The customers break you. The pay starves you, and the stench follows you home." He tugs one glove higher up his wrist, as if the ghosts of breakfasts past might come dripping through the cracks in his armor. "You don't want any of it."

"But pancakes are the mortal equivalent of ambrosia. And look at these decorations!" I gesture at the Grinch cardboard cutout winking from behind the register. "Plus, there's the sunrise through these windows every morning. And tips—"

He snorts.

"What? You don't tip?"

"Of course I do. Generously."

"Well, there you have it. People like you make it worthwhile."

"One decent tipper doesn't—"

"Why can't you be the rule instead of the exception?"

His jaw tightens. "Do you have to do that?"

Am I biting my lip at him? "Uh … breathe?"

"See rainbows where there's only storm clouds. In everything. Everyone."

"And I should what—expect disaster? That's no fun. Should I cross the street at every dog because it might pee on my shoe?"

"Assume it'll bite."

Sweet puppy Fluffy? "It wouldn't!"

Those fingers press at his temples again. "You were *kidnapped*, caged for a week, denied clean clothes and a damn blanket. It's not even the first time that's happened to you.

Assume the worst, Theia. See the world for what it is. Not what you wish it to be."

I stare down at my chipped mug, bright and blue as a bruise.

"Stop believing that if you try hard enough, the world will rearrange itself into something soft. There's no hope. Everything's rotted to the core."

His voice carries something I haven't previously heard from him—emotion. He means it. Truly.

"Rot can be beautiful," I murmur. "Cheese. Truffles. Mulch that feeds gardens. Hope's not a plague. It's a choice."

He wants to argue—I can see the lightning gathering in his eyes—but he smothers it. Leans back, arms folded over a broad chest of muscle and a lifetime's worth of kill orders. Nothing left for me but concrete silence.

Disappointment wells up. I want to fling my coffee at him. Make him feel something. Anything.

"You wouldn't last a night here," he says.

"I can outlast most things." Experiments. Isolation. Starvation. A single flickering lightbulb.

Bringing any of that up will earn me pity, not respect, so I reach for my mug. The handle's sticky with high-grade syrup residue, layered through a hundred generations of pancake fiends. I channel the happy diners who drank here before me. "You underestimate what I could accomplish with an apron, a thousand tiny creamers, and control of the sound system. Mamma Mia all day long."

I think—no—*yes*!—no—that's not a smile. He's spotted the sticky handle. His lip curls in disgust.

It slices. The disgust. Not at me, I know, but there's still a crackle that hits center-mass. Reminds me I've never been anything to him.

Or anyone.

Never a daughter, never a partner, never a pen pal—let alone someone's love. The Moirai, the Fates, wove Drake into my destiny, stitching him into my soul, yet I can't keep him from wanting to bail out the fire exit.

*Keep trying*, the ever-bright voice in my head cheers.

He just doesn't know me. Not yet. Destiny might be slow. The Moirai could be on a much-deserved beach holiday.

I roll the thought around. Picture the glorious Moirai at their cosmic looms, spinning out destinies for every creature—grand tapestries for some, plain cloth for others.

I've never actually met one. Apollo probably hoards them in his sun-soaked temples, draped in gold robes and surrounded by celestial music. Or maybe they're roaming the realm with us. The red-cheeked crossing guard who nudges you along, or the flight attendant upgrading you to first class just as you're about to smash open the emergency exit.

What if, like me, there's only one left, and that's why most creatures wander through life without ever finding their soul-mate, their Fated? Maybe the last Moirai can only watch, powerless as we fumble through relationships, or we burn through lovers, forgetting that matters.

In any case, the Fates made time to tangle my thread with Drake's. "This one", they'd chattered over the crackle of a hearth, "She gets to find her other half. To feel a love unlike any other."

I tap the menu edge, forcing lightness. "If you could do anything, what would it be?"

Astronaut. Everyone says astronaut.

"Look, Theia." Drake's tone takes that turn—terminal cancer, dead Pegasi. "I'm not here to hurt your feelings."

"You haven't."

He sighs as if that's worse. "It's time for you to leave."

I'd rather torch my hair with my birthday candles than have this conversation.

"Let me send you somewhere safe. We'll arrange the travel, destination, even security. Luke can secure you a mortal ID. Rune will set up monitoring."

"Atlas told me to stay," I say, heart like a dropped egg, cracked and oozing.

"Atlas is . . ." He clears the hair from his eyes. "He advised you could stay until you recovered. You're healed enough for a date-night escape. You'll manage on your own. You know that."

"I took Zeke with me."

"Theia." I physically recoil from the tone. His jaw clenches. "It's not safe for you to be with us. Kadmos's sigil—the branded flame on your back—positions you as a target. If Kadmos was killed by someone he knew . . . things are about to turn nasty. A war is coming. We need fighters, not ..."

*You.*

I hear it loud and clear.

I fight tears, staring at the cha-chaing butter.

"No one wants you harmed," he says, soft again. "Isn't there somewhere you can go? Family? Friends?"

Did they have a meeting about this?

Did the entire Blackguard gather around Atlas's war table and debate the gentlest way to ditch me? Atlas probably used phrases like "liability mitigation" while Rune nodded along, already designing a color-coded spreadsheet of rejection options.

Was this Drake's assignment, or did he volunteer? Are these pity pancakes?

"A soft spot for females," Nat had told me, mouth twisted into an offended sneer. Furies are all female, and hold the general belief that males are better buried than endured.

"I have Nat," I say. "Only Nat."

A nod. Almost disappointed. No one would guess this is the same male who hauled my limp body from a collapsing inferno.

I smear my thumb through a streak of something that might be strawberry or might be blood.

"I really did follow the rules," I insist. "Zeke said I'd be safe, and I wasn't causing any trouble, I swear." Mostly because I'd chickened out.

"It's more complicated than that."

"Why don't you want me?" It's embarrassing how I have to choke the question out, how many ways I mean it, how I'm starving for him to answer, to tell me so I can just fix it. Be nicer, sweeter, smell better.

"It's not—Nat agrees with me. You'd be safer if we kept you at a distance. You're not built for the fight ahead. And you don't want this life. It's … you wouldn't survive."

I wait, hoping he'll take it back, talk to me like I'm not a liability.

He doesn't.

Silence sprawls between us. Drake only breaks it to dead-eye the menu, as if it's personally responsible for every murder in this diner since Heracles's seventh wedding.

The table edge imprints a honeycomb grid into my skin.

His gaze flicks from the rapidly healing bruise on my throat to my face. "You shouldn't have been dragged into this," he says, each word heavy. "You shouldn't be a part of it. Let us handle things. We'll secure you in a protected place."

"Safe like a cage?"

"No. Never like that. You'll be free to do as you please. I won't let you be caged again. On my life, Theia."

"I want to stay with you. With the Guard."

"That's not an option."

It's the only one. Sinis—Nat's Fated—is bound to the Guard, she won't leave. "I don't want to go."

"You've been sheltered. The realm is dangerous."

"I love danger," I lie, desperate. "I snuck out. I went home with Rod—Rod the criminal."

"Gregory."

"Right. Rod Gregory."

"No, his name was Gregory. Not Rod. No one's named Rod."

"Then where'd I get Rod?"

His mouth twitches as if he might laugh. He doesn't.

"You won't survive," he says, fingers tightening on his mug until the ceramic creaks. "I'd know. I've seen who does. *What* does. You need to leave before the choice is taken from you."

## 3

# Drake

## HE IMAGINED HER WANDERING, UNSEEN AND UNHEALED

*Don't fucking follow her.*

The command pounds against my skull like a fist. Along with: *Don't even look at her.*

My fingers curl into my leather-clad palms, teeth grinding as I compel myself to stare at anything but Theia's retreating figure.

"Just going to see if they need help," she'd mumbled before launching herself from the table.

No missing the wobble in her chin.

I've upset her.

I expected to, and yet, the feeling gnaws, shame scraping the roof of my mouth.

"A dreamer," Nat lamented to me about her. "My best friend, but she never learns. She'll smile while you gut her."

I didn't believe her. No immortal can be that naive. The world, time, reality—it grinds you down.

Natasa undersold it.

"The Fates will work it out," Theia assured Atlas when he vowed to hunt down and dismember her jailers. She'd meant it. No irony. No edge. Simply that rich, husky voice, as if each word was her first of the day, voice thick from sleep.

I told her she'd been trapped for eight days, and she smiled. "That's over a week without bread. Nat owes me a drachma."

Then there's the brand.

Immortal skin doesn't scar without Divine intervention.

Warped as it may be, the raised flame on her shoulder blade matches the brand seared into my chest. Into all the Kingsguard. A pronouncement that our fealty, for eternity, belongs to our King.

Nat embedded six Divine daggers into Atlas's left biceps when he ordered me to interrogate Theia about Kadmos's brand. The viscous pink blood spurting down his arm brought me wicked relief. Relief that Nat cut him so that I wouldn't have to.

A month of watching Theia, studying her, and none of us are closer to understanding how a creature so breakable survived.

I keep waiting for evidence—the flex of muscle, some glint behind those rich dark eyes, a flicker that she's biding her time. It never comes.

Instead: tears. A wince.

The kind of weak that wouldn't survive Philly's alleyways a single night.

She'd gone limp in that mortal's grip, slack, neck bent to breaking, lips parted, heartbeat trembling at the hollow of her throat. Prey frozen mid-scream. Like Eileen, when the men came. Like Brigid, soft hands and a softer heart, blinking up at me in confusion as she rasped for breath.

I see my sisters in her. They ended up shredded apart, erased, and I cannot let the same happen to Theia. I want her safe.

Which is how things die around me.

*Don't follow her.*

*Sit and wait like the good attack dog you are.*

Fuck I wish I had a collar. A short and sturdy chain.

I can picture her back there, hovering over that waitress, asking what's wrong, convinced one small kindness will set everything right.

Optimism so thick you could choke on it.

Coffee leaches from the hairline fracture in my mug, slowly contaminating the table. I check and recheck my gloves, catch my reflection in the chrome edge of the napkin dispenser. A funhouse distortion of the killer, the fuck-up, the Blackguard who dooms anyone he cares about.

What if she's crying back there? Rubbing her cheeks raw with cheap napkins?

Guilt stings me down to the marrow.

*Don't you fucking follow her.*

Glass shatters four booths down. I go for my gun, then realize it's only a broken syrup carafe, amber liquid pooling in the grout.

Two teenagers are roughhousing, fucking around. One scoops up glass, cuts his hand, laughs as he pats for napkins, leaving bright red dots everywhere.

My skin crawls. The penny scent too familiar to my nose.

One glance at the ketchup-smeared tables tells me the restroom here probably harbors more biohazards than a morgue.

I didn't use to care about germs.

Before they called me Butcher, I would've been in that booth. Doing nonsense with unwashed hands, bourbon breath, sticky with sweat and sex and everything raw, dumb, and mean about youth.

Now, the very creatures of myth piss themselves if I murmur a dark word too close to their ear.

Butcher is a misnomer. I'm a cleaner. A sanitizer.

*What would you want to be?*

Not this.

Not a scourge. Not a curse, or a failed experiment, or the last stopgap for creatures that peel the flesh off old women and vanish before dawn. Not the sad, canned punchline to the world's slowest joke.

I want to burn the rot out of everything and salt the ruins behind me.

I want to be forgiven.

No—just erased. As if I never existed, never touched a thing.

*Don't follow her.*

My phone vibrates against my thigh.

Only three people would text now: Natasa, promising exuberant disembowelment if Theia returns with a paper cut; Zeke, wondering if all mortals smell this rank; or Atlas, checking in.

As the leader of the Blackguard, Atlas would exile me to the curse if he learned I'm sending Theia away. He believes I'm questioning her. Believes the brand on her shoulder is the key to our curse.

I clench my gloves and drown the itch to chase her down, lash a rope around her waist and tether her to me.

Gods above, I hope she's running out the back, sense finally clicking.

A shriek rips through the diner. I lunge from the booth, teeth bared—then freeze as peals of laughter follow.

Shouts, thumps, glass rattling. I sink back, heart racing. It's not Theia.

The teenagers have hit full-blown Dionysian revel, loud enough to rattle the wire racks behind the counter.

I stare holes through the kitchen doors.

Where's the waitress? The cook? Anyone yelling, "Cut the shit, or I'll call the police."

Nothing.

No one.

I'm up then. Weaving between empty tables, vaulting the counter, crashing into the kitchen.

I stop.

Blood.

The floor gleams with it. Fresh and slick, a savage streak flowing from the walk-in.

No screams, no gasps—just the fryer's angry hiss as oil bubbles over.

I check my holster, habit more than necessity. The .22 is there, sure, but it's a pea shooter against anything that isn't human, and even then you have to be willing to aim for the head. What I really want is something with heft, something that can split bone.

My hand finds the block of knives near the fryer, and I draw the biggest one, a cleaver with a blade wide enough to use as a mirror. It feels right. Familiar.

The toe of a sneaker juts out of the thick metal door, partially buried under a heap of flattened boxes.

Panic slinks under my skin.

Theia wasn't wearing sneakers … right?

Or was she? For all my obsessive vigilance, the details slip and slide away from me. Too stuck up on the faded bruise, that fucking brand, too busy scaring her off, knowing if I looked at her, really looked, there'd be no looking away.

Not from those waves, rolling, glossy as silk hanging just so. The mouth always on the precipice of a smile, the ample curves that Calliope would immortalize, the sort that demand an epic, something sung and legend-spun.

Now I'm standing ankle-deep in a crime scene, blaming my dick for letting it all slip past me.

I tighten my grip on the knife.

"Theia?" I ease the door open.

It's the waitress.

Body curled awkwardly, throat a wet scarlet trench, mouth split in a final breath.

Relief ignites and dies.

Dead bodies don't just appear.

There's another killer here.

Where the hell is Theia?

I check my six, study the bent metal shelving behind the body, the fat drops of blood, smears leading toward the back. Drag marks.

I follow, pulse pounding my ribs. Vicious, primal, overquick. Press my ear to the alley door at the trail's end. Silence.

Fuck it. I kick it open, let it slam wet brick and storm through. Darkness blinds me. My boots slap through a puddle and I stagger, knife raised.

Then a noise—a breath, a scuffle.

I blink the night out, force my vision to sharpen.

There.

Crouched by the gutter, hands jammed against a motionless form. Wide-eyed, mouth slack, knuckles slick. Pink stains her cheek, her throat, the notch under her collarbone.

Theia's gaze finds mine through a sheet of curls—terror, hope, pleading.

Moonlight catches her, turns her into something otherworldly—a blood-baptized seraph glistening with that unmistakable pink shimmer. Red mortal blood entwined with Divine silver ichor.

She's a wreck—knees on wet pavement, dress torn, body shaking.

The corpse beneath her is so fresh it still bleeds.

"Are you hurt?" I reach for her trembling shoulders. "Theia?"

She starts. "I—"

A cold barrel presses against my neck. "Stop right there," a voice commands—calm, inhuman. "The female is ours."

4

# Theia

## INSTINCT OVERPOWERED OBEDIENCE

Drake laughs, and it changes me fundamentally.

Raw. Startling. Unpolished. It taps into my bones and wakes me up. Mutes the hunger gnawing on my ribs, transforms the burning ichor in my throat into something almost pleasant.

Almost.

The static edge of my senses won't let go. Ears tuned to every scrape, eyes burning, heart jackhammering, echoing in my skull until suddenly it drops, settling into a deep, unnatural calm. The last ten minutes seep back in, jagged, out of order: hot tears on my face, Mai contorted, neck snapped, hunger buckling my knees, my dash away, retreat to the alley so I wouldn't tear into her. Slamming into the male with crimson slicked around his mouth.

I lost myself then. Heartache, rage, craving collided. Exploded into the kind of brutality forged by survival. Ragged and sloppy and mean.

He's crumpled where I left him. I know what he is without checking for Divine marks, can taste it on my tongue—a sick mashup of blood types, red and silver and pink alike.

He's Keres.

*Keres.*

Creatures from the primal dark, from horror stories. The ones who emptied continents one mortal at a time. Those who crave little glories like peeling out throats with their teeth.

They're supposed to be extinct.

Four are in this alley.

I've killed one.

Two wear expensive fabric molded like armor, every seam severe and unbending, creating vicious lines.

And then—

"Walk away," the Keres male commands Drake, shifting the barrel's aim from airway to temple, pressing until Drake's skin dimples white. "Don't say anything to anyone about what you saw."

Drake's stare doesn't leave me. His posture is insolent, a knife dangling loosely in his grip, but his gaze strips me raw. Sees everything. Too much.

Fury smolders there.

"What exactly did I see?"

He's asking me, but the male answers, almost amused. "Nothing to worry over. A family dispute."

"Is that what this is?" Drake asks, still speaking to me as if the gun at his temple doesn't matter.

The hunger that dragged me out here has fizzled into a dull throb, replaced by something denser, more metallic: fear.

"This is absurd," says the male's partner, checking the mag on her gun. "Quit wasting time on theatrics. Shoot him. The female owes me a debt."

She moves so smoothly in the cover of dark, I don't track her until the muzzle of her own gun presses into my lower back. Her hand lands cold on my shoulder, yanking me to rise to my knees.

"If you want her, you have to go through me first," Drake says.

So simple. So easy it shreds me inside. Like his life is a

throwaway. Like a bullet to the brainstem is just a conversational inconvenience.

The male tips his chin, gun unwavering. The safety's off. "You're surrounded. You're outnumbered. Do not die for her. She is not worth it."

"You've got three seconds," Drake says, emotionless, detached, spinning the cleaver in his fingers. "That's how long it takes to remove your spine. Two if I get to make a mess."

The alley narrows, shadows deepening as if the night itself holds its breath. I catch the glint of blades beneath their coats—not casual wear. Not thugs.

They're imperials. The Emperor's scouts. Trained hunters.

My stomach drops. Nat described them with admiration—the careful way they fan out, the coiled, routine grace in their massacres.

Drake's all but dismissed their presence. As if he's already flipped a coin and chosen which vein to slice first.

The male Keres adjusts his hold, finger tightening on the trigger. "Stand down, boy. Don't get twisted over a female who'll gut you herself before dawn. She's Keres, property of the empire."

Hard, clipped. No trace of bluff or mercy. This isn't a standoff. It's a sentencing.

"Property?" I think Drake might laugh again. As if this is all a joke.

Instead, his gaze skims across my face, my mouth, just an instant, before latching onto the Keres imperials bristling in their brown armor, earth-dark and waiting. "You've been sealed up underground too fucking long if you believe females are anyone's property. Time's up. Who should I start with?"

Me. Again. He's asking *me*.

I don't have time to answer.

The Keres shoots—except Drake is already moving. He ducks under the barrel, twisting so the bullet just grazes his earlobe. He drives his knife into a new home deep under the Keres's ribs. The immortal buckles with a wet sound, and Drake rips the gun away, ditching it in the gutter.

No guns for the Butcher.

The female's gaze narrows at her partner's pink blood splashing concrete. She strikes—boot smacking into Drake's sternum. Air leaves him. She swings again—

He seizes her ankle mid-kick, wrenches it sideways. Her body follows, crashing down. Drake pounds on his chest, struggling for breath when knuckles crack against his jaw. His body arcs, then crumples.

He tries to roll away, to rise.

Boots find him everywhere—spine, ribs, skull—until he stops moving.

The wounded Keres sways, clutching his torso where pink ichor pulses between pale fingers. He roars, half-laughing, half-baying at the moon, and then he spits at the ground. The glob sizzles.

"Secure her," he commands.

My back hits cold brick. I don't resist.

My hunger's vanished, yielding to the strange, numbing shock that comes when reality peels back.

Drake lies motionless against the damp bricks, a thin trail of crimson leaking from his temple. His chest rises and falls in shallow breaths. His eyes stay closed.

Humans believe it's impossible for immortals to die. They're nearly right. Fortified with the blood of the Gods, creatures are tough, but the truth is, we die all the time. Precision, persistence, pace—that's what it takes.

Rough hands wrench my arms behind me, black rope biting into my wrists. "You'll regret every drop you took," she fumes, her breath hot against my ear.

Her partner's boot connects with Drake's shoulder, splaying him like discarded trash.

The groan that escapes his lips slices through me deeper than any blade.

"This one's mortal," he says, sliding the knife from his stomach and driving it into Drake's thigh. Drake gasps. Groans. I jolt forward, seeing red.

The male catches my chin in a grip that says he could snap it if he wanted. "You've violated every protocol. The emperor will have your bloodline for this." His breath is sour with oxidized blood. "Consorting with humans? Feeding in public? We should execute you right here."

"She faces the council," the female says. "For Milos." She kicks Drake's leg. "What do we do with this one? Dumb. But strong for his kind. Gotta be on something. Prop the door, stage it as a feral wolf on the prowl."

The male tugs my wrists so hard I nearly topple. "Too messy. Besides, the court hasn't had fresh blood in weeks. They'll appreciate the offering."

Drake's still slumped against the bricks. Bright red dribbles from his hairline, painting his collar. He could be asleep, looks almost calm, if you ignore the bruises blossoming over his jaw.

A blade scrapes my neck. "You know what happens to rogues who consider themselves above the rules?" the female asks. "What the emperor does to deserters?"

"I'm not—"

"Save it for someone who cares."

Her blade presses deeper, breaking skin. Heat beads down my neck.

My body goes full mannequin. No breath, no twitch. The pain freezes out as the blade nicks my collarbone, pressure so real my stomach lurches. Doesn't register. I'm in perfect compliance.

It's an old trick, learned in front of observation windows. Don't fight when you can't win. Don't speak when silence buys time. My muscles remember how to surrender.

I've never doubted my body's response. Not when it left

me limp during examinations, not when I stayed quiet in captors' arms. Each reaction took me on the smoothest path to safety, to opportunity.

But right now, it chafes. I want to scream and fight, arm myself with talons and teeth, and I can't move.

Drake's right there and I'm stuck.

The male's gaze remains locked on me while he murmurs to his partner. "Milos fought well, Riva. The emperor himself will ensure justice for his death."

"I want to be the one who collects the debt," Riva whispers, voice tight with promise. "When the Emperor grants me—"

"Do you hear that?" I cock my head, interrupting.

Riva's teeth clench so hard she flinches. "Shut your—"

"Do you hear that," I whisper, my eyes widening as I gaze skyward. "That flapping? It—"

"Shut your mouth," she snarls.

I do. Body betraying me despite myself.

The male's fingers slacken against my wrist as his focus fractures, eyes sweeping the gloom above us, but Riva's blade remains steady at my throat.

We all know which creature kept their wings.

The Argos. Winged enforcers. Hera's personal legion, whipped up in a lab or a cave or wherever the Fates deposit nightmares these days.

If Keres are the monsters mortals fear after midnight, the Argos are what wake the monsters up at 6 a.m. and rip open their curtains.

Their mission? Apprehend traitors—any creatures that reveal their true nature to mortals—and bring them to "justice."

Whenever a creature breathes too loudly in public, the Argos descend. Wings. Blades. Unchecked power and a taste for arterial spray.

"There's nothing," Riva hisses, even though her grasp grows twitchy. No one wants Argos attention.

"Quit talking," the male snaps.

"Brevin, you can't possibly believe this pathetic—"

"The Argos do patrol this area."

"She's lying!"

Brevin jerks me against him, voice sinking to a rasp. "If Hera catches us here, we're dead. Heads on pikes. This is her territory. We leave. Now."

"There's nothing up there," Riva insists, but I can see doubt fracturing her confidence. "The emperor expects results. If we return empty-handed—"

Something clicks against concrete at the alley's end—stone on stone, or claws on pavement.

Brevin's entire frame goes rigid, pivoting toward the sound with predatory focus.

"Time's up," he barks, fingers clamping around my biceps until I fear bone might break. My toes barely scrape the ground as he drags me forward. "The mortal stays, Riva. Move."

"I can't just—"

Brevin cuts her off, authority hardening his tone. "The Argos patrols carry bolts. Are you going to be the first to survive Zeus's weapon? We can't afford a confrontation."

Her jaw locks, but she retreats from Drake's collapsed form, her gaze fixed on him with undisguised thirst. She follows orders, falling behind Brevin as he hauls me from the alley into the forest bordering the town.

I trip forward, regaining balance as instinct takes command. My body knows this dance—the precise rhythm of captivity, the meticulous balance between resistance and survival.

Branches scrape overhead. Behind me, Drake lies in his own blood.

It's good that they're leaving him, and yet my chest tightens. Doubt claws up my throat. Each step feels like a betrayal, like I'm snapping something vital between us.

*It's good*, that little voice agrees. *He's safe, and that's what's important.*

But there's this other little voice, a lower octave, a darker tone, that says: *he wanted you gone.*

## 5

# Drake

### HE THOUGHT SHE MIGHT BE AFRAID, DRIFTING THROUGH THE DARK ALONE

Kadmos never dressed me in gold.

The others got to wear it—my brothers in the Kingsguard. They gleamed.

Not me. I've been draped in black since before the curse touched us.

There's no heartwarming origin story for me. No king spotting potential in some gutter rat, no promises about serving a greater purpose. Kadmos knew the monster he was recruiting.

Atlas and the rest—they didn't know I existed until I arrived at the palace, blades strapped to every limb, someone else's blood tacky on my skin.

The memory cuts razor-sharp.

I was in Herzegovina on contract—slop work for twin sisters who paid well—standing in a grimy shower washing away evidence, vodka within reach, when darkness swallowed the room. A single light led me to Kadmos sitting at my kitchen table, his collar crusted with blood the color of watered-down wine, his shirt in tatters, and my own knife balanced on his thigh.

He didn't strike me as a great king.

Just exhausted. Bleeding quietly onto my floor.

He didn't raise his eyes from the cracked tabletop.

Not when I stepped out of the shower dripping wet. Not when I skipped the towel. Not when I finished the vodka. Not even when I reclaimed my knife.

Only when its point grazed his throat did he smile—all predator, no warmth.

"Drake Cosgrave," he said, my name stretched out in his strange accent, vowels split, consonants heavy. "They speak highly of you."

No telling who *they* were.

I counted the steps to my cupboard where a toothpick waited. Pictured the grunt he'd make with it rammed under his fingernail. Spy or a hitman? Murphy's crew had tried similar stunts before.

Then his eyes caught mine.

Reality fractured. Three sentences from his mouth and suddenly Gods were real, creatures breathed in the shadows, and war raged in the hairline cracks between what I'd always thought was real and what actually was.

He slumped in my kitchen chair like a man who'd already lost too much. "I require someone with a particular appetite. They tell me you deliver."

I steeled myself for the trap.

But there's no creeping shadow under the door. No telltale creak from the loose floorboard by the sink. He flipped the empty bottle in his palm—careless, someone who'd already calculated the noise when it shattered.

"I need a specialist," he said. "I've got a war and no time for diplomacy. You'd be killing for me. The bad ones. The ones who make mothers scream at night. You get answers, isn't that what they say?"

I didn't bother playing coy. "What's in it for me?"

"The thing everyone's promised you, Drake Cosgrave. A clean slate." The words hung between us like smoke. "No more scars. No more looking back."

I waited for the punchline. For the devil to appear with a contract and a shotgun.

Instead, he rocked back in my chair, eyes burning with something ancient and exhausted, and I felt it—the weight, the regret, the absolute conviction that whatever insanity spilled out next, I should believe it.

"You want out of this life," he said. "Out of these choices. You want to be the man you were before the Butcher. To wake up and not hate the face in the mirror." He leaned forward. "I can give you that. All I ask is your blade buried in the throats of those who threaten everything I've built."

The word formed before I could stop it. "Deal."

The chair slammed onto the floor. He rose. "Vow it."

I did.

A week later, I stood transfixed before a hotel mirror in St Louis. My skin bore no scars, my eyes held no shadows, every tattoo of my sins had evaporated like morning fog. Divine power hummed within me. Kadmos's royal sigil burned against my sternum.

But the reflection staring back was the same worthless reprobate who'd sold out his family for pocket change. Just with prettier packaging and a fancier collar.

For decades, I honed the art of finding arteries with dull blades. Of knowing exactly how much suffering a body can take before truth spills out. I became the name Kadmos whispered when diplomacy failed, and he needed horrors made flesh.

Deep down, I always suspected that when Kadmos finally claimed victory, when his grand vision of harmony between realms came to pass, he'd dispose of his attack dog.

No place for monsters in paradise.

That was okay. I looked forward to the end, to letting him end me.

Then Kadmos died.

No end. No applause. No absolution. Only the echoing vacuum left behind, as if somebody had hit pause on every reason for me to exist.

Atlas held us together the only way he knew—go to ground, hunt the traitor, outlast the Gods. Our purpose turned into a scavenger's business. A parody of what once was.

But me?

I was a fucking relic. Too monstrous for civilian life, too valuable to the Blackguard to be left alone.

Until Theia. The first time I saw her, bruised and starving, Kadmos's flame burrowed into her back, she barely looked alive.

Suddenly there was a single point of clarity in an otherwise fucked, blurry existence: help her. I hauled her out of that cinder-block hellhole, and the world snapped into clean lines—keep her breathing, keep her safe. If it costs me everything else, fine.

And they fucking took her.

I inhale against gritty concrete, all sound muffled by the blood pooling in my ear. A raw ache opens behind my ribs, filling with static.

Alley's empty, but the knife's still lodged in my thigh. I rock to my side, wrap numbed fingers around the hilt and lever it out with a grunt. Messy work. Crimson fans out, fresh and bright, but I've bled worse.

I grind a glove into the wound, kneel, then stand. Shimmy the phone from my pocket—too smashed to turn on. I ditch it. The alley spins for a second, and I ride it out, hand braced flat to the brick, breath smoking out of me.

They took her.

And now the hands made for slashing secrets from unwilling mouths and peeling truths from screams don't feel so useless. I flex them, rolling pain through each stiff knuckle, and yank my gloves tighter.

Taking her was their first mistake.

Leaving me breathing will be their last.

6

# Drake

## NOTHING THEY TAKE FROM HIM, STAYS TAKEN

I used to think Keres were vampires. They both drink blood, scorch in the sun, and live forever.

I was wrong. Vampires are a teenage fever dream with bloodstained lips, velvet capes, pointed teeth, and coffins. A wooden cross defeats them. A sharp stick. They can't handle Italian cooking.

Comparing a vampire to a Keres is like mistaking a house cat for a tiger. One scratches. The other separates your larynx from your throat before you register the movement.

Theia is not one of them.

They can't be right.

She's *not* one of them.

She basks in the sunlight. She eats chicken nuggets, for Christ's sake.

She must have found the downed Keres and tried to revive him. Tried to do what she always does: fix the world with hope and a gung-ho attitude.

She didn't kill him. Couldn't.

Even Nat, Hades's famed Fury, would break a sweat taking down the emperor's elite imperials.

Theia asked Lev to open a jar of pickles for her. Said *pretty bitty please.*

The idea of her killing is laughable. She can't be Keres. It's impossible.

Only the strongest creatures could shred the throat of an imperial.

I know that better than most.

A hundred years ago, Kadmos recruited me to turn the tides in the Keres war. Twelve years of slaughter, of stalemate, the might of a Divine King and his armies versus a legion of Keres.

I wasn't sent to the front.

Kadmos had better use for me.

Away from the battle, I worked in dank rooms and dungeons. "Find a weakness," he commanded, and then left me with his knife.

Very few made it that far.

Fewer made it out.

The Twelve-Year War only ended because the body count swelled until too few Keres remained to smudge the ground pink. You could almost believe they'd gone extinct, the way Atlas spoke of the caves—as if they'd been scrubbed from reality.

The one lesson every soldier in our ranks learned, even before the screaming began: never follow them underground. Ever.

Keres territory was honeycombed with tunnels that made skin itch and compasses fail, as if Daedalus himself had designed the kingdom.

If you went in after them, you didn't come out. That's not poetry, it's practicality. Atlas repeated it so often it became graffiti, a punchline, a curse, a whispered threat.

Now I'm here. In those tunnels.

If this is what the Keres built from ashes, what the hell was lost?

The halls pulse with quiet, bruised majesty, as if they're mourning themselves in real time and building new masks to cover it. It's not dank like I'd imagined. Neat cleaved stone arches overhead like a cathedral, quartz veins webbing under pin-sized … LEDs of all fucking things. Not a spiderweb's worth of dust. The scent isn't decomposition or cryptlike; it's blood and incense and something fresh, like Downy.

I'm marched through the tunnels not at gunpoint, but with a lone set of cuffs on my wrists. I can't decide if it's arrogance or stupidity that they almost didn't strip me of my weapons.

The males flanking me are decked out to the nines—bone-inlaid armor, skull detailing, boots that could stomp through a bank vault.

The long, dramatic shuffle goes on forever. Tunnels branch and fork. We pass through three sets of suspiciously thick doors, cross two bridges spanning depthless caverns, and arrive in a wide chamber.

Columns spiral up, carved with patterns leading to the throne at the center of the space.

None of it matters.

Because there—quivering—along the far wall, chained, is Theia.

My mouth goes dry, jaw tight enough to snap bone. The chain around her waist could moor a ship, shackling her to a pillar with the creative cruelty to cinch it so tight she's forced to kneel. One of her feet is bare. The other ballooned purple-black, the kind of break that makes you look away.

She trembles so hard her teeth chatter, but when she sees me, her head shakes in a desperate, vehement warning.

Not self-pity or pain in her eyes. Terror. On my behalf. She shakes her head, tries to motion with her whole body—*go, get out*—but all I do is stand, wrists cuffed and bleeding, and stare at her.

The bruise at her temple, the knotted hair, pink blood crusting her hands and chest.

They ripped her dress.

I want to kill every single creature in this cavern.

She looks so damn fragile. So out of place.

Her mouth forms a single, violent, no, begging me to leave.

Not happening. Not a chance.

A ripple moves through the crowd surrounding the throne—a motley patchwork of blood cultists and bored aristocrats, half in rugged armor, half in black-tie finery accented with bone. They all watch me, pupils wide and hungry, hoping I'll sob or scream or shit myself.

I give them nothing. I stare ahead, murder in my eyes. Somewhere deep inside, I know I'm already dead. But not before I repay this humiliation in kind.

The imperial restraining me makes a small sound in his throat, but I'm not waiting around to be noticed. "Your Majesty, I've come to barter."

The male on the throne lets his gaze drift past me. His lips peel back, exposing needle-sharp fangs. "Why is my dinner making noise?"

"He claims Your Majesty has ... stolen his property."

From the central dais, the Keres Emperor rises. He's built like a cinder block: shorter than any of his precious imperials, but so dense with muscle that the air ripples around him. His skin is the absence of color, a sort of violently pale that makes him glow against the black and gold banners and shadowy quartz veining the walls. His face is a death mask: heavy brow, nose flattened by a hundred breaks. Head shaved at the sides, the top left in a thick brown braid falling in segmented loops down his back.

Vasilis Kolaphos. The Blood Sovereign of the Keres. The Emperor.

He's probably old enough to remember when fire was the hot new trend, but there's a slicing clarity in his umber eyes.

"A mortal accuses me of theft?" The emperor is faintly amused. "And has the impudence to demand its return?"

The chamber erupts anew, laughter needling.

I don't flinch. Don't blink. Just keep watching Theia. "Yes."

"And what trinket of yours, human, could possibly merit my attention? Speak."

"Her."

The emperor's mouth splits into a fanged smile, as if I've handed him the punchline to a joke he'll tell for centuries. "You've traveled to my court for my females?"

More laugher, sharp as broken glass.

Theia is silently pleading with me, frantically shaking her head.

There's dirt on her cheek. I hate it.

"I only came for one," I tell him.

He steps down from his throne, and the entire chamber follows where his bare foot touches the stone. He fixes the imperial on my left with an ancient glare. Raised his brow.

"We found him shouting in our territory, your majesty. Drawing too much attention. He submitted to chaining and …" The Imperial exchanges a look with his buddy. "He requested an audience."

"And you did not find this odd?" The imperial's mouth opens, trembles. Vasilis moves on. "Which female?"

"A rogue. Riva and Brevin detained her above. She—"

"She belongs there," I interrupt. "Not chained behind your throne. You took her. I'm here to bring her back."

The Emperor's upper lip peels back, exposing fangs in a rictus that's equal parts hunger and outrage. "You dare to claim ownership of Keres blood? Your kind has always been beneath us, but this is …" His pupils shrink to pinpricks. "Punishable."

I see the muscles bunch in his shoulders, the fine spray of spittle at the corners of his mouth. Something kicks awake in my blood—a reflex as old as the instinct to flinch from fire or duck flying glass. The chains shackling my wrists might as well be tinsel. I twist them once, and the hinges pop. The links scatter to the floor with a clatter that echoes, masking the snarl accompanying his strike.

I duck, pivot, and snatch the gun from my imperial escort, and press it to his forehead. "I wouldn't try that again," I warn. "It'll hurt you more than me."

The realization crawls across his face like ice forming. He straightens, smooths his draped robes, and regards me with a predator's cold calculation. The laughter from the assembled Keres has curdled. Now, they murmur, reassessing.

Clocking the gloves, the strength, the very red blood flowing through my very immortal veins.

His expression shifts—shock to fear to fascination—before settling into that carefully cultivated royal mask worn by those who've spent millennia pretending they're untouchable.

"The Butcher," he whispers, as if speaking my title too loud might summon something worse.

He wishes.

The Butcher has come, and I'm not fucking playing.

Theia's stopped shaking. Her eyes are wide with something other than terror, mouth is set in a small pink line. She might be angry.

Good. Hold onto that. It'll be easier that way.

"I should have smelled it sooner," Vasilis growls. "Kadmos's lapdog."

"Funny. He always called me his secret weapon."

Vasilis doesn't share any amusement. "Drake Cosgrave. Traitor to his own kind. Butcher of men. Killer for false kings. You dare enter my court and deliver accusations?"

He's so close I can smell blood on his breath.

I keep my voice even. "I came to collect what's mine."

The word mine snaps through the cavern like a switchblade. Some Keres stop breathing, jaws clenched. Maybe they remember. Maybe they still have nightmares about it. About me, and the years I spent learning their softest spots. All the ways to force them to talk.

I step closer, forcing him to crane his neck. "I came here for her. I'm not leaving without her. If you want to stop me, you'll have to put me down yourself."

The tension in the room goes from electric to atomic.

I've spent decades perfecting the art of provocation, finding the exact words that cause people to forget their strength and lunge for my jugular.

But I didn't come here for bloodshed.

I came for her.

I release the imperial, discharge the gun's mag and kick it across the stone floor. "I'm not here to make demands. I'm offering an exchange. My life for hers."

# 7

## Drake

### IF ANYONE DESERVED THE GODS' MERCY, IT WAS HER

A hush. The world drops a rung lower.

The Emperor grins, all teeth.

For the Blood King, this moment transcends mere victory—it's the culmination of a decade-long vendetta.

"I could peel you apart for centuries," he purrs, hunger flashing.

I lift one shoulder in feigned indifference. I'll stand right here and let them peel every scrap of flesh off me if it gets her out alive.

I deserve it.

She doesn't.

I knew when I entered these tunnels that this journey was one-way.

The crowd breathes in sync, tasting violence in the air. I keep my hands loose, show nothing, but each muscle in my arms is wire-taut.

It doesn't matter if I want to fight. I'm familiar with how these games are played, and here, in the bowels of the Sunless Kingdom, the role of the executioner is to die ugly.

"The Deep Realm's lessons are bloody and absolute when

it comes to its enemies, but for you we will make an exception," he says. "For you there would be no end."

I look at Theia.

She stands with the stoic, unnatural stillness of someone either about to faint or explode. I can almost hear what she's thinking: Apologize. Say you were mistaken. Leave.

I've bled for less affection, for worse creatures.

Vasilis's coppery breath chills my neck. "Well?" His voice is silk and razors. "Let's hear it, Kingsguard."

This isn't a street corner in Philadelphia, or a filthy alley behind a diner. It's not even a barracks fight in Kadmos's court where every soldier hoped I'd lose. This is worse. This is the point of no return.

"I told you," I say. "She goes free. I'm your problem now."

Laughter echoes off stone, rolls through the cavern.

"You wish for a trade? Beg for it, Butcher." He draws the name out. "Beg for me to break you. On your knees, like the abomination you are."

He wants me to play, wants to show that he has the power, but we both know my offer is one he won't refuse, so I stay standing, shoulders level, chin high.

"Calydon begged, did he not?" the Emperor goads. "Your old friend. We watched as he groveled while the smoke of your king's pyre darkened the sky. He cried out at the end. So weak and alone. We celebrate his piked head every year."

I tamp the urge to defend my fallen brother, to rip his name from the enemy's teeth.

He leans close enough that I see there are amber flecks in his stony eyes. "Kneel to my rule, mortal scum. Or I'll slit your throat where you stand and keep the female for my own amusements."

Something inside me threatens to collapse, but I lock my legs rigid.

"Careful," I tsk. "The last time you took a Guard unwilling, your entire kingdom had to relocate. Or are you ready to rebuild from ashes again?"

His mouth tightens to a bloodless line. "The female," Vasilis commands, fingers snapping behind him. "Now."

Someone says, "Sovereign, she murdered Milos. Custom demands—"

"I said bring her to me!" He can't tear his attention from me, body shaking with eagerness and violence. "You believe you know pain? Blood on the stones is my language. I'll keep you alive until you beg for death and then refuse you that comfort. I'll burn away the memory of every female and child who ever saw your monster's smile." He tells me how he'll hollow my bones, stretch out my skin across the throne, hammer my teeth into his chalice and smile.

I've heard it before. Said it. Done it. More times than I can count.

He expects me to tremble, to sweat with fear. Maybe beg.

"Do it," I interrupt. "Drag me through your dungeons if you want."

His smile falters, frustrated, enraged. He gestures violently for Theia, trying a new approach, searching for weaknesses. "I will do exactly as I desire," he growls. "And I'll make her watch as you scream."

They throw her at the base of the throne, landing in a heap of stained yellow dress, snarled hair and old blood. Pain lances her face, she lets out a husky groan. I feel it in my knees.

Vasilis grips her by her hair, yanks her face back.

I go for the knife hidden in my jacket.

But then he stops. Releases her.

Stares. "You." The word physically hurts him. "*You.*"

For the first time since I walked into this tomb, I have no idea what's about to happen.

She's looking up at me, not him. Eyes so wide. Terrified and angry.

The Emperor collapses to his knees, body slamming the stones, arms limp, useless, at his sides. A sound punches out of his chest, thin and strange.

A sob rocks his body. He's wrecked. Utterly. He reaches for Theia as if she's carved from his own bone.

"My Antheia," he whispers. "You've returned."

# 8

## Theia

### HE WAS TIRED AND TIRED PEOPLE DOUBT

I'm no stranger to hugs, though the list is short. Hard to rack up embraces when you're shuttled between cells, labeled a freak of nature.

Still, I've had a few. Natasa—tight squeezer, Sinis—my head lines up with his belly, and Paul, who took me on that mini golf date and panicked when I leaned in for a kiss, trapping me in what loosely qualifies as a hug, but could also pass for a body slam

But this? This is different.

For starters, my face isn't mashed into someone's armpit or sternum. The Emperor of the Keres stands nearly eye-level with me, our arms crossing at the same height, shoulders almost perfectly aligned.

That part's fine. Nice, really.

Everything else—the sobbing, the squeezing, the violent tremors—stretches into eternity. His entire body convulses—not gentle trembling, but the violent spasms of a system in revolt. Like he's been keeping his heart beating in a bucket for years, waiting for precisely this moment to let it finally break.

"My Antheia," the Emperor—*THE EMPEROR*—chokes out, drawing back to cradle my face between his palms, smearing ichor and blood across my cheeks. His forehead presses against mine, eyes bloodshot and glistening. "My heart. Nyx has found you. She has brought you home to me."

Dozens of Keres stare, slack-jawed.

Drake hasn't blinked in an entire minute.

The Emperor's hands find my cheeks again and I ... I know him. His eyes are the same shade as mine, his hair has the same untamable wave. He's a bit taller, and paler, and he's dressed like he's never heard of cotton but somewhere, in the back of my brain, a memory unfolds. His face, grainy. Almost too hard to see.

I want to laugh. I want to throw up. I want to run.

I freeze, instincts holding firm.

I let him crush me back into his chest, where his scent becomes my world. Burnt copper, wet stone, the inside of an old church where the blood never quite washes off the pews.

Past Vasilis's shoulder, Drake stands motionless, loose fists at his sides like he's forgotten how limbs work. Has anyone in the history of ever looked so mortally offended by an emotional display?

I almost want to check for a pulse or kiss his cheek, pat the top of his head.

Around us, Imperials watch with a shock you'd expect if I'd ripped off my face to reveal a second face underneath.

"My precious child, my beautiful girl, my daughter." Vasilis weeps, thumbing my jawline with hands that could snap spines like balsa wood. "Tell me of the years. Tell me of your life. Goddess, tell me who took you and I will consume their very bone."

Did I hear daughter? Or has my sanity finally packed its bags and left without a forwarding address?

He's too eager or insane to wait for answers. He hauls us both to our feet, chain clanging around my waist as he thrusts our joined hands to the ceiling. "My daughter Antheia Kolaphos, the princess, has returned!"

His people, the Keres, creatures of night, lose what's left of their collective minds. Shouting. Screaming. Stomping of feet. I catch at least three words for "impossible," two for "blessed," one that's probably "bullshit"—and then several insufficiently stifled sobs.

Grown immortals, openly weeping.

I'm still waiting for my mid-breakup pancakes. This is too much.

Drake hasn't moved in the last full minute. He's become a permanent installation. He could be a sculpture: "Modern Man, Suffering." In another reality, I'd hit pause on the chaos and just ... gently place a juice box in his hand to see what happens. In this one, I need a juice box.

His shock says this is real. This is happening. Daughter. Princess. Antheia.

Vasilis squeezes me tighter, tears streaming down his face, my hair getting damp at the root.

It's not so bad.

There's a weird comfort to it, if you can ignore the bone-crushing biceps and half the audience thinking they're experiencing a shared psychotic episode.

It fills a void I've carried so long I thought it was permanent. *Home*, he said, *I'm home.*

Why wouldn't I believe him? When it feels like I've been reaching out for his exact touch for years and now it's here and he's ... happy.

For the first time in my life, I belong to someone. Someone who missed me. Mourned me. Who sees me not as a specimen or a liability, but family.

I'm happy too.

My mouth cracks open to tell him, to let it all out here in front of the court, but I'm cut short. Vasilis stiffens at my side, frame shifting from shelter to weapon as he whirls his gaze over his shoulder.

Straight to Drake.

The temperature plummets. Vasilis's face becomes a mask of hard merciless edges. "Seize the butcher. Decapitate him. Burn the remains. Wipe the ashes from the stone."

The command slams down. Loud enough to bruise my ears. Loud enough to crack my world in half.

Imperials descend on him like shadows with teeth, circling, arms raised, weapons whining. Drake's eyes flicker dark—the green vanishing, only a dark storm left, only murder and promise and the steely refusal to let them have even a bite of him without a war.

I'm paralyzed. Panic stains everything yellow, acid-bright, caution tape wrapping my spine. My limbs go dead. Unmoving. It's like my body's not mine—a puppet cut from its strings. Nothing works. My nerves have gone into full mutiny.

No.

No, no, no, no.

I can't lose my Fated. Not even if he hates me.

Lightning-quick, Drake elbows the nearest imperial in the face. Cartilage crunches, pink spatters the marble. He kicks a foot out, knocks a weapon loose, catches it. Strong, deadly, a warrior. Ferocious.

But it's a numbers game. One imperial swings onto his back, blade slicing down. A boot drives into his torso.

*Don't fight*, I want to yell, *Run!* But only a faint squeak emerges—a whimper, the sound a crushed rabbit makes mid-nightmare.

Drake takes another Imperial off their feet. They hit the floor and roll. He snares his opponent's dagger, springing up only to face three more waiting for him. He slashes, parries, but even as he fends off one, another catches him right at the side of the neck with a blade. It opens up a burning-red gash that soaks his collar.

Everything inside me clamors but my body will not move.

My world tunnels.

My vision collapses in on itself, all air gone, everything spinning.

I black out.

When I come to, everything smells like iron and dust. The chamber's spinning. I'm spilled on the floor still by the dais, bundled against the Emperor, arms wound tight enough to fuse me to his cool, bare chest. His scent is familiar now, like pressed flowers and old coins and the sweetest jelly bean,

Imperials ring us in a barricade of bodies, all straight backs and weapons. Nothing gets close.

One's consulting Vasilis in a low voice, "Sovereign, should we—"

"Leave the Butcher," Vasilis snaps quietly, quickly. "He won't get out. Focus on my daughter. Tighten the godsdamned perimeter."

It's simple, physical safety, from someone who's not calculating my value per gram of DNA.

I sag forward into it, cheek mashed into the Emperor's shoulder. He lets me. Lets me squeeze harder. It's more kindness than I've had since Nat wrote me down as an emergency contact.

I'm in my father's arms. And every time I think it, the thought just sort of ricochets around, making a mess. Daughter. Princess.

Not freak. Not experiment.

I cling to it, wishing I could roll around in this moment like a wet dog in clean sheets but then, through the wall of bodies, I catch a glimpse of Drake.

He's fifteen feet away, alive but absolutely wrecked, breathing hard, hair streaked with blood and sweat, clenching his jaw like he's seconds from biting clean through the next attacker.

My heart twists painfully.

Gods. He's beautiful. And alive.

For now. I mean to defend him, protect him, tell Vasilis

what he means to me, who he is, but all that gets out is, "Please."

It rasps out of me, a shrapnel-pink plea, too desperate, too exposed. *Please leave him be,* I want to say. *please he's mine.*

Vasilis doesn't understand. He snaps at the nearest courtier. "Your cup. Now."

Then there's a goblet, elegant, silver in his hand, as if it's always been waiting for this moment. The Imperial sniffs it, tastes, then presents it to me like I'm the only thing in the room that matters.

It's warm.

Fresh warm.

Thick, a deep glimmering fuchsia, dark as a bruise, glittering under the lights. Blood and ichor.

"Drink," Vasilis says, and it is distinctly not a suggestion.

He doesn't have to tell me twice. I crush the cup to my mouth and open wide. Blood spills over my teeth, sticky and metallic.

The ichor burns, oh gods, every gland explodes, oddly sweet and thick. I cough, sputter, choke, then swallow again. The same insane hunger that makes me eat a scorching hot pocket straight from the air fryer-magma cheese and all.

Painful, but filling.

"All right, my daughter," Vasilis soothes, so low only I can hear. "Drink. Yes. That is better."

It works. Quickly. The ache in my bones numbs, anxiety softens, until I'm left panting, trembling, a little less hollow.

"Thank you," I croak, sucking the leftovers from my extended fangs, closing my eyes, full for the first time in months.

"Drink more," Vasilis insists, gesturing for cup number two. The imperial steps away to gather it, and my stomach drops through the floor as I make direct, and absolutely mortified, eye contact with Drake.

He looks as though he's being dragged backwards through

every bad memory he's ever had. Bleached, hollow, haunted. He looks like he wants to die, and not in a poetic, candlelit way, but in the way a male wants to disappear so thoroughly they'll never scrape up the shadow he leaves behind.

Blood's running down my chin. My fangs bump my lip. I'm a helpless pile on the floor.

And that's when it all lands, detonating in my chest: Drake knows.

He *knows.*

## 9

# Theia

### HE DIDN'T TRUST HOPE TO HOLD HER

Vasilis calls the council to convene, and after quietly promising me he won't decapitate the bastard butcher, he escorts me to the empire's dedicated praetorium.

It's narrow with ceilings that vanish into darkness. Silver murals bleed down the walls—hunters with fangs and spears, Gods draped in flowing gowns, a sun trapped behind bars.

My ancestors' stories. My heritage.

The thought wraps me in the warmest, coziest blanket. I belong to something ancient.

The Keres council members perch on high-backed thrones arranged in a circle. Each chair displays a chain of bones—trophies of varying lengths. The one facing me features mostly teeth—square, flattened.

Human teeth.

"The bones signify honor," Nephene whispers from beside me, and then when my attention drifts to the bluish puck lights pressed into the ceiling ridges, she shrugs. "Batteries. The only tech that works down here."

We discovered we're long-lost sisters an hour ago, but while I'm intermittently dry-heaving, Nephene remains unfazed. There's no time to envy her composure, her onyx nails, or her gown that screams royalty-with-an-edge—because we actually look alike.

Yes, she towers over me with a long, graceful neck and biceps as plump as ripe apples, but I'd bet my life that her dark hair explodes in the humidity just like mine. She thanked me after we met, "If you hadn't left, Vasilis would never have needed another heir." So casual that when she added we're both in the dead mom's club, I said, "Cool."

We're seated opposite the emperor, wedged between males who must wrestle grizzlies for fun. The outcast section. The misfit end.

With Nephene beside me, it feels elite.

Vasilis waits for each council member to settle before taking his seat—a gesture that strikes me as ancient, as if these beings might have watched dinosaurs roam. Their voices slip between English and Greek, as if neither language meets their expectations.

"Princess," I catch. "Daughter." Then: "Killer."

Drake leans against the wall behind my seat, as if I own him. Eyes closed, hands clasped behind his back. No chair for the blackguard, but no chains either.

It's a good sign, I think. They're warming to him. Or at least cooling off.

A muscled female with a bone bracelet rises. "What of the Munera?"

The question sparks fresh outrage. Stomping. Shouting. Vasilis crosses his arms, unmoved.

"Nixa's only worried because her son, Rafil, will compete," Nephene whispers, leaning close. Her honey-brown eyes meet mine. "The next emperor is chosen during the Munera. It's a ..." she pauses, searching for simple words, "tournament, you might call it, and it must start soon if it's to end by the new moon, Nyx's moon."

"Like the Olympics?" I ask, proud to wield at least one Greek word.

"Running?" She's aghast. "No. It is combat based and fought to the death."

"Actually dead? Pushing up paisleys dead?"

"Not all." A crease between her brows. "Survivors must join our hunting parties. Though most die from their wounds, eventually."

"Neat." Because what else do you say to that?

*When do you open presents?*

*Is there a makeover portion?*

I want to fit in. Belong. But I also might puke. Daughter, princess, sister, decapitation, combat death games, and all I really can focus on is …

*My life in exchange for hers.*

*Drag me through your dungeons if you want.*

*I came here for her. I'm not leaving without her. If you want to stop me, you'll have to put me down yourself.*

Drake came for me. Threatened the wrath of an emperor for me.

Now he won't even look my way.

I can feel his presence at my back, massive and vibrating with the effort of standing perfectly still. If I lit myself on fire, he'd let himself roast.

He thought he was saving Theia—Nat's perky, odd friend. Now I'm the creature he once tried to exterminate.

Is he mad that he failed? Or mad that I lied?

I drag myself out of that grim thought, dark thoughts do no good, and turn to my sister. "Why not vote for it? Winner becomes emperor?"

Nephene's thin silver crown catches the light as she glances between me and the heated debate. "The Munera is an honored custom," she explains under her breath, multi-tasking like she was born for politics. "The chosen victor earns absolute authority. Without the trial, our males would reject his leadership. Each challenge is crafted to test both strength and judgment until only the best Keres stands." She dips her chin at a shirtless male listening intently across the room. "Julian will likely win."

I size him up. Cheekbones that could cut glass, dark hair braided tightly down his back, a bit like my father's. He's one of those beautiful males that belong in a protein powder commercial, but the violence in his gaze should come with a warning label. "Heavy is the crown, right?" I gamble. "Or however the shoe fits."

A sharp exhale cracks the silence behind me.

Drake.

Is he ... laughing?

He doesn't open his eyes or move, just lets the noise rattle loose before he sinks deeper against the stone. The male on my left, who smells faintly of raw steak, shoots him a stink eye.

"Something like that," Nephene murmurs, brow arched at me. "I will teach you."

Julian's gaze finds me across the table. His smile is predatory, teeth too white against skin like marble with the faintest flush of rose beneath.

"He's … cute," I manage.

"He's diabolic." She winks at him. "And I will eat him for dinner."

The innuendo—or threat?—reminds me so much of Nat, my heart pitter-pats.

We'll be the kind of sisters who brush each other's hair. Stay up all night talking. I'll buy her a shirt just because, then steal it from her closet.

"It's a trap!" A bull-sized male slams his foot. "She's an imposter! I won't stand for this!"

All eyes swivel toward me.

I guess I'm the topic now.

I swallow the urge to stand and spin, perhaps tip an imaginary hat. Nephene sets her hand on my shoulder, steady as bedrock. Their voices beat down, but she never flinches.

She squeezes, and I feel safe.

We're totally hugging after this. It'll be bonding and therapeutic. I'll journal it.

"What's even the point of this council," I whisper to her as the shouting intensifies, "if you already have an emperor?"

"They uphold tradition. Remind the emperor of ancient ways—though half those traditions he invented himself. They're like guiding stars Nyx uses, but do not worry, when Father speaks, all this noise means nothing. His word alone is law."

I wish I could borrow her calm like a sweater. My eyes drift to Drake.

The muscle jumping in his jaw is the only sign he's alive.

He's not in chains or under guard, but that's pure show. There's no escape down here, not with every Keres warrior surrounding us, muscles coiled tight as springs, eyes promising violence.

But Vasilis promised he won't let Drake die.

Let the council howl and gnash and rattle all they want—the emperor's word stands. I trust Nephene. It'll all work out.

Vasilis rises. "Enough!"

His presence hammers the air, baking the dust of centuries into the stone. "Take witness. Anthcia is my daughter. She is blood of my blood. The next of the Kolaphos. This truth will never again be questioned."

My chest tightens. Only Nephene's hand keeps me upright.

We are so stress-eating a tub of cookie dough ice cream after this.

Vasilis lifts his chin. "As Antheia is my firstborn, she is my rightful heir. As such, she shall oversee the Munera. She will ascend as empress."

Nephene's fingers transform into talons against my shoulder.

There's movement behind me. The soft scrape of Drake

leaving the wall, the subtle change in air pressure as he comes closer, the almost imperceptible sound of fingers flexing into fists.

Vasilis beams at me, as if he's just surprised me with a cream-colored pony. "When Nyx blesses our new moon, and the Munera ends, Antheia will marry."

# 10

## Drake

BECAUSE GUILT WHISPERED THAT HE SHOULD'VE PROTECTED HER, AND THIS WAS HIS CHANCE TO TRY AGAIN.

There is immediate dissent. Violent, nasty dissent. Knuckles crack. Fists slam armrests. Knives flash. The ripple rolls down the chamber. Starts as shouting accusations—liar, abomination—and quickly ignites into bodies colliding.

Empress. Marriage. The emperor has lost his fucking mind.

Theia's staring at her lap as if she heard a death sentence, not a coronation.

It *is* a death sentence.

The sister—Nephene—digs her nails into Theia's arm.

I don't remember crossing the floor, but suddenly I'm behind her, looming. Every muscle wound tight, mouth full of copper. My gloved palm wraps over the back of her chair, ready to wrench her free and vanish if necessary.

Vasilis bellows for order, but the council is crazed with abject fury.

The male next to Theia grabs her hand, crushing flesh over bone, and hisses into her ear. "Filthy usurper. You won't last the night."

*That* is my breaking point.

I tear his hand from hers, and clamp my hand around the

base of his skull, squeezing until his knees buckle. He thrashes and I apply a precise, scorching pain. "Threaten her again and you'll count your remaining fingers on one hand."

"This is Keres territory," he sneers. "You're nothing."

"I'm enough."

"You're a dead king's rabid dog."

I slam his skull to the table. Lean close, mouth near enough he trembles. "What terrifies you most?" I snarl, menacing. "Flesh rotting off your bone? Starvation? Watching your wife fuck your father?" My breath haunts his ear. "No. I see it now. Males like you—who threaten females—you're usually afraid of something specific. The dark. What lurks there. What might reach for you when you're defenseless."

He flails, and I drive my thumb into the tender hollow above his shoulder blade. "Should we find out? Should I tell them?"

He flinches. Stills.

I ease my grip just enough for him to inhale. "Now. Apologize."

He gags out, "Sorry."

"Not to me." I press his face harder into the stone. "Apologize to your fucking princess."

He blinks at Theia, lost, expecting salvation. Shame dances in his eyes, and I should feel pity. I don't.

My thumb finds its mark in the thin cartilage of his ear, twisting until his jaw quirks. "Now. Or you'll do it from your knees."

His breath shudders. "I—apologies, Princess."

"Princess?" I prompt, amazed I can fucking say it while looking at her. Princess. She's a fucking princess. A *Keres* princess.

Theia's voice is quiet in the tumult: "You're forgiven. A mistake, I'm sure."

"One that won't happen again," I promise to the both of them before releasing him.

He slumps, panting as he cradles his cheekbone.

"Get up," I order. "Open the doors for your princess."

He obeys without protest.

Theia watches me with wide, bloodshot eyes, pulse a frantic gallop in her throat.

I know that feeling. The vertigo of realizing that everything you used to hold true no longer exists. That your former self is gone. Forever. The feeling of having your deepest wish granted and discovering it's actually poison.

The Keres will kill her. Sink fangs in. Swallow her whole. She's their next legend, a cautionary tale against outsiders.

She'll walk straight into their arms and let it happen.

I tighten my glove and offer her my hand. "No one expects you here for this."

She doesn't believe me, but still she slips her palm over mine.

I guide her to the hallway where the ceiling drops and sconces flicker against stone. The Imperials on duty straighten, exchanging sharp, unsure glances. I'm their prisoner; she's their princess.

Before they decide whether to cuff me or bow to her, I pull Theia into shadow, prop her against the wall—me between her and them. The relief is instant.

If she's close to me, nothing bad will happen.

Fantasy. Delusion.

"Is that you making friends?" she asks.

Teasing, sweet. I nearly snap at her to stop, to be angry that she's been threatened and hurt, that she was fucking dragged here, but then her fingers hook on the crook of my elbow.

My body responds instantly. Ardently. I move to put at least eight—okay nine—inches between us but she tightens her grip, as if I'm an anchor securing her to shore.

"You don't have to do this," I tell her. "Not the Munera.

Not the marriage. You don't have to be their princess. You can walk away. Right now."

The emperor will strip me to bone, but he looks at Theia as if she's the sunrise after decades underground.

I get it.

Family is everything.

If my sisters stood before me alive after all these years—I'd tear the world open for them.

"This isn't a cell, Theia. You're free to leave."

She lifts her chin with fragile defiance. "He's my father."

"He doesn't understand what he's asking of you."

"I never imagined—" She swallows roughly. Wets her lips. "They're my family. I never thought I'd find them." The words trip and stagger, missing her usual shine. "All my life I thought Zeus made in some weird experiment. I believed the Keres were extinct. That I was the last. That I only survived the war because I was in a cell—"

"They're survivors. Bloodthirsty survivors."

"Do you hate me?" she blurts, husk thick. "You came for me and … I should've told you what I am. But how could you look at me the same? Nat is the sweetest creature and even she has trouble accepting me and—"

"Nat has killed more creatures than the black plague. Sweet isn't in her vocabulary."

"You're wrong." Stubborn as a bruise.

My hand lifts of its own accord, hovering near the silken strands clinging to her damp cheek. I curl my fingers into a fist instead, dropping my arm like it's made of lead. "You're not one of them, Theia."

"I have his eyes."

"These creatures bathe in blood for sport. They slaughtered thousands because change frightened them."

"Tell me then," she whispers, vulnerability radiating from her like heat. "Where do I belong? Who claims a creature like me?"

"Someone. Anyone." I swallow. "Nat."

"You?"

Her gaze locks with mine, a thousand hopes swimming in those depths. Hopes I should crush. Hopes I can't answer. I say nothing.

"You came to rescue me," she clings to that hope. "That's three times."

"Stop getting into trouble," I rasp, close as I'm allowed to tenderness.

"I'm trying." A ghost of a smile. Her arm circles her waist and squeezes. "I'm so tired of being alone."

Me too.

I could tell her.

But I don't.

There's no cure for me but the grave.

Except right now, in this silence, her holding my arm, the rise and fall of her ribs against my arm. She trusts me with her secrets. Relies on me. It does something—I can't explain it.

It doesn't erase the loneliness.

But she's bright.

She's so bright, it scatters the edges of the dark.

I contemplate staying here forever. In this cold stone darkness. Pulling her against me, burying my face in her hair, and whispering lies about everything being okay.

I lock every muscle to overcome the urge.

She looks up, eyes like shattered amber glass—terrified yet hungry. If she moves even a breath closer, I'll become the monster mothers warn about.

Her head tilts. Lashes lower.

Beautiful. Devastating. Forbidden.

Unbearable.

Her fingers slide up my shirt, breath catching like a gasp against my collar. "Drake," she says—it's barely a sound. My name, almost a wish. An invitation. Eager.

I could take her right here. Press her against cold stone until it warms beneath our bodies. Devour that mouth that speaks my name like salvation.

She'd let me. Close her eyes and surrender everything. Because she's lonely and tired of hiding.

The whole world is shoving her to the edge of a cliff, and somehow it's my unworthy hands she asks to cushion her fall.

I step away.

Her face crumples like a discarded love letter. Raw pain. Then she recovers, tilting that lush mouth as if rejection's her oldest friend. "I'm sorry," she whispers, the words like daggers between my ribs. "I thought ..." A broken laugh escapes as she retreats, awkward. "But of course. Nothing's changed for us."

I let the distance grow. It's better this way. Safer.

Even before I knew she was Keres, we were impossible. Now … I don't know how she can stand to be near me.

"Theia." My voice is gravel. "I just want—" *You.*

She presses trembling knuckles to her lips, a queen donning armor before battle, betrayed only by the wild shimmer in her eyes.

She glances down the hall where violence of the praetorium echoes. I wait for her to flee, to demand space, to beg me to spirit her from this nightmare. I crave it like my next breath.

But she's Theia.

Her chin lifts with stubborn optimism.

She smooths wavy hair, shakes out her skirt like she's preparing for a ball rather than a bloodbath, and pivots toward certain danger." I have to go back inside," she announces, voice steady as stone. "They're my family. I want to know my family." Her smile is brittle as frost. "It'll be fine. It always is."

She couldn't be more wrong, but I follow like the damned, devoted fool I am, because the thought of her alone among these predators makes something primal and possessive roar inside me.

Half-shadow, half bad intention, I carve a path behind her as we re-enter.

Experience immediate regret.

Theia hovers at the door, back impossibly straight, chin at some angle between stubborn and sacrificial. None of the council notices. Too busy trying to tear each other's throats out, their hatred a living, breathing entity between them.

Only Nephene clocks our presence. Expression shifting from amused to calculating instantly. She doesn't acknowledge Theia, just purses her lips and sits, smoothly crossing her legs.

Hard to believe they're sisters. She's missing Theia's rolling curves, the faint pock of her dimple, silky waves falling down her shoulders. The life.

Nephene's a shadow of her sister, tall, thin, slightly hollow, too pale.

"If I might address the council ..." Theia's fingernails tap-tap-tap against the wall, sound lost in the chaos.

No one hears. The din crests higher. A male slams an elbow into the face of a female, and in return, she knifes his thigh. Blood sprays.

Theia clears her throat. "Excuse me, if you would allow, maybe we can …"

She's really doing this.

No plan B, no exit. She's going to stand here and play empress for the same crowd that would strip her bones clean if the mood struck.

I want to break everything.

Fuck it.

I surge forward, unleashing the rage I've spent centuries containing.

My right glove comes off first. Cold air bites the exposed skin. I drop the leather onto the table—a whisper that cuts through the chaos. Every single Keres freezes, gazes locked on my bare hand like it's the most dangerous weapon they've ever seen.

It is.

I strip the left glove next, letting it fall beside its twin. The slap of leather against stone cracks like a whip. Beautiful. Potent.

Silence claims the room.

I meet their faces one by one, letting them see the fury lurking beneath my skin. The twitch in my knuckles, the way my bare hands flex, hungry. Let them remember every cursed tale they've whispered about me in the shadows.

"What is it then, butcher?" the sister drawls.

I square my shoulders. Let it fly. "I'm entering my name in the Munera."

## 11

# Theia

## HE THOUGH SHE MIGHT REACH FOR HIM AND FIND NOTHING

I've always trusted my heart.

It's led me to do some bat-shit crazy stuff. From the semi-insane (permitting multiple abductions) to the fully unhinged (enlisting in a medical trial where all the needles were pre-owned), to the downright terrifying (skipping Duolingo's free trial and pledging myself to a full year), and now … now I'm presiding over a gladiatorial blood-Olympics for creatures that'd devour me for breakfast.

If Nat were here, she'd say, "You always take this optimism thing three planets too far." Then she'd rip someone's teeth out for being sarcastic, which, by the way, might be an actual Keres sport. *Dental deconstruction.*

I still can't ask for the toilet in Italian, but I don't regret a single beat of it, because after every insane leap of faith, I have the dream.

It never changes.

I'm cold. Alone. My stomach gnaws with manic hunger. A flimsy dress clings to me like a bad promise; my wrists and ankles throb against iron chains. People swarm around me, expecting something monumental—yet all I hear is the weak patter of my pulse.

Dread coils in my gut like molten rock. My legs refuse to obey. My heart aches in a melancholy drumbeat, as if I'll never taste sunlight again.

Then the shrieking starts. The shooting. An explosion. I clamp my eyes shut, brace myself for the end.

A voice cuts through it all. Smooth and low. Inevitable. A hand at my nape gently tugging me back from the abyss. The chains are still on me, bullets still fly, but my fear evaporates. He's here. My Fated.

He strides toward me through the chaos, a blur of black and white. Nothing slows him. He always finds me. Every. Single. Time. I'll never be lonely again.

I haven't had the dream since Drake shielded me from a firing squad, since he carried me from that burning building, staking his very life for mine.

He's my Fated. I feel it down in my bones.

And yet at the diner … he pushed me away.

And now he's entered the deadly Munera for me. To marry me.

That means something.

An upward turn in this tragic spiral? He could win. We could usher in a new era for the Keres. We could rewrite destiny.

I'm bending over backwards to convince myself I haven't made a grave mistake by staying when Vasilis appears at the far end of the gallery, silhouette etched in the somber lighting.

He's granted me two days of free rein—though he's never far behind, anxiously conferring with his council on ways to disqualify Drake. The elders remind him over and over: the Munera isn't limited to Keres competitors. To withdraw a contender now would enrage Nyx herself. There is no retreat. No mercy.

The butcher must compete.

Drake's taunt echoes in my head, "You don't think I'll win,

do you?" He grinned at the emperor—arrogant, dripping with challenge. "That must be your only objection. At worst, I die quickly. At best, your finest warriors tear me apart. Your next emperor proves his mettle with my blood. Wouldn't that be nice?"

Anger, hot and fierce, clenches my stomach. I am not a violent creature and yet I want to bash him bloody for volunteering. I would if he were here.

But he's been a ghost. My only proof he's still breathing is the way my father's temper flares at the mention of his name.

Vasilis steps beside me before an oil painting of a grim, battle-scarred man—my great-grandfather, Bremon the Uprooter. "A tired-looking fellow," he observes with dry amusement. "Nothing like your vigor, Antheia."

I suppress a grin. Ferocious, I'd call him—ravening eyes ablaze with war. Adjusting the layers of my skirt, I pivot to face him. "You can call me Theia."

He blinks. "Yes, I apologize. I forgot. It is what you prefer."

"It's the only name I've ever known."

He nods, then returns his attention to grandpappy. "I dispatched search parties for you," he tells me when the silence presses in. "My best scouts, every day of every year you were gone. Even when our tunnels burned and I could spare none, I sent them. Where were you?"

The pinch of regret in my choice to stay? It dissolves under the weight of his question, the anguish in his amber eyes.

He searched for me.

He thought of me.

He never gave up.

"I was in a lot of places." I force a tight, courteous smile—the kind you pin above trauma like a brooch. "They captured me before I even knew what I was. Did experiments, trials. I stumped their scientists. They deemed me an unknown creature. Sold me, then sold me again." I shrug, though the memory twists like ice through my veins. "I broke free when I could, but they hunted me down each time."

He stands so still he could be cleaved stone—stare fixed on mine, deadly. "You were only a child. How—" Horror widening his gaze. "The quickening. The hunger—how did you know what to do?"

I close my eyes, tasting the memory of panic and raw need. The quickening is an apt name for the transition from mortal to immortal creature. One moment, I'd been Theia, hobbyist captive, the next, I'd been an unquenchable, savage force they tried to starve into weakness. They fed me through a tube, pureed vegetables, raw meats, crushed vitamins, and when none of it stuck, they left me to wither. When they sensed death creeping in, they sent an attendant in to check my pulse. I lashed out. My first ever taste of blood became my first kill. That night, the dream came for the first time—a black velvet sky crackling with stars, a voice older than time calling me home.

"I figured it out," I tell him. It's the truth.

We drift to the next portrait: a fierce female, wrath inscribed in every line of her face. It seems all my ancestors wore anger like armor.

My father's nose crunches at her face, and then he turns me toward the grand mural spanning the opposite wall. It's bold, alive, glowing with power where the portraits lie stiff and colorless.

"What is it?" I ask.

"This is the first lesson we teach our children: the story of the Keres. Here stands Nyx, who bore us." He traces the silhouette of a female formed from darkness itself, only her gleaming eyes and sharp teeth visible. "Nyx. Our mother. Our beginning."

I can't look away from those teeth.

"Goddess of Night. Creator of stars." Pride radiates from him in waves. "Even Zeus, King of Gods, trembles before her power. And we are her perfect reflection. That's why we must remain pure. Gods do not mingle with mortals, and neither do we."

My tongue brushes against my own pointed incisors, hidden for so long.

"Your fangs are your birthright. You do not have to hide them here." He emphasizes *here*, but there's no need. I know exactly how unwelcome the Keres are aboveground.

He continues the tour of our twisted family tree. There's Hypnos, God of sleep, who father claims suggested counting sheep as a cruel joke to an annoying king, and the God did not expect to be taken seriously, nor widely adopted. Thanatos is death incarnate, and the inventor of the snooze function on alarm clocks. Father calls them 'alarm bells' and struggles to explain how hitting a button to gain more sleep, only that Thanatos views it all as hilarious that mortals flirt with the concept of eternal rest every morning and then panic-reject it five minutes later.

He moves on to Nemesis, Goddess of Retribution, and Moros, God of Doom. Then the Gods of misery and deceit, distress, and discord. Anyone, as far as I can tell, who is associated with cruelty and darkness.

All related to me. All my blood.

"That's everyone then?"

He chuckles. "It is a large family," he says. "You will meet them all in due time."

That's exactly what I'm afraid of. There's not a single God on the wall in front of me I wouldn't pee my pants meeting. That I wouldn't fake an illness to avoid.

"Are you sure that's everyone?" I ask, waiting for a Demigod of kindness or light or cherry blossoms to appear in a corner.

Before he answers, a sound rips through the corridor—a

deep, vibrating gong that makes my teeth click together hard enough to chip. The note climbs higher, louder, until it shreds all possibility of chill.

My father's face transforms—ancient, merciless, hungry. My palms slick with sweat.

The Munera's starting. And I'm the prize.

## 12

# Theia

## ACTION FELT BETTER THAN MOURNING

It's giving mass proposal: barbarian edition.

A horde of lean, rippling males kneel before me, elbows locked at ninety degrees, bowing so deep I can count each vertebra in their exposed spines. Umber war paint gleams wet on their skin, twisted into cryptic sigils, the dye seeping down oversized deltoids in rivulets, sluicing over taut muscles, and pooling in the valleys of their backs.

At the center, stands Vasilis. Maybe a little pleased. A little impressed. Impossible to tell. He's no longer the father imparting history lessons. Here, under the jagged stalactites, he's the Emperor of the Deep Realm, the Last Kingdom, the Sunless Court.

On risers around the cavern's rim, the stands pulse, teeth and hunger and so much anticipation for slaughter. It's a lot.

Too much.

Some of the males are beautiful, sculpted chests, limbs like wrought iron. A few are outright terrifying. Most hover between gladiator chic—veins webbing pink beneath pale flesh, eyes coal black—and homicidal boy next door: long lashes and sinister smiles.

My tongue sticks to the roof of my mouth. The gossamer

dress—fit for a princess—clings so tightly a deep breath will rip the stitches. It's too thin, sticky, a white that is somehow ghostly, emphasizing the extra pigment in my skin, a rare color down here.

I fumble for composure, spine ramrod straight, chin level.

Beside me on the spectator dais, Nephene lounges in scarlet silk. No tiara today, no sisterly affection either. Greta, a councilor who definitely started the stabbing in our meeting, perches on the arm of Nephene's chair, whispering urgently to a circle of attentive females. But Nephene tracks me, waiting, hoping for me to botch my very first public appearance.

Sibling rivalry is a new and highly unwelcome experience.

Her attention shifts suddenly to the endless line of kneeling warriors, and a grin that can only be described as feral curves her lips as she fixes on one particular male.

My stomach seizes.

Drake.

He kneels at the edge of the arena, arms crossed, expression carved from granite. Not bowing, his head is raised, midnight hair tousled in his eyes, curled around his ears as he stares up here. Right at me.

Like the others, his chest is bare. Unlike the others, there are no markings save for a brand over his heart. A cleaner, prettier version of the one on my shoulder. Around him, hulking brutes jockey for position, itching to claim the first taste of his blood. The corner of his lip lifts.

He's not afraid.

He's defiant.

I glance at Nephene, check to make sure my fangs are extended, and smile. If he can kneel in a pit of vipers, outcast and branded, I can too.

The cavern hushes as Vasilis rises. Every eye snaps to the royal dais.

Do I wave? I'm waving.

"The Keres are a passionate people." Vasilis the dad is

gone, body-swapped with a subterranean dictator. "This task requires heart—" He pauses, savoring the moment. "—Apologies. This task requires *a* heart. To advance, bring Antheia a heart. You have twelve minutes."

It's instant. And horrible.

The competitors lunge, bodies slamming together, arms and hands and fangs at necks. No warm-up, no strategy, just violence snap-cut loose. Fangs puncture flesh. Daggers slash cheekbones. Hot arterial spray splatters the railing in front of me. A few drops reach my dress.

It's a meat grinder, bone splintering, sinew tearing. The Keres howl, pounding their concrete seats with fists and claws.

A sickly pink haze mists through the torchlight, slicking hair and skin. It clings to my tongue—metallic and sweet as poison candy.

Nephene's enraptured with the carnage. No flicker of sympathy. She leans forward, mouth gleaming scarlet, and murmurs, "They'll go for numbers—cull early to shorten the events. Favor the brawn."

"Julian's brought a bag," Vasilis notes.

"Arrogant or self-aware?" Nephene wonders. Father and daughter exchange an inside look. They're enjoying this. Bonding. Like she's just taken off her training wheels and he's found her kite in a tree.

I try to watch, but the arena blurs, colors blooming into each other. Limbs tangle, teeth snap, a head rolls away in a fountain of glittering blood. It's beyond horror. It's a waking nightmare seared into my soul.

I shut my eyes. Clench my fists so nails razor the meat of my palms.

Drake won't survive this.

They want him dead more than anyone.

A gong lets out a single, vibrating note. The screams stop all at once, like a switch jammed off. The silence is so pure that my ribs ache. I open my eyes slowly, battling the urge to throw up or curl in on myself.

"Antheia, come," Vasilis commands. "The victor shows his devotion."

My knees shudder as I descend, each step a battle against my own nausea. There are bodies everywhere. Nothing about them palatable; husks, and limbs, some with chests torn open, faces unrecognizable. The tang of ichor slaps.

Julian straightens as we approach him. His brown leather pants are slung low on his hips, the markings on his torso smeared with blood. A pile of gory crushed hearts rests at his feet. Ten. Maybe more.

I backpedal onto Nephene's dress.

Julian grins.

Every inch of him gleams. Hair raked back from his face, skin more marble than living flesh, the design inked across his chest like a curse. The blood-stained band at his bicep glitters with embedded bone fragments, actual trophies, lashed together so the spurs dig into his muscle with every flex. I'm sure he likes the sting.

He kneels with astounding grace, arms spread wide in a perverse benediction. "My princess," he intones, voice a velvet thunder. His eyes are a rush of impossible color: indigo, thawing into silver, then violet, a churning bruise that drinks in every glint of torchlight.

The look he gives me is not worshipful. It's predatory.

He selects a still-beating heart, liquid dripping down his sinewy wrists, and lifts it to me. "For you to feel alive," he offers, fangs out. "I offer you more than any other male. Should you favor strength, know there is none stronger."

Vasilis lays a proud hand on Julian's shoulder. "And none more deadly," he agrees. "A male who can master his people."

I keep my face blank. The sand floor of the arena is crunchy and wet with blood. My toe brushes through something that might be hair, might be nerve. I can't think about it.

My stomach feels ready to turn inside out when a feeling sweeps me, a small tug of worry. I follow it like a dog scenting a bone. Farther, farther, toward the wall where bodies have been dragged, losers being discarded.

Under the harsh light, sprawled like a toppled statue, is Drake.

Flat on his back, pants hacked and shredded, missing a boot. His chest is open. Open. Not ragged and ripped like the other corpses—his is slashed open in a straight, neat line. too precise, too visceral—a silent testament to a blade that knew exactly where to cut. Runny, crimson blood pools beneath him.

Terror bubbles in my gut. My heart stops beating.

In each of his hands rests half a heart, hacked free from his own body. Butchered meat.

A scream claws at my throat, but I smother it.

"He made his choice." Vasilis's shadow falls across me, his words laced with cruel pride. "None but a true Keres can endure these rites."

I'm hyperventilating, crying. "He took a heart," I mutter.

"So he does. We'll prop his body up for the next task." He snares my elbow. "Come, daughter. The crowd is eager to celebrate."

I force my gaze back to Drake's body, desperate for some spark of life—a twitch, a flutter. But he lies cold and motionless, open from sternum to stomach. His innards glisten like blood-soaked velvet, and I taste acid on my tongue

Julian's voice booms behind us: "He fought like a coward."

Hot waves of betrayal crash over me, each sharper than the last. My lungs constrict. My vision drums black. I feel like tearing myself apart, bleaching this horror from my mind. Instead, I stand rigid as stone.

Kill or freeze. The choice isn't mine. My knees lock as I peer down at him.

Why?

Why would he cut his own heart for me? What kind of sickness is that? What hope? What cosmic idiocy?

I want to scream until the world shatters.

I'm mad. I don't get mad; I'm Theia. But I am mad. Bristling with it. I'm more than mad, I'm bloody angry and I can't even yell at him. I'm going to die angry and—

Drake's chest jerks upward in one trembling inhale.

The sound is ragged, raw.

He's alive.

I need to get him out of here.

# 13

## Theia

### EVERY STEP WITHOUT HER FELT WRONG

"Every creature in here is picturing your head on a platter."

I lift a brow and lock onto Drake's molten gaze. "That's how they always look. I believe they're warming up to me."

"They must like me too. We're getting identical death glares."

He's not wrong.

Vasilis sold this as a casual mixer—"Mingle, my dear. Have fun, meet your subjects"—then had a trio of assassin-esque handmaidens lace me into a sapphire gown so tight I can't draw a full breath.

Convenient how he's nowhere to be found now that his subjects show their true feelings.

For sixty excruciating minutes, I've endured:

Male competitors promising Drake's slow demise: "I'll personally hang his intestines like festival garlands."

Suspicious females with thinly veiled accusations: "Strange how you never escaped your so-called captors."

And my personal favorite—power-hungry suitors whispering: "A delicate empress like you needs a strong male ruler. Vasilis understands this."

I sweep my gaze across the room to Nephene, draped in

black leather and brandishing her third cup of blood punch. Her cheeks glow pink, and her eyes sparkling with wicked light. Around her huddle the Keres of high rank. Greta, dark hair woven into a miniature dagger-studded coronet; Malni, whose chainsaw laugh and talon-sharp nails could've inspired Cruella; and that blonde I recognize from Father's personal guard. Nearby stands Julian—shirtless as usual—flanked by his best buddies in the competition, Stav and Varyn, who lead the inevitable charge toward ichor poisoning.

Each new round of drinks, Malni unleashes a bawdy shriek over something vulgar, Greta rolls her eyes, and Nephene recounts grisly tales about ancient battle lust or goat milk and severed hands. I can't follow any of it, but Malni's laugh carries like a chainsaw. Not the most relaxing book club ever.

More than once, I've caught Nephene's gaze flick to me, then to Drake, then to her friends, brow furrowed as if she's compiling a file for some future HR meeting. If the Keres have HR. Probably not.

I'll ask.

Drake's body heat anchors me. He doesn't dare touch me, but that solid presence at my shoulder is an unspoken vow: I've got you. Like a royal wedding security detail—minus the finger sandwiches and any hope of a streaker.

Since he arrived—eight minutes ago, not that I'm counting—no one's dared speak to me, sneer at me, or snicker while pointing at my gown's tight seams.

I don't know if it's good or bad, having a watchdog.

I do know I like it.

"You're bleeding," I say without turning.

"Am I?"

"You should be in bed. Resting."

He shrugs, almost imperceptibly. "This is more fun."

"Than staunching blood flow?"

Another shrug.

I tighten my grip on my goblet. "I wish you'd rest."

Because you cut your heart out—your actual heart—sliced it into pieces like the world's most tedious game of Operation. Because I can smell the blood leaking from your still-stitching wound. Because you should have died. Because I think you did die for a second and it made me furious.

*And what did you do?* The bright voice has taken a bleak turn since yesterday. *You just stood there doing nothing as he bled out.*

Every immortal has their strength. Can't drown a Scylla, can't poison a Keres, you can disarm—literally—a Hydra all day long, but those limbs are ten out of ten times coming back, with even more muscle. But they have their weaknesses too.

Cyclops have zero depth perception, the Boreads swell at a hint of pollen. Sunlight reduces Keres to ash. Just like that. Nothing fancy. A few seconds' exposure wipes them out. No resurrection, no second chances.

All Keres. Except me. I just wind up sunburned with a pounding headache. I add it to my catalogue of freak perks: killer curves and the uncanny knack for finding every high-sodium snack in a 7-Eleven.

But Drake—a mortal remade by the Divine—what destroys him? What makes him stronger?

I begged my father to cast Drake out, to send him away. "If the butcher wishes to die, my dear, you should let him," he'd said.

Did Drake even know he'd survive ripping out his own heart?

The stunned recognition in his eyes when he woke says he didn't.

"I always figured Keres slept in coffins," Drake says, side-stepping my concern. "Seemed like the one thing mortals got right. Descendants of Nyx dreaming about bloodletting in purple velvet boxes."

I nearly choke. "We're not vampires, and even if we were,

velvet's a dust trap. Can you imagine the static cling? Besides, I'm more of a memory foam kind of girl. Gels to your body and doesn't reek too much like a mortuary."

Drake grunts. Which in Drake-speak means "point taken."

He's so close I can feel the warning signal in the air, all voltage and graveyard humor, but not actually touching me. He never does. His self-restraint is Olympic, which is both flattering and deeply infuriating.

I don't know whether to be honored or insulted.

I sip my own blood punch, which, as far as I can tell, is two parts ichor, fifty parts blood, and those hard blue crystals you find in the crevice of a Kool-Aid packet. The taste is crime-adjacent. My tongue numbs immediately, my throat sears. I cough.

"Christ, that's hitting you worse than the roofies did. Stop drinking it."

"No coffins," I retort, "but blood's still a dietary requirement."

He snatches the cup and dumps it into a nearby devil's tongue plant. The liquid sparkles pink against the soil, making him pause. "Is that ichor?"

"Ichor is silver," I snap. "And would definitely kill me. This is immortal blood. I'm not used to it yet."

I steel myself for a barb about my preference for weak veins, or a reminder that he can still see the pink stain on my lips from our breakfast date.

Instead, he says, "Smart."

I finally let myself look at him straight on.

The sight is devastating. He's showing skin. Not in the bold, flaunting way of the Keres with their unashamed muscles, but in calculated flames that feel far more menacing. Two buttons undone at his throat, revealing the tattoo ringing his neck. A strip of skin between his gloves and sleeves. Each exposed inch seems intentional—a warning, even a weapon.

I can't tear myself away.

"Smart?" I echo.

"Kadmos thought the Keres were defined by their brutality," he says, "but it's really their cunning. They never adapted to belong—they broke free of the Gods, slipped Argos's grip. Built their own laws, their own society, and it's outlasted the Olympians. By drinking the blood of other immortals—their only real enemies— they train themselves to crave it, or at least not flinch when it's time to kill. With one notable exception, the Keres are viciously strategic, including their cultivation of a mindless, savage reputation."

"What's the exception?"

He just looks at me.

Oh. *Oh.*

I twist at fabric gathered at my hip. "Still, better to make friends than enemies."

Drake does an almost-smile. Enough to show teeth, but not enough to let you forget the threat underneath. "You really think diplomacy can heal centuries of blood feuds?"

I steal his move and shrug. "Maybe not, but cupcakes might."

"Have you ever seen a Keres eat a cupcake?"

"They don't sell them in the Sunless Kingdom. I checked." I nod toward the buffet: one garnish tray of questionable blue cheese cubes and sixty little glasses of blood. Classic. "When I'm crowned, first order: themed pastries at every event."

"Second order, the Mamma Mia soundtrack?"

"Obviously." I smile at him, and my stomach flips to find he's already looking down at me. "You're a good listener."

His jaw tightens. "I work in interrogation."

Right. Of course. He memorizes everything by habit, not sentiment.

He scans the crowd, half smile riding a knife-edge. "I'm honestly surprised nobody's tried to kill me yet. Welcome wagon in the alley raised my expectations."

"Nyx watches over all contestants outside the events," I explain, garbling and mashing up a bunch of the info I've gotten. "It's a sacred period. Any killing in-between is a Divine no-no."

"Still, not even a knife in the back? It wouldn't kill me, but ..." His lips twitch. A shrug "They're Keres. They'd still enjoy the twist."

Understatement.

The urge for light stabbing is in the room with us. Violence rides the crowd right on the surface in glares and tense jaws, and the occasional flash of fangs.

All aimed at Drake. Unease has me saying, "Please go lie down. Until there are minimal open wounds."

"It's just a scratch." He pauses. "You can really smell that?"

"Clear as a ball. Like the last drop of water when you're dying of thirst." As soon as I say it, my face burns hot, the confession hanging there stupid and raw. "Only in that it's impossible to miss. Like blood on snow or a heartbeat in a morgue."

"You thirsty, Theia?"

My insides do a full somersault. I try not to let it show on my face—which is, I'm realizing, a skill I never developed because no one ever found a way to make "thirsty" sound so ... significant. My entire body lights up like a back-alley pharmacy sign. Cheap, neon. Possibly illegal.

"I can manage," I say, even though the very scent of him —fresh and minty, slightly coppery—is making the blood in my veins fizz like Mentos in soda. The hunger is real and getting worse every heartbeat.

He doesn't break eye contact. His throat is perilously close to my face, tattoo dark as night, teasing. I could lick it if I wanted. Which I don't. But I do. It's confusing. The air between us is electric and awkward, the kind you only get when both parties are thinking about eating something (possibly each other) but no one wants to be the first to bite.

"You look like you could drain me in one go," he murmurs, low, rough. "When's the last time you ate?"

I gesture at the rapidly drooping plant.

"Something that doesn't make you sick."

"I've gone longer than this between meals," I say, which is a lie, but I think I deserve a little dignity.

The corner of his mouth rises. "Your pupils are blown."

"It's called social anxiety," I mumble. "Side effect of growing up in a padded cell. You'd know that if you ever took a BuzzFeed quiz."

He cocks his head, hair scraping his lashes. "You're not even standing up straight. If I nudged you, you'd collapse. Or try to bite me."

"Very tempting." I grin.

A pause, thick enough to coat a spoon. His jaw flexes. "Go ahead."

14

# Theia

## JOY SHOULD BE WITNESSED

I almost whimper. Feel free to psychoanalyze.

Instead, I shake my head. "You're not built for a quick refill."

I think. I'm not willing to test it.

Drake's still looking at me though, chin dipped toward me, voice pitched low. "The guy in the disco hat wasn't either."

Guilt drapes over me like a burial shroud. Of course he figured it out. Why else would a Keres prowl the night. Rod and Theia sitting in a tree, k-i-l-l-i-n-g.

"For the record, eliminating Rod was a civic duty. I was being a good spot. The absolute best. So good, they'll name a children's museum after me."

"Good spot," he echoes softly, that corner lifting higher, twisting almost to a smile. "If you need to feed, Theia ..."

He leaves it there. Not an invitation. Not even a dare. Just the casual, infuriating confidence of someone convinced he's disposable.

Charming. Horrifying

My throat burns. I instantly envision myself going full National Geographic at the crossroads of Drake's neck and jaw, right where the pulse pounds loudest.

*You just had open heart surgery, minus the medical expertise.*

*You're meant to be taking it easy.*

*You're my* Fated. *I'd never take your vein, never risk unleashing myself on you.*

These objections jam up at the back of my tongue, all while my mouth waters so profusely someone might've asked me to suck a lemon.

"Theia?" His glove brushes my skirts. "Are you okay? Should we go?"

His voice is a coil around my spine, tight and unspooling, making every nerve dizzy. My knees wobble. The floor churns like a funhouse and a funeral at once.

"I'm ..." I hear myself murmur.

He stands too close, boots braced wide. For a second, I invent new physics, a reality where it's just us slipping out the back door. I imagine the hush on the other side. Him caging me against the wall, one hand flat against stone, the other fisting my dress tight at the hip.

The space between us? Gone. His lips brush my neck, gentle, patient. I feel his smile there and it's everything. Dizzy, desperate, the way it's supposed to be. His other hand finds my waist, glove gone, skin to skin. He holds me tight, like he doesn't want to let go.

My stomach flutters. My vision halos. Senses go warp-speed, hyper-focus, tunnel-blind: all of me maps the lines of his jaw, the impossible green of his eyes flickering between warning and want.

My fangs snap down.

Hunger slices through—not lust, not hope, but the primal, gnashing bright need. The daydream shatters. I'm back in this dress that strangles, back with every Keres already betting how quickly my corpse will cool. I stumble, shoving air between us, swallowing the thirst. Get control. I clamp my arms around my waist.

"I'd never touch you," I whisper. It's meant to be a vow. Sounds more like a warning.

Drake's head jerks up. I swear he goes a little pale. As if I've just cut the wrong wire on a bomb and we're both about to be scattered across the walls.

He looks ... offended. Not ordinary offended, but Drake offended, which is a special brand of existential crisis mashed with tragic poetry. For a split second, it's written on his face: the horror, the insult, maybe the disappointment that, until now, he didn't realize he wanted me to want him.

I'm halfway to inventing an apology—*I'd actually love to suck your blood, but I haven't mastered not ripping throats out*—when Julian materializes, backed by a wall of fans.

His grin is white as fresh bleach. "Antheia," he greets, smugger than a cat licking a creamsicle. "A surprising number of males finished the first task. All for the sake of your beauty."

Nephene's eyes roll skyward as she drapes her arm over the shoulders of the blond woman who, upon closer inspection, is not Keres. Sun-kissed cheeks, blunt teeth, the edge of alertness, as if she's acutely aware she's a lamb in the wolf's den. Before I can place her—too solid for a Siren, surely—Julian takes my hand in his, weaving our fingers together.

"Princess Antheia," he croons. "The emperor himself has summoned me to prepare you for ruling. As tradition demands, I'll guide you through the rites." There's an unmistakable "and you'll be lucky to have me in the room" subtext.

Drake's arm flexes beside me. A warning shot.

Julian simply beams, star pupil of a remedial flirtation seminar. "Thank you," I tell him. "I feel very … welcomed. And excited to learn our customs."

"I have decades of knowledge to share with my future queen."

"*If* you marry," Nephene cuts in with a razor-sharp smile,

eyes flicking to me. "Who says you'll still be standing at the end?"

Like *I* might not make it to the end of the Munera.

Drake's silence hurts. He's convinced I'll be dust before closing ceremonies.

I straighten my spine and force a smile. I survived a twenty-year stint without sunlight or sugar cookies: I'm stronger than they realize.

"The princess belongs by my side," Julian tells Nephene, near haughty. "It is important for us to bond before we wed."

"Should she fill out a questionnaire?" Drake's voice could sand wood. "Night owl. Mint chocolate chip. Right side of the bed."

Julian's nostrils flare. "Was anyone addressing the blood bag?"

"I'm eager to meet all the contenders," I interject, ignoring how Drake went three for three. "But perhaps it's premature, with so many remaining."

Julian schmoozes on. "Only one will prove himself deserving of your radiance."

Nephene's eyes narrow to slits. "Dial it back. She's flesh and blood, not gold."

"Yet I will handle Antheia as such. As the sovereign requested."

There's a sound behind me—a shift, as if someone's grinding glass under their boot. Drake. He's not touching me, but a deep inhale would bring us into full contact. "She doesn't need a handler. And it's Theia. Not whatever you're calling her."

Julian loses his charm. "You think a human could stand at her side?"

"Better than being a narcissist's second choice," Drake growls. If they had tails, they'd be lashing.

Julian ignores him, tells me, "You should rest before your second round. You look ... drained."

I try to answer, but Drake is suddenly rigid, face locked on something over my head. Not Julian. Not me. The blonde.

Her hair catches the light like polished brass, muscles coiled beneath sun-kissed skin, smile sharp as broken glass. Drake's face has transformed—jaw slack, eyes wide, like someone's yanked the ground from beneath him.

A wet, squishy feeling mucks up my lungs. Jealousy blooming thick and gloomy.

"Antheia?" Julian's voice cuts through, demanding my focus.

I excuse myself, faking a smile, then weave through the packed bodies on autopilot. Down a narrow stone hallway, colder with every step. Drake's behind me. I don't look back, but I know he's there. Heavy, storm cloud energy, practically blocking out the corridor lights with his sheer personal gloom. Typical. As soon as I believe I'm not a total disaster, here comes my favorite audience member, right on cue.

I half-expect a gentle, "You okay?" or maybe something dazzling like, "You shouldn't walk alone, there's a murderer out here," but what I get is—

"Keep your shoulder covered," he snarls, rough and savage. "Don't let anyone see the mark."

I freeze mid-stride, spin on my heel. The chill rattling my bones? Not the drafty corridor. "Excuse me?"

He's shoulder-to-shoulder with me, his sleeve brushing my arm, yet his attention is riveted to the raised skin on my shoulder blade like it personally insulted his mother. Rich, considering he spent the last four minutes practicing drooling over that random blonde.

And why—why is it so much worse that she's not Keres?

If she were Keres, there'd be hope, a thread to clutch, but this—

My fangs are back. Without warning, sharp and ready.

The world sharpens. Sounds amplify, colors intensify, my senses surge, suddenly raw. My body itches to strike, but there's no fuel left in me. The blood in my veins is old, congealed and useless. My stomach empty.

I grab the rock, cool, damp, very supportive, and glare. "No one cares about the mark, Drake. We don't even know what it means, it's probably nothing."

"Kadmos's sigil is never nothing." His eyes cling to my shoulder, then flick away. "It makes you a target. You got it for a reason, and we need to figure out why before anyone else or …"

His sentence ends there. His jaw clenches.

"Why didn't you interrogate me?" I ask. "When the Blackguard freed us and brought us to the safe house, you questioned every other female, except me."

"Atlas handled you."

"Why? Why did Atlas question me, Drake? You're the crown's famed interrogator. The Butcher himself. Nat says you're the best extractor of secrets in the realm. So why pass me off to Atlas? Why didn't you question me?"

"I was busy."

"Then do it now."

His Adam's apple bobs. "You said you don't remember how you got it."

"Then dig it out of me." My fingers curl into fists. I push up straighter. Try not to look like I'm clinging to the wall because my legs are made of Jell-O. "That's your specialty, isn't it? Breaking people apart until they spill? Crack me open. Rummage through my mind until you find the truth."

"Not happening."

"You could unlock what I buried. Tear the memory out."

"I said no."

"There are answers in here," I press, voice cracking. "I could free you from the curse. If you'd only let me—"

"No, Theia!"

His roar makes me flinch. The hallway tilts. My vision fractures. My knees buckle.

Drake's whole body sags. "Come on. You're barely standing. Let me walk you to your rooms."

"Is it because you're scared of what you'll find? Or because you're afraid I can't handle it?"

"I know you can't."

My thoughts scatter. Is he protecting me? Or dreading what I might become if pushed? I swallow hard. "I can take it. I understand the risk."

His face goes cold. "You honestly think I'd take that risk? With you?"

His stare flicks to my mouth—my fangs. Does he think I'd sink them into him? Would I?

I shrink smaller than ever. Lower than mold between bathroom tiles. More worthless than Rod.

Gregory. Whatever.

It could be embarrassment, or deflection, or the fact that I need blood more than Zeus needs a chastity belt, but the anger that consumed me as I watched Drake bleed out sweeps back into me in one violent crash.

"I have no idea what you'd risk, butcher. You swaggered into a Keres party with an open wound. That's as close to suicidal as ripping your own heart out. As close to a death wish as storming the Sunless Kingdom, but if you believe I'll let you kill yourself—"

"You walked knowingly into this mess and expected me not to follow?"

"I expected you to celebrate!" I shout. Not elegant, not regal. "You're the one who wanted me gone!"

Something shifts in those eyes. He opens his mouth, closes it, tries again. "I—" The words catch, and my fury curdles in on itself, a tiny little implosion that renders me exhausted.

I grip the wall for dear life and confess something I never thought could be true. "I'm really beginning not to like you."

"You don't need to like me. Just stay where I can protect you."

My limbs are heavy, lifeless. "Why are you even here? Why'd you really follow me?"

For the briefest, most humiliating moment, I ache for him to confess some grand reason. Destiny. The Fates. A warmth in his heart. The way my eyes glimmer like the lost souls of a thousand dying stars. A reason worthy of wedding vows and pop anthems.

Instead, he meets me with steel. "I made a vow to Nat that I'd keep you safe. That's the only reason."

## 15

# Drake

### THE DARKNESS IS NOT AS SCARY WITH HER IN IT

My gloves peel off sticky and resentful, as if they know I'm about to do something stupid.

Did it. Done it. Will do it again.

I press my thumb to the fresh cut on my wrist, scanning the hallway for prying eyes. Blood beads before the wound seals itself—skin knitting shut so effortlessly that a century later it still makes me shiver. No scar. No proof except the sting.

My chest wound—healed less than an hour ago—still tingles beneath my shirt. Its suturing is the only reason I'm standing here, leaning against cold stone instead of drifting in oblivion.

*Like the last drop of water when you're dying of thirst,* she'd whispered.

My body's still buzzing on overdrive from the Munera. A pulse deep under my ribs, tingling in my fingertips, a faint hum under my skin.

I had to tease her. Had to push. Offer myself as some prize.

The disgust on her face scours. *I'd never touch you.*

Of course not. She's not a masochist.

*Clear as a ball*, she'd said. Confidently. Another phrase mangled beyond recognition. I'd let it slip by because I'd sooner slit my own throat than correct her.

I slump against the wall. Silence except for my breathing. I count tiles and keep Theia's door in sight.

She's not sleeping. I hear the subtle scrawl of her pen, the delicate rustle of parchment as she devours Keres history. Sometimes I think I linger here just to prevent her from serenading the entire damn empire before dawn.

She doesn't belong here.

A sound: glass heels. Nephene emerges from shadow like she was made from it, each step precise. Blink silk clings without a wrinkle, mouth set stern, her eyes burn amber bright.

"Long night?" I ask.

She taps the wall with manicured nails. "She made it back fine then. Didn't get lost?"

I nod, unsure if she's relieved or frustrated.

"The tunnels aren't forgiving to outsiders," she says.

"She's not an outsider."

A soft huff. "You intend to sit there all night?"

"I might stand."

She studies me—measuring, weighing—then drops to the floor beside me with the silent grace of a knife sliding from its sheath. Her hair cascading down her back, the same wave and color as Theia's.

"What makes her special?" Not a question. An accusation. She's staring straight ahead, nails drumming stone.

I say nothing. I'm not supposed to have an answer. I'm a Blackguard, the butcher. I don't believe anyone's special.

Yet here I am, sitting outside Theia's room like a lost puppy when I should be anywhere else.

*It's the brand*, I try to tell myself. I have keep close to her because of that, because the king marked her, and it has to be for a reason. Because she might point us toward his killer, relieve me of this curse.

It's not her unending optimism that makes everything feel shiny and clean. Not her smile, or the fact that she can't use an idiom to save her life.

It's not because I want her. Not because for the first time in decades, I have to physically restrain myself from reaching for someone, constantly remind myself how badly I can hurt her.

It's not because she's a reprieve.

No, I'm chained to her by royal dictate and the scar on my chest, because Kadmos wanted it, and his hand reaches even from the grave.

Maybe she holds the key to this grand unscrewing. Maybe she'll lead us to the bastard who killed him, who cursed all of us to this in-between. Maybe if I keep her in sight, wait for her to remember, I can stave off the pain that gnaws my nerves ragged every time the curse flares up and tries to eat me alive.

But if that's the case, if that's the only reason, duty not desire, why the fuck does it hurt so much to be around her?

Why does the pain sharpen when I hear her moving behind that door. Why does husky word of hers leave me feeling like I've missed a step in the dark, over and over and over?

Nephene's chuckle breaks through the hush. "You're not the only one to want her, you know. But you are the worst choice. You should be on your knees begging to even be near her. If she were a true Keres, she'd slit your throat for that insult."

"You're talkative."

"I'm warm," she says, as if it's a high she only reaches after scaling a mountain. She tips her head to glance at me. Her pupils stretch black, tongue darting over her fangs. "Kareaitho, the oldies call it. Blood drunk. It lights our nerves on fire. Some swear it's an aphrodisiac, some an antidepressant. For me, it's just—" she spreads her hands and lets them fall, "—relaxing."

She leans in. No sweetness in the gesture, only predatory intent. "Is it always like this for you? Obsession?"

I ball my fist. Let the bones grind. "I promised to protect her. I made a vow."

Her laugh is a brittle snort. "Protection? The Munera's a suicide mission."

I sit with that. The silence thickens around us. Nephene stills. No more laughter now.

"You want her for yourself, don't you?" she asks. "Just say it."

I breathe through my teeth. Can't let anything show. "I want her alive."

She tilts her head, glossy strands tumbling over her shoulder. "She's not built for court. They'll snuff her out. She should have never left the surface. Now it's too late. Father will parade her like a newly lit torch, and everyone will want to see how long she burns."

"Is that a threat?"

"It's a warning for my sister. Our father is a sentimental fool, and the council drink from his palm, but this—our caves, our bloodline—it's not the future. Mortals breed like wildfire. They'll find us eventually. We can't just wait for that eventually."

She rises. Adjusts her dress, smooths an invisible flaw. "Stay alert, butcher."

With that, she leaves.

So maybe she doesn't hate Theia, but that doesn't mean she isn't an enemy. Not if Theia threatens what Nephene's built.

The council remains a lurking threat as well. Keres bound in tradition, wary of change. But once Theia's crowned, they'll fall in line. Especially if their precious Julian ascends with her. He's dim-witted and boastful, but he didn't earn ten hearts because he's all talk.

Still, there's another enemy. One I hadn't expected. One I need to clean up.

---

IT'S BEEN fifty years and Lydia hasn't changed a bit. Same bright blonde hair neatly knotted down her back, same rigid shoulders.

She stands in the stone corridor with her back to me, running a honing steel along her broadsword. The same blade she carried when she was mortal. Each stroke is clean, measured. The rasp of metal on metal sings in the gloom.

"Didn't think I'd ever find a Queensguard down here."

She turns, the edge of her blade steady at her hip. Her blue-gray eyes pin me. "Imagine my surprise when the butcher showed up."

I savor the disdain. "You're quite far from the palace, Lydia."

Her nostrils flare. A flicker of satisfaction in her eyes, nothing else. "I go where I'm needed."

"Didn't think the Queensguard had taste for caves. What was it that Kleio said? Aboveground support better suited you." The Queensguard had secured Kadmos's palace during the Keres war instead of fighting in it—twelve years of bloodshed they'd just opted out of. Like a fucking email subscription.

"Angry you got the bad assignment?" she asks.

Yes. Still angry. At myself. Even more at her.

The last time I saw her was through the restless haze of cordite and fluorescent flicker, in the cracked concrete Theia was held in a cage. Lydia and her Queensguard had stormed in after the alarms. Not to liberate the prisoners but to mop up the evidence.

They'd lined the captive females up with surgical efficiency: hands behind their backs, knees bent.

Lydia had stood in front, blade out, not a tremor in the line of her arm. She looked at Theia not as a creature, but as a name to be crossed from a list.

Theia didn't cry or beg. She faced the Queensguard straight on, as if she knew the Blackguard was coming.

My brain burned the image into itself, every cell recording the way Theia's mouth curled upward at the corner as the might of the Blackguard unleashed onto their former allies. If we hadn't intervened—if sheer luck hadn't sent them scattering—neither Theia nor Nat would have walked away.

I haven't had the chance to share my feelings on the issue.

"Remind me," I say, letting the words crawl. "When you were going to kill all the female hostages, was that the good job? Was it your idea to toss the bodies after? Bet you were pissed Kleio brought her guns. Makes you pretty obsolete as weapons master."

Her face doesn't move, but her knuckles blanch around her hilt. "You aren't meant to understand our orders. You're not with us anymore. Then again, butcher, you were never really in the Kingsguard."

I can hear her heartbeat, slow and steady—a metronome for violence. I step forward, closing the gap, unbuttoning my gloves with one hand as the other drifts toward the inside of my jacket. "Are you here to finish what you started?" I ask, low and conversational, as though we're discussing the Deep Realm's accommodations. "I'm tired of the long game. If the play is killing Theia, then let's not waste time. You'll go through me, and you know how that ends."

Lydia rises, every inch of her a threat. "She's Keres. Not your blood. Not your responsibility."

"She's not yours, either."

"I'm not going to lose months of progress with the Keres because she wants to play princess." Lydia squares off, bringing the sword to guard and shifting her weight onto the balls of her feet. "The best thing for everyone is if she disappears."

"What does the Queen want with the Keres?"

"I thought you gave up politics."

"I recently joined back in." I step closer, stripping my gloves off. "Run home, Lydia. Theia's mine. Blink wrong in her direction and I'll show you why they beg me to stop."

"Typical elitist Kingsguard, pretending you didn't fail your only fucking duty. I could kill you, butcher—and no one would care. They wouldn't even notice."

"Oh, they'd care," I let my gloves drop. "You'd be a hero. So go ahead. Kill me."

She stands so close now I can smell the oil she's polished onto her blade, see the tremor in her fingers.

"Come on, Lydia." I flex my bare hands. No weapon needed. "Prove that you sat on the sidelines because you chose to, not because you couldn't keep up."

She strikes. Fast—a lunge, sword tip angled for my ribs.

I pivot just enough to let the steel whistle past, and catch her by the crook of her elbow. Her sleeve is so thin I feel the goosebumps erupt, the immediate fear of contact.

"You're going to wish I'd just killed you," I tell her.

She rips free, swings again in a looping arc. This time I step inside, taking the blow on my forearm and driving my shoulder into her sternum. She grunts but doesn't yield, shoving me off with a twist and resetting her stance.

"You still lead right," I taunt. "You always did."

She doesn't answer. Just comes at me with a flurry of jabs and cuts, each one sharper than the last. It's like we're back in the old barracks, only now there's nothing left but venom and history, all the wasted years boiling up inside muscle and bone. I block, and step with her.

"If it's not me," she gasps, "it'll be someone else. She's too weak. She doesn't belong."

She lunges.

The blade flashes but she telegraphs the strike. I could dodge, let her overextend. Instead I let it slice right across my ribs.

At the last second, my naked hand closes around her wrist.

Skin against skin.

The fallout is seismic.

Lydia thrashes, composure shredded as she cries out. Every muscle seizes, her mouth cracks open.

I warned her.

The world gutters, cold and black at the edges. Her fear is a live wire, an electric undertow. Panic. Shame. Something hidden and sick, writhing in her, coiling up the bones. It's not fear of pain—not her own. Not even death. She isn't scared of dying.

She's scared of failing. Of watching her world collapse. Of the queen sliding into oblivion. Of girls slaughtered in cages, never forgiven for not saving them. Behind her eyes, I see the blood on her hands. Layers of it. She tries to stop it and fails. Every time. Losing and losing. I pull her through fear after fear. Watch her sisters in the Queensguard get gutted, see her parents' bodies burned.

Lydia screams. Not loud, not even human, but the air fractures. Tears race down her face.

My hand is loose, barely touching her, but the darkness keeps pouring through, drowning her under the waves.

She doesn't remember how to fight, too sucked into her fears.

My ribs burn. My head pounds. She shudders against me, struggling—but now the fight is panic and hopeless terror. Her nails rake furrows into my wrist, not to escape but to harm, to kill the source of the darkness.

This is what I am. Just another monster. Butcher. Cleaner. I hurt people because I can—because it's all that ever worked.

I release her.

She collapses onto one hand. Her sword clatters away.

"You go near her, and it'll never end, Lydia. You understand?"

Tears drip from her chin. She nods.

It's not good enough. I still see Theia kneeling before Lydia, so I crouch down and slide my bare palm along her cheek, catching tears and sweat. Lydia begs nonsensically as the fear sweeps in anew.

"You don't hurt her," I whisper into her ear. "You don't even look at her. You're not a cleaner, Lydia. You always watched from the window, praying someone else would do the ugly work. I did it. And I always will."

I rise to my full height, shake out my hands.

It's perverse how my skin tingles, aching for connection, belligerent to the effect it has.

I feel invincible. Like I could take on every Keres in the Deep Realm, slaughter the council, choke out a kingdom. All it costs are my hands, my mind, the wreckage I leave behind.

Lydia twitches on the floor, shoulders hunched, lip quivering. She won't meet my eyes.

I gather my gloves and pull them on, finger the slash across my stomach and turn to leave. "Glad we had this talk."

"Kadmos fucked up when he made you," she spits, staring at the floor, breath ragged. Blood drips from her mouth. Red like mine. She coughs roughly, wipes her face with the back of her hand. "The princess doesn't know, does she? What you've done?"

## 16

# Theia

### LOVE LIKE HIS WAS ALWAYS A LITTLE SELF-DESTRUCTIVE

I enjoy the art of the linger. A dither. The slow meander. The luxurious pause that drives efficiency experts to madness.

When you've spent decades in captivity, where food vanishes mid-bite and showers cut off mid-rinse, you learn to cherish what little control remains. So I dawdle. On principle.

Now? Everything runs on fast-forward.

My mornings begin with the clanging of bells—actual bells, like I owe someone money in a cartoon—while strangers invade my bedroom, yanking sheets, yanking hair, cinching my dress so tight I can taste my own lungs.

Then they shuffle me down endless hallways, past murals that seem to track my movements, into chambers that all look identical yet, impossibly, are not torture dungeons.

No breakfast. Not a single granola bar. Not a whiff of a ham and cheese at lunch.

I participate in "regal amusements," which is court-speak for meeting more creatures in thirty minutes than I've seen in a decade. Handshakes, small bows, a thousand eyes scanning for weakness.

It is relentless.

Every time I drift or even slow, Julian, Nephene or Malni

forcibly corrals me onward, like a sheep with a calendar. "This is your personal armory, Princess. This dagger was forged specifically for your grip, Princess. Stop smiling like an idiot, Princess."

The worst? The orientation lessons. "Find your way back," they command, abandoning me in identical hallways.

I still think maps should label north as "up".

I'm about to become a puddle on the floor when I see the blood.

It transfixes me.

Squabbling voices fade away as I push aside last night's notes on marking rites, and wrap my fingers around the goblet of crimson on my nightstand.

I inhale it. Chase every drop. My tongue chasing remnants along the glass rim until I catch my own wild reflection staring back.

Heat breaks over me. Blood coats my mouth—rich, sweet, whole.

My body vibrates, every cell singing as strength floods my limbs. It tickles my skin, pours light down my spine. I feel good. Full.

Three sharp knocks shatter the moment.

Couldn't even savor that.

I wrench open the door, without my signature grin.

Vasilis is here, which is slightly disappointing when you're expecting a handmaiden or, like, a basket of pastries. He fills most of the hallway, calm and regal and not even a bit out of breath, as if the hallways simply rearrange themselves to deposit him wherever he needs to be.

He scans my face, probably noting the lack of a smile (slacker), the empty goblet dangling from my hand (lush), and the general state of my hair (waves during a hurricane). With royal restraint, he says nothing about any of it, simply extending his arm.

"Today is important, Antheia," he says, voice honeyed but

expectant, in the manner of a favorite professor announcing a pop quiz you'll absolutely fail.

Another task of the Munera.

I'm barely recovered from the last one.

Every step toward the main arena, I lag farther behind.

After years dreaming of belonging somewhere, I've gotten exactly what I wished for: instant and rich royal bloodline, complete with crushing expectations. Congratulations! You're the future empress. Just don't let them see you hyperventilating.

Beside me, my father moves with born-monarch ease, charisma radiating from him so intensely the air quakes in respect. Nephene has that same unnerving pull.

Clearly, I didn't inherit it. At least not from him.

I can't help myself. "Did you compete in the Munera for my mother?"

His sculpted features flicker with surprise. He folds his long fingers over mine. "No. I was of the familial line. The Munera was only for worthy females. The victor vanished the night before our wedding."

"Vanished?"

"Rumor was she'd slipped aboveground on a hunting spree. Back then, the surface was less hostile. We mingled freely; only certain immortals kept to the depths. She was seen leaving the Blood Halls—and then she never returned."

I blink. He is very casual about the whole fiancée-mysteriously-disappearing. "You didn't try to find her?"

"Truthfully, Antheia, I've harbored the suspicion your mother killed her." His tone is casual, as if that's a reasonable statement to drop mid-hallway.

It is. I guess. Here.

Still, I stumble over my own feet. "Wait, what?"

A curve of his mouth. "Your mother was never subtle. But she was the most exquisite female I'd ever known."

My breath catches. It feels cosmically bound that I'm not

subtle either. I cling to this thread of connection. "What else was she like?"

Vasilis studies me, ancient eyes unreadable. After a drawn-out moment, he whispers, "She was … unusual." He closes his eyes, as though that memory still burns. "The council never understood her. Even among our blood, they kept her at arm's length."

Arm's length.

Yeah. That tracks.

My chest tightens. I glance down, blinking back tears that are totally a very normal symptom of high indoor humidity, not disappointment. "Did it get easier for her? To lead?"

His reply is a soft shake of the head. "I do not believe she ever felt welcome. Not truly."

"At least she had you. She was with her Fated."

Vasilis stops cold. Not just a pause. A full system reboot.

He exhales—a seismic breath—and turns from me to stare at the something in the middle ground.

A low drumbeat begins down the hall, pulsing with anticipation.

The people waiting for their Emperor.

I tell him never mind, brush this aside, keep walking in the direction of the death drums, but I can't. My curiosity is too great.

Is he bereft? Is he angry that I brought it up?

Finally: "The Keres do not have Fated mates." The fact drops like an iron hammer, hitting me square in the chest. "Fate and destiny are for mortals and creatures who fear choice. They follow the threads of the Moirai. For the children of Nyx, death is the only certainty. We don't bow to Fate's whims. We decide. We choose a Nevro. We decide to fight. To fall. That is our path."

My heart becomes a small, hard ball. "You don't believe in destiny, a thread?"

"We believe in nerve, my dear. In finding a Nevro and pairing for life."

"Nevro," I repeat, testing it out.

"A partnership that has strength in separation and courage in connection."

"So … no soulmates?" My voice cracks, and I hate how it betrays me, how it keeps striking the wound in my chest.

Vasilis's gaze gentles slightly, as if he can see the pieces of me fracturing. "We are not made for Fate, Antheia. The Keres are too severe for ribbons and threads. It is a fantastical notion that one creature completes another. Nyx did not birth half creatures."

"But …" I swallow harshly. "But I dreamed about—I mean, I've always felt it inside me. That maybe there was a reason for everything, why I was taken, why you didn't find me. Like if I hadn't gone through that, then I—"

"No," he cuts off sharply.

"But—"

"No more, Antheia. It is not in our bones. It is a choice." His hand settles heavily on my shoulder, meant to comfort. "Don't mention the Fates again."

The request sounds simple. Like don't eat garlic bread before swimming, or don't lick the electrical outlet. Only this is more: you get one shot at belonging, don't piss it away by saying the taboo word.

I stand empty, hollowed out. Everything I've ever believed dying like a fish out of water, flopping and ugly.

Destiny was supposed to fix everything, redeem all the broken parts.

Wrong.

No destiny.

No Fated.

Now I'm just a female in a gown, wishing someone would write me a better story.

Vasilis's expression is filled with grief and tenderness, and something else. Pity. No darker—heartbreak. Like he knows he just destroyed my life. "Come, daughter. Let us move on to better things."

---

TASK TWO MEASURES FORTITUDE.

I can think of better ways, including but not limited to: forcing someone to watch a parade of baby animal videos on mute, or locking them in a room with a malfunctioning ceiling fan and a single mosquito. Fates, you could just pour ambrosia directly onto a sensitive area, but that's a bit on the nose.

Instead, the Deep Court picked: a stroll in the sun.

Or, as Vasilis puts it, "Surviving the corridor of death."

The Keres call it "the sun gauntlet." Because, of course, they do.

I peer out from behind the ceremonial curtain—a tangle of velvet, bone, and probably the hair of my ancestors—and assess the gauntlet.

It's ... fine. Perfectly normal. A hundred yards of pure, retina-searing sunlight, streaming in angry wedges through holes punched in the cavern roof. Light pools across the sand in happy yellow puddles. On each side, Keres spectators snarl, hoot and place bets on who'll collapse first.

Several hold parasols. I'd have been less surprised if they showed up cuddling teddy bears.

Nephene stands on the dais in a mauve wrap dress—CEO of Murder, Inc., incarnate. She lifts her arm in that unmistakable "I'm in charge, but I'll snap your neck" gesture I won't master in a thousand years.

The crowd falls silent. Or they just freeze, cowed by Vasilis rising behind me, emanating enough murder-y energy to dry all the rivers in Hades.

Among the biggest, baddest competitors, among males who have lived millennia for this moment, for this bloodshed, is Drake, who joined the Munera like it's a cake toss. Like his mere existence is a cosmic joke at everyone else's expense.

*I made a vow to Nat to keep you safe.*

Which I believe roughly translates to: I wish I were anywhere else. With anyone else. But if I leave, a Fury will *literally* crush me to dust.

Whatever.

It's not as if he's my Fated. Keres don't have those. It's a truth that sears.

If only I could tell my body to get the message. Stop staring at him. Stop caring. Just stop.

I can't.

At least, I'm not sick with worry. This is a challenge he'll crush.

I recline in my chair, experiencing actual, pure relief.

Maybe for the first time in days.

It lasts ... maybe twelve seconds.

Drake steps forward, and my father clicks his tongue in warning.

Dread coils in my gut.

"Ah ah ah, Blackguard. There is no cheating in this kingdom. You will pass through fire."

My dread curdles into horror.

My father gives a nod, and the ceremonial attendant—who probably moonlights as a chemical weapons designer—descends from her perch above the cavern and touches a torch to a trough of pitch spanning the gauntlet's midpoint.

Flames whoosh to life with the satisfaction of Prometheus snapping his powerful fingers.

It's a sheer wall of fire. A living, breathing entity splitting the space from sand to ceiling. Sunlight and fire commingling into a prism of agony.

Drake waits at the ready, one pace from the starting line. In the inferno's backlight, he looks positively Olympic. Or maybe myth-adjacent. Posture ramrod straight, expression set in a determined way that reminds me of old war movies starring guys who always get the girl, never the shrapnel.

The other competitors—moments before posturing and flexing—suddenly shuffle back, unwilling to test their evolutionary fitness against an engineered deathtrap.

And yet.

Drake doesn't. He waits there, gloved hands loose at his sides, the very picture of someone who's been through worse and would prefer not to talk about it.

The crowd, sensing blood and drama, ramps up its ferocity. A pack of adolescent Keres bare teeth and hurl coins at the sand, shouting betting odds in a language that sounds like three languages knife-fighting.

Drake takes a shallow breath, unbuttons the top clasp of his jacket, and—just for an instant—glances up at the balcony.

I can't tell if he's seeking reassurance or just determined to haunt me forever, but I meet his gaze and try to project something useful. Not pity or fear. Maybe a little hope, if such a thing can exist in this torture-festival.

The corners of his mouth downturn. Then, in one fluid motion, he launches himself into the inferno.

17

# Theia

## IF SHE WAS IN DARKNESS, THAT'S WHERE HE LONGED TOO

Drake hits the fire at a dead sprint, and the flames swallow him whole.

I can almost feel the burn myself. A thousand wasp stings everywhere.

It's—

I can't breathe.

He's gone, engulfed in molten gold and orange, and for a second I'm convinced he's been vaporized, reduced to myth.

But then there's a sound—somewhere between a howl and a war cry—and a familiar shape punches through the other side, trailing a comet-tail of blue-hot flame and burning fabric. The crowd loses its mind. They yell, shriek, stampede the barriers.

He's made it. He's alive.

Barely.

Drake staggers as he clears the fire. Skin peels from his arms in wet strips, oozing red-black. His jacket has melded into the flesh of his shoulders, charred and smoking. His pants are fused to bubbled skin as if it's been stitched into him by a sadistic God.

He takes three stuttering steps before his left leg collapses, sending him sprawling to the sand in a spray of blood, ash, and the fine papery debris of dead skin sloughing off in the heat.

He lies there, motionless, an effigy of pain.

My own skin burns just watching, stings everywhere.

He coughs, struggles to suck in air.

I'm running before my brain even receives the memo.

One moment I stand inert on the dais among a hundred pairs of black eyes. The next, I vault onto the flagstones below, dress catching on the rail. My body is all nerve endings, all desperate movement, as if some piece of me has always waited for this trigger, this exact catastrophe. Drake nearly dead.

Stone gives way to sand beneath my feet, fine and hot enough to cook flesh. I skid, slip, right myself. I'm nearly across the arena, can see Drake's chest has stopped moving. I cut through the gauntlet of sunlight to reach him faster.

The sun's fine. Gold and lovely. A first, perfect taste of sunlight after weeks of too-cold air conditioning and dim fluorescents. My skin sizzles lightly. Easy enough to ignore.

Then it changes. Slams into me like a bullet loaded with white-hot mercury.

The outer layer of my skin fries in real time, puckering, then blistering, then peeling anywhere my dress doesn't cover me.

This is not the sun I know.

This is the sun of ancient, vengeful Gods, focused and amplified by the unholy geometry of the cavern roof. Magnified. Weaponized. Inescapable.

I try to run, to bear down and muscle through, but the pain doubles, then triples. My knees buckle. I crash into the sand.

I yelp, but the sound is weak, thin, instantly scorched from my throat. I scrabble at the sand, try to burrow down, but there's no escape. I'm smothered in concentrated sunlight, locked in agony.

The only thing louder than the pain is the voice in my head, cursing my useless, idiotic attempt to help. This is what I get for thinking I'm anything but fragile and breakable. I'm going to die.

No. No, I won't die like this.

Determination like I've never known fills me up, refusal too. I push through the agony, bring my arms under me, panting.

Drake drops to the ground beside me.

The force of his body sends a shockwave of hot air and sand into my face. His hand finds the bunched fabric at my waist—skin so hot I half-expect to hear it sizzle—and he hauls me out of the sunlight and into the safety of his shadow.

Darkness envelops me—cool, rich, and absolving.

The pain cuts off like a bad song.

I collapse under him, inhaling the scorched stink of his hair and burned flesh. He shakes so hard I feel it in my bones.

He stays over me in a plank, elbows in the sand, body hovering over mine, blocking every inch of sun from my skin. He's not wearing his gloves—or his shirt, or half his face, which is currently sporting third-degree burns and a not-insignificant number of open wounds.

He was unmoving. Burned, broken.

And he came for me.

Launched himself like a dying comet, as if his only remaining instinct was to shield me from the sun at the cost of his own body.

"You're on fire," I croak.

He spits blood over his shoulder, grunts. "Stay down. Don't show them."

My brain's on overload—about to short-circuit. Did he just risk his life to save me from saving him? I gape at him, ready to babble that I'm usually sunproof and will be fine in minutes, but Drake's face is so close I can count every fleck of ash on his cheek. His green eyes are molten with suffering, the kind that tears you apart from the inside out.

He presses a blood-soaked fist to my hip, knuckles white with tremors. It's a miracle he isn't collapsing under his own weight.

"Stay," he rasps, voice husky and ragged. "Don't let them see you."

I don't understand. I'm frantic. Adrenaline is all that stops me from screaming his name until my throat shreds.

"Just like that," he mutters, half-proud, half-broken. "Stay. Right like that."

Panic rises, claws scraping at my lungs. "You need—I have to help you. You're burning—you're—"

"Getting a tan."

"You shouldn't be alive."

"Neither should you."

He's … right.

Suddenly I understand.

He isn't shielding me from the light—he's hiding me from my own people.

I should not be alive.

If I were real Keres royalty, grade-A lethal lineage, I'd be dust in the wind right now.

He hid that.

Skin flayed, bleeding, jacket melted, and he thought of me. *My* reputation. Because he knows I want this. The crown, the empire. Even when I'm whiffing hardcore, he keeps lining up the ball for me.

"You know," he says, "I think I will take that rest."

A strangled laugh catches in my throat. "You think? Really? Because you haven't got any skin left?"

"Don't hang up on the semantics," he rasps, but his breath stutters.

I want to snarl at him. Shake him and say what is wrong

with you? Or maybe cry, because who hurt him so badly that he can be sixty percent raw hamburger meat and still joke?

"Maybe you're secretly a lizard. Or a cockroach. Survivability is your only personality trait," I mutter, still cradled under him.

"Yeah?" His breath hisses as he shifts his weight, elbow bracing in the sand right above my shoulder. There's an actual hiss as he props his arm. "Are you calling me resilient, or just ugly?"

"Definitely not ugly." I pause. "At least you weren't. Now …"

"Kick a man while he's down."

"Your poor hair."

"I needed a cut."

We're still a heap. Not in the victorious way; more like a clearance-sale display after a tornado. I can't stop staring at the split at his hairline, singed lashes, the way his jaw is set against so much pain you could bottle it and market it as *Ultra Trauma for Men.*

"You didn't have to do that." I'm whispering, which is dumb, because no one can hear us down here in our cocoon.

A shrug. So casual I could scream. "It wasn't that bad."

"Your skin is literally rejecting itself right now."

"Minor exfoliation."

I laugh. Actually laugh.

His mouth does that particular twitch—the one where you can almost see the male throttling his own smile before it escapes.

Everything in me is tight and fizzy and mortifyingly soft. The urge to fix him, to say thank you, to just hold him until he stops shaking.

He's so close, ruined and bright and real. And he's not mad.

"You're melting. and I'm not emotionally prepared for that."

His chuckle is ugly and perfect. It shreds the air, and somehow, impossibly, he manages to look at me with all that green-eyed focus. There's pride in it. Like he's pleased I didn't crumble into a pile of dental records.

It shouldn't make me so proud that he's impressed I haven't died.

"No igniting in front of the princess. Got it."

"Laugh all you want. My word's law."

"What's the punishment?" he asks. "I already walked through fire."

"I'll host your memorial service. Very tasteful. Keg stand, strobe, a live band. No napkins."

"Just make sure everyone takes their shoes off at the door."

"Clean freak."

For a heartbeat, we are static, smiling lunatics. My clean freak in a graveyard of cauterized skin and smoking blood.

I reach for his face, to wipe off soot and blood. "Don't worry. I'll get you cleaned up."

"Don't," he whispers, warning smaller than it should be. A true whisper, not the practiced threat he can spit over a table of knives. "Please."

I pull my hand back so fast it might as well have been scorched, curling my fingers into a fist against the warm, damp sand.

I feel my face collapse—it probably looks like a rice cake under a rolling pin.

Drake's gaze scrapes past my cheek, as if he can't bear to look.

And I can't fix it. The ever-burning flame in my chest has disappeared, snuffed out in a single sick heartbeat.

I wait for it to revive, for the relentless ember of optimism that could light bonfires in a downpour. It's gone.

I'm cold. Hollowed.

My optimism—the stuff Nat always joked would get me killed—flatlines.

I keep expecting things will improve, that the universe is still on my side, that if I keep crawling forward, I'll strike daylight.

I've been called naive, weak, sheltered, delusional, a walking motivational poster. I never cared. I was always certain the Gods would spot me the difference, that if I kept hurtling forward—kept being good and happy and me—I'd make it. Fate would catch me; my life would break right for once.

Not now. There's nothing.

The only light in these dark tunnels has burned me.

Drake keeps his ruined body between me and the deadly sunlight, the last bulwark left to me in the world, and yet I am suddenly more alone than I have ever been.

I will never be enough. Not for the empire, not for my people, and not even for the broken man who just incinerated himself to rescue me.

Drake doesn't meet my eyes when he speaks, voice almost gentle, like he's laying a blanket over a corpse. "This can never happen, Theia. Whatever you think you feel. Whatever you want … I'm not that."

Despair wraps around me, sticky as blood, dragging me under.

All I manage is silence. For the first time in my life, I don't believe things will improve.

## 18

# Drake

### SOME LOSSES AREN'T MEANT TO BE ACCEPTED WITHOUT A FIGHT

Death is the most common fear among mortals.

There are the deaths that are intimate—poison served by a lover, familiar eyes watching as the blood congeals in your veins, a sickly sweetness coating your tongue as you start to slip away—and there are the deaths that are public, as abrupt and impersonal as a gunshot or a spear through the gut. Then there are the truly cruel deaths, the ones where you see the end coming and can only wait, and wait, and wait for the inevitable.

Working as Murphy's executioner, I became an expert at selecting the most heinous death for each victim.

But thanks to Kadmos's gift, I've felt every one of those deaths myself.

It's gotten to the point where I have to check whether I'm actually dying or just reliving someone else's worst fear. Sometimes, when my power hits like a wave, I lose all sense of time and can't tell what's happening now from what happened decades ago.

I've been buried alive in so many coffins, each with its own distinct grain, its own smell of rot or iron or the residual musk of the last poor soul to inhabit it. Sometimes I drift in the dark for hours before I remember that my body is still, technically, alive, and the pressure on my chest is just a memory, not real dirt crushing my ribs.

Reality and unreality are, when it comes to pain, a matter of degree.

So as I bend over Theia, my stomach doesn't empty at the stench of burning flesh. I don't feel the blisters crawling down my neck. I only smell vellum and vanilla, the fragrance of Theia's skin mingling with the notes she studies at night. I feel only the warm sand under my arm and sun slanting along my back.

Something in my chest shifts, almost a click, like a knee resetting after a break.

I could watch her forever.

The curve of her lip. The way her breath hitches under my stare. Neck exposed, a tiny brown mole right above her collarbone. Hair a dark halo, splayed on the sand. That mahogany ring around her amber iris.

Icarus probably felt like this as he soared closer to the sun, wings melting, unable to slow, drawn closer and closer to his destruction.

My hands are starving and my mind is a lost thing, paddling weakly in the dark.

Her face tilts toward me, pink blooming across her cheeks.

There's a new, greedy light in her gaze, a brightness I have never seen—no, that's a lie, I've seen it on the battlefield, the second before the sword drops, the second you realize you want more than just to live another day. You want to taste it, devour it, bleed for it.

My vision narrows.

She brings her hand between us, fingers poised delicately. She hesitates.

I can't breathe. Can't think.

*Do it. Do it.*

Her fingers on my face are featherlight, careful. Her touch stays light, trailing up my cheek, down my nose.

It burns straight through me. My skin smarts. Everything seizes, and there's this hot, stinging desire at the base of my skull that makes my bones ache.

Icarus never felt this. He never touched the sun. He never knew such pleasure.

Her thumb finds the spot where the skin is especially tender near my mouth. She smooths it with reverence, like it's a holy relic and not evidence of my failures.

The need in me is ugly and feral and loud, a dog chained to the floorboards, howling for something it can neither name nor have.

I want her. Want to crush her into me, fill the hollow places, replace the taste of ash and regret with something—anything—sweeter.

I want to swallow her whole, and she knows it. She wants it too. The hunger in her isn't a mirror but a magnifier, gleaming and ruthless and directed at me.

"See," she says, and the laugh in her voice hurts. "You had nothing to fear. I told you."

"How?"

"Because you're mine, Drake."

I have no words. I want to fuse us together, press her into every broken part of me.

"I've thought about this," she says. "About how wonderful it would be when you finally gave in to me." Her lashes flick up. Her mouth is so close I'm breathing the air off her lips. There's no way she doesn't feel how hard I am against her.

I slide my arm under her hips and pull us together, let the arena dissolve.

"Have you?" She lifts my hand to her lips, kisses my palm. "Ever wondered how good we could be?"

Yes.

*Yes.*

I let my thumb glide over the pulse in her throat. She should be flinching, running. locking every door between us. She presses her forehead to mine with the stubbornness of a child who refuses to let go of the thing she's been told she can never have. "You're not going to break me."

I pull her closer, harder. There's no elegance to it—I catch her by the waist, hitch her up, haul her until we're chest to chest, her spread legs holding my hips.

"Fuck Theia, I—" The words scrape out. "Do you understand what you've done to me? I think you might kill me."

She isn't scared.

She smiles. Brings her mouth to my jaw, brushes along the harsh line, lips damp, heat trailing everywhere she touches. I ache for more. I'm starved. I contemplate burying myself in the sweet, dark space between her breath and mine.

"Drake," she murmurs. My name, but this time it's not panic. It's home.

She lifts her chin. Our mouths are level.

I cup her skull, thumb in her hair, hold her so tight it might bruise. She'll taste like hope. Like everything I swore I'd never deserve.

I pull her in. Inhale her scent. Touch her nose with mine.

"No," she whispers.

It rips through the air, wrenches me back. "Theia?"

She parts those lips and screams.

I'm slammed out of the dream, jarred loose, pain and need mixing until I'm nowhere. The burn crawls over my skin, the inside of my ribs constricted, familiar. Throat like sandpaper, arms too heavy to move. My face is pressed into scratchy sheets. There's the taste of blood behind my teeth and the heat of bruises everywhere.

My cot. My room.

A nightmare.

Of course. She'd never lean into my touch. Never wish for my health or curl into my embrace.

I grip the metal frame. The competitor rooms are pure function—four walls, a cot with uneven legs, the stained table where Imperials deliver food they definitely spit in. Usually milky grits with chunks of undercooked, unidentifiable meat.

My stomach turns over. I shut my eyes, scrub a hand over my face.

Remember how Theia looked at me. Like I could be more. Like maybe I was worth it.

Just for a second.

A fucking dream.

I want to break something.

There's a blanket over my hips, thicker and softer than anything the emperor would grant me. And I know instantly —it's Theia's. Her hands smoothed it there. The pressure at my waist says she tucked it in, careful, as if I'd slip away if she didn't pin down the edges.

"You sleep like the dead," Theia says.

I lurch upright. Every joint protesting. I blink, wipe the grit of sleep away, and find Theia standing by the door, not stepping in, just watching.

Even in the bluish glow of a small lamp, she's blinding. Iridescent fabric clings to her, highlighting wide, luscious curves. Her hair is pinned high, not the wild halo of my dreams. Chin flat. Eyes fixed ahead.

No smile.

"How'd I get here?"

"Dragged."

"Yeah, that's what it feels like."

I wait for the quirk of a smile, that ray of sunlight that always cracks through.

She moves to the foot of the cot, spine ruler-straight. "Thirty-two males survived the sun gauntlet. Julian tied for fastest time, obviously. He told the council that it must have been Nyx herself protecting me from the sun, and that I am undoubtedly a true descendant."

Thirty-two. Too many. An army of bloodthirsty gladiators all eager for a chance at her.

"It worked for the council," she continues. "More or less. They were having a good laugh about what to do with your body. Said your time was slower than half the field."

She stares straight past me into the middle distance. Hand folded. Fingers white at the knuckles.

"Theia." The room deadens my voice. "Are you alright?" Is she still hurt? Does she need blood?

She shrugs, barely there, as if shaking me off is just another task scheduled on the hour. "I'm fine. You should focus on recovering. Julian's ahead. He's strong. He'll want to finish the job." She still hasn't looked at me.

Something is off.

"You don't seem …" How to say it.

"Don't seem what?"

"Like yourself."

A tiny tilt of her head, not enough to betray emotion. "You shouldn't worry about me. That's not part of your vow."

This isn't her. This isn't the female who chatted roofie flavors with Zeke, who thought cupcakes could solve a century of blood feuds.

"Theia—"

She curves around the bed. I tense, instinctive, ready for impact.

She stops as if I've pulled a knife. Backs up. Then recovers.

Leans against the wall, hands locked behind her back. Eyes fixed on the floor or in Tartarus. "I don't want to hurt anyone."

She doesn't look at me when she says it, just keeps her eyes somewhere over my shoulder, jaw tight, mouth a line I want to smooth with my thumb. The pressure in my head extends to my throat, blocking off oxygen.

"I never want to kill. Even Milos, in the alley, that wasn't what I wanted to happen."

My hand hits the edge of the cot, knuckles burning with the urge to smash something. "You shouldn't feel guilty. He tried to kill you."

She tucks her chin, a lone wavy strand spilling forward. "I just get hungry. Too hungry and suddenly lose control. Once I start, I can't stop. I tried, I really did. It's like being erased. Like I'm watching myself from the outside and I can't do anything but keep going. When it gets like that—I don't want it getting to that. So I try to pick people who deserve it. Well, no one deserves it—"

"You let Rod roofie you because you wanted a reason to drink from him. You wanted an excuse to kill him."

She shakes her head a little, nothing like her. "No. I didn't want one. I suspected there might be one. I need to eat."

"I know."

"No, you don't. I'm not like them." She gestures at the hall, at her kingdom. "They laughed while you laid there in the sand, but I … I'm fed here. There's no reason for me to hurt anyone. You don't have to be scared of me, Drake."

I stare at her, and my chest caves in. Scared? That's what she thinks? "I'm not scared of you."

She blinks, lips parting. For a single heartbeat, I see the Theia I know flicker in her eyes, then she's gone. Wiped clean. "No? Good."

I want to fix it. Take her face and make her look at me, make her hear it. She keeps talking, flat, like we're not even in the same room.

"Still. Don't worry about me getting close again," she tells me, voice careful, a scalpel over a vein. "I'll keep my distance. I get it now."

The words twist. I can't even form an answer. "You don't have to … Theia, listen to me, you're not–"

She cuts me off. Not with a fight, but by refusing to fight at all. "It's fine, Drake. You don't owe me anything."

"That's not how it is."

"You don't need to explain." Another shrug, movement so small it's like a glitch. "Everyone's dealing with stuff. I have stuff too."

I catch at the edge. "What stuff? Are you okay? If someone's threatening you, then—"

"I don't need a mortal protecting me anymore. There are thirty-two more capable creatures males fighting to take the position."

"More capable," I echo, numb. Pissed.

"And they aren't afraid of me."

"I'm not afraid of you, Theia."

"Nat told me. I didn't think—I understand now. There are no exceptions. You did your duty. There's no point torturing ourselves." She pushes gently off the wall. "You focus on surviving until I get crowned. Then I'll pardon you or whatever they do down here, and then you can leave."

I grit my teeth at the ring of fire at my ribs. "That's it then?"

"Why drag out the suffering?"

"What happened, Theia? Who's threatening you?" That has to be what this is. Lydia or Nephene wedging into her mind, twisting her apart, making her doubt herself, forcing me away.

I move to stand. Pain surges. The room splinters. The cot lurches. My knees don't work. Briefly, there's only darkness behind my lids, throbbing.

Then nothing.

# 19

## Theia

### THERE WAS NOTHING LEFT WORTH FEARING

Pulling an all-nighter at Drake's bedside, only to be corseted into yet another gown, two sizes too small—definitely on purpose—and marched off to my morning lessons before the stiffness had even faded from my limbs? A cruelty mortals would outlaw.

Here? A princess's daily routine.

Father gestures at the sprawling battle-blotted map on the praetorium's back wall, lecturing on about brilliant formations that saved the Keres during the fall of Ilium. I nod along, afraid to ask which blob of tan paint represents water and which represents land, knowing it would only reset his lecture from the beginning.

Bottom line: Keres are born for bloodshed.

Wars, massacres, raids. First in Nyx's name, then to spite Zeus and his Olympian cronies, later because mortals hunted us, and now simply to exist. My father's witnessed more conflicts than most history books even bother to record.

Why can't history lessons cover cool handshakes and fun group songs?

"Back then, I was just another foot soldier." He takes a moment to look very proud. "Your grandfather conscripted all his children, hoping the field would mow us down and keep him on his throne." My father looks back at me with an uncharacteristically cheeky smile, like *dictators will be dictators*. "His portrait's the one with holes. My brothers used it for target practice before they passed. I haven't yet mended it."

I glance up from my notes—doodles, really. "Top of your to-go list, I bet."

His smile sharpens. "You know me well."

A stray thought pins me: "How come there are no pictures of my mother? In the hall, I mean."

He flinches when I mention her, but recovers quickly. "She was there once. There were objections to her leadership. She asked for the portrait to be taken down, and assured me if I ever forgot her face, she'd remind me." His gaze settles on me. "Here you are. Her exact image."

"Why didn't they like her? Because she didn't fight in the Munera?"

He draws a breath. "They—"

An Imperial enters the room, chin tucked, and deposits a silver tray by the mountain of maps and gooseneck lamp. The emperor waves him off, pushing the plate toward me. "Open it."

Based on this morning's lessons, I expect a severed head or a bouquet of fingers, or some horrible anatomical message. But when I lift the cloche, I frown. It's mangled, for sure, but it's "A … croissant?"

My father studies me closely. "Nephene mentioned you might enjoy it. That you might even miss it?"

I stare at the pastry. It looks like it's been smacked, flattened, and drop-kicked, but it's still trying its best, sluicing flakes everywhere with tragic dignity.

The urge to just grab it and inhale burns strong.

Real Keres don't eat so I summon a careless shrug. "No idea why she thought that. I'm Keres."

He absorbs this, disappointment almost tactile. "Yes," he

agrees carefully. "My daughter, the Keres personally protected by Nyx herself when she falls in battle. The Goddess has good timing, does she not? Especially—"

He's probably winding up for an inspirational monologue about Nyx only blessing mass graves when the door thunders open.

A shadow moves in, tall, draped in black, chains swarming his shoulders and hips, dragging behind him in a clanking song of iron.

I stiffen, every instinct jerking awake, because that cloak is unmistakable. I'd recognize it anywhere. It's etched into the collective unconscious of every living being:

Thanatos.

God of Death.

Soul Collector, Bringer of Eternal Rest, and apparently, massive fan of dramatic entrances.

He doesn't enter the room. He ruptures the air. Kills the atmosphere. Makes the walls wish they were somewhere else.

My chair swallows me. Head spinning.

My father smiles. "Thanatos," he greets, and there's respect in it. Almost warmth.

The God tips back his hood with a flourish worthy of a game show host, revealing sable hair, clear dark skin and a smile of too many teeth.

He's cute. Too cute for a male who probably vacations in ossuaries.

" 'Sup Vas." A chin jerk. He points at the croissant. "You gonna eat that?"

He has a Midwest accent.

Every legend I've heard—razored teeth, soul rending, midnight-stalking horror—wrong. Death, if anything, looks like a male who would get bullied at Keres High for bringing a packed lunch.

I blink, brain rebooting. "Um. No. Please … go right ahead?"

Thanatos doesn't need to be told twice.

He does a sort of slide-step toward the table, all cloak and barely concealed glee, then pinches the croissant like it's a winning lottery ticket. He tears off a chunk, inspects it, and grins. Takes a bite.

The noise that comes out of him is part sigh, part groan, all existential relief. "Divine," he says, buttery flakes falling everywhere. He tilts his face up, practically glowing, and gives a little finger whirl at the room. "*This*. This is living."

He double-fists the pastry, crams half into his mouth, and addresses my father around the chew. "Can't do Friday anymore. Got supremely double-booked on the Phlegethon, and Hermes is deep in one of his moods." He finishes another chunk. "Rain check? You bring the dice."

My father's eyebrow arches, judging a God as if he's got a death wish. "You could have written."

Thanatos shrugs. "Sure, but then I'd miss the joy of spontaneous croissant." He pats the wall beside the map. "Love the renovations, by the by. Almost can't tell you were blown to bits." A sweep of his cloak chases the flakes to the floor. "Good talk. See you at the next game or when you die. Whichever."

He's gone before I finish breathing out.

The air snaps clean.

I look at my father. "You … play board games with Death?"

"Backgammon. Doubles. We're undefeated. Thanks to clear strategy and weighted dice." He watches me very closely, smile gone soft. "Thanatos is the closest family we have outside these tunnels. You should feel free to call him kin."

I can think of forty things I'd sooner do, including skinny-dipping in the Phlegethon, but I nod anyway. "Sure. I'll keep it in mind."

His attention returns to the map, but I don't bother pretending to focus. The walls are closing in. Drake pushing me away, the lesson, the pastry, the knowledge that I am absolutely, terminally weird—not just in a quirky, lovable way, but in a *let's-just-admit-you-don't-belong-here* way—it all presses down until I feel hollowed out.

"I'm not feeling well," I say, and before he can object, I slip out.

The hall is colder than I remember. My lungs suck in the chill, which helps with the rising panic.

I just need some sleep, and I'll feel better—

"Oh good, you got my signal."

Thanatos, God of Death, Bringer of Eternal Whatever, sidesteps from shadow with a flapping swirl. Whatever reaper effect he's going for is slightly undermined by the white crumbs in his hair and the butter glistening on his fingertips.

"The Dread Queen is looking for you."

My stomach falls to my feet. "The dread *what*?"

A slow, delighted chew. "Persephone. Queen of the Underworld, Consumer of Pomegranates, eternal busybody in the springtime. She's searching for you."

All I can do is repeat: "Persephone?"

"The Queen worries about her sweet Fury's friends, and you are on her list. I'll send word you've been found." He pauses. "Be glad she's not in residence, or she'd have Hades collapse these tunnels."

My nod is shallow, mechanical. "Cool. Okay. Thank you for the heads-pup."

Thanatos flashes all thirty of his teeth. "No problem, little fang."

He waggles the last croissant chunk temptingly, so close I can practically see the warmth radiating off it. "Sure you don't want a bite? It's transcendental."

Oh, I want it.

I want it so bad it hurts.

My mouth does that desperate little purse.

"I'm good, thank you."

He shrugs and pops it into his mouth. Chews with euphoria bordering on indecent. Then he licks his fingers. Every one.

Not even a little sorry.

"You know …" He studies the crumbs in his palm, something soulful flickering across his youthful features. "They bring Charon drachmas. There are sacrifices and prayers for Hades. No one ever leaves so much as a crumb for me. I'm the one doing the heavy lifting. Personal soul escort. Can't just break for brunch. It's granola bars and energy drinks."

"At least you have backgammon?"

A bright, crinkling smile, deep and genuine, crow's feet blooming, as if Death has made laughing a habit. As if there's nothing more serious than joy. "You're right. It's important to make time for the things you love. Goodbye, little—"

"Wait." My hand is already out, halfway to his sleeve, before I remember who I'm reaching for.

A fraction of his face falls. He erases it quickly. "Yes?"

"Do you—did you know my mother? She died."

The sigh he releases is forged over centuries, tired and splintered. His face ages in a heartbeat. "I didn't escort your mother. There was so much death during the war. Celia went direct with Hermes to Elysian Fields per the sisters' wishes."

Celia.

The name rings in my head like a struck bell.

My mind spins.

The sisters. He must mean the original Furies—Nat's aunts who judge souls on the banks of the Lethe.

Has Nat met my mother?

"The Messenger gets all the good souls," Thanatos says with theatrical resignation. "Such a glory hound."

It's the first kindness anyone but my father has expressed about her. It touches some deep part of my heart. "I …" Am I crying? "Thank you for telling me."

"My honor, little fang," Black eyes dart over my shoulder

with the sudden alertness of prey sensing a predator. His chains clank as his cloak billows dramatically. The transformation is instant—hood up, voice deepened to sepulchral tones. "May our next meeting be over cheesecake and not a pyre."

Then he's gone.

Three solid strides down the hall and he disappears.

No rest for the wicked.

*Celia.* Her name's Celia.

Before I can grapple with the information, a group of males rounds the corner, all muscle and monochrome.

I recognize the male in front. Varyn, Julian's friend and fellow competitor. "Princess." He bows, his companions following suit. "Care to join us in a bit of training? Any true Keres must be restless without proper exertion."

What I want is sleep. Or escape. Or to curl up with a bag of gummy bears and pretend none of this exists.

But that's not the Keres way.

I make sure my fangs are extended before smiling. "Love to."

# 20

## Drake

### HE SUSPECTED A TRICK AND REFUSED TO BE A FOOL

There's water on the nightstand, beading with condensation. Next to it—new gloves, resting side by side. Theia. She's the only one who'd bother.

She knows I won't want to touch anything without them. Not even myself. My stomach twists. I dig my fingers into the cot, but my hands won't work. Body's still not firing right. Every breath rattles.

*They're not afraid of me*, she said.

Fucking hell.

I drag water to my mouth. Swallow. It burns; everything burns. My skin is raw, shreds clinging to the muscle. My throat's the worst, like I inhaled fire itself.

The memory unrolls, ugly. Theia's rigid shoulders, her detached stare. Practically a stranger.

I reach for my gloves and freeze.

A shape fills the doorway. For a heartbeat, I think it's Theia, but no—too tall, too pale, and straight as a blade.

Nephene. Arms crossed.

She's been waiting.

I shift beneath the thin sheet, blink at her, let a beat pass to see if she'll leave.

She doesn't.

Her stare is surgical, cuts everything else away.

"You should be dead." Her voice is calm. Almost bored. "If you were mortal, you'd be a scorch mark. What'd Kadmos do to you?"

"Improved me."

"In whose opinion?"

Not mine.

I press my tongue to the roof of my mouth. My thigh's shredded, but I swing my legs off the cot anyway. The movement's stilted. New boots wait on the floor. Right size, midnight black.

Theia.

I pull on clean pants from a pile. That's her, too. She got them from somewhere. Folded them where I'd see.

Nephene doesn't blink.

She's waiting for the answer.

I move slow. Tug the pants up, mindful of the fresh skin on my hip. The pain is there, of course. It always is—a hackle-raising burn, a million needles working the underside of every muscle. My vision tunnels and light sparks behind my eyes.

But pain is just a place in the room now. A chair you don't sit in. A lamp you never turn off.

"Do you feel it?" She hovers in the doorway, arms crossed high across her chest, hair loose, no tiara. Just the searchlight gaze and growing contempt, like maybe if she glares long enough, I'll decompose on the spot. "When your skin burns off. When the bones break, when your heart stops. Do you feel any of it? Or did Kadmos turn it all off?"

I stare at my hands, fresh clean skin. "I feel it."

"Then why'd you jump in front of her? How? You could barely stand."

I haven't asked myself yet. I haven't had time. Now that I circle it, I taste the answer on the back of my teeth, a stab of something I'd call desire if I were still the kind of man who earned that word. All I know is how the sun bent over her bare skin. I just moved. I had to.

She'd been down there on the sand for *me*. Running to me.

"Odd way to thank me for saving your sister," I say.

"Who says I care what happens to her?" Mildly offended. "She stole my crown."

"She's a victim of circumstance, just like you." I flex my hands. "If you truly didn't care, you'd have killed her already, immediately, I'd guess. But you do care. She makes people care."

"She is not built for this. She's not like us. She can't endure the crown."

I force my heel into my boot. "That's not your call, is it?"

"She doesn't belong here. We both know it. The entire realm knows it."

I keep my face blank, hands moving. Snatch a trio of knives from the table, fit two at my hips, one in my boot. "She belongs to herself."

"That's not an answer."

"It's the only one I have."

I want her to belong anywhere but here. But she wants it and so I want it for her. Even knowing it'll hollow her out.

I finish with my gloves, plant both feet solidly on the floor.

Nephene stalks to the door, stops inches shy, gaze slanting back to me. "Lydia believes it's guilt that drives you. She whispers it around court, calling you a devil paying a penance, says you shouldn't be considered a threat."

"Then she won't see me coming."

A smile, predatory. I almost see Theia in it, if she had the edge. "Why would you owe my dear sister your sword? What would you have to feel guilty for, Blackguard? And what does it have to do with the brand on her back?"

"Who knows."

"I think you do," she purrs. "I think you and Lydia are

keeping secrets about her. About that mark, her disappearance, the whole damned war—"

"Then kill me," I snap, a dark feeling taking hold.

She firms her mouth. "You're making Theia a target. The closer you stay to her, the less they see her as a princess, more as an enemy. They hate outsiders. They hate you even more."

"They can hate me all they want."

"Eventually, she'll hate you too."

"I already—"

A scream. One word. *Stop.*

Not loud at first. Not at this distance. But it grows. Repeats.

Fear cracks straight down my sternum. I know that sound. I'm moving before I'm conscious of it, shoving Nephene aside, breaking down the hall for her.

The screaming stops. And that's when I sprint.

I slam into her door shoulder-first. The hinges nearly tearing off.

Theia's on the floor, back to the wall, knees up to her chest, arms locked around her midsection. Blood drips down her temple.

My guts crawl out of my body.

Her eyes are wide, not even crying, just shock. Pink pools under her nose. Her hands are shaking so hard I fear her bones will break skin. She's cradling her left arm.

It's bent wrong, snapped in three places.

Rage ignites, hot and furious. I drop to my knees. "Theia, sweetheart. Look at me."

Her chin lifts in a nervous jerk, pupils blown wide, black moons drowning any spark of reason. She's not here. Not really. Lost somewhere beyond pain. Somewhere darker.

"Who did this?" My voice comes out black, death at the edges. "Who attacked you?"

She shakes her head, curling tighter into herself. "No one.

We—I …" She shrinks away from my outstretched hands. "I can do it. I'll fix it. I have to."

She rocks against the wall, teeth sinking into her lip until blood appears.

I ache to grab her, haul her off the floor, force her to let me help. I can't. "Fix what? Who hurt you?"

"You don't understand. They said—I have to do this."

"Who? Who said that?"

"I'm going to take care of it," she grits out. "I am."

Sweat beads her forehead. "I'm Keres," she rasps. "We don't cry. We don't need anyone. This is nothing."

She tries to realign her arm, whole body shuddering in agony. She yelps, and winces, inhales a sob.

I want to kill everyone who told her this was right.

"Stop. You don't have to prove anything."

She glares at me, breathing heavily, each inhale a little whine. "If I don't ... they'll know. I'll be weak. Keres don't need healers. I'm supposed to be strong. Be Keres."

Every word is shredded by agony. Still, she tries moving the snapped bone. I can hear the sickening crunch.

Fury blossoms in my chest, an inferno of helplessness. "Tell me who did this. Who. Theia. Now."

She shakes her head, tears flooding. "I wanted it. I asked to join the training. I wanted to be better. To fit in."

Her face screws tight, a mask of suffering and embarrassment and something else. She's not looking at me. Won't.

My temple throbs with heat. My jaw locks. I taste bitter iron. This is my destiny: to stand by while she savages herself for acceptance, while she bleeds to prove she belongs.

"You screamed. I heard you. You told them to stop."

"I asked to train—"

"You're allowed to change your mind!"

"But—"

I'm too furious to temper my voice. "But *nothing*!"

Theia recoils, squeezes flat to the wall as if I'm the next in line to hurt her.

I go still. Will the terror from her eyes to vanish, to let reason burn through the haze.

"I'm not here to hurt you," I say. "I will never hurt you, Theia."

It sounds stupid in the charged air, but I say it anyway, over and over, in case repetition is the only thing that gets through. My pulse slams behind my ribs like it's trying to crack bone. I focus on her arm. Bent wrong. Nasty. Pure panic still radiating off her.

My body's weak, flame-burned, every nerve reminding me I shouldn't be upright. Doesn't matter. The world narrows to her face, that impossible, shattered look.

"It's okay. Just breathe for me." Gently, as soft as I've ever managed. I touch my palm to the ground near her foot. Let her see my hands, covered and safe. "You can hit me if you need to."

She won't look at me. She's keening, low in her throat, biting her lip to keep the pain from boiling out.

I'd tear apart Tartarus to stop her pain. Instead, I edge closer, a slow crawl, always watching her, waiting for the flinch, the no.

She doesn't move away. Doesn't move at all.

"Easy, sweetheart. You're safe. I won't let them touch you again. You can hate me later, I promise. But first, let me fix this."

Her arm lies at a grotesque angle. I cradle it in gloved hands, trace each jagged ridge. Three clean snaps.

Not a training accident.

Whoever did this wanted her ruined.

Rage sits with me, patient and cold as an empty grave.

I brace her head with my other hand, fingers tangling the damp strands of her hair. "Ready?"

No answer.

"On three, Theia. Can you count? Here we go, sweetheart. One, two—" I set the bone.

Her shriek is pure agony. I have to restrain her. Do it two more times.

Hate myself.

I think I might be fucking sick, but I make myself whisper, "It's over. It's over. You're all right. It's over."

She sobs, barely conscious, blood mingling with tears on her lip. Exhaustion hums, the brief calm after a storm.

Gently, I tuck damp hair behind her ear, careful not to brush bare skin. "Who hurt you, Princess?"

"Training accident."

She's protecting them. I wish it surprised me.

"I need the truth. Or it'll happen again."

"S'okay"

Her chest quakes with each ragged breath. Honor? Fear? Pride? Whatever it is, it's devouring her.

There's a cut on her cheekbone. Long. Angled. From a ring. I know the shape of that wound, have put it on enough faces.

Not a fucking accident.

"If you tell me," I promise, my voice low. "I'll make it right. I'll keep them from hurting someone else."

She clamps her arms around herself, head bowed.

It will happen again.

They'll do it again.

Hurt her again.

I draw in a gasping breath and make the choice I swore I never would.

One glove peels off, then the other.

She flinches—the barest flicker of hope in her eyes.

"Drake?" she whispers.

"Don't worry, sweetheart." I flex raw skin and broken cuticles. Pain lances, but it means nothing. "It'll be done before you know it."

She blinks, confusion draining into something else. Fear? Disbelief?

"Trust me. This is a bad dream. You'll wake up and it'll be like it never happened."

She stares, mouth parted, then the fight seeps out. A nod.

"Here we go." Gentle as I can, I reach for her cheek with my bare hand. Her eyes shutter closed and before I can find the mettle to touch her, she leans into me, tips her face into my palm.

The contact is—

Euphoric.

It crashes over me, fever-hot and wild. I shut my eyes and drown in the gentle curve of her face, imagine pulling her into my arms whenever I please, weaving my fingers through her hair, crushing her to my chest.

Then it fractures.

A snap in the darkness, and the nightmare unleashes.

I'm plunged into horror: Theia sprawled on cold stone, screams shredding the air while three males peel her arms from her torso. A boot drives into her arm. Pain blossoms in my own arm and I choke it down. Etch their faces into my memory: the crusted blood at his hairline, the malicious curl of another's lips, the cruel flex of a fist around her wrist.

I burn her attackers into my veins, let their hatred sear me alive.

Theia's screaming.

And it's not a memory.

It's here because of me, raw and unrelenting. I wrench my hand away.

She lashes backward, body colliding with the wall, eyes rolling white in pure terror. She shrieks like an animal caught in a trap.

My palm hovers above her shoulder, desperate to comfort —but that's not anything I can offer. I back off. A butcher, not a healer. "It's me. Theia. I'm here. It's over."

I wanted to fix this.

I'm an idiot for thinking I could.

One final, broken whine drifts from her lips, and she crumples: limp, silent, as if her entire soul gave out.

I stay on my knees, dig my nails into my palms, drive down until the pain has a shape I recognize.

Force myself to breathe.

Force myself not to touch her.

I wait. Thirty seconds. Maybe a minute. Maybe an hour.

Slowly, color returns to her lips, her cheeks. Her arm lies straight and strong—she will heal.

It's supposed to comfort me.

It doesn't.

I want to punch a hole through the foundation of this entire kingdom, but I have one job right now.

I slide my hands under her, careful to touch only fabric, not flesh. Unconscious, she curls into me, like if I let go, she'll shatter.

I place her on the bed. Untangle the sheets. Settle pillows under her head, the soft blue one she prefers. I roll her to her side, mindful of the arm newly set, the ribs that might be cracked, the dark bruises emerging.

Her blood marks the floor and wall.

I scrub until no trace remains.

I turn on every light, banishing every shadow.

Arrange clean clothes for her in perfect, obsessive lines at the foot of the bed.

Find a cup and fill it for when she wakes.

Adjust her blankets. Again. And again.

Check her pulse. Examine her arm.

Adjust her blankets.

Wrench the knife from my boot.

Leave my gloves on the nightstand.

Become the monster she needs.

# 21

## Theia

### HE COULDN'T TRUST THAT LOVE COULD SURVIVE IN THE DARK WITHOUT HIM WATCHING

The flush builds under my skin. Slow. Sinister.

Dangerous and thick.

All-consuming.

Not desire. Something rougher, with serrated edges.

Warmth whispers along my nape, tingling. I bite down on my lower lip, pulse racing in my veins. My fingers slide from the swell of my hip into the curve of my waist, over the soft valley beneath my ribs. Every inch of my skin screams for a need I can't name, can barely imagine, but am certain will kill me if I don't get it.

I rake my nails up my sides, desperate for sensation that makes sense. All it does is fan the inferno.

My hips shift against the bedding, and I almost whimper. It's not just the simple ache of wanting; it's starvation.

I'm ravenous.

My fangs throb so violently I moan.

The covers are too much. I kick at them, a frustrated hiss escaping me, animal and involuntary.

My thighs are slick, fevered. I can't tell if I'm in agony or ecstasy. My spine arches against the bed, some unseen force is pulling me apart, dislocating every vertebra, stretching me so thin I'll snap.

My mind is hazy, sticky and pink. Just sensation.

Fury and possession wrap around me. Burying me. I roll again, shove off my blankets. Groan against the next surge of emotion. Drag in a breath all the way to my hollowed-out stomach, and then—

A hum. Low. Dangerous.

The sound is so specific, so utterly Drake, I could pick it out anywhere.

I go statue-still, fangs tingling, thighs slick and wanton. I blink hard, and my eyes snap open. The world is all flickering sconces and shadows and—

Drake.

Settled comfortably in the wide armchair by the door, watching me. Black, blue and green bruises scatter his skin, blood splatters his throat, the left side of his face. His hair drips shiny pink, expression between haunted and homicidal.

His gloves are off.

I'm suddenly sober. Awake. Aware.

He breathes out and I feel him do it. In my chest and my core.

The scent is overwhelming. A sugary tangle that irritates my nose, and a copper tang underneath it, savory and impossible to ignore.

His gaze latches onto my mouth as if he knows precisely how close my fangs are to slicing my lip open and he wants to lick it better.

I'm in crisis. I scramble upright, ready to do literally anything except broadcast how I'm one caress from an orgasm, when he speaks.

"Go back to sleep." His voice is wrecked. Not just tired, but post-apocalyptic, like someone hit 'puree' on his soul and then dumped it back in his body. "I'll watch over you."

I blink. Reset my face. It takes two tries.

"You're in my room," I say. Not a question. Just a fact. Verifiable. Like the square root of sixteen.

"I am."

"Because there was a massacre in yours?"

"I had to make sure you were safe." He leans forward, forearms braced on his knees, gaze locked on mine. "And now I can't seem to leave."

I blame the big, overwhelming feelings and the scent of fresh blood for how long it takes to come back to me.

The training room. Varyn and his buddies offering to spar, all smiles. Them charging at me, even after I fell. Ganging up until my body broke open and reknit. Pushing me to my feet and shoving me toward my rooms, telling me a true Keres wouldn't cry about broken bones.

Drake found me, stitched me back together.

The breath I take is embarrassingly loud, desperate, an effort to use oxygen to drown out the keening ache haunting my bloodstream. It doesn't. It just lights me up again, all exposed nerves and molten hunger, so intense my hands actually shake on the sheets.

He sees it.

Of course he does.

His jaw flexes, the veins in his forearms thick and shining with blood not yet dry.

He watches me as if he's waiting for me to tell him to get out, head cocked, face half-shadowed by the messy tumble of hair. The ends of which are faintly singed.

There's an edge to him, humming with danger and patience and the scathing certainty that he's already imagined this moment a thousand different ways.

I follow the trail of congealing blood sliding down his bare biceps. Pink, almost neon. His skin is sizzling, little hisses where the ichor sticks. "No shirt?" I rasp.

"Tore it."

"Oh." His chest and arms, the flat ridge of his stomach

are muscle-packed, bulging and sinewy. A trained warrior. A killer. "You've got something on your …" Everywhere. Blood everywhere.

"I like the way it feels."

"But syrup on a menu makes you recoil."

"I didn't know whose syrup that was." He leaves it there, the unspoken: *I do know whose blood this is*, hanging between us.

"Drake—"

"Sleep."

Not happening. Because I know whose blood it is too. Not the pink glitter, the dark red along his wrist, dripping down his palm. Everything inside me begs to crawl over and sink my teeth in, claim him, mark him, make it stop hurting.

I can't. Too risky. Too much.

He's out of the chair now. He never needed it, was never really resting. It was simply his best vantage point, the perfect place to watch a female fall to the edge of her sanity.

Here in my room, he's the predator Nat warned me about. The butcher, the executioner, the torturer, the Blackguard. Blood-covered and not a lick of regret.

It's almost funny how I'm not afraid. I catalogue him. The weight of his steps, the precise aligning of violence in his posture, his eyes never straying from me.

My fingers curl around my stomach, need roiling under my skin, gnawing.

He's beside my bed before my brain recalibrates. I'm still sticky and hot, fangs vibrating like personal embarrassment sirens, and he just stands there. Not breathing hard, not gloating. Just there.

He looks me over—not hungrily, but carefully, seriously. The way people check for damage. The muscles in his forearms quiver. "How are you feeling?"

"Good." It's true. A deep, liquid ease has settled in my bones, like someone finally remembered to put oil in the engine. "Really good."

He nods, giving me an intense stare that makes me want to cover all my vulnerable, bitable bits. "Good," he repeats, as if he doesn't quite believe it but would punch the first person to suggest otherwise.

He takes the cup from my nightstand and holds it out to me. "They brought this for you. You should drink."

Blood scents the air. Red. Delicious. It should steal the show.

I can't look away from his hand. It's bare.

I can't remember ever seeing his hands bare. Not once. Maybe in the arena, a flash of wrist and bone under burning leather, but it's blurry from too much panic.

Now? My eyes soak them in, greedy.

They're huge. His hands. Thick knuckles and wide tendons, like he stole them from a statue and stitched them to his own wrists. Strong enough to crack plaster. Or snap necks. Yet, they look ... nice. Tired. Veins shot through like blue lightning.

I want them.

I want them to touch me. Or possibly not. I don't even know anymore, because my brain is, at this exact moment, a big frothing cauldron of "feed now, think later."

I take the cup, hand shaking not because I'm weak—it's the opposite. I'm so strong with thirst that it's a miracle I haven't attacked him.

"Drink," he rumbles, voice pouring straight to the center of my spine. "It'll help."

I do.

I tip it back and let it rush in hot, and the taste detonates behind my teeth.

It's everything: sweet, alive, a red streak of lightning. Richer than I've ever known. Fresh, but with a polish, a luster that slicks down my throat and floods hollows I didn't know I had. It wipes out the static, the old tears, the mortar in my cracked bones. Heat climbs my cheeks, and my hands stop shaking.

The dull throb in my skull, the lingering pain in my arm? Gone.

I suck down the cup in one go, relishing the sweet, metallic, completely illegal rush of it.

My fangs are out so sharp even my lips tingle. Blood stains my mouth, but I don't have the coordination to care about messes right now.

Drake watches with the kind of focus that could strip paint.

There's a tautness in his jaw, as if he's the one restraining a wild animal now. "They won't bother you again," he tells me. "The males. The ones who ... They can't apologize tonight, but they will."

I don't know what to do with that.

I lick the glass's rim clean, slow, regretting the rush, not caring how rabid it looks.

Drake doesn't look away.

"You've got a little ..." he says, and his hand comes up, bare and bold, to wipe the wet from my face.

I flinch. The cup almost goes flying.

Terror. It coats me head to toe, scorches my cheek right where he touched me. It's not the fun, scary-movie kind. This is white-out, edge-of-panic, nightmare terror.

Drake becomes dead still. Then pulls back, inch by inch, rewinding time, backing off. His face shuts down, mouth becoming a hard line.

"Sorry," he says. It comes out strangled. "I wasn't going to—I won't do it again."

The air between us goes brittle. My hand is welded to my cup. Teeth sunk into my lip.

Nat told me Drake wouldn't touch anyone until he felt comfortable, until they knew what it meant. I'd thought ...

I'd thought he was sensitive. Touch averse. Private.

His touch destroys.

*Don't*, he'd said to me. Begged. He pulled away, stepped back, every time I've tried for connection. My brain is racing, pulling moments between us, and remapping them with new information. Drake wasn't disgusted with me. He was protecting me.

"I am sorry, Theia," he says, firm now. "I should not have done that. But I …" He cuts himself off, shakes his head. I think his eyes might be glassy, might have tears as his hand makes a fist. "They hurt you, and you may not want to hurt anyone, but I do. I enjoyed hurting them for what they did to you. I might even hurt them again if I can tear myself out of your room."

"Are they ..." I can't finish the question. "Did you ..."

He slides a look my way, green and sharp and so honest it almost guts me. "They're breathing. But now they understand the word 'stop' isn't optional."

"You taught them ... basic English?"

"I showed them what it feels like when someone ignores their request. They'll never want anyone to feel like that."

"But they're definitely still alive, right?"

My attempt at lightness crashes against his granite expression. "They were competitors. Killing them would disqualify me from the Munera."

And that would mean he'd lose his one chance at freedom. My stomach plummets. "Funny way of showing they want to marry me."

"They wanted a kingdom." A shrug. "Now they won't survive the next task."

It's so male, I snort.

"You shouldn't doubt my success rate."

"The next task could be balloon arranging or charades, or—"

"Irrelevant."

"Are you especially adept at balloon animals, *butcher*?"

"I can make a noose, *princess*."

He's serious. He'd party-planner murder them. "You can't just kill them. They were only training me to fight."

"Stop justifying what they did."

"It's Keres culture."

He shrugs. "It's not mine."

"This isn't your home. You don't make the rules here."

"I realize exactly how powerless I am when it comes to you, Theia."

I am suddenly, acutely aware of every molecule in my body sitting on the bed, wearing a thin nightgown. I scrub the last streak of blood from my mouth, daring myself not to look at him.

I fail. Heracles-hacking-off-Hydra-heads-level fail.

"How does it work?" I ask. "Your touch? Did you see everything I did? Is that how you found Varyn?"

His head snaps up, not quite startled, more like guilt caught off guard. "Yes."

"All of it?"

Me huddling on the ground? Sobbing while they laughed. My shouts for them to stop even before they'd attacked.

He doesn't smirk. Doesn't gloat. Just answers, blunt, like any other answer would be too much. "Yes. The strongest fears manifest first, those sitting at the front of your mind. The longer I keep contact, the deeper, more undiscovered, and twisted fears arise. The darkest ones. I stopped as soon as I could with you."

His hands curl tighter, knuckles white.

"So you know what they did?"

A nod. "Yes, and I felt everything you felt." A swallow. He looks away. "Decided to use it to my advantage."

As the king's torturer. All the information on how to ruin someone laid bare with a single touch. No wonder they're all scared of him.

Drake's voice, when it comes, is as rough as gravel. "You really should rest."

I feel like laughing. Or sobbing. Something hysterical, something that shakes the kingdom to its foundation and pops a couple bricks loose in the realm above.

Instead, I say, "Can we talk? If I try to sleep right now, I'll just ... think about things." Like the blood, and the males, and the fact that despite all this, my body is still humming. "Come on. We both know you're not leaving until you've finished monitoring my REM cycles. Too worried I might launch myself into a knife fight."

I can see the flicker of options behind his eyes: "No," "Hell no," "That's an actual nightmare," "Go back to sleep," etc.

I give him the world's most battered puppy stare. "Please?"

He sighs through his teeth, then, in a voice that could sand the finish off a desk, "Lay down."

I go flat in a heartbeat.

He crosses to the door. He's not limping, not exactly, but there's a heaviness to every step. Like the room can't decide if it wants to let him pass or just snare him at the ankles and see what happens.

He checks the lock. Three times, maybe four. When he's satisfied, he says, "I'm not actually from Boston." His voice is low, reluctant. "The Butcher of Boston? Not me. I was born and raised in Philadelphia."

"But it's your name, your thing. You're the butcher." I roll onto my side, hair fanning everywhere, trying to arrange myself to see him while hiding the goosebumps on my arms. "Everyone calls you that. *You* call yourself that."

"Everyone's wrong." He shrugs one shoulder, turning off the light. "It could've been a copycat. Or someone forgot where I lived. Maybe it just sounded good. I was working a job, and suddenly I'm being introduced as the Butcher of Boston."

"And you went along with it?"

He stops by my bed, looming. "Fear is mankind's oldest emotion, and its strongest. The name inspired terror. So I kept it."

"So you're basically a fraud," I say, unable to hide my smile.

"I'm not."

"A reputation thief. A knockoff."

"The title may be borrowed. The skills are not."

"And somewhere," I sigh dramatically, snuggling against my pillow, "the real Butcher toils in obscurity while you swagger around with his glory."

A shadow crosses his face—almost amusement, but darker. Makes my pulse skip.

He takes the edge of my blanket between his fingers, folding it with surgical precision across my hips, then pulls it higher. The air between his skin and mine crackles with possibility, yet he maintains that careful gap. The blanket rises to my ribs as he leans closer, his breath warm against my collarbone.

We're two magnets held at that perfect distance—close enough to feel the pull, far enough to resist it.

I swallow, attempt to control my overactive pulse. "All this time I believed I was in the presence of the great Butcher, practically swooning, and you're just some imposter with good PR."

"Disappointed, princess?"

"Entirely." I fight a giggle. "I was promised a monster, not someone who probably rescues kittens and knows how to French braid. I'd like to speak to the manager."

He's still leaning over me.

I'm tucked in. The lights are out.

"You think you're funny, yeah?" His thumb grazes a strand of hair on my pillow.

The almost-contact sends desire coursing through me.

"Am I?" I'm whispering now, my chest rising and falling too quickly. His weight shifts, the mattress sinking under us, bringing him a fraction closer.

"Yes, Theia. You are."

"So, what exactly was this job?" I ask, pretending my pulse isn't racing.

"What job?"

"Before. You mentioned a job, not in Boston."

His shoulders tighten. "I was in the Murphy mob." He lifts away from me, gaze fixed on something invisible in the corner. "I did whatever they asked. I was good at it. By seventeen, I could break a man's fingers one by one until he remembered where he'd hidden the money he'd owed. I was who they called when they needed the dirty work done."

I want to ask if he means "dirty" as in "shoveling coal" or "dirty" as in "hey, could you harvest the kidneys and alphabetize them by unwilling donor?"

But his face says, *please, Nyx, just let me have this one moment of dignity*, so, for once in my life, I shut my mouth.

Eventually, I can't stand it. I need noise, even if it's the sound of my own impending doom.

"Sooo … " I wait for him to stop me. He doesn't. "The mob have a sweet retirement plan? A good work-life balance?" His look is withering. "Why'd you join?"

"You want the gory details? Or just the headline?"

"I'm a big girl," I say, which is a lie. "I can handle gore." *Lie.*

"I was a dumb fucking kid who thought working for the bad guys would keep them away from my family." He leans against the wall next to the bed, Adam's apple bobbing once as he stares at the ceiling. "The first time I killed someone, I threw up for an hour after. By the fifth, I could eat dinner right after. The next ten actually made me hungry. My youngest sister was twelve when they threatened to send her my fingers if I tried to leave. My oldest was engaged when they put her fiancé in the hospital because I had the gall to ask why I needed to cut apart a priest."

"You have sisters."

"Had," he corrects. "I might have stolen a name, Theia, but I earned every letter of Butcher."

He says *butcher* not like a threat but like a wound that's never closed.

"You should sleep," he murmurs.

I stare up, let the pulse in my throat show, let him watch the way it works beneath my skin. "Are you going to stay?"

"Do you want me to?"

*Yes*. The truth shudders through me, warmth pooling in my belly like a reward

"I feel better with you here," I say, so quietly it barely counts as sound. My face heats. "You can ... if you want, you can lay here with me."

I pat the bed. A weak attempt at casual.

He doesn't even glance at the mattress. Doesn't flex, doesn't twitch, just firms his jaw. "No, princess."

"It doesn't bother me," I press, greedy for closeness. "It'd be nice, actually. We can use the sheet as a no-touch barrier. I think I'll sleep better if you're close."

He grunts, a low, fraying sound that resonates between my legs. "Better for you if I'm not."

He returns to his chair across the room, crosses his arms. The quiet between us has weight. Motion. The urge to call him back, to crawl into his lap and bite him until the world stops burning, grows worse.

I flip over, burying my cheek in the pillow. "I'm still hungry."

It slips out, humiliating. The need's so strong I can't keep it caged.

"Yeah?" A rumble. It doesn't make it easier. He sounds like he's daring me.

"Yes."

"You never did get your cranberry pancakes."

"Vampire's Delight."

That low, sensual hum. "That's what I said. That kind of food doesn't fill you, though."

"Of course not."

"Then why eat it?"

"Brilliant marketing. Targeted. Poignant. It *is* the season to indulge."

"Go to sleep, princess."

I pick out his silhouette in the dark. "I eat it for the same reason you don't like when your hands are messy. So, I can pretend everything's normal, like I might not be a killer."

"Drinking blood doesn't require killing, Theia."

"Neither does torture."

We hold each other's eyes—two killers that might not be if we had greater control.

From his spot in the dark, he says, "It shouldn't have to, but sometimes it's better that way."

The words hover.

I want to kick at the covers and tell him, "No, it's not better. You're wrong. Group hugs and cat videos are enough to overcome anything." I want to say that nightmares, and bad feelings aren't forever. That people get to choose.

But I don't. Because for him, maybe they are.

A male who everyone fears, who can't even find solace in an embrace.

Optimism isn't sufficient armor for me to follow that thread, to wonder if he's ever wished he hadn't woken up.

I fall asleep with Drake sitting there, my guardian at the gates, and all that heat in my veins, the wild animal throbbing quiets. Just calm enough to let me rest.

I don't dream. Or maybe I do, but it's not the kind with plot or helpful metaphors. Just flashes: teeth, blood, light. Hands.

Big wonderful hands.

I wake to hunger. A velvet, writhing ache, deeper than bone. My body's flushed, wet between my thighs, fangs crowding my mouth before I open my eyes. The longing's so sharp, I try to throttle it with blankets, only to realize I've torn the sheets to bits, rolled half off the mattress.

I consider burrowing down into the memory foam and making a life there when I smell it. I lift to my hands and knees, wipe the hair from my face.

There's a cup on the nightstand. Another on the dresser. More. Teetering on the frame of the mirror, balanced on the footboard, next to the lamp, on the arm of the chair.

And in each, filled to the brim: blood, deep as rubies.

Still warm.

# 22

## Theia

### HE CHECKS IN, TAKES CARE OF HER, EVEN WHEN HE SHOULDN'T

We have a lake.

The news hits me the same as if Nephene had said, *we have a Pomeranian named Mopsy*.

I didn't believe her, and yet—there it is. An expanse of complete stillness stretching under a ceiling of black stone cleaved so sharply it reflects every drop.

The lake gleams pure silver. Not water with cheap body glitter drizzled on top, this is thick and creamy and molten. Pulsing in the dimness.

It's ichor.

The Divine blood of the Gods, as if Zeus double-tapped a vein and forewent the mop. The brightness burns my eyes, and the air so saturated with cloying sweetness it hurts to breathe.

The effect is disorienting. If Nat were here, she'd say, "Don't look directly into the hell sauce," and then pretend to push me in as payback for that time I signed us up for Smash Mouth karaoke.

"Bet they don't have this above," Nephene says from my side, as if we're at a wine tasting and not the epicenter of generational trauma.

I'm this close to hyperventilating.

Have they killed a God?

*Can* they kill a God?

Did they stick a tap in the crook of Apollo's elbow and leave it to age it like a horrifying cabernet?

The council filters onto the railed ledge behind me, not a single cloak or boot scuffed, bristling with murder-happy anticipation. "Hate this one," Orielle, one of my loudest dissenters, says. "Takes forever."

Ripples of agreement. I can't face them.

"It's not Hestia," Nephene says, moving to my side. "Although if we could watch a God bleed out on our stones, I'd pick her. Goddess of hearths? What a waste."

"Not Apollo?" I ask. "He represents everything you hate. God of the sun, of prophecy, of healing. Hestia protects the home."

"Everything *we* hate," Nephene corrects. "And Hestia didn't protect our home. Apollo at least carries a weapon, though the bow is a child's toy." She lays her arms over the rail and inhales deeply. "We strain the ichor from our hunts. Some creatures possess more than we want to drink, so we filter it out to our preferred ration and spill the rest in here."

A lake of their dead enemies. *Our* dead enemies. A monument to violence that they use to style an empty room, like it's their great aunt's old leg lamp. My stomach cramps uncomfortably, queasy.

Nephene mistakes my horror for reverence. Her voice turns almost fond. "We have two others, though this is the biggest."

I tear my attention from the lake to my sister. No gown today, or tiara. "There are no spectators for today's task," she'd explained on our walk over. "No reason to pretend I give a shit who lives and dies."

She gestures with her chin toward the lake's edge. "Each male must cross the steppingstones"—she indicates the pale flat rocks barely visible above the surface, glinting like the most obvious bait box for disaster—"and ascend the pedestal where he will face his true self in the waters of Narcissus. If he wavers at all, a flinch, a gasp, the stone collapses. He falls."

"Into the ichor?"

A nod. "Death by divine. Ichor dissolves bone whole. No one's ever been fast enough to swim to safety." Then, with a casual shrug: "It's a mercy. Some call it a cleansing."

A cleansing, and she's explaining it like the features of her mouthwash. I massage the sting in my throat.

"Father does it every year under the autumnal moon," she adds. "A trial of will and responsibility. If the emperor cannot conquer it, he doesn't deserve to lead."

Greta appears at Nephene's side before I can ask questions one through thirty. There's a knife woven into her hair, and two streaks of black accenting her eyes. "You look better," she says, giving me the up and down. "Almost like a Keres."

I glance over my shoulder. "Me?"

My sister laughs and Greta nods. "Yes, you. You're still soft and weak—"

"Greta," Nephene chides.

"Relax, Effie. I'm just saying she looks less sickly. We're fixing what the surface dwellers broke."

*Effie?* My jaw drops.

Nephene unwinds a hank of hair from my bun. "You do look quite good."

"I said *better*," Greta points out.

"She's my sister. Half my blood, do you not think she's stunning?" The sleek arch of Nephene's brow feels like a loaded gun, like if Greta says no, Effie—*Effie*!—will sucker-punch her, but if she says yes, Effie will sucker-punch her.

I try to say thank you, but it's wasted effort. Greta and Nephene have already moved on to make outrageous, slightly offensive observations about the competitors as they file down a narrow metal landing to our right. Greta says something about Rafil not being able to keep his own fangs sharp. Nephene snaps back that at least he's not built like a mortuary mannequin like Yvet.

She has a point.

"Here he comes," Nephene murmurs as Julian steps in, demonstrating perfect posture. The markings on his skin shine like jewelry. His hair is even more perfectly coiffed than usual, braided in spirals like he just did product placement for *Hemoglobin Extra Hold.*

What's missing is the little fan club that's usually glued to his side.

I cut a glance to Nephene to see if she notices that Stav and Varyn and the other one—*Daryl?*—who all have impressive upper arms and the collective personality of one (1) damp dishtowel are very much not here.

Because of me.

But her mouth only curves up. "They decided conscription would be less dangerous," she informs Greta of the missing males. "Or maybe offered a more attractive an end than the Munera. Either way, they swapped allegiances. A wise choice, really. They wouldn't have survived this task."

"Cowards," Greta snarks. "Wonder what scared them."

"I can think of a few things." Nephene does not elaborate, but a small, deliberate pause hangs in the air. In case I want to add specifics.

I don't.

I absolutely know what scared them. It involves several snapped bones, a blood-soaked Blackguard, and the phrase "no means no."

"He doesn't seem very ..." I gesture at Julian, who manages to look delighted about being the lone wolf in a shark tank. "Upset? Aren't they his friends?"

"Julian doesn't want friends, only rivals to break," Greta says, as if the distinction is one of taste rather than pathology.

I expect Nephene to disagree, but she lets the observation

stand. "He will make a fine emperor. Not overly clever or terribly commanding." Her eyes flick to me, measuring, gauging if I am absorbing the lesson.

Greta nods. "He wants to be seen leading without making actual decisions. Like Menelaus with a higher body count."

"He'll never threaten the crown. Will do as he's told."

"Looks like a conqueror, folds like a napkin."

I can't tell if it's a eulogy or a sales pitch. "He seems kind," I offer, mostly to reassure myself.

Nephene moves her ring around her finger, the closest to fidgeting I've witnessed from her. "Exactly. Julian *seems* kind but he'll rip the throat out of any dissenter. The council requires a proud and violent emperor to bow to, but the real power must stay with the bloodline."

"The Empress's word is law," Greta agrees, admiring Nephene's hand.

Nephene turns to me. "*Your* word."

*My word.* Because I'll be Empress. The one to marry. The one to rule. The one they'll try to smother in my sleep when they find out I eat banana bread and freckle under the sun.

My body goes into full crash-cart mode. Scalp prickling, tongue marshy, wrists burning, heart beating so fast I swear it's about to cut out early. But then it passes.

And Drake enters.

He's at the rear of the incoming pack, hands buried deep in the pockets of his combat pants, as if he can't be bothered to put on a show. If anything, he looks bored, just finished with the idea of time as a concept. His black hair is messy and falling into his eyes, hiding the green and making him appear twice as threatening as the last time I saw him. Which is saying something, because the last time he was covered in blood.

He's cleaned himself up for the task. Not a fleck of blood, not even a pinkish crescent under his ear.

He regards the lake like he'd love nothing more than a bone-melting swim. Dismisses it. Finds me.

He is, objectively, outrageously handsome. Not the pretty, glass-blown symmetry of Julian, but the old-world, raze-your-city-and-take-your-children kind of beautiful. It's how he stands, overconfident and steady, as if he isn't surrounded by his sworn enemies.

Last night's warmth sinks back into my skin, dips into my stomach. His hands compressing my mattress, the low, fragmented hunger in his voice, the weight of his body caging me in, barest scent of eucalyptus on his neck. My chest contracts with the sudden, involuntary ache of lust. Heat strokes my throat, cheeks, the backs of my ears.

Imperials seal the doors at the back of the chamber. A latch barricades them with a slam. The noise is final.

Greta purses her lips. "A shame to lose the butcher in this round. I'd have liked to hear him scream."

"He's going to make it." I have a strange, steel certainty about it. I watch him shake out his gloved hands, crack his neck.

"You don't really believe the butcher will pass this, do you? He betrayed his own kind, he bowed to a mad king, he's tortured—"

"That's not his name," I say. "And it doesn't matter. He'll pass. The certainty burns through me like wildfire.

Drake knows exactly what kind of sinner he is. Every drop of blood on his hands, every scream he's caused—he owns it all. Wears it.

There is nothing Drake Cosgrave does without knowing the consequence. He won't flinch at the reflection because he knows who he is.

The villain.

The word should repulse me. Instead, it wraps around my heart like a caress.

Villains don't break down doors because a mortal's getting

handsy. They don't chase after abducted females. They don't join the mob to protect their sisters.

I meet his gaze again. The other males stare up at me with hunger or calculation, but Drake watches me like a storm he has no hope of surviving.

A pool of flesh-dissolving ichor? He doesn't waver.

A princess who slices her lip with her own fangs? Pure terror.

I can't help but smile at that until Nephene's cool fingers encircle my wrist. "A reminder, sister," she murmurs against my ear, a hint of warning. "Kill what you drink or give it up cold. Anything else would result in the cruelest torture."

# 23

## Drake

### SHE MADE HIM RECKLESS, UNAFRAID OF PUNISHMENT

In the center of the room, Theia's dancing.

I watch from my place against the wall, holding her drink.

I've invented twenty ways to kill her partner.

Just a matter of time before I pick my favorite.

My hand tightens behind my back until the leather of my glove creaks—a quiet, traitorous sound the music swallows.

I try—really fucking try—not to watch her.

No one's going to jump her in the middle of the celebration.

Yet each time she disappears in a throng of swaying bodies, my muscles seize.

The serpentine cavern must hold the entire Keres empire. Each bend hosts a cathedral-sized chamber supported by massive, veined columns of limestone. Stalactites drip in tiered clusters from the sky-high ceiling, shivering with condensation. They're strung with a million LED pinpricks, making it look like the Milky Way is punching down through the stone.

The string quartet plays from a hollow above the flowstone dais. Their instruments are ancient and ugly. Probably handcrafted by a Keres artisan who desperately wanted the wood to remember pain. They play without sheet music. It's a tune you couldn't hum if you heard it a hundred times.

A harmony so decadent, it hurts my bones.

No—that's the curse. It writhes around my wrists, my ankle, circles my throat in a continuous, pressing sting. It's done waiting for Theia to give me answers. It demands I take them.

Too many unknown enemies surround Theia for me to even register the pain, even if it would cripple another male.

"The pining thing is pathetic," Greta says, her high, smarmy voice coming from beside me. She collapses against the wall beside me, sipping from her overfilled chalice.

She's wearing what many of the males have donned: brown slacks and a fitted upper harness, midriff bare, hips exposed, shoulders and back painted with ceremonial markings. The Keres tuxedo. "That vein's about to burst in your neck. Then this whole inane celebration will turn into a real party of who gets first taste."

Theia twirls back into sight, navy skirts clinging to her legs before spinning wide. Her hand rests in Rafil's grip—a male with the personality of a chair and the strength of an Echidna.

"Wanna guess what we used to do when the final sixteen competitors remained?" Greta doesn't wait for an answer. "Ritual sacrifice. Each of the ten finalists captured their biggest enemies, *outside* the Munera, and slaughtered them right up there where the musicians play. That was something. That was Keres. Now the emperor feels our numbers are too low and our Imperials too vital to cull, so we're dancing instead. Like the fucking Charites."

"There's no threat of anyone confusing you for a Charite," I say. "They're charming and beautiful."

Her glare could peel stone. "Would've been too easy if you just fell in the pool, huh?"

"Yes."

She huffs.

Did she think I'd cower when faced with who I truly am? Horrified by the devil's reflection? When I touch someone, their nightmares become mine. The second, third time I touch them, *I* become their nightmare. I see my own features pinch with malice, my own laughter echoing while I pry them apart.

I was never going to flinch.

Theia spins again. Her partner's hand slides lower.

My weight shifts forward, instinct overriding discipline, every fiber of my being aligning toward one singular, catastrophic purpose: remove the threat.

My fingers twitch.

One step. That's all it would take. One step and I could—

Greta clicks her tongue. "It's suffocating. All the preening and bloody nauseating decorum. It makes me want to stab my eyes out."

"Do I look like I want company?"

"You look like you're going to pluck the ribcage, bone by bone, out of anyone who touches our precious Princess Theia."

Anyone who looks at her, actually.

I force my hand to unclench and return to the wall. It's exactly where I belong. Close enough to kill for her, far enough to never touch her.

He pulls her closer.

I make myself watch. Remind us both: "I'm forbidden from harming the other competitors."

That's who she's dancing with. The finalists, her suitors, potential husbands. This is her seventh dance, her sixth partner, and *that*, right there, is smile number seventy-nine.

So sweet and lovely, even fucking Rafil smiles back.

"No," Greta says. "You're not allowed to kill them. Injuries are on the table though. I saw what you did to Varyn. He had to write his Imperial vow of service because he couldn't speak it. Two days and his jaw still hasn't healed."

"Hard to turn dust back into bone."

"Lydia's not in the Munera." Greta tilts her head. "Hasn't the Queensguard got a bounty out on you?"

"She's Vasilis's guest." And I'm already eating spit in food. I don't need it poisoned too.

"The emperor wouldn't blink if she became a stain on the floor. She's Nephene's guest."

The music wanes, then quickly waxes. Movement flickers in my periphery—partners trading, cups refilling, Nephene's mousy friend cackling horrendously.

Rafil takes Theia for another turn.

His hand grips her waist.

I grit my teeth. Remind myself of my purpose. "Why is Nephene talking to the Queensguard?"

"Because until two weeks ago, butcher, she was to be empress. Told she would rule since birth. Arguably the only reason Vasilis stomached her dreadful mother. Decades of strategy don't just lose momentum because a princess shows up." Greta drinks deep. "Look at how she clings to her, like a helpless lamb. I need to puke."

"Why stand here watching then?"

Greta sighs. "Because she'll never marry me. Never pick me over her kingdom. Even though I've accepted that, and even though the healthy course of action would be leaving this terrible music and nauseating crowd, I'd spend the entire evening away from her wondering what she's doing, who she's with, if they treat her as well as she deserves. I'd rather know than wonder."

I glance down at her, surprised by the vulnerable tone, the openness. Then she glances up at me and smirks. "No. Wait. That's why *you're* here, butcher."

"Funny."

She finishes her drink. "Lydia's a scorpion. Kill her before she stings you."

She's gone before I can tell her to fuck off.

I certainly can't say she's wrong.

I rub my knuckles hard against my mouth, consider pouring out the drink in my hand. A fool's errand.

I don't. Just in case.

I stay and watch her dance, winding guilt around my lungs until I'm out of breath. Close my eyes. None of it calms the violence in my chest.

Quick as a breath, I'm reliving last night, the sound of cracking bones ringing in my ears as Theia sits up in her bed, as she gasps at the devil in the corner, only to relax at the sound of my voice. As if it comforts her. As if I'm not doused in blood and stalking her in my spare time.

She lets me see the pulse at her throat, the way it beats beneath her skin. When she asks if I'm going to stay, I don't have to think. "Yes."

She whispers that she feels better with me here, almost inaudible, then offers the bed.

She believes I have the control of a Titan if she thinks I could share a bed with her and sleep.

I'm happy when she shifts away, sheets wrapping around her knees. Happy—fucking elated—to remain in the dark, arms crossed, half-dry blood crusting on my skin, digging under my nails. Because I'm with her. Happy to hear her even breaths in the quiet.

"I'm hungry," she whispers. Soft. Needy.

The confession rattles me.

I can fix it.

I can picture it perfectly: slashing my wrist open, blood pooling in my palm, dripping along her floor as I stalk to her bedside, as I beg her to lie back and open her mouth, admire the rise and fall of her chest as she arches for me. Crimson drips onto her lips, splashing, messy and crude, and I have to bite back a groan, stop myself from rattling off indecent, pent-up fantasies. Her breath scalds my palm. I want to lean in, drink, let me ruin her.

But even in my head, I don't touch her.

I just hold my arm out, a dumb, distant offering. I wait, entranced, as she tips back, lashes low, mouth open, tongue ready. The first drop would hit her lip. She'd lick it away, slow, and go soft in her own bones.

I want it. The want is volcanic. Devastating. I want to see her take me in and never stop.

I open my eyes, shut down the fantasy, blink away the haze. The crowd has shifted.

She's not there. Not in Rafil's arms, not under the gold lights, not at the edge where Nephene holds court.

I go rigid. A fierce darkness whips through my chest. I reach for my knife and charge forward.

"Looking for me?"

I twist, my cup splashing red on my sleeve.

Theia's brows lift. She stands close, hands folded, head tipped, watching me with a patience that doesn't suit her. Her cheeks are flushed, brown eyes sweet.

"Finished dancing?"

"Unless they finally take my ABBA requests."

Smile eighty-two. I lean my shoulder into the wall. "It appears you have me cornered, Princess."

Her brow arches as she mirrors my pose, the draping, sheer sleeves of her gown bunching. "Princesses do not corner. We kill." A smile. "Nephene's giving me lessons."

"Have at it then."

"You don't think I will?"

Part of me craves it—her fangs bared; her full strength unleashed against me. "Show me what you've got."

She's fighting smile eighty-four. "I really could."

"Not a chance."

"Even if I used all my tricks?" She traces a pearled vein on the wall between us, stopping just before it disappears under my elbow.

My throat burns. "Let's find out."

She laughs.

Fuck.

Her fangs catch the light. Predatory. Ravenous.

I'm already there, aren't I? Ready to slit my own throat for her just to have a taste.

She doesn't even realize it.

"I think Rafil's my favorite," she confides. "He used to be a scout, so he's spent time with mortals. Didn't need me to explain my reliance on coffee to understand my 'still the beans' tangent."

"Good."

"You do that a lot."

"Converse amicably? I'm working on it." Really fucking hard.

"Let me say it wrong. Rafil corrected me. He's not even mortal, and he knows the phrase is 'spill the beans'." She pauses. "You were mortal. And you let me go on saying it."

"I got the gist."

"I do it on purpose."

I misheard her. "You do what on purpose?"

She places her cheek to the wall, the puff of her curled hair a cushion. Smile eighty-four is playing at her mouth—small, private, like she's letting me in on something she's never said out loud before. "I say the phrase wrong. I know the right words."

"You …" I stop, reassess. "Why?"

"Are you sure you want to know? You won't look at me the same."

"I assure you, I will."

"I … I don't enjoy conflict, but some creatures really *really* deserve to be bothered, and these are precisely the ones who are driven mad by fumbled wordplay. It's good for changing topics too. They fixate on the mistake and forget what they're saying. Oh, and it's very useful when meeting new people. I get to see who corrects me, who laughs, who uses it to feel superior." Her gaze lifts. "Who lets it slide."

A strange laugh breaks out of me without my control. "You let them think you're—"

"Naive? Whoever would call me that." Eighty-five.

She's magnificent.

She's developed her own system to instantly categorize every person she meets. A useful tool for someone who didn't have the time between kidnappings to really get to know someone.

Even better, she lets herself be underestimated, dismissed, considered nonthreatening. Everything a secret Keres had to be to survive among other creatures.

"You're right," I say. "I'll never look at you the same." I lean forward, catch the vanilla on her skin. Inhale. "Don't marry a male who corrects what you say. Next he'll be correcting your clothes, then your behavior."

"That'd be Ozren." Her nose wrinkles. "He said I looked hungry. Offered me a bite."

He did? I'll launch him into the fucking lake.

"I told him we'd burn that bridge when we get there."

Another laugh tears up my throat. It's so rough and clunky, a passing Imperial stops to stare.

And then Theia laughs. Crystalline and devastating. I lose control, lean into her, gloved fingers taking the ends of her hair and tugging. "Are you hungry, princess? Is that why you're here with me?"

24

# Drake

## DOUBT CAN BE LOUDER THAN A GOD'S COMMAND

Her eyes snap up. She's so close I catch the heat from her skin, the slight hitch in her breathing. "You were sulking, I thought I might cheer you up," she says, watching my finger in her hair.

"By telling me your darkest secret."

"Please. If you knew that, I'd have to hunt you down." She peers up at me through her lashes. "You don't want me to hunt you, do you, Drake?"

The scrape of my name in her throat. I nearly break. I let the silence stack bricks on my chest, and when I breathe, there's only her, filling every empty place.

"You're welcome to try." I look at her mouth. Don't bother hiding it.

"I bite. Remember?" Her shoulder brushes mine, and that single point of contact ignites a line of fire under the skin, crawling down to the palm hidden in my pocket.

It yanks me back to fucking reality.

I thrust the cup at her. "This is for you. Pure stuff, though it's cold now."

It's still warm.

She's noticed the cup. Same way I've noticed the fangs she

keeps pricking with her tongue, but she waves it off. "Thanks, but I'm fine."

"You need your strength."

"It's time that I broke blood with the others."

"The ichor makes you sick."

She contemplates the party, refuses to look at me. "I can learn to handle it."

"Theia—"

"Wasn't it you who told me about building immunity? That micro-dosing poison was smart?"

"Smart for *them*," I counter. "Just like Zeke's naked moonlight yoga keeps him sane. Doesn't mean you should try it."

"Why not?"

"The cold for starters—" And I'd slaughter anyone who saw her bare.

"That's not what I meant. Why should they drink it but not me?"

"They're playing defense. Doing it out of self-preservation."

"I need that too."

"Yes."

"So then why shouldn't I—"

"Because you have *me*." The declaration rips from my throat, tearing flesh on its way out. My chest heaves as though I've been gutted.

The space between us empties.

"I can't."

"Why not?"

She fidgets. A flush rises up her throat, hotter than anger, denser than shame. "I know it's your blood, Drake."

I'm on the verge of denying it, but then she says, "I'd recognize your blood anywhere. I could find a single drop in the ichor lake. I know it's you. It tastes like You. I've always known." She watches the dancers like it's her job. "I shouldn't have drunk it before either."

"You didn't say anything."

"You didn't either," is her sharp reply. "It seemed like you didn't want me to know."

"You told me not to."

"We both know I have zero control over you. If I did, you'd have …"

"What?"

She sighs.

"You like it," I say. Maybe ask.

A laugh. "No, I like diners and Broadway, your blood is …" She doesn't finish, just shuts her eyes. Her throat works as if she can taste it right now. Taste me. Her fingers grip her wrist until her knuckles pale.

I fucking like it.

More than I should. More than breathing and independent thought.

I lean in. Can't help it. "You do want it. Good. I want you to have it."

"Obviously I want it." She runs the tip of her tongue over one fang. She studies my hands. Closes her eyes. "That's not the problem. It's not fair to you."

"Take it anyway. I'm immortal. There's plenty more where it came from."

"No."

She spins from the wall, paces, and comes back. Shakes her hand, has little fists at her sides. Turns back to me. Crashes into Julian.

He's all teeth and grace, sweeping her into him as if he paid for the honor. Hands at ease on her elbows, steadying her. His tux is pristine, not a drop of the real war anywhere on him. He slots between us. Theia amongst the music and dancers, me condemned to the wall.

"Antheia," he croons, velvet smooth. "I was beginning to think you'd deserted me." His hand caresses her cheek, brushes back a curl.

Color spikes across her face, and Julian chases the dark pink with the tip of his thumb.

My teeth grind.

"My future bride," he says. "This is the color you'll wear to our wedding."

She blinks, "Isn't black traditional?"

"We will defy tradition." He's touching under her chin now, stepping into her, tilting her up. Forward. Too forward. "We will shock them all. They will be putty in our hands."

"You don't think they'd be mad?" she asks.

He's planning their wedding.

I've torn through men for less. Snapped bones by accident. Crushed throats without thinking. Left fingerprints in places no one survives pressure.

Julian murmurs more ideas to her, extolling the virtue of setting a precedent for their reign. Theia nods.

I catalog his weaknesses out of habit—center of gravity too high, right side slightly exposed, grip firm but untrained. I could break that arm in under a second. Put him on the floor before Theia gasps.

Planning his death helps.

Until Theia covers his fingers on her neck, sets her palm on his chest, and nods lightly.

Julian's lips land on hers.

He smears her lipstick.

I nearly shatter the cup.

I hope it cuts me.

Maybe I'll bleed out right here. It would be easier than watching this.

Her face tilts up. There's a glint of fang, but she keeps her lips together, lets him roll her face with his thumb like he controls her.

He doesn't.

He never will.

Theia breaks the kiss with a gentle retreat. She steps back, a line between her eyebrows.

"Forgive me, princess," Julian purrs, beaming like his tongue is still in her mouth. "I could not wait for our wedding night."

He licks his fangs and winks, showy. I'll knock his teeth in.

"Right," Theia says softly, practically breathless.

"I hope I didn't overstep, my princess."

"No." A laugh, thin. "It's not you, it's me. I've just realized I am exhausted. The task and the dancing, I need to punch the hay."

He studies her. Allows the mistake to pass. "Of course, princess. Goodnight."

"Goodnight, Julian." She spins on her heel, heading for the stairs, and in a voice almost too soft to hear, she calls, "Come, Drake."

# 25

## Theia

### LOVE MIGHT BE STRONGER THAN DEATH

The burning pain. The hopelessness. The fury. The *lust.*

Even the calm, centering confidence.

Clues I should have noticed.

This. The thrumming fury, the wrenching pull in my stomach—it's more than the confirmation I was searching for.

It's a sentencing.

## 26

# Drake

### ONE GLIMPSE WAS WORTH ETERNITY LOST

It should be me.

My mouth on hers. My hands cradling her face.

I wish it were me.

I'd kill for the chance.

But these confessions remain locked behind my teeth.

Julian sucks. But he'll be good for her. As her consort. He's a homegrown boy. Her father's favorite. He's the kind of male Theia would love. Driven, polite, kind in the Keres *makes-sure-you're-dead-after-he-stabs-you* way.

He can give her the life she wants. The family, the home, stability.

It shouldn't sting, realizing it.

But it hits like acid.

Still, I follow her.

It's automatic, a subtle collapse of my own damn dignity, legs moving before my brain cracks into gear. She doesn't look back to check if I'm coming. She guides us down a stubby hall that narrows to a point and, without hesitation, disappears into a gap of cracked stone.

I lurch forward, chasing after, jamming sideways through the opening, so narrow I have to wedge in behind, the edge of the rock chiseling a line up my side. Only Theia's sparkling dress train guides me through.

On the other side is a galaxy.

Theia waits on a ledge no wider than a doorstep. A half-broken guardrail, the only barrier between us and a plunge directly into the abyss of the party below. From up here, the celebration blooms in the shimmer of a million hung lights.

Stalactites surround us, tiered and dazzling, glinting with the weak blue LED stars. They cluster so dense and uneven, we're living in a constellation.

Theia leans onto the banister, absorbing the view. "My father comes up here when he feels helpless," she says, face up to the lights. "Nyx makes each star in the sky. The work is so tedious and thankless, so repetitive and endless, that she loses sight of what she's accomplished until she steps back and the entire night beams down at her, cradled in her darkness. A kingdom is not built on emperors and proclamations. It's built by its people. So I won't break the kingdom if I become its empress."

Is this what she frets about at night? Not being good enough to lead?

I've never met a man, creature or God in charge who wasn't convinced it was their fucking right.

"You won't." I set her cup on the banister. "Like Nyx forming each star, you can mold every person in your kingdom as bright as you want. The fact that you worry means you'll be a better leader than most."

A huff of breath escapes her, as if the compliment is a punch she didn't brace for.

I clutch the banister, hating every inch between us.

*Don't look at her mouth. Don't.*

"Was it good?" I hate that I ask.

She turns. Arm against the rail, cheek aglow with a thousand piecemeal stars.

It's too much.

"Did you like kissing him?" I can't stop. The words topple out, raw and jagged. "Can you do that for the rest of your life? With him. Will you be happy?"

"Would it bother you if I did?"

"No." Meaning *yes*. Meaning *Gods, yes.* Meaning *it would destroy me, but I'd rather be shattered than make her lie.* "There are worse males to choose."

Her eyes flash. "Like Ozren."

"Like me."

Surprise pulls her eyes wide.

I'm not right for her. Never was. I'm not suited for fairy tales. It's written into every scar under my skin, every nightmare waiting if I let the gloves slip. I know this. I do.

But I want her. Want her enough it's a sickness. Jealousy rots me. Desire chokes everything else out. The desire is so loud I can't see straight.

"Julian is a good choice," I tell her, voice so flat it can't possibly matter.

For a heartbeat, there's just the sound of the party.

"I don't believe you," she says, a steely defiance in her tone.

"It's fact. Nothing to believe."

Her gaze lifts to mine. Something feral gleams there—pupils wide, cheeks redder than I've ever seen them. "I can feel what you feel. When I drink your blood, I feel you."

Shame's a weight in my palm.

I stand there like I've been lashed. I thought I'd raised a wall high enough. Granite, steel, mortared with years of reluctance and the absolute certainty that no one, ever, could get past it.

Exposed is too mild. Flayed would be better.

I let the admission settle on my tongue: the idea that when she tastes me, she drowns in the filth I've spent years coughing up.

Shouldn't hurt. Shouldn't. But it's the worst thing I've heard in decades.

"Fuck." It stumbles out, a bladed syllable in the meat of my throat. I could paint the word on every wall in the Sunless Kingdom. Fuck. Fuck. *Fuck.*

She flinches like I hit her.

My mouth opens, closes. The banister creaks under my grip. Nothing comes. There's not even a memory of what talking should feel like.

She realizes. Of course she does. She can fucking *feel* it. "I'm sorry, Drake. I should have told you when I figured it out."

"You felt that then? Just now."

Her tongue flicks the corner of her mouth. "I ... what?"

I can't tell if she's sparing my pride or genuinely confused.

"When he kissed you. You felt what I felt. You felt my jealousy. My hunger."

"Yes."

"And you still let him kiss you."

"It's not as if you'll do it, Drake. You've made that extremely clear."

"If you think that's what I'd do with you, Theia, if granted the opportunity, you are critically mistaken."

# 27

## Theia

### THE LINE BETWEEN FAITH AND DELUSION HAD WORN THIN

I expected jealousy would feel cold, like water dumped down your spine. But this isn't cold at all. It's heat, liquefied and mean, branching through every cell.

"You think I'm anything like him?" Drake's voice scrapes. "You think I'd let you go cold between dances? Let you fend for yourself? Stand there while your fingers tremble with hunger?"

He steps closer, cornering, predatory.

I grip the rail before I melt.

He's been restraining himself. No longer.

Mindless desire emerges in my chest like an invasive species. It's in my blood, my teeth.

"You think I would let you go? Apologize for kissing you?"

He steals every inch of air between us, taking it for himself. His gloved hand rises—not slow, not gentle—and hangs, suspended between us like a threat.

There's nothing clinical in how his gaze rakes over me, nothing reserved, just lust, greed and a tension so pure enough to slice diamond.

He's losing it.

He's mainlining whatever flavor of jealousy gets you

banned from all future charity events and elementary school bake sales.

I'm drowning in it too. Jealousy that's black and muscular and wet with need. It's fucking unhinged. I want to bathe in it.

Gods Above, we're both losing it.

His hand braces against the banister beside my hip. The scent of his blood, rich and potent lives in the back of my throat, but this close, I smell his skin, fresh and minty, almost like spearmint but sharper.

His voice breaks low at my ear, raw as an open wound. "An apology would imply regret, Theia. You suppose I'd regret my dream coming true?"

His free hand cages my other side.

My lungs can't expand enough for words. Not when his head drops, midnight hair reaching for me.

"Julian touches you like an ornament. Like you're for show. He'll parade you and forget where you are when the spotlight fades." The possessive note turns surgical, like he's dissecting his own rage for the council. His breath heats my ear. "He wants to keep you, sweetheart. And I just want to survive you."

My heart ricochets in my chest. Nyx, he can probably hear it.

He slides his hand over my fingers, up my arm, higher until leather catches my chin. Tips my face to his.

"You know what I'd do, princess?" His voice is sandpaper and midnight and some deep, adult thing that should come with a warning label. "I'd never let a single fucking hand touch your skin without your approval. I'd treat you so well the thought of another male would turn your stomach."

My head falls back, useless. Nothing left to keep it up but Drake.

Down below, the party rages. Boots and blood. Malni's

hyena-cackle. I barely register it. Drake's got all my RAM now, and he's on the verge of crashing my system.

He dips his mouth to mine. Doesn't kiss. Just hovers above me, dangling my fantasy. Goosebumps rush down my spine.

"Would you like that, Theia?" The words slide right to my core. "Would you want to be adored? Would you want to feed on me while I fucked you? I'd give you every pint, every inch. Make up for the century I spent alone with you."

I try to say yes. What emerges is breathless, unclassifiable.

He does not appear to notice. His thumb brushes right where my jaw meets my ear.

"I'd revel in you. Your touch, your breath, the skips of your heart. Those fucking fangs. I'd let them cut me everywhere. But that's impossible." He pulls back to let those green eyes rove over me. "So instead I'll revel in the screams of your enemies until their blood sings for you. Then, maybe, you'll look at me the way I look at you every night. Like you want to tear it all down. Like you're starving, and you finally believe there's enough of me to fill you."

Everything goes molten. I forget the ledge, the railing, the party. There's only Drake's brutal confession, his closeness, the black-leather grip, and the feeling that an entire new universe is waiting, teeth bared, right behind my next word.

His mouth is positioned so close that the air between us is basically theoretical. "You know what I long to do to you, Theia?"

The hunger in his voice frosts my bones and melts them all in the same instant.

"I want to undo you. So slow you'll forget your own name." His gloved hand spans my throat. Right at the spot just beneath my pulse. Waiting. Measuring. Checking it doesn't gallop, doesn't scare.

A torturer who knows precisely how to push limits, trained to shove past them, perfectly keeping me within mine.

"Do you want to know my secret, Theia?"

"Yes."

"I don't get jealous. I *am* jealous. I am jealous of the sun on your cheeks, the rock beneath your feet, the cup at your lips. Since I met you, I have been jealous."

"I … I haven't felt it." Not all the time, like he's saying. "Not like tonight."

"This isn't simply jealousy, princess, it's an illness." His hand tightens at my throat—heady and unyielding. Not pain, not even close. It's a claim, bright as neon sign in the night: *This is mine. I could break it, but I won't. Unless you ask me to.* "It's a poison. Fuck, it's Greek fire. It claws me apart. Makes me want to hurt for you, bleed for you. All that's in me, all the Keres down there—their hunger is nothing compared to mine."

The party below could collapse into a pit of fire, and I wouldn't find it worthy of a glance. If Julian or Nephene or a row of Imperials watch from the shadows, I genuinely cannot bring myself to care. I want none of them. Only this. This thing between us.

"Don't worry," he murmurs, pulling back slightly. "I won't touch you."

It feels like he's opened a window in my chest and just let the storm crash through.

His hand constricts on my neck, and it's not even about power now. It's about restraint, and the fact that I can feel every molecule of it vibrating through his body, hissing at the edge of mine. He's keeping me upright, not because I'd fall, but because if he let go, we'd both go straight through the floor. No survivors. No regrets.

I try to swallow. "That's ... good?" It comes out like a question.

He huffs. The sound is predatory in the way a midnight wolf is predatory: almost bored by how easy it would be to just take. "If I could touch you ..." His thumb presses in, just so. "It wouldn't be good, Princess."

He says it like—*you'd die if I fucked you. Or worse, you'd like it.*

I pinch together the last of my functional brain cells. "Do it anyway."

Bold. Possibly unhinged. I don't care.

The muscles in his jaw flex. There's a crowd, a ceiling full of spikes, and one very persistent quartet of violinists. But for a second, I think he might. Actually. Lose it.

He doesn't.

He releases me, steps back. "I can't."

Air rushes in. Icy, full of humiliation.

"Why?" I ask, tips of my fangs throbbing. "It's not because you don't want to. I know that now. Is it because of your promise to Nat? Because the council might be watching? Or because you're scared of me? Of what I am?"

He doesn't answer. Just stares, jaw set, every muscle cabled under the thin black fabric. His emotions churn in my stomach. Anger, jealousy, a shadowy shimmer of self-loathing. Lust so dense it's practically a new state of matter. Fear, too, but not for himself. Never for himself.

Not from the male who clawed out his own heart, who walked through fire.

I wait, feeling ridiculous in my dress, chest heaving like I just ran sprints for the varsity bloodsucking team. I wait for him to cave.

But he doesn't.

He won't.

My heart sinks.

Of course he doesn't.

Drake is not the kind of male who caves.

The butcher doesn't indulge his desires. The executioner does not succumb to poison. The Blackguard's dark spot does not bend.

He looks like he might shatter a leg by holding himself back.

I want to ask again. Keep asking. Beg. Fall to my knees.

My dignity's been missing with this male since he broke me out of a cell, but it doesn't matter.

I can bleed myself empty, crawl on all fours, and he'd still never take what he wants.

Telling me is all he'll ever do. Judging by his expression, he hates that he even let that slip.

So I give up. Not the dramatic, 'call him a coward' kind, but the quiet, real kind.

Exhaustion swallows me, making way for heartbreak.

The Fates don't care about Keres. Nyx would curse me for wanting a former mortal.

I open my mouth to tell him to go rest, to stop torturing us both, just ... whatever.

But then he says, "Turn around. Hold the banister. Do not move."

# 28

## Theia

### LOVE ISN'T SOMETHING YOU SURVIVE

I heard him, but hearing and processing live on different worlds now.

Drake doesn't look at me. He tucks the hem of his sleeve into his glove, then repeats the process with the other hand.

It's not sexy, objectively.

Except.

I can't stop staring. Can't stop remembering those bare forearms splattered in pink blood.

He makes a ritual out of it, every inch of skin treated like a landmine.

When he's finished, green finds me. "Turn around, Theia."

I spin, slow only because I'm trying to process, and numbly brace my palms on the ebony banister. It's cold, seams raised enough to imprint upon my palm.

Below, the Bloodless Court hums with dancing and politics.

A hand slides over my waist, drifts lower. No warning. One moment, I'm reminding myself how to breathe, and the next, black leather slices through the slit of my dress, strokes my bare thigh.

I make a noise—a whimper as I jolt.

He doesn't pause. His other hand lands solid over my stomach, pinning me to the railing like I'm prone to spontaneous flight. "Hold on tight."

His hand crests higher, riding up the bare skin under my skirt. I push into his palm, thigh flexing, core wet. Needy.

He doesn't gloat like I would. Only tightens his grip on me.

"You can let go anytime you want. But if you do, I'll stop."

My fingers dig into the banister.

I might leave claw marks.

I might not care.

Black leather glides upward, bold now. No delicate "let's check if we're still welcome". This is, "oh hey, there's my favorite flavor, let's see if it's still on tap."

It is.

His hand splays over my bare hip, skirt drawn obscenely high. "There he is," Drake murmurs. "Your biggest admirer." He tips my body slightly right, and I spot Julian, a head above his brethren, goblet in hand, Nephene shaking her head at him.

"You let him kiss you. Will you let him touch you like this?"

I don't answer. Can't.

He exhales a soundless laugh that sounds like, *you're torturing me.*

He strokes higher. Exponentially higher. Skirt hiked, glove splitting up the line of my thigh to cup the curve of my backside. He owns me, right down to the shiver that starts in my ankle and explodes behind my sternum.

"Do you wish his hands were on you right now? Are you pretending I'm him?"

Never. I shake my head.

He strokes between my thighs, catches the side of my

underwear and promptly sweeps them aside. "Do you want him to see how you're falling apart for me?"

Yes. No. Ask again later.

He chuckles at my silence.

If anyone looks up here, there'd be zero question as to what we're doing.

Pride seethes through me, a strike of it, greedy and ruinous.

*His*. His pride.

Proud he's the one touching me.

He strokes once more. Not gentle. Not rough.

Worse: he's deliberate.

His fingers pass over my core, pressure that makes my vision go magenta for a second. I want to say something, anything, but I'm past knowing any words at all. I'd be better off speaking Italian.

"Do you think any of them could do this to you?" he asks. "Do you think Julian could make you this wet just by looking? No." A chiding click of his tongue. "No. You already know he doesn't. He'd try to please you and end up missing the clench of your thighs, the hitch in your breath. He'd stir you but never get you there. Not even close."

Gloved fingers bracket tight against my hips, forcing me to arch until I'm on tiptoe, his hand an indelicate bulge under my dress.

Strong fingers caress slick heat, every part of me caught and held and used. He's a master at sensation. A male who's learned exactly how to make a body sing.

He's hard against my back.

Done hiding it.

"Look at him." He cranes my neck so I have no choice but to stare down at the main floor. "He wants you. But not like this. Not the way you want."

"He wants a crown," I manage, words all consonants and broken vowels.

I try to grind backwards into him, but he stops me with his thigh between my legs. With friction. With what I need. *I'm here*, it says.

A growl right into my ear. "You deserve a fucking crown."

I shake my head, frenzied, trying to work myself on his thigh. "I just want you."

"Hands on the railing."

I didn't realize I'd been slipping, reaching. "Drake."

He pushes his thigh against my core, rubbing, teasing. My feet are nearly off the floor. "That might be why he marries you," he tells me, low, threatening. "But he wants to fuck you because he knows you're better than him. He wants to own you."

I'm not sure which part makes me lightheaded—the two fingers circling my clit, or the image of Julian groping for relevance while I basically set fire to the banister.

No.

It's Drake, not even trying to hide how badly he's shaking with desire.

My brain wants to linger, wants to savor, but my body is, for once, wildly on task. Especially since his hand is—

Merciless. First grazing small, perfect circles against my clit and only when I'm pushing back at him, rolling up and down his thigh, does he work one long, gloved finger inside me.

He thrusts into me like he invented the concept of stamina and then overachieved. Every motion precise, never too fast, never giving me enough to fall over the edge. He keeps me balanced on a pin between collapse and implosion, demonstrating how much willpower he's been hoarding for exactly this: me, at his mercy.

And I am. Completely and humiliatingly at his mercy. My legs quiver. My entire body feels like a toy on the verge of malfunction, seconds from shorting out on the banister.

He doesn't make a spectacle of it. Not Drake.

He doesn't wrench my chin to meet his gaze, doesn't narrate his conquest.

He simply dismantles me, quietly, ruthlessly.

My job? Stay upright and try not to lose the thread of language. Both of which are going poorly.

Pleasure builds low in my stomach, then my spine, and Drake unleashes a helpless groan as he pushes a second finger into me. His gloved fingers maintain their slippery friction, and my every nerve sparks like "hey, maybe this is what we're for?" I dig my nails into the railing. My thighs tremble. My whole body bows into his touch, shameless, impatient, all that suppressed, ridiculous desire at last finding somewhere to belong.

Then he closes in, chest pressed to my back, a wall of heat, and leans in. Lips at my ear, voice raked raw. "Is it everything you wanted, sweetheart?"

It detonates in my head, crackling down my spine, as though finally someone has recognized my true calling: banister decoration, moaning mess, entirely his. I'd sign up for another round, no hesitation.

"Time to let go," he says then, and my mind fizzles out.

The orgasm rips through me, savage and dreamy, dismantling everything in its path. I fall for what feels like forever, world fracturing into white noise and ferocious pleasure that makes seeing colors optional. Drake works me through it, hand unrelenting until the pleasure overloads, my core locked around him, pulsing.

I hear myself keen, embarrassingly loud, reckless. Hear Drake tell me *I'm good, so good, better than he's dreamed*, until I'm twitching, spent.

When finally, finally, I sag, he catches me, arm braced firm around my middle, careful and steady, as if letting go would mean I'd tumble straight through the floor into Hades. And wow, okay, I absolutely would.

I'm gone, pulse pounding between my ears, cheek pressed to the railing, panting, undone.

The Keres below seem so irrelevant, like if the world ended now I'd greet it with a "hey, at least I got to orgasm on the emperor's balcony."

Drake retracts his hand carefully, as if stepping back from a crime scene. The loss is a shock. The air immediately feels too cold. I twist to look at him and lose my breath at his tousled hair, his angled cheeks, green eyes so stark and starved, they knock me back.

I go to touch his cheek.

It's so dumb. I know it's dumb, but I can't help it.

He jerks back fast as a whip-crack. His whole body jolts, arms yanking him, chest heaving like he just ran a marathon.

Shame gnaws at my stomach. I want to melt into the floor and die, but then I remember his touch.

The fear consuming me.

It's not me.

He wants me. He's proved that.

It's not fear or disgust or "that was a mistake, let's never speak of it again," forcing him to push me away.

It's his curse. He cannot touch me without dragging me into a nightmare that'll claim us both.

I let the silence stand: one breath, a lash of suspended time.

Then, somehow, laughter bubbles up—an uncontrollable, cracked thing—and I wipe my face with the back of my hand.

I have everything. A family, a kingdom, a soulmate who cares for me. I won't be upset about a no-touching rule.

It's fine.

I tell myself it's fine.

I say it out loud. Again.

Drake must think I'm having a breakdown because he says, "Theia."

"It's okay." I dredge up my smile. "I understand."

I do.

This will work. We will work.

But his expression isn't as full of hope as I want. It's as if he's realized he's opened a dam and now has to put all the water back upstream.

No.

I force down the heat in my cheeks, arrange my skirts, ignore the wetness dripping down my thighs. "It's great, really."

He doesn't argue, not with words.

I take it as verdant agreement. "I've spent a century alone, Drake. That was … this is more than enough for me."

"Is it?"

"You know it is. You've seen what you do to me. I felt—I heard you too."

Because I did. I felt the intense, gutted-gasp of pleasure lock his body to mine. That animalistic groan he thought I wouldn't notice.

He came too. Just as powerfully as me.

He barks out a laugh. Coarse, filthy, as mean as a bite. Drags a hand down his face. Harsh, as though he's reminding himself there's still a body attached to this want. "Yeah, sweetheart, it's enough."

If I could glow, I think I would.

He plucks the goblet off the banister and pushes it into my hands, fingers brushing just enough to let me sense the tremor.

"You still want me to drink this?"

His chin drops in a decided yes. "Do you?"

I could scream yes. Instead I drink.

He watches me guzzle, no attempt at subtlety, grinning like a wolf who just stole the last good steak. "Is that enough?"

It's our new favorite word.

"Yes. Good."

There's banked approval in his eyes. "It is good, Theia."

I want this male. Forever. But no time for that—not now. "Fun and names are over, Drake. You need to win the Munera."

## 29

# Drake

### HOW COULD HE LIVE WITHOUT HER

Vasilis knows I cannot win this task.

There's no outwitting this, no brute forcing it, no clever trick, no riddle. Not even my curse—the one thing that turns last-ditch chances into survival—will save me now.

The knowledge sits so firm in the Emperor's core, he's smiling as he stalks down the corridor, robes billowing, beads of his bone necklace clattering against his bare chest.

"This is not something your people are known for, is it?" he asks as he strides past, on the verge of flouncing. He's as happy as Zeke with a blue raspberry slushie and a full clip.

"I've overcome worse odds."

"No, butcher. You haven't. Because there's no chance in this realm or the one below that you will win my daughter."

The lone door at the end of the hall opens. Theia's laughter rings out—sweet, lethal. It slides under my skin like a knife wrapped in velvet.

Ignoring the line of waiting competitors, Vasilis spears a finger toward me. "The butcher goes next."

I fall in behind him. The males can't resist a last flash of their fangs at me, a few gory threats. Only twenty of us left.

Nineteen after I go.

The tattoos on my wrists and neck twinge harshly. The constant stinging louder as I walk toward death.

Vasilis sweeps into the room without a backward glance, but I catch the amusement lurking in the set of his jaw. He's orchestrated my downfall and fully intends to enjoy it.

The room is a bruise: black slate, shadows penned in by a few dancing candles. Bleak, except for Theia. She sits alone on a violet cushion, knees bunched, arms loose. Her hair tumbles prettily over the lace of her dress. Eggshell blue, the same shade as her favorite pillow.

Not a streak of gloom touches her.

"Another already?" she greets her father, accepting a black folding fan from him, and immediately beating it at her face. I can't look away.

Sweat sheens the hollow of her throat. The room runs oddly muggy, unlike the rest of the kingdom, damp stains mark the walls.

I'm covered foot to throat in battle gear—leather gloves, a chest harness, shoulder harness, steel-toed boots.

Vasilis didn't want me to go out with dignity.

He kisses his daughter's cheek, strokes her silky hair. Doting, loving. Hard to believe he's the same male whose sole purpose is to end me.

Less so when he passes me and says, "Consider what comes next your last words."

Then it's me and Theia.

Alone.

She points her fan at me and smiles. "Hello there. Would you care to join me?"

*Yes.* I nearly crash into the chair waiting for me in front of her in my eagerness.

That's all this room holds. Two chairs, three feet apart.

She has no idea that in fifteen minutes, I'll be kneeling for her father's sword.

I sit. It doesn't matter. The end result is the same, but at least seated, she won't crane her neck.

"Hi," she says again, secretive, sweet. As if I wasn't fucking her with my gloves last night. She waits, eyes lit from within, skin flushed.

And I've got nothing.

I'm fourteen minutes from decapitation.

This morning when the emperor lined the competitors up in the gallery, I'd been filled with this ridiculous hope.

The air reeked of ichor and sweat. The walls holding Theia's ancestors, faces cold as ice. The emperor paced around us, silent, his council watching, faces stuck in permanent scowls. His instructions came clipped. Each male gets fifteen minutes with the princess. During which, he must make her laugh.

"She is my star," Vasilis said. "Make her shine."

And I stood there, knowing godsdamned well there's not a cell in my body built for joy. I'm not cheeky. Not funny. Not charming. I'm a brick wall. Blood and nightmares and the urge to protect. That's it.

If I had to crack a joke to save my life, I'd just claw my heart out to save time.

Which, all things considered, is still preferable to what's coming.

There's so much I want to say to her and none of it matters now. The knife's already on the block.

"I hope the others have been treating you well."

She winces. "I'm not allowed to say. It's cheating, and I don't want you disqualified."

Would it matter? "So …"

She cuts in before I mention the weather. "Can we just ... not?" Her voice stays cheery, but underneath I hear the splinter. "I've never talked to so many people in a day and it's ..." She shrugs, the motion draining her shoulders of tension. "Exhausting." She shakes her head and buries her face in her hands. "It's *so* exhausting smiling and thanking and sitting like a princess."

She yanks the pillow from beneath her and chucks it at the corner, "I'm like the princess and the bee. It's—I hate it."

"We can be quiet, Theia."

Making her laugh might have been a shot in the dark when conversation was on the table, but silence? That's a shot with no bullets, no trigger.

Silence wraps around us. She tips back, spine a question mark against her chair as she shuts her eyes and fans her decolletage.

The breeze ruffles the damp curls at her hairline. She shivers when the air hits the sweat on her collarbone.

It shouldn't make me this hard.

"This is what I wanted," she exhales. "I wanted family and friends. Now that I have them—" She opens her eyes to me, unguarded. "You must think I'm ungrateful."

"I don't."

"I've got everything I wanted and I'm so …" She trails off, pinches her lips together.

"Exhausted."

She nods, mouth creasing with shame.

The confession makes me cold. I know that kind of fatigue, the weight of keeping course not because you enjoy it, but because you set it.

"I think it's an enormous change," I say. "Going from solitary confinement to leading an empire. No one adapts to that overnight."

She snaps her fan shut, folds it in her lap, plucks at the seam. "I was so lonely. I spent days dreaming up dinner tables and birthday parties and being tucked into bed at night." She looks up, eyes rimmed red from sleepless nights. "I imagined a sister to fight over sweaters with, and a dad who'd put his hands on his hips and roll his eyes when we were brats."

I'm supposed to make her fucking laugh, but she needs this. I hum for her to continue.

She does. "I waited for all this. For so long. For someone to come."

"Waiting is the hard part, Theia. The rest will come."

I get a skeptical breath. "Will it?"

I slide my chair closer, snag the fan from her lap, pop it open and start a methodical sweep through the air. Her hair lifts, dark strands tickle her cheek. "Orpheus didn't wait, and you know what happened to him when he got what he wished for?"

"What?"

"Twice the pain, and an eternity of loneliness."

Her brows lift. "Wow. Thanks. I feel better."

I swat her thigh with the fan. "Orpheus's wife, Eurydice, died young and suddenly from a snakebite. Rather than accept his grief and mourn his beloved, Orpheus marched into the Underworld to steal her back. On the shores of the Lethe, he sang for Hades, begging for Eurydice. And Hades, God of Darkness, Ruler of the Underrealm, granted him the boon. Orpheus could walk out of the Underworld with his wife right behind him. They'd be free to have the life that was stolen from them. On one condition."

She waits.

"Only one. Hades would allow Eurydice to leave so long as Orpheus didn't look back until they reached the mortal realm, and—"

She cuts me off, amusement slanting her mouth. "I know this story. Orpheus looked back."

Of course he did. "Yes. He turned. Orpheus was the son of a Muse, and he never sang again after losing her the second time. He gave Eurydice hope and then stomped on it. Doomed them both."

"Why do you think he looked back?"

I don't even pause. "Same reason he went down into the

Underworld. Hubris. Selfishness. He believed the commands of the Gods didn't apply to him."

Theia smiles. "That's not why."

"It is."

A shake of her head. Her eyes are bright. She leans forward, liberates the fan from my hand, and gives it a little flourish. "Orpheus was so excited to have her back that he started running. He ran so fast that Eurydice couldn't keep up. When he felt the sunlight, the mortal world under his feet, he spun around to hold her and never let go. Except, she hadn't made it out. He turned one step too soon. He lost her. Because he couldn't contain his love."

No one in the cosmos would champion Orpheus's ruin like this. Hope as armor. Desire as weapon.

"If he'd slowed down," she murmurs, voice feather-soft and iron-edged. "If he'd been a little less eager, tempered his longing, he could've held her. But love isn't tempered, it's reckless. It races ahead, desperate for tomorrow."

"He got her hopes up and then crushed them."

"He loved her beyond reason, and she got to see it."

"He loved her so much he destroyed them both."

"He braved Hades for her."

"He *ignored* Hades."

Her mouth quirks. "You're a Debby Clowner."

Fuck, I like her. My ribs tighten as I lean in, breathing vanilla off her skin like a lick of ambrosia. "More of a Negative Chancy."

"A Gloomy Fuss."

I yank the fan back. Return to cooling her. "It doesn't matter why he turned. It's the same damn ending."

"Maybe, but he tried. He breached the Underworld's gates. Battled for her soul. Laid bare his devotion."

I should leave it.

I should study the dark rings in her irises, the near red

bloom of heat on her throat, how her hair sticks to the ridge of her collarbone.

But I can't. She needs to understand that this story is a tragedy, not a romance. "Devotion didn't resurrect her. It ruined Orpheus. He couldn't live without her. He let the Maenads rip him apart rather than move on."

She lifts her chin, brown eyes alive and daring. "I'd want someone to run for me."

I nearly flinch. She's a hopeless romantic. That's who I'm falling for. With the fan's edge, I brush a stray lock of hair from her shoulder, let the fan linger on her skin. "I'd walk for you, Theia, but even then it wouldn't matter. Chasing the impossible only means you die twice."

"I'd still run. Every time."

I believe her. She's sure. Even if it cursed her, she'd want her love one second quicker than allowed.

All joy and hope. I stare at her, raw and open and shining, and realize—Vasilis was right. I have no chance. None.

Now I just want these last minutes.

No more arguing.

A hush coils between us.

I want her so much it hurts to breathe. It's pointless to confess now, but maybe I've got enough Orpheus in me to sabotage myself anyway. "Theia—"

"They're not even fighting for me," she whispers, small and broken. "It's the crown they want. They don't want me. It's never me."

"You're wrong. Again."

A smile, though she doesn't want to. "I don't even remember their names."

"They remember yours."

"Because I'm the princess."

This, then. If this is what there's time for, so be it. I hook my boot on her chair leg and reel her into me until my knees trap her thigh between them. The fan ghosts up her arm. "No, not because you're their princess, because it's you." I swipe my tongue over my teeth. "The first thought I had about you? I'll never be able to verbalize how beautiful you are."

She swallows. No escaping the twitch in her jaw, the way her throat tightens and releases. I want her to believe it, to see what I see like a sunspot after a blindfold comes off.

"Every day it's gotten worse. There are more things I notice, more things I want, no need, to tell you. Words have become this barricade I can't kick down …" I trail off, unfinished. This is the closest I've been to rambling since Murphy picked me from the gutter.

Time's up. Any second the door will swing open.

I let the silence spread. It's almost okay. I almost told her.

I wonder if Vasilis will have his sword already drawn.

Theia watches me.

Covers her mouth.

Snorts. A rough, husky sound. It gets rounder, builds into a roll. A chuckle.

Then she's laughing.

Outright laughing, trying to swallow it down but failing spectacularly.

I stare, dumbstruck, as she clamps a palm over her mouth, shoulders shaking.

"I thought you were—" She chokes on a laugh, forces out a long breath. "I thought you were disgusted with me." Her voice has gone to tatters. "I thought you couldn't stand me. You kept pulling away and going silent. I told myself you hated me." Her smile doesn't break, not at all. "You were really just ..."

"Awestruck?"

"Inarticulate."

A flare in my chest tells me to be insulted, but it smothers itself quick. She's laughing again.

First in splinters, then cracked wide open.

I know what it is to be flayed open, to be striped to raw sinew, have every regret peeled back for someone's amusement, but I've never known the soft, razing sensation of being the reason someone else's world is less bleak.

It's a problem.

Not just that I like her laugh.

It's that I'd tear myself apart to keep it going.

## 30

## Theia

### GUILT WHISPERED HE WAS FAILING HER AGAIN

"So, wait. You've really never punched someone in the face?" Nephene's aghast, and also deep in her cups. I've called her Effie twice, and she hasn't threatened disembowelment.

"Celebrating," she'd explained, each syllable sloshing. "I've chosen a Nevro. Nyx blessed the match, and we've bled on it. It's done." There is a pinkish bandage wrapped around her left pointer finger, and the nail is cracked and black at the cuticle.

I might've asked who if Greta weren't perched on the arm of Effie's chair, wearing the same blood-drunk grin.

"How about stabbing? Have you stabbed someone?" Greta twists the fastener on her hip sheath. "Clawed? Slapped?" She's horrified by my inexperience, like she's discovered I eat my own hair after it clogs the drain.

I shrug, half watching Imperials roll a body off the raised platform in front of us. "It's never come up."

"Are we even sure she's Keres?" Greta stage-whispers to her Effie.

I bite back a laugh, because she looks truly distraught that the next Empress of the Sunless Kingdom has never sucker-punched anyone. I might as well confess to recycling and see how long it takes for her to shove me into the ichor pool.

"She's as soft as a …" Greta stops, taps Nephene. "What are those horrid human things?" A snap. "Emotional support blankets!"

"Blankets can smother," Nephene assures me diplomatically. She's smiling, teeth glinting, brown eyes glittering with the mean delight Keres specialize in.

The only thing I've ever stabbed is a mozzarella stick I dropped behind the couch.

I could make a compelling case for food-based violence. But this isn't the time.

Tonight, violence is king.

This task of the Munera is segmented, ten males sectioned into pairs to face off in brutal hand-to-hand combat.

Only ten.

Because the other ten were dragged away from me by imperials, one after another. Shouting. Thrashing. Blaming.

Each failed.

Why? How?

Everyone before Drake passed, received my father's approving handshake. They bestowed me deep, satisfied bows.

Everyone after Drake—

What'd I do?

What'd Drake do to me?

*Rip out your heart and take it for himself?* Yes.

*Awestruck*, he'd said.

It all blurred after that.

The round's barely started and Drake's already got his opponent on the defensive. No pageantry, no circling, not even a dramatic monologue about their ancestors—the male lunges for Drake's throat, and Drake simply steps aside. Not even a flex. Just pure, clinical efficiency.

He hasn't even taken off his gloves.

"Rip and rend!" A councilor cheers.

"Tear him up!" Malni. Paired with her signature cackle.

They want carnage, more of the gore we saw in Julian's round, and the two before it.

Drake doesn't do gore. His opponent Vin,  a slab of muscle and markings, comes in hot. Classic Keres jugular strike. Drake glances him aside, nothing like a shadow cut loose from the wall.

The audience hisses for violence, gnashing air. Boots scuff the tile. Tension ripples off Nephene's closed fist.

Drake's expression? Not bored, exactly. More like a butcher lamenting what's left behind after the cut.

He doesn't crave this fight. This is a job. He's detached, methodical.

Not like the other night. Doused in blood in my room. That was a battle he hungered for, savored. Revenge. For me.

He feints left, pivots, and then the other male's face hits the sand so hard a fang goes spinning. Pink sprays.

The arena likes that—the splatter. Drake pins him, gloved hand around the neck, the other twisting the Vin's arm back until the socket nearly pops.

"Finish it," Nephene whispers.

He could. Right now. Squeeze a little harder.

Instead, he rips the hem of his shirt off, knots the fabric around Vin's wrists.

Leaves him breathing.

The silence drops like a knife that never stops spinning.

Fangs click, someone asks, "Why's he tying him up? That's pathetic."

Another sneers, "Kill him or don't show up at all."

They're wrong.

This isn't weakness.

It's discipline.

I know how difficult restraint is. How little it satisfies.

Smooth, gooey warmth coats my insides. Pride for the male who asks to worship me. Who became a killer to protect his family. Who used his messy skills for good. Who now dismantles that part of himself to save my people.

And still sees Orpheus as the villain.

There's an actual chorus of "pathetic!" and "shame!" and a few more poetic insults about cutting throats and what a real male is. All the Keres classics.

The worst is my father, who looks on with a single brow arched like a challenge's been thrown, and he knows exactly how to crush it.

Down in the sand, Drake steps back, tightens the straps on his gloves. His best weapon tucked away.

"He's won, right? It doesn't have to be to the death?"

"Right." Nephene's lips flatten. "It doesn't."

"He hasn't killed any Keres." I sound smug. I am

Green eyes find me. Cool. Calm.

I shouldn't smile. My fangs aren't out. The council is seething, Nephene's scowling. My mouth curves anyway.

Until a gagging sound echoes.

Vin rolls—no. He convulses.

Vomits a stream of silver and pink. Hacks at the sand. Heaves. Spasms. Bucks in his binds. Goes utterly still.

I jerk out of my seat. "What the—"

"He's dead." Nephene sounds disappointed. "He swallowed his fangs. It's a fail safe if we're captured. Cut his own throat out."

Greta holds Effie's hand. "He'd rather die than lose."

I step closer to the dais edge, unable to look away from Vin's body.

The Keres—my people—they're drinking it up. Cheering. My stomach turns inside out.

From over my shoulder, Lydia's voice slices through the cheering: "Now that's a real Keres. A male who could've been emperor."

She slides into the open space beside me, decked out in black and green, blonde hair nested in braids over her shoulder. She takes in my lilac gown, lingering where fabric bulges too tight, as if to say, *you really don't fit, do you?*

I remember how Drake stared at her. They have history. She fought for Kadmos. They're probably friends. She's everything I'm not. Direct. Cutthroat. Comfortable as an outsider. Like Drake.

But he's not awestruck by her.

"I'm sure this is what the butcher planned," she says.

I pretend not to hear her. Shove the thought down.

Don't picture Drake grinning over a broken male.

"You know what real mercy is?" she asks, not waiting for my answer. "Not playing nice for the crowd. Not pretending you're above the kill. Mercy is ending it quick."

"No one needed to die. Vin could be with his family right now. He chose his path. Not Drake."

"Please. He'd be shunned and tossed in the sun by his family for getting bested by the butcher." She taps her fingers on the scabbard at her hip. "I met him during the Twelve Year War. Only a day old in his immortal body. He didn't need any time adjusting—vicious from the start, absolutely heartless. You would've been young. Barely a few years old back then, right?"

Down in the arena, Drake is frowning at the corpse by his feet.

"That was a hundred years ago," I murmur. "I barely remember."

Lydia barrels on. "Let me enlighten you, then. No one believed the Keres could fall. They are creatures built for war, trained to withstand siege, eat their victims. Relentless, barbarous soldiers. But it was a new, unimaginable ruthlessness that felled them. From one Great King and his handpicked monsters." Her eyes flick down, grazing the scar on my shoulder.

I twist away.

"That Blackguard you're so fond of, princess?" Her voice is a venomous purr. "He butchered your people."

No. I'm shaking my head, watching Drake kneel beside the body as Imperials storm the platform.

"He tortured them. Keres after Keres. Body after body. His was the last face they saw. Smiling. Laughing before he dumped them aside."

Drake's untying Vin. The Imperials are shouting at him. No one looks at us. Lydia's words curl into my veins. "And now he's returned to the Deep Realm, under the protection of the lost princess. Quite a shield. I wonder how long before the council starts asking if he put that mark on your skin as a sign of your loyalty. Kadmos couldn't exterminate the Keres, so the Blackguard will ruin them from within with a brainwashed heir."

"No."

"You're not one of them. You don't belong here. You don't even look Keres, and they all see it. Wonder where exactly you've been these hundred years."

"Stop. None of that's true."

"They'll figure out who kept you shackled so long—and why you walked free the moment the regime was on the verge of change. Just poised for a takeover."

I'm shaking. "Stop."

She snatches my wrist, whispers, "Wake up, Princess. You're not a prize. You're a Trojan horse." Her grip is talon-sharp, not letting go. "You'll gut this kingdom before anyone sees it coming. All because you were fool enough to trust him. A monster like him never stops."

I wrench back, pushing at her hold. She clings harder, lowers her face. "He'll cut you open and leave the Sunless Kingdom starving—"

"*Stop!*" I snap, shoving, twisting, throwing myself back, needing to get away.

I stumble into Nephene.

My sister's face is cold as ice, pupils contracted to pinpricks. The temperature around us plummets. "Let go, Lydia," she commands. Instantly, I'm released. I press fingers to my wrist, rubbing raw skin.

"I should remind you," my sister says, "that your continued presence here is by my invitation, and that the Princess, our next sovereign, the future empress of this kingdom? She is my sister."

Lydia recoils, chin ducking. "I meant no offense, only to explain—I thought she deserved the truth ..."

Nephene closes in on her, fangs peeking, "Do it without harming her next time, or I might forget to show you the way out of our great kingdom. Hmm?"

A nod, a stammered apology. Lydia flees.

Nephene doesn't ask if I'm alright. Only mortal wounds garner that question from a Keres. But she does linger, gaze touching my exposed shoulder. "Lydia overstepped. But she's not entirely wrong." She looks down at the arena. "Few here celebrate your return, sister, and most see that brand as a reminder of the persecution that decimated us."

Guilt tears at my stomach. "I don't know how I got it, I swear, I didn't ask for it. I'm not here to ruin us. That's ..."

"I believe you, Theia. But he did. He asked for that mark. He fought. There's no reason he should be here."

# 31

## Theia

### HOPE HURT HIM MORE THAN FEAR EVER DID

I've never been drunk.

That's not to say that I haven't downed six spicy margaritas at a matinee showing of Twilight: Eclipse, it's just a hazard of being Keres. Alcohol, drugs, all the lovely poisons can't touch me.

But I think this is how it would feel.

Knees wobbly, a tremor in my hands, the floor tilting and rolling like it's trying to shake me off. Walls pop up from nowhere. My forehead pulses angrily and there's a spot in my vision.

I stagger down the corridor, no princess gliding, only the frantic scramble of someone who can't stomach what just happened.

I blink and see Vin's body.

Hear Lydia's snarling voice.

Everything in this kingdom is life or death. Every breath, every conversation, a battle.

My heels slip. My skirt wedges in the door and nearly tears. I trip and careen into my room, rubbing at the sizzle on my arms, crawling up my throat, desperate for a moment alone, a second to rifle through my feelings to sober up.

I can't.

Adrenaline slams into me. My vision pixelates.

Someone's here.

Two weeks ago, I'd have called out a question, excused myself, offered assorted candies in a brass dish.

This is the Bloodless Kingdom. They're not here to bum a skittle.

I lunge for the nearest weapon—a wall sconce, brass and leafy and cute in a gaudy way—and rip it down, brandishing it like a sword.

This is how those girls die in horror movies. Drunk one second, hunted the next.

Except they don't have Divine vision.

Or hearing.

They can't hear the pulse of their attacker, can't track the hulking figure as it moves along the wall, aiming for the door.

I turn hard, aim for the gut. All-out attack.

Only to have it caught an inch from making contact. "Alright, I'm leaving. I get it."

"Drake!"

"Are there other people breaking into your room?" He quiets, nearly smiles. "No, I already know the answer to that." He flips the sconce, and though it took all my strength to wield, he twirls it like a toy. Turns on the lights. "Redecorating, princess?"

I blink away the light and when I register how close we are, I step back. He's in his kicking ass uniform from the arena, hair raked back on his head, curling around his ears. Chin dipped down to look at me, features hauntingly handsome.

I throw my arms up at him. "All I hear about is how many creatures want me dead, and I'm supposed to not arm myself?"

"With a sconce?"

"Exactly. Hit them with the light, then crush them. That's

the plan." I grin to cement my confidence in the strategy's success. "Save the hand-to-hand mishmash for when I really need it. Throw the intruder off-balance, then dazzle them with violence."

He laughs, a flash of teeth. "No point in violence without dazzle."

"Right, and—"

"Who's trying to kill you, Theia?"

He asks it like he's asking for a grocery list. Bodies to check off.

I shouldn't smile.

But I do.

I twine the ribbon belt of my gown around my palm, nerves burning. "Yes, who would dare? The council of course. Apparently all of my suitors. Lydia's at the top. Malni would like to dance on my grave, but I don't actually know if we do graves. And that's just the surface level. If we expand—" I smell it then.

Don't realize how I missed it.

I cross the room in a blink, closing the space between us. Drake's too preoccupied with my enemies to register, just tilts his head down at me. "What'd Lydia say to you?"

Who cares anymore? "Did you leave me blood?"

Third time today.

"I do this thing where I make more of it. Almost without having to think about it." He shrugs, very casual, brushing off the fact that he's got me on a steadier diet than I've ever been in my entire life.

"Yes, smarty-lamps, I'm aware, but—" I move quickly, faster than my attack, faster than even the great Blackguard can track, hand snapping out to clutch his sleeve. I rip it down.

"Theia." My name is a curse, an exhale of warning. He tries to snatch his arm back.

Doesn't get far.

Drake may be a Blackguard, an immortal, a killer, but the blood in his veins is red. Mortal, beneath all the trappings.

I'm Keres, an apex predator, thrumming with the bloodline of Nyx, family to Thanatos, daughter of the emperor. I dig my fingers in, hold him still. "This is fresh," I murmur, attention glued to the precise cut on his wrist, a lone red drop gathering as the skin sutures itself together.

In my heels, we're lined up beautifully, my eyes right on his pulse, the scent of eucalyptus calming and steady under the rich tang of his blood.

He could throw me off, but there's no way he'll risk wriggling and brushing up against my skin. He's trapped, the whole of him tense as I examine the wound.

It'd be so easy to bring his wrist to my mouth and drink, to sink my fangs in and taste.

I crave it on a molecular level.

Instead, I grab the hand towel from the nightstand and press it to the gash, treating it with an unnecessary, obsessive tenderness. The bleeding's already stopped, but I keep at it, making slow, circular dabs.

Drake shudders.

Not a quake, not a flinch; just a single jolt through his arm, as if my touch pours lightning into his veins.

He won't look at me. Stares at the wall, jaw locked like he's getting ready to explain he doesn't need the help, but he physically can't because it'd send me out of his sight.

There's this microsecond where I consider saying something meaningful. Like "you don't need to cut so deep" or "no one has ever tried this hard to keep me alive."

But what I say is: "You're not helping me fit in."

"I'm not letting you drink something you hate. Not when all it costs me is a scratch."

"Only you would call this gouge a scratch. I meant, I already don't fit in the dresses they give me."

"Tell them they're the wrong size." Flat, like it's obvious.

"They're the *Keres* size." I point out, waving at my hips. "Haven't you noticed everyone's like Nat, tall and carved, muscle in place of curves. I am not standard issue."

He doesn't answer immediately, watching as I sweep the rag across his bare skin.

"No," he says at last, voice neutral in that way that means it's anything but. "I haven't noticed."

Heat travels up my spine and rushes to my face. I believe him. That he doesn't notice anyone but me.

I clear my throat. "They're sharp and effortless, size six, and I'm guzzling double helpings of the extra rich stuff, sticking out like a sore numb."

He doesn't take my bait for levity.

Just grinds his teeth together.

I take one last pass at fresh skin, stripping away blood that's no longer there. I fold it into a perfect origami lump and set it on my pillow, absolutely normal, not-at-all-deranged behavior.

He doesn't budge, watching me squirrel away his things. "They've spent centuries sculpting themselves into what they think they're supposed to be," he says. "You didn't."

"Trust me, I'm well aware."

His heated gaze slides down me. "You became something else. Something they don't understand and can't replicate. It's got to infuriate them, realizing they picked wrong."

My pulse kicks.

He drags down his sleeve, turns away. "Rest now, princess. I'll be on watch."

"Stay." It comes out less like a bold, seductive plea and more like the sound of a Keres toddler's tricycle brakes locking up at the bottom of a hill.

Still, he stops. Objects. "You've had a long day. I know you want alone time, not me clinging to you."

"No!" His mouth twitches, not quite a smile. "I mean. I do want to be alone. Just … not from you."

A shift in temperature. The air recalibrates. He moves—not quickly but as inexorably as a tidal pull, back across the room, into his chair. The one I see him in when I close my eyes, always with blood on his wide palms and something like victory pressed to his skin.

Silence folds around us. I take the cup he put out for me. I try to sip, but I fail, drinking deep, draining every drop. A slow warm wave washes over me. It isn't desire I feel from Drake—it's a yearning. The moon's ceaseless pang for the sun, the itch to touch what's always slipping away.

My shoes come off at some point and I fall onto the bed, legs tucked, bare toes curled in the sheets, skirt spilling around my knees.

From across the room, Drake smiles—a new shape, not a weapon, not a mask. Something softer.

I've never seen it before.

I want to know it.

"What?" I ask, my own little smile creeping onto my face, as though I'm in on the joke.

"Nothing."

"What?" I laugh, real, sudden. "Tell me."

He wets his lips, gaze dropping briefly. "I just want you," he says. Simple. Unadorned. "I want you so badly. If this is it, just this, I'm happy."

"Really?"

"Really."

"A chat and a drink, that's all it takes?"

"With you?" His eyes meet mine. "Yes."

"And if I just fell asleep right now, you'd be just as happy?"

"Yes."

Skeptical, I arch an eyebrow.

He doesn't waver. "I'd get to watch over you."

I'm caught on that. How simple a pleasure, how it brings him comfort, knowing I'm safe.

It makes me bold.

The clasp at my sleeve comes undone, fabric sliding heavy and slick down my arm. I unknot the belt and let it curl lamely on the bed. The dress comes off with tugging and wiggling. I strip out of the rest, self-consciousness kicking in like a brute, but I turn, needing to see—

Drake's eyes are shut, gloves curled into fists on his knees.

"Drake?"

A resonant note answers, torn out of him, dark and guttural.

If I had a conscience, maybe I'd pity the male.

Tonight I'm Keres. "I thought you liked looking at me."

"You're trying to kill me." His voice is sanded down to rags.

I study him, seated at the foot of my bed—a living monument of restraint.

When did he close his eyes? Was it the sleeve dropping? Or when I shimmied to get free of the skirts?

"Open your eyes."

Green: unguarded, hot, nearly crude.

He's so wound I can taste it. Metallic and slick, coating the air.

"Theia," he chokes out, voice mangled.

His aching desire nests in the pit of me, searing my core. Delightful heat rattles low in my stomach, and I will not cage it tonight.

He braces himself like he's prepping for a ritual, gloved hands clenched so fiercely the cords in his arms stand out like ropes. I wonder how long he can hold together?

I stroke a fingertip against my throat, between my breasts.

He wants out—I see it in the clutch of his shoulders, the silent plea for an easy escape, for the comfort of distance. Not happening.

My hand slides down my stomach.

His chest lifts and falls, thigh muscles drawn taut. "Didn't realize you were so mean."

"Should I cover back up?"

"Fuck no."

A laugh breaks out of me. "Should I stop?"

He considers saying no.

Wants to.

His mouth's a flat slash. He hasn't blinked. "Don't stop sweetheart."

I slide two fingers between my thighs to stroke light against my core, let him see how the shiver travels through me. Spread my legs wider for him, catch him in the V of my knees. His eyes are everywhere: my parted lips, taut nipples, the swell of my stomach, the movement of my hand. He tracks the wetness dripping down my inner thigh.

Nyx probably felt like this when she gave life to the stars. All-powerful.

"You deserve better than to perform for the devil," he rasps, but it's for him, not me.

I drag my fangs across my lip, fingers teasing. "If the devil came for me, you'd tear him apart before he got close."

He exhales raggedly. "Fuck."

I grind my fingers harder, gathering wetness that lives in his presence and rubbing until pleasure scorches my spine. Lifts me off the mattress. The frame complains with a whine.

Not princessy, not sweet, not anything delicate.

Drake drinks it in, entranced.

Good. I want this sight to burn into his memory forever—me sprawled and fevered all for him.

His hand's between his legs now. Almost forgetful, the rough edge of his palm pressing against his zipper, hard, as if he'd rather carve out the ache than feed it.

He's fracturing.

Unraveling.

Beautifully.

Incrementally.

Gnawing the inside of his cheek. Clenching his hand

against his thigh. His boots scrape across the stone floor as he shifts forward in his seat.

When his breath hitches, I push two fingers into my core and moan at the graze of his tongue over his lips, as if he wishes he were there, tasting me. His eyes darken as I thrust into myself. Three lines cut across his forehead, deepening with every thrust.

He's being tortured. The notion catches fire in my mind. Followed by: he likes it.

The torment, the tease, the stress of being denied. It's bitter and bright in his blood.

I should've guessed.

Drake's not built for comfort. He's a master of writhing and white-knuckled self-denial. For the kind of caustic ache you catch in the lungs, every inhale sharp as glass.

If there's a one-percent chance something might twist into discomfort, he'll pick it over happiness, every time. Destroy his own delight.

He's done it at every turn in the Munera. Always chosen the rougher road. Sought out the unendurable, again and again. If the path's slick with thorn and pitch instead of sunlight, that's where he'll roam.

Every. Single. Time.

Which explains why he's still locked in the chair, only watching his naked, panting princess.

It's safer to say no to happiness than to risk getting close and losing it. This moment might as well be a knife to his throat.

I need him to try anyway.

Need him to destroy the flex in his jaw, release the strained biceps.

So, I don't hesitate as I rub quickening, obscene circles with the pads of my fingers, sticky with desire, and hold his gaze like he's the last light in the dark. His stare is green fire, acid bright and punishing, I have to shove my tongue at the roof at my mouth to keep myself from begging.

Begging him to let go.

To give in.

To try. For me. For us.

It could be how I gasp, or jolt, or accidentally nick my lip until dark pink falls down my chin, but Drake splinters.

Mutters something like *fucking hell*, or *you're magnificent*, voice warped with need. He palms the line of his zipper, wrist flexing, and if there's anything pretty about it, it's the sheer violence in his restraint.

I arch, twisting my fingers, thrusting at just pressure and speed I need. Sweet pleasure gathers in my veins, my stomach, my chest. Glass-green eyes drowning in hunger lock onto mine, and the tension climbs to cable-bridge tight, strung across some terrible, beautiful void and he's the gravity at the bottom.

"Drake," I gasp, fangs out. "Come here."

He exhales. Just sound, no words, his jaw working. "Unwise, princess."

"The best things rarely are."

His expression shifts, weighing ruin against restraint. "You don't want me to touch you. You want the fantasy."

Nyx, his voice undoes me.

A shudder barrels through me. "No touching," I agree, against my wishes. "Just come here. I want you closer."

"I—"

"Should I ask Julian?"

Aside from murder, it's the cruelest thing I've ever done.

Something ferocious and deadly slashes across his face.

He rises, a tower—a mountain, no, a force of nature transposed into flesh—and crosses the gap. The whole mattress bows as his knees press down. I nearly tumble, not out of gracelessness, but elemental draw, like Nyx reeling the stars to form constellations.

He hesitates over me, boots hanging off, intense gaze lingering on my mouth, throat, breasts, hips, hands.

"Lie down," I whisper.

He does. Obedient as a knight.

I settle astride him, bracing bare knees at his clothed thighs. There's nothing left but blue silk brushing my ankle, and the relentless intent between us. Heat pushes through his clothes, an entire singularity of longing under his belt.

I yield to my desire. Grind downward, unapologetic and overly wet, painting his trousers, his thighs, the rigid outline beneath. I want my clean freak to be filthy with me.

His gloved hands lock onto the frame. His last defense. "You're killing me," he mutters, almost reverent.

I laugh, sweat on my skin, and roll my hips, grinding down on him. "Drake—"

My fists tangle in his shirt, greedy for what's caged under the cotton. "I—I need—"

He breathes a curse, hips snapping up, eyes wild. The abrasive fabric rubs at my clit. Each rotation of my hips tearing me apart.

I bend down to him, bare heavy breasts against his dressed chest, shameless as I ride him. His body is a tense muscle beneath me, hips involuntary thrusting up against me, steel length rocking my center. It's too much; it's not enough.

He's rigid beneath me, face an expression of false control. His hands fist the sheets so tight he could strangle a God. He refuses to reach for me. Will not.

Denies himself his greatest pleasure to protect me.

Gives his life, his pleasure, his promises away for me.

I don't last any longer.

My back arches, contorting, breasts crushed against him. My hand's wedged between my thighs again. Frantic, sliding slippery. My hair's in my mouth. I don't care. I moan. Louder this time. Past caring. All that's left is pleasure.

Drake's voice fractures against my skin, "Like that…

*Christ*… look at you… so fucking perfect… so beautiful… keep going …"

Release slams into me. Hot. Cataclysmic. I jerk on his lap, legs shaking. I sob his name. Once. Again.

And he's right there.

Right with me.

Growling through it, finishing with a powerful snarl. Grip clawing the mattress, hips thrusting up. His cock, thick and insistent, surges against me as the last threads of his discipline snap. We're primal, both of us.

I'm naked from head to toe, fangs sitting lazy on my tongue as I lay my cheek on his sternum. He hasn't shed a thing. Gloves, jacket, belt—even the boots are still on, marking up my sheets. Doesn't matter.

It's enough.

He's right.

I could stay like this. Tangled above him, sticky and flushed, his name echoing off my tongue. Forever. I could do this every night and never bother the Fates for more.

Optimism. She's here, a gold coin in a palm full of IOUs. I clutch her tight.

We'll make this work. I believe it. Even if I never get his hand on my bare skin, I am full anyway. Giddy. Euphoric. My smile is a busted strawberry, smeared and wild and sweet.

"And to think, I've been spending my nights on the floor in the hall." His voice is guttural and dark.

"You're too noble."

A chuckle. "Nobility has nothing to do with it."

"Protecting me isn't noble?"

His thumb scrapes my thigh. "Not the way I do it."

I twist, chin digging into his chest, to look at him. He's watching me, black hair overlong in his eyes, as if waiting for me to push it away. He lets out a quiet, humorless breath. "You'd hate what I've done in your name. If someone ever got past me and got to you …" He pauses, thumb stroking. "I don't know who I'd be after that. Maybe nothing but the butcher. You'd hate me."

"There's nothing you could do that would make me hate you."

His touch pauses. "You're seeing rainbows in storm clouds again, sweetheart."

I press my cheek to his heart. "Rainbows are made by storms, you know."

---

"YOU COULD WIN," I blurt, casting off the sprawl of sheets to brace myself on my elbows, the linen pooling down my spine. "The Munera. You could really win."

Drake's lounging against the ebony headboard, gloved fingers weaving through the ends of my hair. He hums low, a sound so gravelly it vibrates my soul.

I smile. Count on my fingers. "Only four males left standing. My father says by tomorrow night, it'll be over."

"What dreadful amusements will I have then?"

"Wedding planning, obviously." I trace invisible patterns on the sheet separating us. "I've got a dozen mood boards you'll despise, but eventually pretend you loved all along. Baby pink and vanilla cream."

"If it makes you happy, princess."

"Yeah? You'll wear a tux and tango with me?"

"I'd wear a leash and collar and crawl for you, if that's what you want."

Delight glows inside me. I smile, filled to the brim with happy. "Such devotion could turn a female's head."

"Took you long enough to notice."

A laugh belts out of me, the sound ricocheting until it feels like the whole room spins with it.

"I love your laugh."

It's a compliment but it hangs like a farewell gift. My

insides scrunch into a ball, breath snagged. I twist to get a full view of him.

His expression is distant. "Theia." My name sounds like a wound. "Your father would sooner gut me than see us wed."

"No, I've done my research. The law is clear. The victor claims the bride."

"The *Keres* winner. Not that it matters. Your father is the law. He'll rewrite it in my blood if he has to."

"He's a romantic," I defend. "Did you know the war started for love? My mother vanished and he tore the kingdom apart for her. Like Orpheus. He braved the sun to get her back. For love."

"Your mother didn't disappear," he says. "She was stolen. By my king."

"Your king, not you."

He shakes his head. "Doesn't matter. I wore his crest, carried his banner, spilled blood for him. There's no separating it."

"My father believes love can conquer anything—"

"Orpheus came back broken, Theia," his voice is suddenly harsh. "Eurydice's death hollowed him out. Losing her again destroyed him. Wrecked him. Your father isn't a grieving musician hanging up his lyre. He's a killer."

"No."

"Sweetheart, be realistic."

"I am." My voice is surprisingly stern. I touch his arm, feeling the iron cord of muscle tense. "I've had this dream since childhood, where everything's falling apart, I'm terrified, and sure I'll die when someone walks through the chaos for me. They find me, scoop me up, and carry me away. They protect me. The Fates don't deal with Keres, but *you're* not Keres. Maybe that's why I saw you. I'll just tell my father that you're my destiny. My Fated. He'll have no choice but to bless our marriage."

A void clangs between us, eats at the air.

Drake is still. Too still.

"What?" The word claws through the hush. Ugly. "What did you say?"

I rise to my knees, limbs reckless, sheets puddling around my hips. "You're my Fated," I whisper, the certainty unyielding. "Drake, it's you. It's us. I've never felt anything like this. Like you're my home, my happiness. It's you and me. It's always been. It's predestined."

I reach for him, the most natural thing in the world, except he jerks away, crashes into the headboard. "Don't."

I clamp my fingers around my thigh.

A careful shake of his head. "The Keres have no Fate."

"The Keres don't walk in the sun either," I throw back. "They don't eat. You said it yourself, I'm evolved. The Moirai could steer me. Gods above, even without Fate in my blood, I know it's you. You have to feel it too."

His mouth opens, then draws shut, bruising the words before they can crawl out.

"It has to be you," I say, relentless now, stubborn. "The way I feel when we're together … There's no other explanation. We were made to be together."

The green in his eyes is the darkest I've ever seen it.

"Drake?"

The door doesn't so much open as explode, the metal lock blown into shrapnel.

Boots hammer the floor. Shouts slam my ears. Cold blue light slashes the room. Four imperials storm inside, formation close, weapons out.

Drake reacts first. Always. Charging from my side, putting himself straight between me and the threat.

But they don't even look at me. They go for him. Four pairs of eyes, four guns, all for him.

No.

I wiggle in the sheets to launch for the imperials.

Drake catches me with one arm, stopping my attack. He

wraps the blankets back around me, tight and rough until I can't get a single hand loose. "What are you—have you lost your mind?" I snarl at the males watching. "I demand you leave."

"This doesn't concern you," the leader barks, gun leveled at Drake.

"Rest," Drake tells me as he rises. "I've got it handled." He squares his feet, pulls his shoulders back.

I smile.

He'll tear them in half.

Except, he doesn't move. Doesn't even twitch.

His hands don't curl. His eyes don't flare.

Cuffs snap onto Drake's wrists. And he just lets them. Lets them pry his arms from his sides, lets them shuffle him from me, lets them bash at his kidneys, kick him in the knees.

"You want to see pain?" One spits, wrenching his arm until there's a pop. "Fight back, Blackguard."

He doesn't.

"Don't," I beg of him. "Please, don't."

*Don't give up.*

*Don't stop fighting.*

*Don't destroy this.*

He does though.

For the first time, he chooses the easy path. The one away from me.

# 32

## Drake

### HOPE, SMALL, STUBBORN, AND DESPERATE REFUSED TO DIE WITH HER

The lockup doesn't surprise me.

Neither does the Imperial's fist driving into my gut, his boots grinding my fingers, or the way I careen into each doorframe we pass like they're aiming to dent me. Even when they flip my own blade and drag it over my cheek—I could have predicted it.

I've been the one holding the chains before. I know this dance. This dismantling. It's old routine, worn and familiar as the clench in my jaw.

The stripping of dignity, layer by layer. Creatures excel at this particular cruelty, despite hating it the most when it's done to them. We thought they were empty growing up—vampires, mermaids, demons. Heartless. Mindless. Cruel.

But when you tear humanity from a creature, what's left isn't emptiness.

It's hunger. Ravenous. A hole that consumes everything it touches.

That's the point of all this Keres pageantry. The metal biting my wrists. The chain woven around my forearms, the parade down their precious halls, our footfalls echoing like the heartbeats they pretend not to have. I contemplate this irony while they yank me by the throat and knee my back, their message spelled out in black and blue.

I let it happen.

A distraction.

Just enough pain to drown out the image of Theia on the bed. Not freezing like she usually does in the face of a fight, but striking and scratching, all for me.

So I let myself be taken. Let each blow dig deeper. Don't even blink when someone smashes my face against cold stone, hissing, "Look alive, butcher." They're begging for a reaction. They want the real devil, the one who broke the Keres before the war even started. That bastard. That's who they're afraid of.

I let him sleep.

Instead, I bleed quietly. Taste iron and savor the warmth leaking from my skin. The heat of Theia's body clings, the faint scent of vanilla lingers.

Fated.

Not to me.

Nat warned me. Before the blood, before the chains, before regret stamped itself across my knuckles: "Theia believes in a prophecy. That she'll be saved by her Fated. She's waiting for him. All or nothing. Once she chooses, she burns."

Theia—the princess of Icarian optimism.

She'll bind herself to one name, dig her heels in so hard they'd scrape the floor bloody if she thought it was right.

She thinks it's me.

I want to tell her she's delusional, break the fantasy, force her to swallow the ugly truth until she chokes on it.

She already knows the Keres aren't destined for Fated pairs and I'm certain no one deserves to be shackled to me. What soul could be condemned to a partner they can't touch without unspeakable pain? What crime merits binding yourself to someone whose very essence corrupts everything it meets? The Moirai's cruelest joke.

I clench that misery between my molars and chew it until it's dust. The cuffs bite. My ribs throb, foot swelling where they stomped it, but it's nothing next to the taste in my mouth when I remember Theia's voice. Soft, unreal.

*You're my fated.*

Said like it'd fix the world.

Bullshit.

She deserves a sunrise, not the stalk and slash of butcher hands. She deserves a home with laughter, a male who won't crush her with nightmares or bring fresh scars every time his skin is bare. Not this. Not me.

She deserves to be a princess, to live as royalty. Crown and castle. With her family.

All of which I cannot give her.

Instead of telling her, I let the Imperials guide me deeper into their labyrinths.

They toss me into a dark cell populated with Julian and two others from the Munera. The air thick with sweat and apprehension. No one speaks.

We just sit there.

Julian tosses his hair back, perfectly serene, even as the collar of his shirt glitters with someone else's blood.

I taste blood on my teeth and hate that it makes me think of Theia.

Hate how I want to let it pool there, right on my tongue, just for her.

Nobody cracks a joke, no one flexes threats, not a single Keres opens their stupid mouth. Just the hush, and the shared certainty we're not marching to a grave but to something meaner: competition, the lure of victory, and Theia waiting at the end.

Julian stretches his fingers, polishing a bone ring with his thumb. "Smile, Blackguard. It's not your funeral yet."

Now this is Fate. The sick, animal grind of it. If ever there was a punishment suited for the likes of me, it's sitting shoulder to shoulder with the male Theia will marry.

The bastard sprawls, king of the cell, host to my torture.

He's missing his usual pressed shirt, the lacquered hair, the clean smile.

He cracks his neck, hair shifting like a curtain. I feel him examining my profile. "You come by these wounds honestly, butcher?" His gaze skims the bruise under my left eye and my coat, torn down to the lining.

I grunt. "If I said you looked better, I'd be lying."

He smirks, fangs shining, and methodically smooths his cuffs—though we both know the iron is meaningless. A breath, a heartbeat, and we could snap free, bolt before the metal hit the ground. But we don't. This is Keres theater.

A last bow of deference.

"Didn't expect to see you go down easy," he concedes, picking at a flake of dried ichor in the seam of his elbow. "But then again, you're not known for style. Or self-preservation."

I don't answer. I let my head thud back against the stone, stare at the ceiling. A curse word burns within me, but I swallow it, let silence settle like dark water. He waits, that diamond-hard smile a trigger.

Finally: "You're seething because I kissed the princess."

His self-righteous smirk demands a response.

"Without asking," I clarify, as if I'd be fine with him and her if he had manners.

A fucking lie.

He scoffs, digs at a blood speck beneath his nail. "She doesn't want me."

He's got that fucking right. She moaned my name as she came. Fuck, I'm wearing her orgasm. I bet he can smell it.

"She needs me," Julian says before I erupt. "She needs what I am and who I know. I can give her a crown she doesn't have to bleed for. I can teach her to survive the swarm of councilors." He tips his chin up, eyes catching a fleck of light, casual as betrayal. "The empire needs that too. Needs us. The lost princess who crawled out of the realm above and the loyal male everyone recognizes."

"That's all you bring then? A plain face?"

"I've been an imperial. I've been a scout. I've trained with or bled for every damned body in this empire. That's how you earn respect here."

"That's your permission? A few cuts, some calluses, and you're entitled to kiss her? That's the magic formula?" I'm indignant now, snarling.

"We're not the grand match of Nevros, but fuck, Nephene and I weren't either. Theia and I, though? We could be compatible. I'll protect her, embrace her."

"You want her crown."

"Why not take her too?"

His eyes glint, too polished for what he's saying. If I ever needed a reason to cave his skull in, it's this.

"She's not a crown. She's a female. She doesn't need you. She doesn't need anyone. She just wants to breathe, and you're already plotting how to suffocate her with politics."

He laces his hands behind his head, just so. Like he's playing at relaxed, like his spine isn't a steel girder waiting for my next move. "She gives me a crown and I'll give her a people. They'll accept who I marry."

My laughter's thin, scraping the walls like a layer of old paint. "How fucking magnanimous of you."

"The heretics keep the old stories alive, but there's nothing left of the tradition. Your king killed it. The Keres want more. They want it now. Theia is an agent of change."

"She's not a bomb."

"Of course she is, butcher." He leans in, voice honeyed, like he's telling a bedtime story and not setting a house on fire. "You think the Munera is about strength? The Emperor hasn't lost his thirst for power, he's just tired of using his own hands. He wants blood without the migraine of cleanup. All this?" A tidy wag of his finger, pure councilor showmanship. "It's the old order getting slaughtered and dressed up for dinner. Vasilis is emperor in name only. This is succession by extermination, where the survivor gets to wear a crown and pretend he's civilized."

He's got a point. I hate that he's got a point, but there it is, spitting and snapping at my ankles.

Julian grins wider, teeth a shade of "This Could End You." "Any other generation, they would've torn you limb from limb, then pissed in the crater," Julian says, which is true, and also a special kind of annoying, because now I have to agree with him. "But now? The next round, the one after that, it's about optics. Survivability. Whoever fits the throne best, who the realm above might stomach."

I stare at him. The urge to respond is, frankly, subatomic. "Maybe you should've kept your stylist, then."

He grins. "I could run this kingdom in a bathrobe. Theia would love it."

Of course she would.

Bathrobe brunch would be a weekly holiday.

But she's not wired for the throne room. She's not even grounded for it. More like the circuit's open, the juice is live, and everything in this kingdom is one accidental puddle away from catching fire.

"She'd prefer movie nights to bloody feasts. She'd rather untangle council drama with, I don't know, cake and stories than whatever the fuck this—"I gesture my cuffs at the room, at the chains, at Julian's face.

I take a deep breath. "Why are you telling me this?" I ask, voice flat, not bothering to hide the edge. Let him hear it, let it drag through the silence like a file across bone.

Julian steeples his fingers all prim. "You're not stupid, Butcher. You know you're never making it out of this room unless the emperor wants you to. And what the emperor wants, you are not. He needs a smooth transition. A face the people will eat up like blood pudding at a child's funeral."

I roll my eyes. "That what you are? A side of sugar to help the poison go down?"

He flashes those fangs, then stalls—the first blip in his confidence. He drops his voice so the others have to crane forward. "You need to let her go. I could be good to her if she let me, but while you're around, she won't."

# 33

## Theia

### LOVE SHARPENED INTO FEAR, AND FEAR MADE HIM RECKLESS

"Once you recite the oaths, they will not just kill for you, they will die for you."

I suspect Nephene's attempting to comfort me. It's having the opposite effect.

"I just want them to live," I say.

Nephene rolls her eyes, shoots me a look that says, "Oh, honey, you must be new here." There's fondness behind her eyes, but also savage disbelief, like I've wandered into Keresville with a tote bag full of kittens. "If you want kindness from this court, you'll have to invent it yourself."

"You're kind."

"Wrong. I'm pragmatic and loyal."

If that's what she needs to tell herself, I let her.

But she's more than that. No one else searched for me this morning. No one else tore away the drapes, saw me unshowered, sleepless, starfishing across the floor and offered me four seconds of complete commiseration before demanding I "strap up and ship out".

Beneath the fangs and leather, the bone earrings, she's as sweet as a Nymph.

Now we're speeding along the corridors, half walking, half

running. Our dresses—umber orange (me) and onyx (her)—swish and slap behind us.

I haven't slept. Not a wink. Just spent the entire night concentrating on the feeling in my stomach, the low throbbing horror, the flashes of disgrace and pain, the only proof Drake might still be alive.

I keep replaying his face, the way he recoiled when I called him my Fated—how everything in him twisted away, absolute misery in his eyes. He'd sooner eat a bag of wasps than believe in anything as dumb as destiny.

And still it didn't stop me from worrying.

But he's not here.

Nephene shoves me down corridors at a full clip, heels biting marble, her braid a whipcord against her spine. We're late. Every imperial we pass does a double take.

We break into the main hall, where reaching pillars are draped with banners signaling the end of the Munera. A wall of drums and strings reaches us.

Nephene muscles me through a knot of courtiers; they split for her like she's carrying disease or flame. I stay small and out of sight. My dress is wrinkled. I feel it, and I don't care.

I have no desire to play princess today.

The music becomes muffled as we enter the arena, drowned out by cheers and stomps. The spectator stands spill over, bodies jammed together scrounging for carnage.

The arena floor burns brighter than usual, every torch cranked to max, red dancing light wriggling across the sand.

Ahead, my father's voice floods the cavern. I follow it straight to the dais. Nowhere else to go.

He shines with ancient power. His dark robe open to display muddy paint streaks and tokens heavy on his chest. His smile is full tilt.

Beside him: rows of councilors, Imperials, and, inexplicably, Lydia, whose grin competes with his.

It takes me a second to understand why the crowd is so keyed up.

"... the true test," my father is saying, "always comes to this. What is an emperor, but a creature willing to crawl, bloodied and shamed and unmade, through every misery to rescue his empress from the jaws of doom? Who will outwit enemies, outlast damnation, shoulder humiliation beyond comprehension, until there's nothing left but claws and teeth and blind force—a drive to drag her back from the edge."

Nephene curses. "Nyx help me." She scans the arena, calculating odds, risks, and outcomes.

Who I'll have to marry.

I spot Julian first. He's dead center, brazen as a spark thrown into dry tinder. He waves like the world's brightest candidate, hair knotted and shirt knifed into his belt, chest bare, the usual chaos of blood-marks gone.

He grins at me, then pivots to bow to my father. Every gesture soaked in pride that stains the sand between us, even from twenty yards.

"He's showboating," Nephene says, voice flat.

"He's proud." He's made it through impossible tasks.

"He should set the tone, not mug for the crowd." She nudges me toward the seats reserved for royals.

"They obviously love it," I defend, because Julian has been, in all truth, a good male to me. I smile back at him, noting the cuffs locked on his wrists.

That can't be the task.

Breaking a chain? That's not Keres.

There's no blood, no death, no fangs.

I twist around the throne. Dread slithers into my chest. The chains aren't the task.

The task is what's opposite him.

The body suspended over a nest of daggers, two stories below.

No safety net. No pillow, no secret escape hatch.

Nephene tugs me forward. "We're late."

I can't move though. Every competitor, every male who spun me at a ball, who swore marriage under the stalactites, is shackled and staring down someone they love teetering at the edge of gruesome death.

Screams ricochet, desperate, the way the dying always are. Females, males …

A child.

No older than thirteen, straining against the rope at her waist, face soaked with tears. The threads of the rope are frayed and splintering, dropping her inch by inch toward the sword aimed for her skull.

The logic clicks, ugly and immediate. I might be sick. "Is this why the competitors were taken last night?"

"Of course. Who would let Imperials just take their loved ones? Not a future emperor. There'd be a slaughter. Easier to restrain them." Her voice is a yawn of indifference as she falls into her seat, beckoning Greta with a curl of her fingers.

I tumble into my seat, bodice eating at my ribs with each inhale. The councilors are waxen, bent forward.

Their families are out there.

And they're watching.

It's grotesque. Horrendous.

I should leave. I want to. But there's a thorn at the heart of this: a snag, a hook-in-the-lung kind of problem.

I can't find Drake.

I rake my eyes across the lineup once, then twice, a third time, half manic.

There's Rafil, attempting to shake his manacles off to get a head start. Julian with that smug smile, weighing whether brute force or a grace will win him more adoration. And Ozren, poor thing, is staring at not one, but two of his family dangling above their death.

No Drake.

Not anywhere.

Sweat beads down my back, ice cold. Nephene presses her palm to my shoulder, jaw ticking. "He's not with the others. Maybe he never made it back from the lock-up."

Terror flares.

In front of us, my father's voice unfurls—liquid poison. "To prove your worth to rule, you will rescue your own blood from the gates of Hades. Only the fiercest will survive. The weak—it does not matter. A ruler only shows mercy when he must. Bring your loved one home."

Julian pumps his fist. The stands roar.

Greta takes her perch on Nephene's chair. "It's time," she says, hand spreading over Nephene's.

"But I don't see ..." I'm bent in my seat, searching for something—anything—but find only empty sand and echoing void. I scavenge the walls, even the ceiling. No green eyes. No black leather.

My stomach shrivels, curling on itself in fear.

I'm meant to sit and smile, keep a pretty face for the empire while my father endangers innocents. Meant to applaud at the brutality ahead of me.

I panic instead.

I bolt upright, nearly tipping the chair, skirts hiking indecently high, etiquette flailing and trailing in my wake as I half-run to my father's side. The imperials jerk, ready to strike, then sag when it's only me.

My father's voice pours out, flooding every inch of the arena. "...for the one who would rule, let it be known: love is not passive. It is not delicate. It is a blade, and only he who grasps it by the edge may ever claim a crown."

He's speaking to his empire, but his eyes are on me. "Witness the final proof. Their truths."

The bell rings, a nightmare klaxon that explodes through the crowd. The stands shake with the riot.

Anxiety turns my blood fizzy. Lydia cheers with open glee, like she'd buy popcorn if it wouldn't ruin her lipstick.

The task begins. The competitors hurl themselves at the obstacles. Drake is nowhere.

I grab my father's arm. "Where is he? Where's Drake? What have you done?"

"Calm, my dear. He is competing." His arm clamps over my shoulders, warm and heavy.

"What? No. He's not—"

There's motion above the stands. A dark thing, swaying—

No.

*No.*

He's there.

Hanging, inverted, stripped to the waist. Arms contorted behind his back, metal gnashing his wrists, ankles buckled, every line yanked taut, his entire spine cast into a vicious arc. His head hangs forward, hair a dark sweep glued to his forehead. Sweat and blood run in shiny, stiff ridges down his chest.

The chains holding him have teeth. Serrated nasty teeth. They bite around his neck: a lunatic's necklace.

With every minuscule shift, the links knot tighter, grinding in, jagged edges gnawing for arteries.

I taste iron at the back of my mouth and don't know if it's his blood or mine.

The wrongness burns through me. I rush for Nephene, clutching at her. "Stop this. He'll die."

"It's the task."

The calm in it stabs. I fall back, betrayal and terror crashing together.

The task. As if this is busywork, not execution.

"Fuck the task," I snarl at her. At my father. "Stop this."

My father's eyes tear at me. "Calm, dear. We couldn't find anyone for him to rescue, nor any who wanted to help the butcher, so he'll save himself. Ingenious, isn't it? The harder he resists, the deeper the chain lacerates."

"That's not the task then!" I shriek. "It's not the same! You can't do that!"

"It's better." My father shrugs, casual as a God snuffing out stars. "Let's see if he can grow his head back on."

My knees falter. My nails rake my palms. "Call it off. Stop this. Please."

"That wouldn't be sporting."

"You said the Munera was a test, not a sentencing."

"He was warned. Win or die."

Breathing feels like a scream. "It's barbaric!"

Nephene snares my wrist, hard enough to jolt. "There are rules. The Munera cannot be interfered with, not even by the emperor. Not until a victor is chosen."

I stare at Drake. Dangling like something discarded, shadow blotted with crimson.

No one's even looking at him. They're lost to their own nightmares and puzzles.

Rafil, left shoulder shot through, strains to build a ladder, sweat and blood race in twin lines down his arm. Julian, knife wedged between his teeth, dismantles the obstacle of spinning blades under his mother, muscles shaking but precise.

Panting, hands limp, Ozren just paces as three Imperials haul his grandparents down. He's given up. He'll be joining the Imperials soon, taking the vow in shame.

All the while, Drake writhes. Agony fractures his features. The slow tilt of his chin as he braces to take more. Stillness is his only hope—all he can do is dangle and bear it. If he shudders too hard, the chains will slice his head clean off. Execution by inches, artful. Made for the audience. Made for my father.

I whimper, "He'll die."

That's the point. That's what everyone is here for.

The dais detonates with applause—a thousand bloodthirsty cries. They want violence. No, they want a message: the Blackguard gets nothing. Not even pity.

Panic drags me under.

For the third time in my life, I don't freeze. I run.

Off the platform, toward the sand. Nephene's yells at me, but I'm already knee-deep in sand, landing with a thud. The stumble rubs grit into my knees. When I stand, my hair sticks to my lips and fangs.

Before me, the obstacles are horrors. A pit rimmed with broken glass, a volcano of acid, hissing green.

I look up. Drake's face is gray with exhaustion. All the concentration in the world won't stop the chains.

Julian's in the obstacle next to him, partially pulled together and sort of heroically battered. His mother, already freed, fusses panting at his feet, gag loose around her neck as she curses him out in Greek. There's a brief, beautiful moment where her boot connects with an open gash on his shin.

The pain doesn't even dent his smile.

"My bride!" he calls, smile flooding his face. Owning the moment. Milling it into spectacle.

Above us, Drake hangs.

A slab of muscle, blood, resolve.

I crash into Julian's side, skirts in ribbons, pulse hammering, barely tethered to reason. "Help me! Please. Drake—they chained him up. I don't know how to save him."

Julian glances up, completely unhurried, gripping me at the elbows. "Wasn't that the point?"

"But he'll die!"

"The butcher's not my concern."

I go fucking mad. Wrench my hand in Julian's hair and yank him down to me. "If you leave him up there, it's as good as killing him yourself."

"That's the tradition. We rescue our own. He has no one. It is the way."

"Save him," I beg. "I'll give you anything."

Julian's brow cinches. "I want him dead, Princess. There is nothing else I'd ask for."

"She just said anything," Nephene yells, appearing at my elbow like a vengeful hall monitor. "Your biggest fucking desire, Julian. Say it!"

That's when Julian's mother explodes, ramming past an Imperial to swing at Nephene. "Don't you lecture my child. We honor the old rules. You want mercy, go back to the nursery and cry for it. Here, power's a currency, and not everyone gets to spend it."

Nephene whirls, braid snapping like a whip. "If you want him to rule, he better be a male worthy—"

I can't listen. Not now. Not while Drake's blood rains onto the sand below. I clutch Julian's face, gentler, knuckles trembling, smearing pink across his cheekbones. "Save him and I'll marry you."

"But we already—"

"Rafil's still fighting," I grind out, watching the final competitor hack through his little brother's restraints with desperate fury. "End this now. I've chosen the victor. You're the emperor. Just save Drake."

Chosen. The word rings in my head—something Nephene said in the council. The empress chooses the victor. I am to be empress. I am choosing.

I raise my lip at him, ready to shout again, when his mouth breaks into a predator's grin. "As you wish."

He steps away. Goes straight for carnage.

First he cold-clocks the nearest Imperial. Fist to helmet. The blow lands with a sick cartoon crunch. He doesn't wait for a response. He takes the Imperial's gun, turns, cocks it. Aims.

Fires.

The bullet drills Drake in the shoulder. I scream.

His body jerks hard, corded muscles buckling under the

brutal whiplash of agony. The serrated iron chews a new groove into his flesh.

He's suffering. Again. Always.

It's my fault.

The word "no" tries to crawl up my throat but only bile makes it out. I lunge for Julian to rip him to shreds.

Julian recalibrates. Re-aiming the gun, slightly higher. He fires a single perfect shot that rips clean through where the black chain is anchored to the ceiling. Gravity grabs hold.

Drake plummets.

He strikes the ground with a sound that knocks the breath out of me.

I sprint, heart a sodden, ruined fruit. "Drake!"

Except Julian cages me.

He twirls me into him, lifts our entwined hands high. A showman's finish, prizefighter's victory. "Smile, wife."

34

# Theia

## THE LAST TIME HE REACHED FOR HER, HE LOST HER

I snap backward the instant Julian's grip falls away. Nephene's there to catch me, hauling me tight in bracing arms, and I cling to her, nerves raw, the aftershocks screaming down every cell.

Imperials circle Drake in the sand. His face is buried, one green eye slicing up at me. The chains around his wrist and neck are in pieces where he's ripped them off. His crimson blood stripes the sand.

Father folds Julian into an honest, proud embrace. He might call him son, might welcome him to our family, the next Kolaphos.

I jerk against Nephene, only to have her yank me back, hissing. "Don't. He's alive. That's enough. Don't make a scene. It's not the way."

Fuck the way.

The *way* is a coffin. The *way* is bowing while the realm shoves your face into the dirt and thanking the Gods you didn't get your fangs in their neck. The *way* says you let your kind—let your heart—bleed out for the comfort of cowards and dynasties. The *way* means you smile, you curtsy, you pretend not to notice when your lover's blood stains the Imperial carpet.

I'm so fucking tired of doing everything everyone else's way.

I love that male.

Love him in a way so feral, Zeus should take notes. In a way that feels like something I should get on my knees and apologize to Artemis for. I love that male who thinks being a shield for me is all he's worth, who'd let himself be shredded for me without blinking. Who's so convinced he's a devil, he doesn't realize he's the only one who's never, not once, tried to chain me or shape me into something easier for them to palate.

It's always been my choice with him. My decision, Drake following in lockstep.

He's mine.

He's always been mine. Only now, it's time to show him. Make him feel it, bone-deep. I want him to know that his dry, deadly jokes ricochet through my head for days, his laugh props up the cracked beams of my soul,  his smile sets my fangs on edge.

Makes me want to bite.

He gets dirty for me, wrecks himself, tears through the world. He'll die for me.

I won't let him.

Blades and guns spike the air around Drake's prone body. The pure red leaking out has more than one Imperial strung tight, ready to end him.

What's left of me is slashed sunset skirts, snarled hair, and throbbing fangs. I bull through the wall of imperials. "Stand down," I order, dropping straight to the sand at his side. "Clear out. Now. Give him space."

The nearest Imperial flinches, shuffles back. He's never heard me snarl, never seen my fangs bared.

I'm not the odd princess now. I'm Keres. Relentless. Untouchable.

Sand skids up my knees, the sting grounding me.

Drake's body is a ruin on the ground. There's blood everywhere, viscous and wild, staining the mangled state of his shoulder, the gash under his ribs, the outside of one trembling thigh. It puddles dark beneath his fingers. Not pretty red. Ruddy brown. Old, dying.

I want to scream.

He's not even struggling. Just sprawls, shuddering, cheek mashed against the grit, jaw locked up like he'll bite straight through the planet to keep from moving. The chain's still wrapped around his throat, blood slicked from where it nearly cut him apart, the light sucking darkness of his tattoo hardly visible.

His breath shudders, ragged, empty, grinding.

I reach for him and flinch midair.

His gloves hang in shreds from his wrists like the remains of a flag after a bad war. Torn to pieces trying to rip off that chain.

His beautiful hands are ruined, gashes and burns crisscrossing the bare skin, flayed open in a testament to what it costs to keep breathing.

My hands hover above him, useless. Shaking.

Inches from wrapping around his shoulders. Millimeters from wiping that blood away, from threading through his hair. From pulling him against me.

I bend over him, air caught in my throat. "Drake?" His name breaks between my teeth, a prayer and a plea. "Drake, it's over. I've got you. Stay with me, okay?"

He won't meet my eyes. Or maybe he can't. His face is a disaster, sand caked to a raw cheek, blood streaming through stubble. At last, one green eye finds mine, unfocused. There's no pain in it, not really: only loss, only shame. Devastation.

He finds the words—the effort nearly kills him, voice torn to wet paper: "Stay back. You can't …"

"I *can*," I snap, sliding my body closer, careful not to touch. I will. For him, always.

I set my fingertips to the shoulder that's still covered by fabric, just barely. Gentle. How Nyx would caress a dying star.

I want to comfort him. All I manage is a shudder.

"I'm not going anywhere," I say, and the promise is soaked, flooded, salt coursing down my cheeks before I know I'm crying. It stings.

"Theia."

It's too serious, my name on his lips. Too much like a last request.

"Look at you," I stutter, the laugh breaking, half-mangled. "Blood, dirt. You must be horrified."

He hums, eyelid twitching, defiant even at the edge of the abyss.

I wiggle closer, just to see if I can scandalize him into consciousness. "The real butcher would never just lie there and let other people do the mopping up," I say, swiping at my wet face. Panic pushes down on my chest, my own body nothing but the echo of his pain. "He'd be up, destroying everyone's evening, demanding hand sanitizer until Imperials dragged him off."

I know it's weak, but my pulse is hammering and he's leaking blood by the gallon.

"Come on." I dare to go closer, dress hitched mid-thigh, not caring that the Imperials are getting a clear view.

Drake's head thumps sideways away from me, stubborn still, dignity bleeding out but not yet dead.

His eye shuts.

I strip every ounce of softness out of my blood and snarl, "Someone get me gloves! Now!"

A beat of clean, slicing silence. No one moves. The spear

nearest my face dips, but the hands stay floating, gloved and nervous and too aware of all the rules.

It's Rafil who cracks first. His voice arcs out: "You heard the princess. Give her what she needs." He's a mess, nursing a broken femur a couple yards away, but his brother is tucked safely under his arm.

An Imperial yanks off his gloves, and I reach for them like I'm about to accept a newborn baby, when a shadow falls over across the circle.

"Maintain your uniform, scout," the Emperor says. He's close enough that his sandal touches my knee, scuffing sand into the wound on Drake's thigh. "She is not yet your ruler. She must be wed."

I go still. Grit and blood staining my knees, the taste of sand ground into my molars. Everything in me beg to show my father what real power is. As if any of this—the suffering, the misery—is a victory.

He stands in front of me now, all obsidian and molten silver. His hand opens toward me, cordial as Aphrodite accepting a lover's note at her altar. "He has lost, my daughter. Rise. Go to your groom."

Go to my groom? While my soulmate bleeds out on the sand at my feet.

He waits. Eternity in a single, unmoving palm.

"No," I rasp, furious. "I demand mercy. Unchain him. He fought harder than any of them."

"Mercy is not the Keres way." A line in the dust, hard and final. "Seize him."

Violence floods the circle, blades out, guns shouldered, that metallic stink of coming ruin. Everything folds inward, compact and crushing.

I don't hesitate. I snatch the broken, jagged chain, my closest weapon, and bare my teeth. Let them try to take him. I'll become the Keres of myth, harness a brutality to topple Gods.

Except—

A blur tears past me, air bending around Nephene's speed as she appears at my side. The ultimate Keres, the perfect weapon, she reaches Drake first, hand spearing into the wreck of his hair and wrenching him from me, forcing him to his feet.

I'm still on my knees when she grinds the muzzle of her gun into his ear.

Standing tall under the empire's complete focus, she is not my sister, not Greta's Nevro, just a blade with a heartbeat. "This is how it must be done," she says. "You've made your choice."

Drake doesn't struggle. He could, but he lets it happen, blood pooling beneath him, endless and dark. He bows his head, not in defeat, but in the way you lock yourself in to take the hit that breaks your bones clean.

It cracks my soul. Father I may have understood, but Nephene …

"Let go of him, please," I beg of her, throat thick. "He's not a killer, Effie. He's not." I crawl to them. Crawl through his blood, as low as I've ever been. "Spare him. He's not the male you think he is. He's—I love him. I love him, Effie."

Nephene only shakes her head. "He is, Theia. You don't know—"

A sound steals her words. A laugh. Merciless. Oil poured over ice. The laugh of the Deep Realm's emperor. My father's eyes are not his own, not the male who cradled me, who welcomed me, taught me, they're primordial. Heinous.

He studies me, head cocked as if to better see the misery writhing under my skin. "He has deceived you."

"He has not!"

"You defend a liar. You protect an unworthy king's executioner—a beast so vile, he has entranced an innocent female to attack us again."

I want to sink claws into his throat and tear out the rot he's spewing. But my mind cuts sharper than my teeth. I spit my words, needlepoint, venom-tipped. "I am not so innocent—"

"He killed your mother."

No.

Bile scorches my throat. I shake my head. "You're lying. You're a liar."

Has to be.

The emperor dips his chin. "Lydia. Speak the truth required."

The blonde glides forward, sleek and soundless, horrible smile on her mouth. "It's true," she says, all gravitas and gloating. "I saw him. The king summoned his torturer specifically for the Sunless Empress. After the butcher finished hacking her apart, he dragged your mother's body from the dungeons and down the halls of our palace for all to see his work."

I whip my head side to side. "No."

I find Drake, no longer waiting for the death knell, but watching me.

"Tell them they're wrong," I rasp to him, desperate, scratching for a truth that doesn't cut like a hook in my chest. I'm on my knees in the sand, dirt in my teeth, bloodied pride flooding my mouth. "Drake. Tell them you didn't."

He stares at me, green eyes feverish, pained.

"Drake," I beg for denial, a ghost of it. Instead—

"I didn't know who she was," he croaks, not to the crowd, but to me, pulling against Nephene's grip to come nearer. "Kadmos—"

Lydia scoffs. "Kadmos tortured the empress for years and when he couldn't crack her, he brought in a mortal expert, who promptly killed her."

Something's wrong with my chest, my stomach, something wrenching. Guilt, raw and flayed. Drake's.

"No," I mutter. "No. You weren't there."

He reaches for me. "I buried her under Nyx, just as she asked. I—"

I jolt backward, stomach full of razor wire, lungs chemical. "No. Her death started the war. You weren't there. You were mortal."

But even as I say it, I know. I can feel it, the marrow-deep truth, Drake's shame sinking me.

My father lowers to the sand beside me, features buckled in pity. "No, Antheia. You started the war."

## 35

# Theia

### HE WOULD RATHER BE DESTROYED THAN CHANGED

There are pictures of my mother. Of Celia.

Three. Worn thin.

Not painted. Not gilded, reverent portraits like the ones hung in our gallery, just three sun-shot photographs, faded in the corners and creased down the middle.

Father hid them. Once I'd have been angry. Now I understand keeping secrets just out of sight. Some truths are too heavy to revisit.

I shuffle the photos across the council table like tarot cards, waiting for them to give me answers. The praetorium's not cold, but part of me expects my breath to puff white. There's a goblet of blood in my left hand, coppery enough to trick my nerves into thinking I'm safe, but the scent is wrong. Like wilted lilies in a grave.

Like a lie.

Not the right stuff. Not Drake.

I strangle the thought. Can't go there. Can't think about how they hauled him away and he just went. Agreed. Compliant as I used to be.

Julian watches my every micro-flinch from the bone-clad

chair beside me. Perfect posture, not a hair out of place, not a single muscle betraying boredom.

Nephene's been locked out of this meeting, but not Julian. He'll be the emperor. He's privy to everything now.

All the kingdom's secrets.

Sand powders my palms and blood stains my knees. The only clean on me is my father's robe draped over my shoulders.

The usual boisterous debate that echoes this room is absent. I glance up at the elder counselors, trying to determine if they're learning new truths like me, or airing dirty secrets.

I look down at the photographs.

The first shows her laughing, teeth big and wild hair everywhere. The next is blurred, a streak of white slicing in front of her —a hand reaching to fix her hair. In the third, she's reserved: eyes like mine, skin a darker shade of brown, a comet-bright smile.

"She gave up the sun," my father breathes. Very, very careful. "For me."

I stare at her smile. "I don't understand."

He glances at the council, weighing what he can say. "Your mother defected to the Keres. Nyx made it clear what that meant—for any Keres to have a partner like her."

I run my finger over the photo nearest me. Her eyes are a perfect mirror. Same tilt at the corners. Same stumpy bottom lashes.

A whole person I will never, ever meet.

Someone who loved me, who carried me, probably patted her stomach and whispered me stories.

"I still don't get it."

"Keres blood doesn't mix. We dominate. Always have, always will. Any child from our line comes out pure Keres. No matter who they mate, Silenus, Oceanid, Gorgon, the baby will be Keres."

Julian's nod is a shadow-tilt. He already knows.

"So?" I say, still confused. "What does that have to do with Drake, or the war, or her?"

"Your mother was Moirai—one of the Fates. She defected for me. And when she had you, you were not Keres."

"I'm Moirai?" It comes out as a question, but it's not. I feel it in every fiber. The early mornings I strolled in the sunlight unscathed. The dreams that felt real. How killing never felt right, not even in the depths of starvation.

I pull the photos closer.

The realization is a punch.

I'm Moirai.

Except … "But I'm not," I say, unsure, voice barely there. "I have fangs, I need blood. I can't be Moirai."

"You are half," my father says. He ignores the stress sweeping through Julian, the council's averted eyes. "Half Keres and half Moirai. The first of your kind. I did not think you'd survive even one moon. But you did. Look at you. You thrived."

Julian shuffles forward, gaze pinning me in place like a biology specimen.

I know this feeling. It brings an odd comfort as the truth settles in my chest.

All the loneliness. The bite of not-belonging. The reason they look at me like I'm a cracked egg, leaking something foreign.

"You don't fit because you can't. Before you, no Keres ever mixed blood. But then came Celia. The day she strode into my camp, she announced we'd be wed. Said she'd seen it in the thread."

My tongue goes sandpaper dry. "Did you believe her?"

He exhales, mouth bending to memory. "I tied her up. Thought she was a spy, a threat. But she just waited me out. She was so alive. A force. By the time I freed her, she'd already made herself at home. She liked to tease me about it. We could've had a month more if you'd only listened."

Tears brim. He lets them.

The table vibrates beneath my palms. I skim my thumb over my mother's face, the slope of her brow. Something tightens at the base of my spine, explodes into understanding.

I am two warring natures: the ruthless Keres keeping me alive, while the persistent Moirai compassion fills me with hope.

My hands tremble. I hide them in the folds of my dress.

Silence lingers, viscous.

I force down the knot in my throat. "So I was never going to be enough. From the beginning, I was the wrong thing."

"No." My father's answer stuns me and some councilors. "You're more. You were born battling. You are Keres by strength, by ritual, by what pounds in your veins. But you're also Celia's. A child of Fate. Two legacies united."

My mind snags the next question like a burr. "What does this have to do with ..." I don't say Drake's name. "With the war? With my mother?"

My father's palm lands on my shoulder, but Julian speaks for him. "You're living proof the mad king's vision had merit. Kadmos wanted to integrate all creatures. The Keres refused, wisely. For the realm's sake. Kadmos needed proof that the Keres could be diluted. Made less dangerous. He needed evidence."

*Diluted.* Like a stain to rinse out. Made weak. Like me.

My father picks up where Julian stops. "The false king believed your mother held the key. That she possessed a secret to domination. So he stole her. He stole her out of her own kingdom. Imprisoned her in his wretched sun-drenched palace. Tortured her, broke every code."

The next bit sticks in his throat, a chunk of history he will never digest. "She never broke. Not once. Held through years of torture."

"And after?" I ask. "What did they do to her then?"

The council stirs. Hunger or horror, it's hard to tell.

My father's hands curl against the table, knuckles pulsing a weird, washed-out blue under thin skin. "They brought in a mortal. The butcher. She survived only days after he arrived."

The butcher.

I want to dissolve backward through the wall until the air isn't wet with this story anymore. But I can't. I lock my knees around the chair until pain blossoms. I almost like it.

"She suffered because of me."

"Because she refused to abandon you. Because when she was taken, Antheia. you were stolen too. A babe, barely days old." He's crying. "Somehow she hid you. Protected you."

"How?"

Nobody answers. The silence is final.

"We do not know." There's anger in the confession. "We fought and fought, until the war was dust and cinders. Half the realm burned as we pushed to get you back. But Kadmos lied to everyone. Swore you both vanished. Said nothing remained, not even a stain. No bodies."

Julian says, "Now we know what happened."

*Who* happened.

Drake.

My vision goes blurry, sloshed with the colors of ruin: black, rust, greasy gold. I drill my focus onto the table, the photo of her laughing, hair like dark fire, eyes so brilliant I nearly wince.

"The Queensguard has shed an abundance of information to prove herself a worthy ally. She tells us that Celia got you to freedom, and that she did not last long after." He breathes once, shallow as a grave. "My Nevro. My only. Strong until the end."

*My Nevro.* I never thought I'd hear it in his mouth, like a curse, like a sacrament. Like a history that lived inside him, chewing out his heart cell by cell.

"She saved you," he whispers, as if repetition makes it matter. "And I—the empire fell and, in the ruins, I lost you."

He clings to the tabletop like it's the only barrier between him and the abyss.

Julian brings him back with a pat on his shoulder. "You held the kingdom together, my sovereign."

My chest twists.

He'll be a great leader.

My father stares at the photos. There's hatred, sure, and longing, but underneath—the flayed, shredded hope that maybe, someday, stolen miracles are returned. "Kadmos never figured it out, anyway. Couldn't. Not a male who ruled with nothing but spite and greed."

"Figured out what?"

"You."

# 36

## Drake

### HE WAS SELFISH, TOO FUCKING SELFISH TO GIVE HER PEACE

The gleaming tip of Lydia's sword never leaves my spine as she forces me deeper into the dark.

The message is clear: move or die.

Though it's not like her to give options.

Ahead, our guide, an imperial outfitted in umber scout armor, silently guides us through the maze of the sunless kingdom. They're whisper-quiet, swift as a cut. Not once do they check behind them. Not for someone lagging, not for approval. They take corners sharp, confident. Not a wasted glance.

Done this a hundred times.

A smuggler. A traitor.

I ought to be grateful to the smuggler saving me from going mad in these halls, but all I think is of how they're betraying Theia.

Committing treason.

I'm a full-circle hypocrite.

I follow anyway.

Lydia jabs me between the ribs, an amuse-bouche of pain. I don't flinch. Just continue the trudge. Needing to move forward and away, never enough distance behind me.

Each corridor swallows us. Walls slick with weeping condensation, close as a strangler's grip, dyed in blue-black of old bruises.

They could be leading me to slaughter and I don't fucking care.

Beneath my ribs, an intense pressure spreads out like a living thing. Clotting, nesting in the cavity where my heart might still be. I'd open my own veins across this floor, but it isn't enough. The destruction doesn't match the crime. Nothing could.

I've been trying not to let it crowd out all thought, but that's pointless. Every time a torch sputters or a tunnel twists, I remember—

The female. Bound to my wall.

Brown eyes a little brighter than normal, even when bloodied. A voice that stayed level through every misery. She wouldn't give up her name. Wouldn't talk of her kingdom, wouldn't acknowledge her child. Wouldn't betray them.

Not even when I was the one prying.

She was the first creature I killed.

My experiment. Do creatures unravel like mortals? Do they cry and beg at the end? Call for Gods?

She didn't.

Tears would stream down her face. Pink would drip from her lips and she'd ask for more. Tell me someone was searching for her.

Each night I fell asleep convinced I was an imposter. That maybe the butcher only sliced red, mortal meat. and Kadmos would slaughter me for failing. So each morning, I returned to her cell, resolved to do better, push harder, get answers.

She was Theia's mother.

Not fucking practice.

Her mother.

I should have known. As soon as Lydia threatened me,

stared at me with that ace in her pocket to destroy. I had a feeling. I just wouldn't accept it.

Accepting it meant telling Theia.

When Lydia hisses in my ear that I am filth, that I deserve nothing but death, it lands with a clean, satisfying click. A brick slotted precisely where it ought to go. Fresh mortar sloughing into old wounds.

I don't deny it.

She pushes me. "Go any slower and I'm fucking leaving you here to let the tunnels have their way."

Fine.

Doesn't matter.

I'm not getting out. Not really. Even if we break the surface, I left everything that mattered in the Munera.

*I love him*, she sobbed.

"You never had a chance," Lydia snaps. "You're nothing. A black mark in history. The only reason they're not dragging your corpse through the Deep Court right now is because they want her to choose your end. Watch their empress swing the blade." Warm breath scrapes my neck. "I would have done it myself."

"You should," I say.

My voice is gone, buried under the mess of my own making. I can barely speak. But it doesn't deter Lydia. She just shoves me on, outpacing mercy, toward whatever waits at the end.

Last time war battered these tunnels, it was my hand on the blade. I used to tell myself it wasn't personal.

It always is.

At the next junction, she wrenches me to a stop. The smuggler floats just ahead. Then nothing but silence, water trickling through the dark.

"I hope it fucking haunts you," Lydia spits, hate naked. "How you killed her. Every time the princess looks at you, that's all she'll see. That you stripped her of her family. Her mother." She leans closer. "She couldn't believe it, but it's exactly what she should have expected, isn't it?"

Yes.

But Theia believes in things. She believes long past reason, until it breaks her. She's so strong, so fierce in her convictions. It's what draws me to her. Why I love her.

Lydia doesn't care about my opinion.

She doesn't want an answer.

All I can do is keep breathing, a torture all its own.

"You're not a hero," she whispers, crowding my back. "You crawled out of the sewers. Just because you killed for his name doesn't mean you have a soul. You're a fucking coward."

Maybe.

Probably.

Why sugarcoat it?

The only thing—I mean the *only* thing—that stops me from throwing myself on her blade is that Theia might feel it. The pulse of pain. The ache of my dying. I will not leave that stain for her.

She doesn't deserve that. Not from me. Not ever.

And Gods, I hate myself for caring even that much.

The smuggler dives through a hole in the wall. Lydia slams me after them, no warning.

Bone meets concrete, shoulder forcing through a space my body was not built for. Pain flares. I suck in air with a hiss; let it rip the inside of my lungs bloody.

Lydia hits again, deeper, throwing me forward. Pain wipes everything else clean. Shame threatens its own collapse as she jams me. No mercy for the pieces that don't fit.

She wants a fight. I've got nothing left. She spits venom. I take it.

"You know what you really are?" Joy threads through her voice now. "A liar. Filth. The Gods should rain every plague they've got down on you for tricking her the way you did."

Denial's a joke. I clamp my mouth shut, tuck my chin down, and let her speak.

A sound, almost a laugh. "You think you're so clever. Manipulating her. Convincing her she loves you. Like you're a fucking gift, a damn miracle." Her breath hits my ear, electric, mean. "You're nothing. She's so much more than you'll ever be. And you used every second of it. You twisted the knife, just for fun."

The air down here curdles with sweat and rot. My boots sink deep in muck. I keep moving anyway. One step. The next. The next after that.

"All for what?" She's relentless. "For your own pathetic redemption? Did you get off hearing her beg for you? Did you enjoy the way she forgave you, even when she didn't know what she was forgiving?" A jolt of pressure in my ribs as she digs the point home. "You belong here. In the dark. With the creatures you always considered yourself better than. The legendary Blackguard. I swear, I will never understand how any of you sleep at night."

The Blackguard. The word lands heavier than the rest.

They'd probably cut me out, too. For hurting her. For gutting the only hope we ever had at peace.

"You lot always thought you were saints," Lydia seethes. "Holier than everyone else. You wanted to keep the wars to yourselves because you couldn't stand the idea that some female might show you up in the killing. Sexist. Elitist. Miserable." A hard exhale. "You're exactly where you belong."

"All those years hunting the king's targets. All that righteousness." She whips me toward the black, blocking escape. "You were the worst of them. You were the monster they measured by. The others just followed. You set the pace. You made the evil."

I tune her out. She's not telling me anything I don't already know. If I die down here, it won't be Lydia Faber's voice in my head.

I think about my mother. My sisters in their taupe everyday dresses. They raised me. Taught me to stand up, open doors, take the beating. Above all, never let women pay the price—not out of some myth that women were too weak, but because someone had to draw a line in the dirt. Someone had to be better.

Because our father hadn't been.

If they saw this? If they knew? They'd have wrapped Theia up in a decade's worth of wool and made a trade: her happiness for my head.

They'd love Theia.

They were the same. Kind-hearted, sweet.

Lydia's voice snaps back to me when she mentions Theia. "She's weak. Clinging to you, guzzling your blood, acting lost and helpless. She's a joke. She's not going to last a month as empress. Not unless she's got a male to fix her mess."

The muscles in my neck pull tight.

Anger, crude, searing anger tugs in my veins. Hot. Alive. Sudden.

"She's not even Keres. She's a fraud. All those years in the cell, you'd think it'd toughen her up. Turn her into less of a disappointment. But no. She tosses it all away for a sob story."

She shoves me again. "Dreaming of 'family' and 'hope'. I've seen children with more sense. She could have shredded you. Made you beg. But she's so soft and empty. When this place collapses, she'll be the first body—I promise you that. She can't even keep herself upright. Too busy pleading for someone to save her."

I might've let it go.

If she'd just stuck to the initial insult.

If she hadn't tried to piss on hope.

But she did.

And then she threatened Theia.

A burn ignites at the base of my skull. Spreads. Tears into

my stomach. I spin, clean and quick, and knock Lydia's sword aside. The clang is loud, almost a gunshot in the wet dark.

She looks stunned. Doesn't matter. I drive my fist into her chest, just below that Queensguard badge, and slam her back into the slimy wall. She wheezes. Surprise and anger twist her face.

I get in close. I want her to taste my fury. "Talk about me all you want. Call me filth, monster, traitor—it's true. But you don't breathe a word about her."

Lydia thrashes. I increase the pressure to her throat.

"You think you've seen war? Seen suffering? You don't know half of what she's lived through. You stand in the dark because your queen told you to. She was born in the dark. Lived her whole life there." My voice drops lower. "The difference between you and her, Lydia? She's never stopped fighting. Even when every single one of you wanted her gone."

She tries to kick. I've got my weight pinning her.

"Call her weak again and I'll end you." The words grind out through my teeth. "But if you even think about hurting her, I'll tear the tongue from your mouth and hang you from the ceiling. Keres-style."

Her pulse stutters under my hand.

She tries to spit. I twist harder.

"Theia is better than any of us. She could have picked power. Could have let any of us die. But she didn't. She saved lives. She forgave her enemies. She forgave me."

"And you hate her for it. Because she has faith in creatures, whatever the world throws. And you can't fucking stand that."

She nods. Barely. The agreement of a cornered thing.

I want to break her. The impulse is pure, raging. I could snap her neck, easy.

She feels it. Now, she's afraid.

And I savor it. Stop fighting the current. Press harder.

Steps rattle behind us. A voice slices through. "Break it up."

I don't let go.

She's on us, then. A whisper of motion, grip to my shoulder—not a challenge, just force.

My brain does the math slowly. The speed. The voice.

Not an Imperial. Not a smuggler.

Nephene.

I release Lydia. She falls, coughing, catching herself on a wet exhale.

Pulling the umber cowl down to her shoulders, Nephene steps between us, calm as midnight. "If you're going to kill each other, save it for the surface. There are no rats down here to scavenge the bodies." She turns. "Otherwise, follow me."

Lydia scoops her sword from the mud. She glares at me. Then at Nephene.

Nephene shows her sharp fangs. "If you can't handle him, get lost. This isn't for the weak-hearted."

The silence? Dense.

Nephene takes the front, black braid and posture like a death sentence. When she walks, it's soft, swallow-the-echo soft. She doesn't care about hurry. Doesn't fear what might echo back.

The walls change from muck to formal cut brick. Some ancient Keres ambition eroded by time. Nephene drags her fingers along the stones, reading them, memorizing the raised veins.

She's reading a map.

That's how she does it.

Ancient Greek Keres Braille.

Eventually, the question rips from my mouth, straight at the back of Nephene's skull. "Why are you doing this?"

Her shoulders cinch. She doesn't turn right away. "Why? You gonna write me a thank-you card?"

"I'm out of stamps, Nephene."

"*Princess*," she corrects like a whip. "I owe my title to you, don't I? If you hadn't killed the first empress, my mother never would've fucked Vasilis. No copulation, no me." She flashes a cruel smile. "So, in some batshit cosmic equation, you're my fairy godmother."

"That's not it."

She walks on, kicks silt off her heel. "The council wants a spectacle. They want you bumbling through gunfire in a panic. They want an example of Keres justice." She says it like a hangman talking shop. "It'll take the spotlight off Theia's coronation."

"Then put a noose around my neck in my cell and stage a suicide." I stop. For the first time since they yanked me out of my cage, I stop doing what I'm told. "Show them I'm worthless. Parade the coward. Dump the body. You're strategic, Nephene. It's easier to call me a coward than risk letting me run. Why help?"

She stops. Turns.

The fire that lives in her—it's not there. She studies my face, searching for something she doesn't even want to find. Turns back to the wall, fingers restless.

"You want honesty? Fine." Her hand flexes. "You're not the only one with secrets. I grew up with the rest of them. The court. The elders. The fuckers in charge. Playing nice, playing formal, always toeing the line. Because I believe we can be great, but we aren't yet." She pauses. "I understand that if you want to make change, you have to make sacrifices. I did things I don't talk about. So did you. Sweet Nyx, I'll probably do more."

"You didn't kill the empress, Nephene. They won't drag you into the ichor pit."

"I know that. I'm not sympathetic, Drake." She leans in. "But I think if you'd known what it would do to Theia, you'd have said no to your king. You'd have let them kill you first."

I say nothing, but the thought bruises, leaks in, discoloring everything.

"She's my sister, Drake. Half of me, and half something I

will never *ever* understand. When she's around, I'm not so ..." She swallows roughly, glances at her feet. "She's going to have enemies. You are not one. Therefore, it's better if you're alive."

Tactical.

I'm not surprised.

But then she says, "And she gave me Greta. For that I owe her."

Greta. The mouthy violent one. They're Nevros. Can be together if she's not married to Julian.

It's the love story Theia wanted.

I drag a hand down my face. "Alright. What about you, Lydia? Has the queen issued us a pardon? Forgiven us for crimes against her husband? Are we allies?"

"You freed them," she says. "The females in captivity."

"The ones you tried to kill."

"We get orders too, Blackguard. And we've seen what happens to a guard that doesn't follow them. I don't want a curse around my neck." She frowns. "You set them loose. Now we're even. That's why I haven't knifed you."

"This is as far as we go," Nephene says. "The surface is twenty paces straight, first right. Latch between moss and slate opens to the realm. You open it and don't look back. Never set foot in my kingdom again. Understood?"

"I ..."

"She'll never leave her people for you, Drake."

"She's only half Keres."

A new kind of sorrow fills Nephene's stare. "Would you have left your family, Drake? If you got them back right now, could you walk away?"

37

# Drake

## HE WAS MISERABLE

There's no sunlight.

The air's gone heavy, thick as a storm, all humidity and the thrum of insect wings. The press of night embraces me in a dark crush, seeps under my skin, oily and devouring. Above is a canopy of black oak leaves, firefly strobes, an owl tensing for its hunt. Not a lick of moonlight makes it through.

No Dryads would be caught dead in the shifting shadows.

Not when *they're* here.

They cut through the forest in tight formation, weapons drawn, armor buckled and layered. Kevlar, leather and Divine steel.

Zeke's up front, the white streak of his mohawk a phosphorescent beacon. He uses the goo of a broken glow stick to mark each tree he passes. Our leader, Atlas sticks at his tracker's shoulder, black hair tucked around the point of his ears. A tactic, like everything he does, meant to make any enemies second guess themselves when they see he's Chire.

Rune and Lev fan out in a perimeter sweep, two hulking bodies loaded with silencers they don't need, moving like a dragnet, checking for tripwires and bogies.

Sin holds the back line, ready to counter attacks from

behind, eager to show off for his Fated, Nat, who stomps in the middle, strong and tall, radiating murder. Peeking under the gleam of her red Drakon armor, is a slice of bare stomach, showing the news she carries.

They're surgical: sweep, mark, move. "Clear," Atlas murmurs every fifth step, careless of the wind stealing his voice. Zeke marks a branch. Rune drops a puck sensor without breaking stride.

I'd bet anything Luke is nearby, tracking those in the driver's seat of a getaway vehicle and furious he's been relegated to a computer.

I watch from behind a vine-strangled trunk, mud frosting my boots, shame digging a pit in my stomach. They're searching for me.

As if I deserve finding.

I almost let them pass. Almost disappear. Pretend I never left. The desire burns so fiercely, the tattoos on my neck and wrists tighten painfully. A reminder my service to Kadmos will never end.

I grind my boot into the mud. Clear my throat. "Zeke."

Six heads swivel, Guns up, blades out, an instant threat assessment.

Zeke sweeps the empty space to his left with his Katana. "Marco?"

I step forward, hands loose. "Put the toys away. It's just me."

The tempo shifts. Gravity eases. Weapons lower, breaths release, relief rolls through them like a tide. Lev grins, Sin's posture falls into a slouch. Even Atlas relaxes, lowering his twin .22s.

Nat? Not so much.

Her eyes burn coal-hot, zeroing on me. She has my collar in two strides.

"Where is she?" She scans the copse behind me. "Where's Theia?"

Answering tears something vital loose.

"She's not coming back." I force it out. "She's the next Empress of the Deep Empire. Daughter of Vasilis. She takes the throne on the new moon."

Nobody moves. The wind dies, as if even the Anemoi need processing time. My back throbs where Lydia's sword dug in. Feels right.

Atlas blinks once, lids heavy. "Run that again."

"She found her family. She's staying with them."

"Her family."

"The Keres. She chose them." I'd rather be shot than say it again. I can't look anyone in the eye. "I didn't stop her."

Nat's fist smashes into my temple.

She drives me back, slamming me against tree bark, pins me there, vambrace crushing my trachea. Only a millennium of ruthless training keeps her from brushing my exposed skin while delivering maximum damage. Her rage burns elemental, the tornado before the hurricane.

"Repeat." she can't form full sentences, she's shaking.

She endured torture, hunting, leashing to rescue Theia just months ago.

I promised protection. But I have to say it again: "She's not coming back."

She slams her helmet into my nose, drives her knee into my groin, rams her elbow across my face. I don't resist. I keep my arms tight to my torso to keep from losing my arms.

It takes three of the Blackguard to pry her off—Atlas, Sin, Lev. Not gentle, but careful. Sin locks her in a half-nelson while whispering how beautiful she looks. Lev restrains her arms, his bulging biceps straining.

"Don't stress the baby, my love." Sin purrs. "I'll rough him up later."

"Now!" She writhes in their grip. "Cut him to pieces. He promised! He made a vow!"

"Calm, my bloodspiller."

"Shut the shit, demigod. He lost Theia!"

"The stress—"

Nat spits. Ichor streaks my cheek. Sears. "Nothing can stress the baby." She jerks against their hold. "She's half Fury. She's built for this. This makes her strong."

"*She*?" Sin's voice drops into pure wonder. "Did Eros tell you? Did Hades?"

Nat tenses. Recalibrates. Her gaze finds her Fated, care for him banking the fury in her chest. "I don't know. She must be a girl, right? To make me this sick?"

Sin kisses her, ignoring that she's restrained physically. She allows it. Lev coughs, suddenly fascinated with Zeke's green flip flops.

I wipe my face.

Atlas inventories my injuries: face, ribs, the trail of blood on my thigh. "Are you going to drop on us, or can you keep up?"

The truth comes too easy. "I can't feel a thing."

38

# Drake

## AND PATHETIC

The curse doesn't work on me, if I nick my cheek with my palm, no choking fears drag me under.

I figured it meant I was fearless.

What had I to fear? A man with nothing. No family, no hope, a skillset most wouldn't wish upon their enemies.

Now nightmares hound me. They slither in and latch on each time I've convinced myself the horror is past, that leaving her was for the best.

I don't need to fall asleep for them to come. Pen wedged in my fist, white-knuckled, still mid-sentence, the ink sunk into the stationery. I freeze, palm leaving oil on the page, my back knotted like a hangman's rope, and my wrists ravaging me.

It's the same.

Theia waiting with a patience that makes me sick with longing. She smiles, arms held open. The kind of embrace I always knew I didn't deserve and could never accept. She beckons me forward with that glorious grin, and I think maybe if I walk to her, if I let her pull me in, I'll get to stay there.

Then she tells me she wishes I was never born.

That we'd never met.

That I'd been shot that winter, on my knees in the alley Died at my peak as a worthless pickpocket.

My pen snaps in half. Paper shreds in my grip. My heart jackhammers.

I roll my wrist, my neck. The burn has morphed into a steady sear. My pain tolerance is high, but the curse has descended deep, intent to pulverize me.

I keep writing.

As if the words will magically appear. As if in the turmoil of this fucking anguish, I will find a way to ask for her forgiveness.

I keep going. Hours slide past while I hunt for reasons to make this all go away, to take back what I did, to convince Theia to give up the family she's always wanted. The father the sister, a kingdom, her people—for a fucking butcher.

It's her fault.

She made me believe the devil could be redeemed. That my hands could hold something and not break it.

She gave me fucking hope. Not Kadmos, not any Olympian, no Titan, no sunrise or miracle. *Her.*

And I tore it out of her.

I started my first draft within hours of returning to the Blackguard safe house. Convinced there was a reason to turn around, a reason for Theia to look at me like the way she did before.

There isn't.

Every day that passes only makes me more certain that leaving was the only good thing I've ever done.

She chose Julian. I might want to kill him, but I heard him when he said he'd try for her. No one will have to try for more than a day to fall in love with her.

Sin checks in, even after I threw a steak knife at his throat for trying to cheer me up with his ability to manipulate emotions. Atlas opens the windows each morning and shuts them at night like a personal warden. Lev asks about my shoulder, if the curse chafes. Luke sits with me, typing on his phone, telling me when my stomach growls.

I can't eat.

I can't put on my gloves.

I let ink stain my hands, watch it crust in my nails.

"Luke'll hang you when he sees this mess." Rune looms in the half-lit doorway, surveying the carnage of my life.

"Do you need something from me?"

A body to bury, a truth to rip out, a fear unlocked and named, ready to exploit.

He glides—as much as a six-five Viking can—into my room and plops his ass on the corner of my desk. The weight of him vibrates the cheap particleboard, and sends the plain black Bic to the floor. He's in his usual uniform: navy polo shirt, sleeves rolled; dark jeans; sneakers double-knotted, looking every inch the straight-laced suburban dad bringing orange slices to a kids' soccer game.

Rune glances at my hands, then at the streak of blood across the lampshade, then at the torn pages in the overflowing wastebasket.

"You couldn't screw in a lightbulb right now," he says. "What help could you be?"

My body's a tangle of barely-healed wounds, my mind a howling chasm. I squint out at the room The bed I haven't slept in, the laundry heap next to it sand-covered and bloody. My mouth tastes like metal, my shirt's stuck to my back.

"I'm sorry." I scrub a hand over my face. "I'll take a shower. I'll get it together. Just … what's the job?"

Rune raises one blonde eyebrow, the most expressive muscle in his face. "Is that the only reason you'd expect me? Not to say hi. Not to check if you're still breathing." He plucks a dog-eared sheet from my pile, brings it to the window, and peels back the blackout curtain. Evening sun glares through the glass. Fuck. I've lost an entire day.

"You're not good with words," he says, thumbing through my scribbles.

I crumple the page in my hand. "Thanks."

"You're spiraling."

"Is that a diagnosis or are you just bored enough to psychoanalyze me now?"

He peers over the paper, narrows his eyes. "It's an observation."

I flip the desk drawer open, grab a fresh pen. "Do fuck off."

He shrugs, leans back against the glass. The sunset stains him burned gold, and for a moment he looks a thousand years old, the lines in his face shadowed and deep. He holds up the page and reads, monotone: "What could I do? Sing for the God of the Underrealm? Swim through the Styx? Soothe Cerberus? Would any of it sway you? Would any of it matter if I were still the snake that bit you? Would it make you look at me with any less contempt, for even a second?" He lowers the sheet, fixes me with a stare. "Not exactly Dickinson."

My hands close into fists, only to loosen as the curse sizzles, creeping up my forearm like a live wire. "Then don't read it."

"If this is true, what are you still doing here? You're not a writer, Drake. You're a man of action. Go get her. Bring her back."

I press my fists into my eyes, see white bursts. "You think I don't want to?"

"How would I know? You've spent the last hundred years taking orders. I don't think you've ever done what you want."

"I want to bring her back. I want to—" My throat closes. The words jam up, heavy and sharp. "But she deserves better. She has better."

"That's it?" he asks. "You're the bad guy. You're evil, and she doesn't want you. You're the monster who can't even hold down breakfast, can't sleep, has kept himself locked up, self-flagellating—"

"I'm not—"

"I see the curse gripping you, tighter and tighter. You've left scratches on your throat, you're limping. You don't feel it because you're too fucking heartbroken."

"I feel it. I deserve it." He doesn't understand. None of them do. "I killed her mother," I hiss. "Rune. I broke her world. Every day she spent locked up, every time she suffered, every lie, every wasted hope—it's on me. They put her in cells, they hurt her, they made her believe she was alone, and you think I shouldn't fucking suffer?"

I realize I'm shouting then, bellowing like a madman at a friend who only wants to help. The shame comes in hot and fast, a fresh layer on the endless lacquer applied to my soul. I collapse at the desk, anchor my elbows, and scrub at my face. Bare skin to skin, only then registering that I'm not wearing my gloves.

Ink and sweat and blood sting as I push my palms into my eye sockets, blotting out the meager light. "I'm sorry," I manage in a hoarse scrape. "Fuck, I'm sorry, I—"

"Save your apologies for her."

"That won't fix this," I admit in a mutter. "Even if she forgave me—huge fucking if—I still have nothing to offer her. No home, no family. I'm a cursed mortal asshole who can't even touch her. Can't brush a tear off her cheek, can't hold her in my arms. She needs more than what I can give. Deserves more. You have no idea what that's like."

Rune gained immortality not from Kadmos, not from the selfish, transactional currency of a king's whim, but from an actual God—as a reward for acts of Divine heroics. He's a hero, born and reborn. Could've spent immortality on Olympus but chose to stay in the mortal realm. Could've had wealth and wives and abundance, never raised his axe again, but he joined Kadmos because he believed in doing the right thing.

He's never felt unworthy a day in his life.

Except he stands. Looks at me the way you look at a dying fire. "Actually, I do."

He must see the surprise, because he lets out a breath and sits again. "Did you think you were special? That you were the only one who's ever been broken, who's ever let someone down? Who's ever lived in shame?" He's not angry, not even disappointed. Just tired the way old gods are tired, worn down by the sheer repetition of mortal tragedy. "I was twelve when the crops went. Our best men vanished on a hunt, and every day the village shrank. But I had a spear, some basic tracking knowledge. I could find prey, snare it. But I didn't. Told myself I'd do it when the snow melted, when the wind calmed, when the moon widened. Every possible excuse."

His voice is simple, stark. No flourish, just the facts of memory filtered through the long, hard sieve of survival.

He looks past me, out the window, as if the memory is a ghost that might reappear if he waits for it.

"The blizzard hit and every trail vanished. The jarl told me anyone who left would freeze in ten paces. My stomach was acid. I had thin clothes, a dull knife, two fingers already black with frostbite. I was so desperate I went out anyway. Walked until my feet bled, my eyes watered so much, they iced over. And when I finally gutted a boar, and dragged it back to my village, I didn't feel like a hero. I looked at their thin faces, their shivering frames, and I felt like a coward."

I take a breath, chest tight. "But you saved them."

"I saved those who were still alive to eat." He rubs the callused webbing between two fingers. "But not the others. Not the ones who waited too long. I let them starve. I watched for months as they wasted away because I was scared I might fail. It's abhorrent." He turns his gaze back to me. I see the raw, weathered truth of a man who learned that fear kills. "You—Cosgrave, you did what I couldn't. You have always tried, without hesitation, no matter what it cost you to help the people you love."

I look away, not because I'm ashamed but because the words cut so deep I'm bleeding inside. "But I failed."

"So you regret trying?"

"No," I say, and for the first time in days—maybe centuries—the word isn't a shield but a blade. "If there was even a chance I could have saved them, it's worth any pain."

I'm not sure if the ache in my chest is emotion or the curse, if the trembling in my hands is from lack of blood or hope. But Rune just lets the words sit in the space between us, heavy as judgment.

My eyes roam over the sheet of paper in front of me, the one I mangled under my fist. The words I wrote, desperate and doomed, collide with the ones Rune just tore out of me.

Then he says, "New moon tonight."

It's a gut-punch, dead center. "Tonight?"

It's been two days. I've been locked up for *two* days. My thoughts scramble, hunting for purchase. The wedding. The coronation. Centuries of tradition about to be set in stone, and I'm here—barely able to see straight, arms shaking, shirt pasted to my ribs—while she's out there, probably writing her vows to fucking Julian.

I won't let it happen. Not without speaking to her first. Not without trying.

If there's a one in ten million shot, it's worth it.

I jolt upright, scattering papers and pens. Turn to Rune. "Let's go break up a wedding."

39

# Theia

## MAYBE ORPHEUS NEVER REALLY WANTED A LIFE WITH HER, JUST A GOODBYE

He doesn't belong here.

There are a dozen things the father of the bride should be doing right now. Multiply that by a hundred if you factor in that he's the emperor.

And he's about to abdicate.

Yet here he is, not drenching himself in applause and fanfare, not letting history douse him in legacy, but stalking the hemmed velvet of the temple's privacy alcove.

Tonight he steps down, and that's it. No seat on the council. No voice. Royalty stamped on his skin, but the pulse of power shunted elsewhere.

I'll outrank him.

The thought sits wrong, like swallowing glass

The closer we inch toward the ceremony of the century, the more I want to rip off this silver tiara and wedge myself under a table.

My father's ditched his crown for black on black, no gild, no bones, just a coal-dark shirt, and the kind of brooding presence that can only be reproduced in a lab.

Is it inappropriate to request an emotional support toad? Or passage to Saturn?

He's staring at me. Not in the "I want to see my beautiful daughter in her special dress" way, but in the "I can analyze which psychological trauma is making you sweat through your clothes right now" way.

Keres. The original therapy dynasty.

I pick at my sleeve's embroidered cuff, which I'm told is a blessing from Nyx but mostly looks like squiggles. My stomach drops and flips. Has been. For days.

He gestures to the chair beside me—a mini throne, hewn solid out of something blacker than despair. "Sit."

He's kept close since the Munera ended. Checking in, offering blood, confirming, double checking, triple checking whether I'm sure.

Of course, I'm sure.

Drake is—

No. Doesn't matter what he's done.

He left.

What other choice is there?

I sink down in the thronelet. A goblet waits on the narrow table between us. Blood, dark as heartache, probably a good vintage, a famous artist, a muse. My gaze catches, snags.

I try not to look.

Fail.

My fangs ache, a twisty, hollow pain that leaches down to my marrow. I roll my tongue, pretend I don't want it.

Look back. I want it. Desperately. But imagining the taste makes everything shrink.

My father clocks the glance. "You can still change your mind."

No one warned me this would be the hard part.

Captivity, injections, chains, the sun. That's a walk in the park without the pollen.

This? Looking my father in the eye and admitting I have no idea what I want? My lungs forget their job.

I used to have this pull, a guidance system in my chest that reassured me: *this is right, hang on, steady the course.* Constant internal confirmation that it was okay to be a prisoner. I'd get out, I'd discover cherry popsicles, and my life would be brighter.

Nothing guides me now.

"You don't have to do this," he says.

*I know. I know that.*

But if I don't, it burns.

If I do, it cuts.

Either way hurts.

I want him to forbid it. Want an order. For him to tell me not to and I will.

But I made it clear I wasn't taking orders anymore.

And he's losing his position to argue.

"I do," I lie. "I want to."

He doesn't buy it. Why would he? He's seen straight through me since I drooled over a croissant.

He doesn't argue though. Not his style.

Instead he reaches for a silver box and sets it on my chair's arm. "Then I want you to have this."

Inside: a necklace. Ancient-looking, extra-heavy, violet, nearly indigo gem pendant, held in a spiderweb of silver thread, strung so tightly it looks alive. Moirai work.

My throat closes. "Was this my mother's?"

He nods. "She was wearing it when we met. It is a mark of the Moirai, a piece of her life thread. Tradition, she told me, since those who control destiny can't know their own. The three sisters slice it, away and the Moirai must live always guessing what's missing. A friend, a death, a lover." He traces the web. "The necklace reminds them to seize the moment. Not so very different from Keres."

The words settle with an exhausted thump. I pick up the necklace and it's cold, almost spiteful, like it can sense I'm an imposter. Or just highly unqualified for the next forty-eight hours.

"I can't wear this."

He loops it over my head anyway.

The chill bites my neck. If I were full Moirai, maybe it would sing. Instead, it sits.

"She would want you to embrace what you are," he tells me. "You *are* Keres, my daughter."

I don't move. Not my jaw, not my hands, not a single muscle. But inside, it's chaos, a jolt along every nerve. Like someone slammed a car battery to my ribs and wished me luck.

The dress, my dress, the one I spent hours being fitted for, fighting for the yellow that's too bright for Keres halls, a waist that drapes elegantly, embroidered sleeves and a winding train —the dress marking the start of the rest of my life suddenly presses in.

Celia's necklace burns on my collarbone, heavy as fate, and I sit frozen, seconds from crawling out of my own skin.

His words hang like hooks. Keres. Not maybe or almost. Not a question at all.

I could argue. Present all the evidence: I'm not Keres. I'm not even Moirai, just a glitch.

But all I do is breathe.

"You *are*," he repeats, willing belief into me. "You survived what would have ended all other creatures. You do not break, Antheia. You do not endure from stubbornness or luck." He touches my heart. "Keres is not in the blood. It is in the soul. In the refusal, in the fight, in the way you choose love even when it is impossible. You are Keres."

My eyes sting. I drag a knuckle across my lashes. The necklace catches on my hair. My knees suck together, wrinkle my skirt. If I move, I might unravel completely.

But his gaze won't release me. "The exile, the crown, the years they tried to kill you and failed. *That* is Keres."

My laugh comes out dull, nothing like the glass-breaking

joy I want to give him. "So, it's not the fangs, then?" I swipe my sleeve across my nose. "Not the taste for drama?"

His smile is quiet, and still knife sharp. "Drama is our favorite tradition," he tells me, kind, so kind to me. "It is not how you are born. It is how you live, how you walk the realm, how you die. You are Keres. You are home here. Always."

His stare could tack a God to the wall, could gut a Demigod on sight. It surgically peels me apart, strip after strip, all the way to my marshmallow fluff center.

My hands shake. I stand, awkward, entirely too tall for once, dress pouring down my legs.

I hug him

Vasilis, Emperor of the Sunless Kingdom, Commander of the Keres Imperials, Sovereign of the most fearsome creatures, children of the Goddess Nyx herself, wraps his arms around me.

He leaves his chair like gravity doesn't exist and folds me in, a shroud of cold, undertaker chic all around me, and for a second, my world narrows to his starched shoulder and whatever blood cologne Keres are genetically forced to secrete.

I hug him hard. Full force. Fangs out, arms cinching, fingers digging in.

He holds me back. Fiercer. Like releasing me means something terrible will blast us apart again. His chin finds the top of my head.

"My dcar." Thc murmur vibratcs through mc. "I lovc you."

I didn't think I could break anymore, but he manages it.

My chest pulls tight. Feelings crashing in: love, loyalty, an ache for something lost and then found and broken but still ... mine. Family, in the truest sense. I almost beg him to call this off. Say it's too much.

But he shifts just enough to tip my face up, eyes rich brown like mine searching deep. "You will change this world. You will lead a rebellion. Remake a kingdom. You will alter how creatures see Keres forever."

My heart skids sideways, a sick spiral of panic and love and awe crushing me. "You want creatures to think we're soft?"

A huff of real laughter. "No. I want them to see us walk in the sun and realize nightmares aren't limited to the dark anymore. I want them afraid."

"Ah, yes." My laugh has a brittle twinge. "Your ulterior motive."

"Perhaps. My only motive for the past century was finding you, and now I am to step down. Perhaps I'll join the kottabos league. I hear it is cutthroat."

He squeezes tighter, a male who could strangle a Primordial with one arm and cradle a newborn with the other. I want this to last. I want to dawdle in this moment. "No one could be a match for my father."

He blinks. Releases me. Holds me arm's length away.

His face detonates—a smash of pride and amusement.

It's the first time I've called him that, and he's ... elated. By one tiny, greedy little word.

It puts a stupid grin on my face.

He grins back, all fangs. "Your mother was Keres too. She ruled as empress even when they called her traitor. She was more Keres than any of them. I see the same in you."

My hand fumbles for the necklace. It still stings, but not as bad. Just the ache you get when you finally, *finally* fit the shape of your own skin.

"There's something else, dear. Something that your mother would want you to know."

## 40

# Theia

## HE NEVER BELIEVED HE DESERVED HER

No one stands as I walk down the aisle.

They do stare.

Rows and rows of eyes, not one warm, dissecting my every step.

Nephene told me when a Keres walks down the aisle, she only looks forward. It's a sign of commitment. No, conviction. Or tradition? It's possible she said it just to keep me from crying in front of the empire.

I'm holding a bouquet. Actual flowers, not the severed femur or knuckle bones strung on ribbon that is traditional. Nephene probably ripped these dahlias out of the hands of a terrified mortal florist. She insisted every detail be perfect, down to the black silk wrapping each stem.

My dress sweeps the air behind me, as defiant and raw as a sunrise. Twelve seamstresses stayed up all night to bring it to life, pinning, stitching, and draping. The train could double as a fire exit, and I guarantee it's the brightest thing that's ever entered Nyx's temple.

I'm a stain, a blight.

I keep my head up.

Every Keres who ever wanted a throne, every councilor

who wrote me off and whose mutters scraped that "she'll never last a week," lines the halls. Lips painted, fangs shined, eyes rimmed in charcoal, clothes darker than the inside of a crypt.

They're wishing for me to trip.

I focus on the magnificent dais ahead, where the throne for the future emperor—or as of tonight, future *empress*—awaits. A smaller chair for the consort waits beside it. Both pushed back, not the focus. They come later. After the wedding.

Father stands, waiting to surrender his crown. No smile now, no tears. Julian occupies his right, genetically engineered to win at weddings. Perfect hair, smile dialed down to a careful simmer.

I take a step. Then I take another. Pass Greta—heart pinching at her thin lips, bloodshot eyes, and blotchy skin. She's been crying all night.

I can do this.

This is the right thing.

My stomach knots. I ignore it.

I narrow my focus: carpet, altar, the pulse of candle flames. I am a machine built to walk forward, hips locked, steps even, yellow dress burning in the temple's monochrome. Everything slows—the sweep of my dress, the tap of my heel. I can feel their thoughts, thick as syrup. *She's not Keres. She's a mistake in yellow. She's not one of us.*

I don't care what they think.

I am battle calm.

Nothing exists but this walk, ragged and all-consuming.

This *is* the right thing.

And I'm proud. Proud of my decision.

Before I can splash around in the feeling, it vanishes.

A storm sweeps into me, strips my calm, floods my chest, my stomach, flares at the base of my spine. Hunger, hate, want, pain. Fury.

Possession.

I stutter-step, barely catch myself, rattle the bundle of flowers.

Several rows of Keres snicker, delighted.

The candles flicker.

Snuff out.

Darkness detonates. Not a gentle extinguishing, not a velvet-curtained fade to black—total annihilation. Consuming shadows leap from the walls and meet in temple center, smothering every trace of light.

The music, so steady before, ends with a shorn note that does not echo.

There is nothing. No color. No shape. The hush before the axe falls.

Then: chaos.

The Keres do not scream.

They shout. Voices spearing upward, overlapping commands volleying off the stone-tiered ceiling. Metal shrieks, the bitter whine of ritual knives unsheathing in unison.

Something's about to get butchered, but nobody's sure who.

Light punches back in.

The room snaps into stark relief.

It's the same.

Except—

There.

At the altar. Not Julian.

Standing alone, face etched in grim lines, hair in a feral tousle, jaw shadowed with a spray of pink sparkling blood, is Drake.

41

# Drake

## HE NEEDED TO TELL HER ONE MORE TIME

Theia is dawn incarnate—Helios himself must've torn night's veil to drape her in molten light. Every loveliness in the cosmos in one heartbeat, one pulse, one radiant body. A fever-dream goddess ablaze in yellow silk, unashamed of her brilliance. She burns the world away, and I want to drown in her glow forever.

Nothing else exists. Not the Imperials closing in from the wings, not the entire Keres Empire baying for my head, not the desecration of a primordial temple.

It doesn't matter that Leni's got a pistol fixed on the emperor's throat, or that Zeke's got Julian face-down in the carpets, humming "Ding Dong, the Witch is Dead" like it's a lullaby.

My universe contracts to one merciless point: Theia.

This is what hope tastes like—sweet, fierce, all-consuming.

If this is all I get, this look, her defiant glare, then it was worth it.

I'd do it again. Risking Zeke's life—he volunteered—to bait Thanatos and then begging the God of Death for access to the Deep Realm.

We stormed in silent and precise: no one killed, no one

broken, barely a ripple. Zeke ran the op like he was ordering pizza. In, out, clean.

Too easy. A God on our side, a path lit straight to the temple, Imperials who fought like novices.

Maybe it's a trap.

I don't care.

I can't look away from Theia.

I crave a thousand lifetimes to memorize the tilt of her jaw, the way her fingers curl white around that bouquet, stems bending under her grip. Every eye weighs on her, but she refuses to duck, refuses to shrink.

Unbreakable. My princess.

The crack of a gunshot shreds the air, and pain explodes in my shoulder. I stagger—and straighten. Pain registers dim, background static. The true agony pulses inside, the shape of her in my head like staring into the sun and hoping not to go blind.

Shadows reel up around me, eager, from the spymaster's side, but I shake my head no. Not now—not when her light has finally found me.

I don't reach for the wound. I'd rather bleed out than break this spell.

Let me drown in this pain. Tear me open. As long as I get to keep staring at her.

She's incandescent, furious.

The crowd veers to chaos. Not my problem.

Another bullet finds me in the frenzy—white heat tears through leather and flesh tearing across my hip.

Theia staggers, pressing a trembling hand to her side, a tortured groan tearing from her throat.

I lurch, scanning her for blood. There is none. It's mine. *My* agony, echoing in her.

Oh Gods. She still feels me. Desperate hope erupts in my chest, followed by rage.

They're hurting her. The Keres don't see her bending,

folding—they don't care. They surge forward with knives, full bloodlust.

"Touch her and we kill your emperor!" My voice booms across the temple.

To emphasize my point, Leni shoves her gun harder into Vasilis's throat. He hisses. "Try me, and I redecorate the dais," she says. "Revenge for my male."

Shadows coil at her feet, snake up her arms, and the male behind her in the same Kevlar I've got smiles like a besotted male. A Fated pair.

The Keres howl for justice. Weapons glint. Zeke's laugh whips out. I palm my Glock.

Theia's voice glides through the tension. "Stand down. No one dies today—not on the new moon. Honor your empress and your Goddess."

The hush is instant, absolute.

She smoothes the dress down her thighs, sucks air through her teeth.

Pride flares in me. She is born to rule them all.

Words clog in my throat. Apologies, explanations, everything I need to tell her.

She stalks toward her throne, and pivots, finger stabbing at Julian under Zeke's boot. "Release him. Now."

Doesn't spare me a glance.

"Theia," I try, miserable, clutching my chest. "Please, let me explain. Let me apologize."

"This isn't the time. Give me Julian. Now." Another command. Beautiful. Unfuckwithable.

Blood pools under my glove but I blink through the haze. "Don't marry him. Not without—just please listen to me first. Let me explain. Please, Theia."

She's over me, ordering Leni to drop her weapon, firing instructions at Zeke.

I should stop. I'm bruised, bleeding, embarrassing myself in real time. I beg anyway.

My knees hit the base of the altar. The pain radiates up the bone like a warning, but it's nothing, less than nothing, compared to the panic that she's about to disappear from my life forever and this is my only shot to claw her back.

"Don't marry him," I beg, voice breaking. "Hate me if you must—but don't—"

She shakes her head, curls dancing. "Give me Julian."

I won' t look away. Even on my knees, I reach for her with every shattered piece of me. "Please. One chance. Just listen."

She glares past me. "Zeke, really, keep it PG. You're ruining Nephene's wedding."

I hear Zeke's "Awe, but I was having fun," before his boot leaves Julian's back.

I try again, words scraping out of my chest like they have claws. "Please, Theia. Just one chance to talk. I need you to hear me. Just once."

I am so locked in on her that Julian scrambling upright doesn't register. I don't hear Zeke's muttering or the loaded silence of every Keres plotting my murder. Then it hits me—

Wait.

"What?" My brain lags, drunk on agony. "*Nephene's* wedding? You're not marrying Julian?"

Theia glares at me. I think Theia's going to hurl her bouquet at my head. But the anger releases, leaving only hurt. "You think I could? You think-"

A sweep of white, so bright it's nearly violent, carves through the mob. Heads snap around. Through the columns, through the fog of dead quiet, Nephene descends. "Unhand my father or I'll have your skulls stuffed and mounted. This fucking nonsense will not be the start of my glorious eternal reign."

## 42

# Theia

## LOVE REFUSED TO STAY BURIED

Keres weddings unfold in three strict acts.

The first is the most mortal. Witnesses gather, a reading of rites and promises that bind, a father gives away his child, pride and sorrow at war in his chest. That's the threshold. Then the part that tastes most Keres: burning ichor into the palms of the consenting, branding flesh with commitment's bite.

And lastly, the step Hera herself demands of wedded pair: consummation.

Down here, it is the groom's sacred responsibility to prepare a space for such togetherness.

Julian's penchant for flair spills over every surface.

Zeke shatters the silence first, nostrils flaring. He sweeps his gaze across the crimson-streaked room we've been herded into and declares with exaggerated flourish, "I'll say it—the art of interior design isn't dead."

Across the room, Leni's tattooed fingers tip a goblet—gleaming iron, rim smeared with emeralds—sending thick pink droplets onto the table. Disgust twists her mouth. "I thought this was a wedding. It feels more like an execution."

The tall shadow lingering at the room's edge—the spy, the

stranger—lets something out like a snort. "This is a practically Keres Disneyland."

"It is not," I snap, wrenching the ceremonial blade from Zeke before he summons Hecate. "It's—" My gaze catches on desiccated petals, paired bejeweled goblets, knives laid casual as cutlery. Heave a sigh. "It's romantic. For Keres at least. It's sweet Julian put in such effort. Especially since Nephene already has a Nevro."

"Sweet as sugar," Zeke confirms.

"Right. And—" My body betrays me, eyes flicking to the door. To the one party crasher who hasn't spoken since Nephene banished us here.

He's a wreck.

Blood seeps from two visible wounds and a dozen more I can smell. His black shirt glistens with the sweat and gunpowder. Black, messy hair curls under his ears, falls into his eyes. No gloves.

He was willing to use his best weapon to get to me.

His pain thrums jagged in my gut.

Last time I saw him, his face was crusted with sand, wrists chained as they towed him away. Now he just stands there, an open wound clad in Kevlar.

My hands itch to reach for him, which isn't fair, because I should be angry, not tender.

"What were you thinking?" I demand, tone sharper than I intend. "Bleeding out on the nuptial runner—you could have died. They all could've."

"I told them not to come."

Leni snorts, leaning into her spymaster. "We've all taken bullets for love. Still breathing."

"Preach," chimes Zeke, mouth packed with dead dahlias.

Fierce affection swells in my chest.

They're a mess. Dirty. Underdressed. Manic. Perhaps insane. Grifting cutlery, threatening my father. But they came for me.

This is the rescue I craved.

I wish I could bottle this moment, mail it to my past self for comfort on those particularly aggressive Mondays.

I'm about to thank them, emotionally, profusely, when Drake's hand finds the small of my back. Warmth and need crackle through fabric. My focus shrinks to that touch.

"Entertain yourselves," he growls at his team as he steers me through a side door, clicking it shut behind us.

It's a bedroom.

There's enough silk and shadowed candlelight to summon Aphrodite—if she were into the whole haunted-cave aesthetic. The arched headboard is centered, gaudy, bedecked with fluffed pillows and crisp white sheets, seduction so loud it might as well scream, "Witness! Bang here!"

Heat flames my cheeks.

Drake releases me, plants four solid feet between us. He doesn't even look at the bed. Like if he pretends hard enough, he can un-invite every memory of us tangled together. "I knew the risk coming here." His gaze locks onto the wall. "I knew I might—"

"Die?" That's his thing, isn't it? Risking everything for me, then fleeing when the danger passes.

He flinches. "I thought—I had to try to-"

"You actually believed I'd marry Julian?"

He nods.

"I'd never marry him."

His face does a thing, surprise and then this weird, wounded hope. "But you agreed to be his wife."

"To save you!"

He shuts his eyes. "Without him … Theia, you can't give up the empire."

My jaw drops. "Are you serious? You think I'd sell myself for power? Marry anyone with a pulse for a crown?"

"That's not …" he starts, but I barrel right through.

"Is that what you believe?" Hurt thickens my voice. "That

the moment I could, I'd swan-dive for a throne and leave you in the dust?"

He takes it. Stands there, shoulders hunched, blood sliding lazily down his arm and into his cuff. He looks ready for me to rip him open, let his shame pour free.

"Is that what I am to you? Some female who values a title more than a soul?"

His jaw works. Pain flares in his eyes. "That's not how I see you. I just—I know how much it hurts to want those things and lose them." His voice is ruined. "I thought if I made myself go, you'd have the chance to belong. To have everything."

"I only ever wanted one thing," I whisper.

Green finds me, haunted and fierce. Nyx, he looks terrible. "I haven't had one sane thought since I walked away. The second I was free, all I did was look back—to you."

The confession sears.

"You deserved the life you asked for. The family, the home. But *Christ*, I lost two days spinning excuses to come back—any scrap of reason—because you're the only thing I want, Theia. You're all I want."

Oh.

He lays it bare, and it shreds me.

Right there. The only thing he wants.

My hands splay over my stomach, squeezing just to check I still exist. "You're not allowed to say things like that," I mutter hoarsely. "And why didn't you tell me about her? My mother."

Haunted eyes lift. The regret there ruinous. "I didn't know. Fuck, Theia, there were enough reasons for me to keep my distance without you being Keres, without you being royalty. I didn't need to look for others. But then Lydia threatened me, said something that made me think … and you started mentioning the war, how Vasilis spoke of his wife—it unlocked something. I knew before I let myself know. I pieced it together."

His hands flex. He watches the middle ground, whispers, "How was I supposed to tell you that it was me? That she asked me to?"

"She asked you …" My mouth dries, understanding bitter. "She asked you to kill her?"

He doesn't answer. Can't. The silence is ugly and hot, the kind that makes your skin crawl and itch to be ripped clean. Drake plants his fists on the dresser, head bowed for sentencing. "She wanted the war to end. She wouldn't give anything up, not even her name, but she said that as long as she lived, fighting wouldn't stop. She asked me to stop it all ... and I did."

It doesn't hurt how I expected. My bruised heart thumps with pride and relief, the throb of surfacing for air after drowning. My mother chose him. Surrendered only to spare her people. Creatures who hated her, and she used Drake as her blade.

I swallow. No words come.

"I'm sorry," he whispers, like he hasn't apologized with every wound he's taken for me already. "I'll never deserve you, Theia. Never. But I can't stop loving you. I want to—I *should*—but I can't. Every step away from you felt like a death, another wound of my own making. You're not something I can survive losing. You are the measure of my life, and without you, everything comes up short."

He draws a ragged breath, shadows dancing on his face. "So yes—I came down here accepting it would end me. I came knowing they'd punish me, ready for pain. I accepted your hatred might be the last thing I ever saw and your father's fangs might bleed me dead."

My heart tightens. "You've always been too brave."

"It wasn't bravery," he insists. "It was refusal. I couldn't live in a world where I had the power to reach for you and chose not to. If my end waited in these tunnels, then at least it would find me walking toward you, not away."

If I could, I'd pin eternity right here and make it promise never to hurt him again.

"I would do it again," he vows, eyes blazing, "just for this. For another look."

I try to wrap my head around it—the idea that this haunted, aching, gorgeous mess before me is the villain in my family's story. The butcher who killed my mother and crumbled my kingdom.

My mother must have known. A Moirai gifted with prophecy, she had to know who he was, who he'd be to me.

"Drake." My hand hovers, useless, before I give in, grab his sleeve, pull him closer. "You're apologizing for giving my empire peace."

He's never looked more pathetic. Or more beautiful.

"I'm apologizing for everything," he murmurs, voice a caress against my skin. "I'll keep apologizing, every hour, every day, if you'll let me. Let me try to fix it. Let me try."

He looks at me like he's already decided he can't survive my answer.

"I'm not good at this." A shake of his head. "But I'll try. I'll try forever if you want." He moves closer, not touching. Air swirls with his scent, eucalyptus and soap and the tang of copper. "My brothers in the guard, my skill with the blade—every shard left in me—they're yours.. I'll wear a gold chest plate or set down the fight forever. Just tell me. If you want to stay with Nephene, have your father lock me up and just promise you'll visit. I'll never leave again, not unless you tell me."

I think I'm smiling. "I won't," I whisper, though he's past listening.

"I'll carry you when you're tired. I'll crush anything that hurts you. I'll dedicate eternity to making you laugh. I swear it."

"You only need fifteen minutes."

"Say you'll let me." His voice is a hitch, a wound. "Say you'll have me. Let me be yours, Theia. I've been a weapon my entire life—let me be your shield instead. I love you."

I'm definitely smiling. I was a fool to think Drake and I were merely Divine chance. We're deliberate design, destiny crafted with precision, sealed in blood and history. My mother's last twist of fate—a secret message for me alone, delivering this male straight to my arms.

My chest folds inward with longing.

I rise on my toes, meeting those sea-green eyes. "No." Nyx, it's easy to say. "I don't want your servitude. I just want you to be with me, the both of us as happy as we can possibly stand."

I don't warn him. Don't blink or think. I lean—happy, light, a female in a pretty dress and the male who descended into the Deep Realm to reclaim her—and I capture his mouth with mine.

43

# Drake

## THE DARKNESS WAS NOT AS SCARY WITH HER IN IT

I don't even breathe at first.

Her lips are soft. Her hands lock firmly in my shirt.

Carefully, I let my palm anchor at the curve of her waist, flat and safe, the fabric bunched between my fingers.

I pull her closer.

She melts up into me, reckless, dazzling, leans in further, takes like I'm the last of air before the world ends.

So careful. So tender.

Then she tilts, parts her lips. Her fangs catch me, drag along my lip—

And that's it, I'm gone.

Suddenly there's not enough time, not enough skin, not enough Theia. I pull her to me, greedy, just this side of desperate. Her mouth opens into mine, drawn tight with hunger, with this force. All of it hits me in the chest like a shot of morphine chased with Adderall, and it's so fucking good. I've never been this hard, never this hot, heart never beat this fast.

Fingertips, smooth as a petal and warm as the sun, stroke my jaw.

My pulse detonates. Glass fills my lungs, everything turns

cold. I break away, back slamming into the wall, chest heaving. The curse, the trigger, old reflexes light up like alarms—

But Theia waits, joy pouring off her. She's pink-cheeked and breathless and her lips are wild with color from where I had her. "What?" she asks.

I can barely get it out, panic chewing up my thoughts. "Are you okay?"

*No*, my brain says. *She can't be. You touched her, she touched you. You felt her fingertips on you—she's in untold agony, that's all you bring. Ruin. Everywhere.*

Her curls bounce, brown skin luminescent in the candlelight. "I'm fine." And then brighter, like this is a joke she gets but I don't: "Drake, I'm fine."

I shake my head. "No. My hands." It stumbles out, a mess. "I touched you, you touched me. It should have—it should have hurt, scared you." I taste the bitterness of it.

Did I block it out? So distracted and obsessed with touching her, holding her, I shoved her fear to the side? Is it bloodless from the bullets? No, they're already healing. Fuck.

I kick off the wall, scrape past the bed, put distance between us. "What have I done?"

"*I* kissed *you*."

"Don't do it again." I can't look at her. Is she shaking? Is she hiding it? What if I broke her? Logic and plans, all that careful speech—it's gone, burnt up in the space between us.

"Drake," she says.

"I'm sorry." I'm sorry, I'm sorry, I'm sorry. Round and round. Two minutes after promising to protect her, I shatter her instead.

I ruin everything.

Like always. Like I said I would. Orpheus in the Underworld, can't hold what I love. Can't follow the fucking rules. Couldn't take the greatest gifts the Gods ever gave.

"Drake, honey."

I glance up, try to read her. All the small changes, the

barely-there tells: tremor in the jaw, tightening around the eyes, that stutter of fear that always comes.

But her voice is steady. "Drake. Really, I'm okay."

She's about to fold in on herself, to fracture. Any minute. A whole-body recoil. Horror and—

"*Butcher*!"

Something snaps. I jerk upright, looking for a fight. But it's only her, cheeks lit up, all that glow, breathing hard, looking at me like I'm the best thing in the room.

She's not afraid. Not even a little.

Zero evidence of agony, of horrors seeding under the surface. My curse is a hammer; it doesn't miss. The curse never misses. It should have unmade her, spilled her open, but it didn't.

I rub at my scalp, try to find words. "You should be …"

Theia's smile could bend iron. "Should be what, Drake?"

I gather myself, taking a step, trying for control. "Reeling. Broken. Scared out of your mind."

I come closer, careful, collecting evidence, waiting for the moment fear will upend her. "You should be afraid."

She just stands there. Soft and warm in candlelight, one palm fixed on her hip, the other clutching the edge of the mattress like kissing me knocked her equilibrium sideways. Her lips curve into a smile that would stop a war.

"You look like you're waiting for me to turn into a bat." She tilts her head, that infamous edge of mischief brightening her eyes. "Even if Keres managed that, I'd end up flapping around as a pigeon."

My throat won't work. "You'd be a dove."

"Stop that look," she tells me. "I'm fine. Still in one piece."

I want to believe her, but chemically, biologically, it does not compute. I grind out my disbelief. "That isn't possible." Each step forward is deliberate, as if she might recoil, show the classic micro-expressions of terror I've learned to expect.

She does not flinch. Just glows. Not even a hint of fear in her eyes.

I'm terrified. "Theia. I touched you. That should have done it." Breathing comes in ugly snatches. "How are you still–" The sentence snags, clots. I feel physically nauseous.

She shrugs. The casual roll of her bare shoulder. "I don't know." Still no tension anywhere; her body only speaks anticipation, the quiet, drowsy twist of her smile making it look easy. Like surviving me is her best party trick.

I close the gap, cautious and clinical, as if a tremor or a wince might finally surface. I brush my fingers along her jaw, half expecting electricity, horror, a plea for mercy.

She closes her eyes.

She fucking leans in. Soaks it in.

The erection's back.

She tips her head again, tiara glinting, and sighs into my palm, a gesture that could bait a titan into war.

"How?" My voice cracks up the middle. "How is this possible? There's never been an exception. Not one. Not since the king's mark. The curse. Every time, it ends the same." My hand shakes against her cheek. "I should have hurt you."

She looks up, all bright, helpless affection. "I have a theory," she says, quiet, like she's bracing for ridicule. "But you're going to say I'm naive, or ridiculously optimistic."

"Go on then," I mutter, thumb coasting along her cheekbone. "Enlighten me."

She looks up, lashes gone star-bright, like she's actually nervous I'll disagree.

"I think my greatest fear is losing you." Theia says it like a confession—the kind that could double as an invocation. "And when you're right here, in front of me, suddenly there's nothing left to be scared of. Which is … weird."

Impossible not to react to that. My insides twist, revolt, and settle into a melt. No clever rebuttal, not when her hands are circling my wrist, not when she's watching me as if I'm the answer she's been writing in the margins all along.

I am wholly unequipped for this. But the next inhale is easier, and her cheek under my palm is so slight I'm afraid even air might bruise her.

My self-control crumbles. "You are—"

Perfect.

Perfect. Perfect.

I haul her to me, distance erased, fist in her hair, mouth on hers.

Theia's lips fit mine like Divine architecture. I lose the physics of my lungs, hunger folding in on itself, inescapable. Her hands find my jaw, my hair, my shirt; now she's clutching at the back of my neck like she is one hundred percent certain I will vanish if she lets up for a breath.

And she's right.

Every time she pulls me closer, the marrow in my bones burns hotter. I anchor my hands at her waist, lever her up against me, chest to chest, both hearts hammering, riotous, every beat a double-dare, a promise. When I taste her again, her mouth is open, fangs slicing at my lip, her whole body tense and alive.

"I've thought about this–dreamed about it, every permutation of what we'd do if I—if we—" I kiss her again, rough, deeper, gather the dress at her hip in my palm and pull her up. She climbs, arms locked around my shoulders, tongue sliding against mine, legs spread around my hips.

Theia sighs, and somehow the sound sticks to the skin of my neck; my whole spine vibrates like she's tuned it with a single, perfectly shaped moan. My hands are everywhere and nowhere at once. Her hair, along her tiara, her back, spread across her ribs, her throat.

I walk us back until her knees hit the mattress edge and our weight tips. Then she's under me, my body in the cradle of her thighs. She pauses, pulls away enough for me to memorize her, hair tousled, cheeks flushed, radiant. As if she's seen something she can't unsee.

I can hear my own voice but it doesn't sound like me: "At night. In the morning. In between fucking breaths. Every minute, every second in the cracks between the life they let us have." I grind in closer, nose to nose, lips grazing, not kissing, not yet, but bleeding tension into the space until she cants her face up, needing it, and I say, "All the wicked things I'd do if I got the chance."

"Yeah?" Breathy, husky.

I fight the urge to kiss her again, fuck my confession. "I wrote it down. Everything I'd do. A ledger of where I'd suck and lick, find what made you scream versus beg, which flavor of you would ruin me first, which ones I'd have to work up to." I breathe in vanilla. Sweet. Beautiful. "How I want to take you apart with just my hands, bare, no fucking gloves, until you come undone so many times you forget what it's like being whole. I catalogued all of that. And the rest too."

"The rest?"

My hands go north, tracing the line of her spine, every vertebra a sacred bead in the rosary of her body. "The quiet things. Tracing your cheek, having your hair brush my chest, tucking my face into your neck and just inhaling. Covering your heart with my palm, just to feel how it beats. Just—"

Loving her.

There's a catch in her breath, and her hands go gentle, thumbs on my jaw, smoothing me down, sculpting her devil into something almost beautiful. I can't look away from her, and I don't want to.

Then she says, "I've imagined biting you."

It's a sledgehammer straight to the solar plexus. I almost want to bust out laughing, or maybe drop to my knees and beg, but instead, I grab her by the jaw and crash our mouths together until I can't feel my lips. It isn't enough. It'll never be enough.

We're already tangled up. She goes for my neck, arms tight, and I'm steering us higher on the bed, crawling over her. Her thighs clamp around my hips, greedy, and she's yanking at my shirt, clearly not satisfied with anything less than skin-on-skin. She whines into my mouth. Nails bite my abs.

What's the word for craving someone so bad you forget what normal ever felt like? There should be one.

All I want is for her to remember this, the precise way I am making her lose her mind. Like, centuries from now, after we're both toast and the world's decided to get fancy and carve our names in stone, she'll still remember how much she wanted this.

My heart pounds. I'm kissing down her neck, her collarbone, pulling her dress. The pounding is so hard, so loud it fills my ears.

No.

That's not me. It's something external. Next room over. Some idiot slams a door. Glass shatters. Shouting, rough and urgent, slicing through the moment like someone drop-kicked a grenade on the pillows.

Then, a bullet bursts through the door.

# 44

## Theia

### LOVE IS RECKLESS

No way and never again.

The days of Drake volunteering to play bullet sponge on my behalf are over.

I burst through the door before he can close it, crash into his bare back, then stumble into a room, that twenty minutes earlier held zero bloodshed.

Zeke's got a fistful of his own bicep, cheery pink blood seeping through his fingers. Leni—all tattoos and hair dye—is mid-apology.

"It's about time, really," Zeke assures. "Haven't had a fatal wound in almost ten hours."

"Fatal wounds require you to die." The male wrapped in shadows rolls his palm over the barrel of the gun in Leni's hand. "Honestly, I think you're getting better," he murmurs to her, which is either Stockholm syndrome or true romance. He disarms her with the same tenderness most people reserve for kittens and fancy cheeses.

Drake's hand finds mine, locks our fingers together and reels me into him until we're flush, shoulder to hip. "And why are you shooting at each other?"

Zeke shrugs, delighted despite the pink leaking down his arm. "That one got all fangy," he says, nodding at the door.

"It's not my fault, she's trigger happy," Greta cuts in from the open doorway. Her dress is brown and billowy, with gossamer sleeves but her expression is sharp enough to fillet a mosquito. "And I didn't 'get fangy'. I *have* fangs." She flashes them; tongue skimming the points. "That bullet didn't get within six feet of me. Good for your aorta's sake, and bad for my entertainment."

"I'm glad you're unharmed," I tell her, bridging the gap between my insane rescue squad and my Nevro-in-law.

She lands on me instantly, eyes skimming over my disaster hair, the wrinkled dress, my portable support system named Drake. "There you are. Finally. Nephene demands your presence. There is, technically, still a wedding taking place."

Right. That.

My cheeks burn. Full heatstroke, up through my ears and down my neck.

Got slightly distracted trying to swallow Drake's tongue.

"Yes, okay. Of course! I'm coming. Give me a moment to freshen up."

But drake's already on it. Straightening my sleeves, smoothing the ruffled carnage of silk at my collar, flattening creases from my hips. There's nothing we can do about the big red stains everywhere his hands have been, but still he licks his thumb to wipe blood off my cheek, tilts my chin to check my hair for shrapnel.

It's innocent. And thrilling.

His touch lingers at my wrist, my throat, that soft, ticklish divot beneath my ear. I could melt through the floor. Then he pulls back.

His mouth curves into something small and smug. "Perfect."

The unspoken message blazes between us: *perfect* when

you're disheveled because of me, *perfect* when you're dizzy from my hands, *perfect* when you threaten to bite.

I short-circuit.

"Ready," I announce, radiating 'faking normal' so hard I'm surprised no one throws confetti.

Greta makes a disgusted noise. "No. Her Imperial Highness-to-be wants you both." She gestures impatiently at Drake, exasperation reaching new heights. "And she's not known for patience."

Both of us?

"Not to be weird," Zeke says, no longer staunching his wound, but jabbing at it, "but is anyone else worried that the last time Drake was in that room, he got shot?"

The memory overtakes me—Drake face-down in the sand, Nephene's gun at his head.

His hand rips away from mine like I burned him.

His eyes go dark with something I don't have a name for. Did he just—

I was afraid.

And he felt it.

# 45

## Theia

### LOVE BEGS TO BE SEEN

The knot in my stomach unwinds when I see the bow.

It's monstrous. Ridiculous. An actual ivory chariot's worth of silk, stitched to the back of Nephene's dress in a feat of engineering that must've reduced a dozen seamstresses to tears. It's so big it flirts with the horizon.

Unspooled, it's long enough to lasso an entire pack of Lycaons and drag them straight through the Shadowlands.

Nephene owns it.

She stands at the altar, chin up, jaw ready to shred any critic to pieces. The white layers of her sleeves catch every flicker of candlelight, turning her shoulders gladiator-broad. Her hair gleams, big sweeping curls pinned down, waiting for the crown, and somewhere in all that perfection is the bow. Bright, unrepentant, flipping the bird to every ancestor who ever muttered about tradition.

"If I'm going to do the fucking wedding thing, let's fucking do it," she'd insisted. "Make. It. Bigger."

She never budged.

Each time a seamstress sobbed into her pincushion, Nephene doubled down. More. Bigger. Bolder.

Every ounce of froth and silk became a dare. I watched it

with a growing disbelief simmering in my sternum—not horror, but awe. Because every time Nephene threatened apocalypse unless the lace was two shades whiter, the sleeves more voluminous, the bow itself approaching weaponized, Greta would smirk.

A private joke hovered at the corner of her mouth.

Nephene saw each one.

Heard each snicker, each hiccup of glee.

Almost as if the only reason Nephene demanded the gown of the millennia was to help Greta get through the ceremony without crying.

My sister is a killer, but she is not heartless.

I want to reach back, tear a strip off Nephene's train and wrap it around Greta's heart so nothing can bruise it. But progress is slow. The Munera is not open to females. Not yet.

Nephene will change that.

She'll sweep in progress, raise the Keres from the dark and lead them to conquer. For now, she'll live two lives. One with her husband as a leader. The other with her Nevro as a partner.

"Get up here," Nephene snaps. She doesn't even bother to lower her voice.

Drake tenses beside me. For one terrible second, I wonder if he'll turn and shoot the door off its hinges so we can bolt. But no, he squares his shoulders, grabs my hand, and leads me back down the aisle.

Every single Keres tracks us. The emperor. The councilors. Some female with a hat that looks like it ate a squirrel. My chest does this horrible up-down flutter, like a sparrow staged a coup in my ribcage.

Nephene taps her foot on the dais, hands folded in front of her, sleeves massive and white and totally uncompromising. Julian flanks her, looking like he wanted this to be over three hours ago. Behind them is our father, who is actually smiling, really smiling, like Nephene and I are five years old in matching pigtails.

"You took long enough," she tells Drake, voice carrying to the back row and the black tunnels beyond. No threat of death. Not even a slap. "How much easier could I have made it for you to infiltrate? Glow-in-the-dark signs? You waited til the last minute."

Julian's eye twitches. Father is unsurprised. Someone in the peanut gallery makes a noise suspiciously like a gasp.

"I heard a gunshot," she says to me.

I hear the unasked question. "Greta's fine." She eases slightly. "It was—"

"I do not care. It's time." She flips her hair, waving for Julian to move slightly left and gesturing for me and Drake to fill the gap. "Since you two are here and already attached at the soul, we might as well do this."

Drake's hand clamps tighter. Not pain. Just the weight of him, sure as anchors and old myths.

"Do what?" I ask.

Nephene rolls her eyes like I've just asked the difference between a femur and a tibia. "Get married, sister." She glances at Drake, who stands so still it's like someone forgot to animate his spirit, then back at me. "A proper Keres ceremony. No mortal half-measures."

I blink. "But I thought–"

"You're Nevros, aren't you?" She deploys the word like a classified weapon. "I may not be omniscient, but I am trained to identify my enemy's pressure points." She angles her head at Father, a dare in her eyes. "With your approval, Sovereign."

Vasilis looks at me. The intensity is like a chemistry experiment gone off the rails. "Is this what you want, Theia?"

It's the first time he's called me that. Theia. Not daughter, dear, princess.

"Mother would approve," I say, necklace burning against

my throat with sweet pain. "He's more than my Nevro. He's… everything. I think she made it so we'd meet."

He has reservations. Objections. But he learned not to second guess his Nevro's prophecies. He nods. "It is done then. My last act as emperor."

I start to turn, already happy about a thousand things, when a flash of panic scurries through my head: Did anyone ask Drake? Is this a shotgun wedding? But he's already looking at me, nodding. His thumb circles my palm, the tiniest drag of skin to skin, a private communion.

A universe opens in the space between his thumb and my palm. Warmth, static, the burn of new nerves catching each other and taking flight. I imagined a wedding would feel like this. Dizzy. A little violent. Like being chewed up and spit out by Fate's teeth. Every inhale tastes brighter, easier.

It goes fast.

Drake's fingers stay locked around mine as he makes Keres promises, Divine vows, mortal platitudes.

Tears salt down my jaw. I repeat everything I'm supposed to. Drake adds his own line to the end.

I echo that too, "I love you."

And then Imperials rush in, guns drawn, knives out. "Siege!"

# 46

## Theia

### LOVE DOES NOT WALK AWAY

I imagined my wedding day about one million times. Embracing on the bow of a cruise ship in matching speedos. Floating on an iceberg sealed with a nose kiss. In a log cabin surrounded by my friends turned family, toasting with roasted marshmallows.

Never once did I imagine the Blackguard present in a kill formation at the treeline, every last one of them locked and loaded and radiating wedding-crasher energy.

Except. Here they are, the sunrise banking behind them.

Lev, most likely to break necks first, ask questions later, towers with his arms crossed. Atlas stands with black hair slicked back smooth, grenade launcher slung casual at his hip. Sin hunches over a crossbow the size of a toddler. Nat glowers beneath a gold helmet that looks imported straight from Sparta, spiked and mean as a heart attack.

Drake's hold tightens at my waist, the dank smell of the tunnels falling off his skin. "Stand down. We're good."

"You're good?" Sin's voice drops low, disbelieving. "That's it?"

My Fated shrugs. "The Emperor gave me his blessing."

Zeke holds up his arm, hole and all, cheery: "I did get shot, though."

With lethal calm, Atlas asks, "By whom?"

Leni tips her chin at Zeke. "Me!" she says it like a badge, like she'd drill him again right now if a blue ribbon was on the table.

Lev makes the sound of a freight train. Atlas is all cold assessment, tracking with a tense jaw how Drake rotates to shield me—a reflex baked into bone.

Sin rises to his full height, ditching his arrow in its sheath. "Beautiful. All together again. Big happy family. Right, babe?"

Nat yanks her helmet back. "I was promised carnage. My one chance to poke the swarm of Keres."

"Babe, you can't keep instigating wars in this state."

"Don't you tell me what to do." She snaps round to me. "And *you*!" She pauses, zeros in on my hand clasped in Drake's, skin to skin. "What the fuck? You're touching him?" Three strides and she's on me, clamping my wrist, peeling me away. "And what—what's that on your hand?"

She jerks my hand up, thumb scraping the red spiral burnt into the palm. The mark of a Nevro pair, the swirl of night, branded using Nyx's ichor. It's beautiful and romantic, a match to the mark my father painted on Drake's hand. Nat looks ready to commit a massacre.

"What have you done, butcher?" she snarls, full tilt fury, glaring over her war helmet like I've tattooed 'please avenge me' on my own forehead. "I'll crack your bones with my teeth and feed you to the river Lethe."

My heart swells. She's gonna be a great mom.

Drake covers his male parts.

"Babe," Sin's voice is honey poured over gravel, soothing as he places wide, ring bedecked hands on her shoulders. "We like Drakey, remember?"

"He hurt Theia. I'll kill him."

She's so sweet.

I throw my arms around her neck and squeeze.

Drake thinks I have no concept of self-preservation. *I* think homicidal holes in hearts can be patched with tight hugs.

She's tense as a caged thunderstorm, but I hang on, cheek pressed to her breastplate, voice muffled. "I knew you'd come. I'm so happy you're here! I missed you."

She shakes, full-body, as if I tackled the wind out of her. Wrestles my arms off, takes a hard look at my face, searching for signs of trauma. "You're not hurt?"

"Nope. Not even a scratch." I waggle my hand at her, showing off the spiral, proud as Demeter with a fresh sown field. "I said please and thank you for this. Please don't decapitate anyone."

"I don't just decapitate everyone," she grumbles.

I gather her back up in a hug, clinging like a barnacle to a warship. "There is *so much* I need to tell you. There were husband trials. My grandpa was a conqueror! Oh! I have a sister."

"I thought we were sisters." She's grumpy. Maybe jealous.

Good Goddess Nyx, I missed her. "No, see, to be sisters you have to almost marry the same male that neither one of you really wants."

"Never did that with my sisters."

"Huh, I figured we'd have that in common since we're both cave dwellers."

"The Underworld is not a dingy cave. It's a majestic realm that—"

I've heard it before. "Wait, wait—the ichor pool! That's where to start. It's so creepy and it smells like you."

I peel back to beam at her big scowl. Find her kill stare fixed on Drake and tug at her gold vambrace. "How's my little wittle future Demigod? Aren't you supposed to be resting?" I turn my own glare on Sin.

He shrugs it off like a mosquito.

"Resting." She spits the word. "I'm a Fury. Avenging my friends is like naptime."

Only a Fury could mean it. I collapse, boneless, into her arms, cheek to her collarbone, letting her rage eat the world for me. "I could nap for a month."

Sin lounges at the edge of the kill-ring, mouth slick with a grin, catching Nat and me like pay-per-view. "She hugs better than you, babe."

"Your taste in hugs is suspect," Nat returns, but she relaxes a millimeter, like maybe, just maybe, she's not going to commit homicide tonight. Unless provoked.

None of this registers for Rune, who's been staring at me with a religious awe, except more like he's just spotted Typhon at the company picnic.

I smile at him.

He trips, actually trips backward. "Your fangs. Holy Hestia—"

Oh right. I slap a hand over my mouth—or, I try, except Drake snatches my wrist midair and pulls it into his side, leaving nothing between us.

"I see you checking out her mouth like that again and I'll take a blade to your spine," Drake says. No rise or fall. Just death on the tongue.

Rune nods, a bit haunted, but Atlas is on to the next, unimpressed. "No more unscheduled trips, yeah?"

Drake's nod is stone, his hold on my shoulder becomes a fortress, tender and unmovable.

Sin tucks an arrow behind his ear. "So a Keres, huh. Excellent choice of lover. The nastier the better in my opinion."

Nat slams an elbow into his ribs. Sin grunts. Keeps the smirk.

"Half," I correct, wiggling tighter to Drake. "Half Keres, half Moirai."

Atlas's head notches up. "The Keres don't have half-breeds. Kadmos—"

"Found her," Drake cuts in. "Kadmos discovered Theia existed and branded her himself. Snatched her mother to dissect the anomaly—to replicate it."

"He branded her?" Nat's furious again. "That fucking—"

Atlas interrupts. "Theia would've been an outcast. The Keres wouldn't tolerate a half-breed. They'd have made her an example. They're too emotional, too bound by dogma. Kadmos taking you saved your life."

I envision the gallery of leaders, absent of my mother. Atlas is right. "I suppose I should thank him."

"For locking you away?" Drake asks, oddly sharp. "Kadmos swore to end the hiding. To stop apologizing for creatures' existence and then shoved you into a cell."

Atlas answers hushed, head low. "He didn't promise kindness. He promised certainty. One future, united. No wars, no in-betweens. Theia could resolve everything."

Zeke stirs, chin lifting. "I bear the sin so they might live." The words slide through him, raw and scalding, like an exorcism. He stands with bullet-mangled hand raised to the horizon in a mock salute. "I will take the first step. I will bear the cost. I will be the shield, but I will not drag you behind me. Walk with me. And if I fail you–then let history call me monster so long as it never calls you forgotten."

The speech clings to the forest, resin-thick, caught in the cracks of every gnarled tree.

Atlas's head tilts, just a hair, calculation in his navy eyes—counting costs, weighing a future with a monster at the helm against a present full of ghosts. Sin's mouth is twisted up like he's biting down on a memory, refusing to swallow it. Leni's eyes go distant as she considers this. Even Nat, who hates speeches the way most people hate food poisoning, lets it wrap around her.

Drake is somehow closer than before, arm tight around my waist.

Zeke's hand wavers, turns until he's staring at his palm, as if there exist answers in the lines. Or the glistening hole. "That's the speech that made me a believer," he admits, voice shrunk back to its normal octave. "Leaders have to make hard choices, or someone else does it for you."

"Theia's life was never his to decide," Drake argues in a tone none of his brothers have heard from him. Too passionate.

Nyx, he's sexy when he's overprotective.

I kiss his palm. "It's okay. I'm here now. In a way, Kadmos brought us together." I smile at him, then at the infamous Blackguards. "Not that he ever needed to study me. I know exactly why I'm not all Keres."

Atlas and Drake snap up straight, stiff-backed, like generals sensing a surprise attack, shoulders set in carbon copy. Sin's face is suddenly, violently attentive. Even the forest seems to lean in.

"What do you mean?" Atlas's tone is soft, but there's a bullet in the chamber, ready to fly.

I try to think of the right way to explain, Something poetic, or at least not embarrassing. Instead, my mouth coughs up, "It's never made sense that the Keres can't have half-bloods. I mean, every other creature has them. Scylla marry Dryads, there are Maenad-Minotaur hybrids, Silenus and Chimera cannot stop populating the realm. But not Keres. Never Keres. Isn't that strange?"

They stare. Silent.

I raise my chin. "Isn't it obvious why? The Keres spat in the Moirai's face—they denied prophecy."

"What does destiny have to do with genetics?" Rune asks, arms folded so tight his biceps bulge.

"We're not mortals. Not ruled by cells and code. We're shackled by Divinity. Every creature feeds a prophecy. But the

Keres forsake prophecy, blaspheme the Moirai. Why would the Gods grant them children tangled with Fate? The Gods loathe independence, unless they grow bored and want a new flavor."

Sin smirks. "Go on, tell us how you taste."

I ignore him, determined not to blush. "My mother was Moirai, my father Keres. They should have ripped each other apart. Instead? They fell in love. Their union was Fated. Thereby defying tradition by setting a Keres on a path of destiny, toward belief in the Gods. That's how I exist."

Zeke lets out a reverent little whistle. Like he just watched me pull a rabbit, a coin, and possibly the next emperor out of my sleeve. "So you're, what, God-touched? Like Achilles?"

I shrug. "Touched, slapped, possibly kissed by a Muse. It's not Keres biology that rejects outsiders. It's their hubris in dishonoring the Gods, and being too fucking terrifying for anyone to punish them. When Vasilis bent to Fate, the Gods rewarded him. With me."

I brace for questions. For disgust. For a light exorcism. Drake too. Arm cinching like a tourniquet, thumb moving over the burn on my shoulder, again and again, as if physical repetition might remind him he likes these people and loves his king.

Nat frowns. "So the Gods made you out of spite."

"It seems so."

Nat smirks. "Fucking love it."

All the tension falls away.

Drake kisses my forehead, as if sealing the fact of me. "Now stop staring at her like she's grown a second head. This is Theia. You know her. Extra loud laugh, all the optimism, still convinced pony rides solve blood feuds. Only difference is now she's my wife."

I consider a happy dance. *His. Wife.*

Leni says something. Maybe 'also a princess,' and Lev

might add that I do have fangs now, but Atlas nods and Sin's smiling. None of them see how Nat's begun to vibrate.

I step between her and Drake, hands raised. "Now Nat, remember to be calm for your health and that you also fell in love—"

"Did he say *wife*?"

# 47

## Theia

### AND HE'D MISSED HER

"Stop with the face."

Nat makes the face harder, arms folded tight, death stance softening slightly as she adjusts her elbows around her pregnant belly. "You got married without me."

I've already offered her my best defenses:

"You would've slaughtered the entire guest list."

"Blood triggers your morning sickness."

"It wasn't exactly planned."

But she's demolished each excuse with classic Fury logic: "Not you." "I have a bucket." And "I don't believe you."

Time for the nuclear option—the friendship trump card. "Can you remind me which one of us fell madly in love with a literal Demigod while I was waist-deep in dungeon dust?"

Her eyes flash, slit-thin, nostrils flaring. "At least I didn't elope."

"Sweet Gods, you're as unreasonable as Zeus!"

She snorts, a hair's breadth from violence, but her arms loosen, elbows easing around her stomach. She won't admit it, but my shot hits the mark.

Sin appears at her left, cutting a circuit on the makeshift dance floor waiting room, a bottle of merlot in his grip. He's impossible to miss: crop top, flower-printed jeans, a beautiful cocktail of reckless joy. "Darling, don't hassle the bride."

Natasa growls but lets him fold her close. "If you say the word elope again, I'll drag you out of here and make you run laps."

I surrender, hands up. "Never again."

She tips her chin up, watching me, totally undeceived. The glow in her eyes isn't anger anymore—it's pride, maybe, or something like love, dressed up as menace. She radiates so much power, even standing still, that all the dogs in the wire pens angle their muzzles toward her, reading her as the new pack leader. Which, let's be real, she probably is.

A terrier in a cone rockets past my heels, yipping. High on Sin's steady stream of joy, it full-body wriggles until it upends an entire tray of bandages and syringes. Nat watches the mess, unimpressed. She's immune to her Fated's ability.

"That one's got your energy," she drawls to him, nodding at the dog.

The furball has a lazy eye, a glob of drool, and a wagging tail.

I grin. Maybe I can't get drunk, but Sin's gift gives me a floaty, weightless buzz.

Strong arms catch me from behind, warm and certain. I fall into the wall without thinking.

Maybe it isn't Sin at all.

I melt against Drake and his minty earthy scent, letting him wrap me up too tight, too greedy. I tuck my nose to his throat, press a kiss there, breathing him in. "And where have you been?"

"Arming myself with tranquilizers," he tells me, voice rumbling sweetly up my back.

I laugh. "Tranqs won't slow Nat."

"They're for me. I want to be knocked out when she tears me limb from limb."

I twist in the circle of his arms, lock my hands at the base of his neck, refusing anything but full contact. "Imagine ever thinking you couldn't make me laugh."

He glances away, mouth twitching—not quite a smile, more like he's swallowing the urge. "I thought terrifying you was the greater risk."

"And yet. Here I am," I say, hands perma-linked behind his neck, fingers combing his hair. We're married now, which means the rules have changed: I'm allowed all the clutching, the public displays, the obscene flirtations.

A loud, drunken whoop echoes from the other end of the clinic. Sin has coaxed Nat into a sort of dance; he attempts a half-spin, but is only semi-successful, owing to the facts: 1) Nat is encased in full battle armor; 2) she never agreed to tango; 3) infuriating him is how she flirts. Liquor sloshes across the floor. The terrier laps it up, fueled by chaos, cartwheels into Nat's boots, then springs up.

Nat glares at the dog, then at me, then at her Fated. I watch her try to not smile. She fails. The edge of it is pure homicide, but there's a genuine curve in the middle, where the violence gives way to something softer. She lets Sin spin her.

Romance. It's in the air.

The slightly wet-dog-scented air.

Yes, the vet clinic's waiting room is my wedding reception. Not a joke. This is it: civilization's best and only option, in all its harshly lit, beige-splashed glory.

Dogs and cats—an extremely fat rabbit—in various states of cone and recovery frolic across the tile, all of them basking in Sin's charm, and strung out on the cannolis dispensed with open bar abandon.

We didn't have many choices. No last minute venue but the local vet would ignore heavily armed creatures. The place is run by Asclepiades, who deworm ferrets by day and unknot Gorgon hair by night, committed to healing any and all. For a price. Atlas paved the way with his rescue donations flowing like bribes. Not to mention, the Blackguard practically funded their mobile neutering van with what he spent rehabilitating the females they freed with me. Factor in Nat's blood oath not to invite any of her homicidal sisters, and the deal was officially sealed. party commence.

It is not, I repeat, not a Keres party.

Every surface is sticky with celebration. Every cup filled with Sin's signature cocktail—nuclear bright crème de menthe served in beakers. Music bleeds out of a Bluetooth speaker so old it might pre-date the Titans. The bass makes my ribs vibrate—and Luke, who seems to know the words to every song, and has had enough of the neon concoction to loudly prove it.

Nat's laugh bounces off the tile, echoes so wild that a mutt behind the counter howls in support. Sin bows grandly, sweeping Nat toward collision with a circle of Asclepiades drinking straight from test tubes.

They dodge. Sin apologizes. Miraculously, Nat doesn't break his neck.

I watch, waiting for that old, bitter edge of jealousy—the flavor that's haunted me my whole life, the reminder I'm forever on the outside peering in. It isn't there. Not a trace.

My heart is delightfully light. I chase the new feeling, let it work itself into every battered, newly mended piece of my soul.

If you'd told me a year ago I'd end up here—in a vet clinic, post-wedding, complete with full-service dog bar, black and pink confetti, emotional support limoncello, and the finest creatures in the world—I'd have called an ambulance for you.

Nat's doing a brutal two-step with Sin and half-demolishing the floor. Dogs trip in circles. Healers sway in corners. Lev and the spymaster wrestle on the floor for custody of a muscly lapdog with a purple cast. Leni sits luminous, neon-pink heels neatly crossed, shadows wrapping her like a cloak as she hustles an unsuspecting vet-tech.

Rune is hacking a karaoke mic with a dental drill. Zeke

has built a cone-of-shame hat pyramid on the check-in desk. He's bleeding from somewhere, the pink shimmering in the disco light.

This is my life.

I'm not the Empress of the Sunless Kingdom, or a Moirai oracle. Not an experiment in a cell.

I'm just Theia. Preferably lowercase. Preferably with nap breaks.

And all of this—all the wild and mess and nonsensical violence—is mine.

Ours.

Drake's arms cinch around my waist, wedging him so close the static of my thoughts pops and settles. He's suctioned to my back, chin tucked against my shoulder, breath hot behind my ear. I want to climb him like a tree.

I lean back into him, full force, until our ribs slot together, puzzle pieces with a mutual vendetta against common sense.

"Nephene would love Nat," I say, and *wow*, the feeling that gives me could knock a couple planets off their axes.

Drake hums low in my ear, sounding like someone forced to imagine a breakfast meeting between a chainsaw and a tornado. And if that feels like a wedding toast, well, welcome to our world. "They would have the Titans on a leash by, what, Wednesday?"

Probably.

And I'd make sure it was rhinestoned.

"This is it," I tell him. "This is everything I dreamed of."

His mouth finds my throat, heat and stubble dragging against my pulse. "You always wanted a groom with bullets still inside him and no ring?"

"Rings are for mortals." I tip my head back, meet the hollowed dark of his gaze. He follows, kissing the side of my jaw, the soft beneath my ear, the spot that might have been made just for his mouth. It's better than the swirl cake, better than sugar. "And I like the scent of your blood. Almost as much as drinking it."

He smiles—a real one. His fists tangle in my hair, winding, refusing to let go. "Then drink it."

I scoff at him, but the ache is already there, a pressure in my gums, fangs extended. "There's only graduated cylinders left, and I don't want the taste of you diluted by bleach and bovine sedatives."

"So, drink from me." The offer burns against the shell of my ear, and this is how it feels to have the world tilt, or just the vet-clinic linoleum? My knees may or may not be functioning, which is inconvenient, as they're the only thing between my butt and a pile of K9 Recovery blankies.

Drake makes it worse by carding his fingers through my hair, slow and a little too reverent for a male who's just been shot and married, in that order. "Drink from me," he repeats, patient and insistent.

"You're still healing. And what if I drool? I'm not staining this poor vet's floor. Or your shirt."

He shrugs, unconcerned, and cradles my chin in his palm. "Stain it."

We're moving lightly, swaying to the music. Our first dance.

"Please sweetheart. Drink from me." It's a plea. A dare. A Divine commandment, his lips lost in my hair, his hard length at my back.

The entire clinic is noise and chaos—dogs yapping, Nat and Sin waltzing like a murder-suicide pact, Luke and Zeke howling karaoke straight from the jaws of Tartarus. But everything inside me shrinks to this: Drake, skin so close it chokes, eucalyptus scent like a personal spa retreat, and the constant hungry red heat running from the base of my ribs to my tongue.

I want him. I want him now. I want to taste the thing that ruined me and rebuilt me and clawed itself behind my heart.

It's overwhelming. There's so much hunger, it could paralyze an elephant, swallow the clinic whole, devour the sun right out of the sky. My stomach does a triple barrel-roll, hyper-bright and white-hot.

And beneath the need, something else ebbs. Something black and spiky and mean. The memory, the echo of what happens when I let myself drink, not just for pleasure, but for real.

Fear, bitter as spoiled roofies, surges up behind my teeth.

Drake doesn't seem to notice. Or scratch that. He does. He's just fearless, or accepting that if I kill him, then that's how he'd most like to go. He tilts my chin up, and there's this look in his green eyes—a look like he's already decided he's going to let me bite him, let me do anything, if I just say the word.

I sigh. "I love your eyes. The endless green."

A raise of his dark brow. "They're brown."

"What?" I spin, grab his cheeks. "No. No way."

"I guess my ma called them hazel, but not green. Never green."

It's not the best lighting, but—"Oh, I guess there is some brown there. I only ever noticed the green."

He kisses me, light, wonderful, sets our foreheads together. "Yeah, I believe that." A beat. "Bite me, sweetheart."

It should be hot. Should set the whole room on fire, melt my spine, short-circuit my brain. It's my fantasy.

But the second he angles his throat at me, my body slams on the brakes. Suddenly I'm not staring at Drake at all—I'm staring down at a body on the ground, limp and white and absolutely, unequivocally dead. Not a scratch of warmth in his cheeks, not a ghost of green in his gaze. Just an empty vessel.

I jerk back so violently I almost catch him in the jaw.

The fear flows to him through our connection, but Drake doesn't let go. He takes my hand, pitches his voice low, no room for argument. "Anyone you want to say goodbye to?"

"Everyone," I blurt. Lame, but one hundred percent true. "I mean. This is our party. Shouldn't we stay? There's cake. There's a cannoli bar. If we leave now, Leni's going to win the poker tournament."

"She will," he agrees as he hauls me through the party. A distinct shake of his head at anyone approaching sends them away.

"This is one party where everyone expects us to leave," he tells me over his shoulder, gaze on my mouth, my neck, my body. "A place for them to kill time until we finish."

"Finish?"

A smirk, a squeeze of his hand. "If we can find it in ourselves to stop."

48

# Theia

AND HE COULDN'T BEAR FACING
THE SUN WITHOUT HER AT HIS SIDE

"Is this your kink? Freaky bathroom stuff in front of the mirror?"

"Do you think this is how I'd break it to you?" Drake asks, guiding me past the threshold with steady hands at my hips.

On the drive over, I'd anticipated a mauling in the driveway, the front door shouldering open in desperation, both of us stumbling up the stairs, clothes torn and scattered.

But Drake, despite never really letting me go, he's kept us at arm's length. Opening my car door, unbuckling my seatbelt, hauling me into his arms to carry me into the Blackguard's safehouse. Not setting me down until we're inside his rooms.

It's not much. A desk smothered in paperwork, a bed so crisply made it looks fake.

And he steered me away from all of it.

"Are you one of those people who needs to shower before sex?" I ask. "Because I don't mind the blood on you. Or the sweat."

A sly smile ripples across his mouth. Then, seamless, he lifts me, palms curling around my waist and sets me on the counter beside the sink.

He plants a palm on my thigh, so broad it nearly spans it. A barricade in case I try to bolt.

As if.

Sunlight angles down from the skylight, a flood so gold it bruises, and I tilt into it, greedy for the glow, letting it burn right through me.

Drake's reflection darkens in the mirror behind me. He stares, just stares, like I'm a sunrise that makes his retinas ache.

His thumb drags a lazy line along my thigh. The contact brands. "You're beautiful," he says, soft, almost self-indicting. "I don't know how you could ever have considered giving up the sun. Not…not when it loves you like this."

"I went without it for decades. I survived. I don't know how *you* ever thought you could give up me."

Drake shakes his head, jaw working, hands flexing slightly too tight, like my body is precious cargo he'll break if he tries to hold it all at once. "I didn't last an hour, Theia. Not ten minutes before I realized doing the right thing might fucking kill me."

A rush floods my chest, wild and sharp and happy as hot coffee at three a.m. I catch his shirt, yank him closer just to breathe his air. "I never wanted that. I didn't belong there. They didn't understand me."

"They're not exactly a happy-go-ducky crowd."

"Happy-go …" My laugh chases a smile up my face, my heart stinging with want. "I love you, Drake."

A kiss. Too light, too shallow. He murmurs, "I have loved you, Theia, and I will keep on loving you until Thanatos claims me."

He kisses my cheek, delicate. My jaw, gentler.

I rake his hair back, smoothing it out of his eyes. "Still can't believe he's my family."

"I'm your family."

Another kiss, deeper, beautiful. Lingering.

Then: "It's time, Theia. You need to drink."

My fangs drop instantly, but I say, "I'm not that hungry. It's only been a few days. I've gone longer."

"Not anymore."

Just like that.

I touch his cheek. "You need time to heal."

He doesn't answer. Just shrugs out of his jacket, movements deliberate, rolling every muscle in his shoulders. The black long-sleeve is next, peeled up and pulled over his head. Anger breaks through me at the bruises along his chest, the bullet hole above his belt, still leaking.

"Drake," I say, a chide, but he grabs my hands and lays them over his chest as if I'm the only thing he wants against the ache.

"The curse is slowing my healing," he admits, voice rough. "But when you're touching me, that's all I can feel."

Beneath my palms, his heartbeat is thunder, muscle rigid and ready. His torso is all stark planes and deep-cut valleys. I trail my hands along each carved ridge, delighting in his shudder.

"How many teeth marks do you think you could fit on one body?" I murmur, hypnotized by the way his stomach tenses. "Is it possible to run out of space?"

Drake's mouth twitches with something dark and owned. He rocks forward, both hands bracing my hips, his hair messy and onyx dark in daylight. He's got me caged, utterly, and I'm not pretending I want anything else. If I could have him branded across every cell, I would.

His fingers slip behind my jaw, tilting my face up. He kisses me. My toes curl in my shoes, my palms finding little homes on the hard edges of his stomach. His tongue brushes my fang, and reality blurs.

"Drink," he murmurs against my mouth.

"Drake—"

"We're in a bathroom where it's fine to spill. You won't stain my shirt. If you take too much, you know what I'll do?"

I shake my head, mute.

"Die fucking happy."

"That's not funny."

He's already kissing me again. Drugging, dark. "I'll stop you, sweetheart."

"You can't." We both know it's true. "I'm stronger. I'll—"

Another kiss. A bribe. A dare. He wants me to taste him so badly I can feel it crawling up my veins. He smells so good there should be a warning label. "Bite me, Theia," he hums.

He gives me a look I will never, never not crave, and drags my hand up to his throat. "Here," he says, offering the best part of himself for me to ruin. "Come on, sweetheart. Don't make me beg."

I've seen him on his knees enough this day. "Last chance to change your mind. You sure you don't want to, I don't know, say a prayer to Apollo or put down a towel—"

Drake does the not-listening thing. He takes my wrist and lays my palm over his pulse. It's a drumbeat, the swift rhythm of "I absolutely mean it, thanks." He tips his chin, exposing the line of his throat. If the ceiling collapsed, he'd still be sitting here, waiting for me to snack on him.

My lungs don't work, not even a little.

My fangs slip, sharp and ready.

He waits.

Once upon a time, drinking felt like nothing. Not real. Like standing behind the clear glass at a gas station, watching your tank fill, knowing the number's climbing, but you're not "you" for any of it. It's someone else. Some possessed version, mouth moving, body set to autopilot. It filled me up, but it left a bad taste in my mouth, like I'd just spent too much on too little.

This is different. Real. I'm here. If I hurt Drake, it'll be me.

"Do it," he says, voice the definition of wrecked. "I trust you. Trust me."

I do.

I fit my mouth under his jaw, tongue first flicking to taste, to savor, to make completely sure this *is* real, and I am allowed. My fangs cut in, slide in insanely easy, and the effect is immediate.

Fireworks. Inside my skull, behind my eyes.

Blood rushes into my mouth, and for the first time in my life, I'm not watching it happen from the other side of an aquarium.

I'm present. Hyper-present.

It's not just blood—it's him. Everything Drake is. The ache, the need, the intense, reckless devotion, all of it spiking absurdly hot.

I surge into him, draining deep. His arms lock around me, and I'm not perched on a counter anymore—I'm floating. Correction. I'm airlifted. Big hands clutch tight under my thighs as Drake draws me closer, like he needs every curve of mine glued to him. He keeps my face at his neck, anchoring me so I can take and take and take.

It's not enough.

My arms wrap around his shoulders, squeeze tight, then tighter, at risk of leaving handprints. Or maybe dents. Drake doesn't complain. Doesn't even grunt. If anything, he brings me closer, gives me even more, as if he's obsessed with the mess I'm making.

Neat freak Drake doesn't care that I'm sucking too hard, that fat drops of his blood slip from my lips, past my jaw, skate down my throat.

I'm slurping, body rolling against him.

My fangs sink a little deeper. His breath hitches. He's hard.

"Go on," he murmurs, voice molasses-thick. "You're doing so fucking good, Theia. Don't stop."

My heart explodes into confetti. My thighs cinch around him, ankles locked at the base of his spine, and I press down, crush him to me.

I drink until I'm shivering with it, still wanting more, needing more, when Drake murmurs, "Now kiss me."

I'm a moth to flame.

I don't think, I pull from his neck and crash my mouth into his.

His kiss is fierce and greedy, tongue coiling with me, his hands everywhere, like he's checking if any part of me escaped intact.

It's messy and hungry and so, so delicious.

He walks us, effortless, down the hallway, like I'm weightless or a particularly unruly bathrobe. I barely notice the change in scenery until my back hits a mattress and he untangles me.

The rush of air over my over-hot skin slaps. I groan, reaching for him, and then panic when he steps back. I shove up to my elbows.

Ruby-red drips down his neck and over the rigid brand on his chest. His feet are planted, solid.

"Did I take too much? Are you alright?"

He nods.

But he's not.

He's wired, alive, staring at my mouth, possibly developing a new version of lust, mid-arterial leak.

"Drake?"

He shakes his head at my worry.

"You didn't take too much," he says, voice rough, but not in a call-the-paramedics way. More please-do-that-again-and-then-again-and-then-possibly-several-more-times-for-the-sake-of-science." He skates a hand over his mouth, staring.

There's blood on his mouth, from mine. More on his chest and stomach. My hands leave prints on the white sheets, wrecking his space, desecrating the untouched.

He only looks at me. Gazes like I'm daybreak after too many lifetimes in the dark. Like I'm startling. Impossible.

Finally, he says, "We should wait."

Wait for what? Blood regeneration? A return to sanity? The sun to implode? Genuine confusion stutters through me. I don't know what world he's in, or what kind of patience he's summoning.

Then I understand.

"We've waited." We've starved.

Then he says the thing I never, ever thought I'd hear: "This scares me, Theia. I feel like Prometheus handed me fire and walked away. I don't know what to do with it. I want to touch you, but what if I get it wrong? What if I burn this all down instead?"

The truth rattles my teeth. The way his voice shreds itself on the edge of honesty. The way his hands tremble, not from pain, but from the terror of being seen. All the nightmares, all the Keres wars, nothing compared to the idea of disappointing me. Us. Now.

I catch his hand in mine, admiring the bare skin, caressing it.

"Drake," I whisper. "I'm not going to burn. I could never burn because of you. I am …" I'm a solar panel, a pizza oven, every weird and dorky thing that needs heat to function, and all of it is his.

I try again: "Do you want to let me go?"

He's braced over me, arms stiff, jaw locked. If someone held a gun to his head, he'd look more relaxed. "Never."

I card my fingers through his hair, up the tender nape of his neck. Watch green shatter and reform in his eyes. There's a war in him: fear versus desire, both refusing to yield. I drag my mouth over his, fangs grazing. "Then hold on to me tight, Nevro."

## 49

# Drake

### ORPHEUS BRAVED THE UNDERWORLD BECAUSE HIS HOPE REFUSED TO DIE WITH HER

I'm not new at this.

As Murphy's most vicious suit, power clung to me like cheap cologne. Women chased that scent, believing it might erase their husbands' debts or fill their children's empty stomachs. Some simply wanted leverage—to have the suit on a leash.

They never propositioned me directly. Just approached with chins high and eyes sharp, shedding clothes with false bravado, declaring passion they didn't possess.

As suits, we were told to indulge. Do the dirty work, claim the perk.

But the filth accumulated.

On my knives, my fists, in the grooves of my palms, under my nails. Evil seeped into my skin until only the most desperate women approached, trembling like leaves, offering flesh for mercy.

They didn't need more grime on their skin, so I abstained.

Then Kadmos came to me.

Now—

The last females I touched were Lydia and Nat. Their

fears manifested so vividly, I never registered whether their skin ran warm or cold.

No need to wonder what they felt.

With Lydia, it was failure. Collapsing walls, knives thrown at her chest. Her shrieking as Empusas dragged her brother to his death. Her body—mine in the nightmare— slumped on the floor, stomach hacked open, nothing to do but watch. Just a sopping mess as my family died in front of me.

Nat's vision was neater. Efficient. I stood over Sin, blood lighting the world like a signal flare. My hands came up, wet and dirty. The fear was cold. Absolute.

It blazed down inside me.

A hundred years I've been burning without any warmth. Without kindness. Only the slow accretion of misery, layering over until the only thing left is the urge to shield. And the certainty that even with that shield, I won't save anyone.

Theia wraps her hand around my fingers, and not once does her grip tremble.

Not once.

There's no fear in her, not even when my hands shift from her cheek to her hips and I haul her down onto the mattress like I'll die if I don't. She goes with it, eager, a laugh in her mouth as she rakes through my hair and pulls me closer.

No dread. No wariness. Her body is soft and keen, rolling up to meet me, frantic for every inch. Velvet at her hips, skin popping with heat under my touch.

I flex my hands, as if to prove I'm not dreaming.

She kisses me. And fuck, I kiss her back. Hungrier, harder. I need her to feel it. I need her to know nothing else matters.

I stroke her everything. My thumb at her jaw, my palm at her throat. I press her back into the sheets, watching breath balloon in her chest, full breasts rising under all that yellow. Gods, the dress only Theia could wear. Brighter than Zeus's gold crown.

She giggles. Licks into my mouth. "I always knew it would come to this."

Fate. She's a Fate. Untold power thrumming beneath her skin.

Fate wrote it right into our skin.

"I'd come for you again," I kiss down her neck, nibble her ear, "even if it'd only mean I could see you in this dress."

"Should I leave it on?"

"Absolutely fucking not."

She laughs. Breathless, star-bright.

"Are you sure about this?" I ask, voice rough.

"I've imagined every scenario." My words sound infinitely better in her mouth.

"You still have a choice, Theia. You're only half Moirai—destiny may claim part of you, but the Keres reject predetermined paths. You don't have to follow the threads."

She rises, pressing her forehead against mine. "I think it's my Keres blood that wants to devour you whole. The part of me that knows how to take what it wants."

If the universe has ever written a more beautiful threat, I haven't heard it.

I want her to say it again.

I want her so much I forget how to speak.

She rolls us over to straddle my hips, big bouncy curls falling into her face. Amber light from the bedside lamps caresses her, dancing over her brown skin like she glows from within, as if her entire being has a vendetta against darkness. Maybe it does. Maybe she was always meant to blind out the night.

Her hands plant over my heart, pupils blown with excitement, smile sharp enough to cut through realms.

Her weight is heaven on my hips, her thighs pinching my hips. I have to check three times that this isn't a trick, a hallucination, some mean streak of hope that the Fates are about to rip away the second I'm stupid enough to believe.

I summon bravery and reach for her, fingers skating down her arms, over her breasts. "You really want this?" I ask in a voice that would get me thrown out of every church in the city.

She laughs—not a giggle or even a gasp, but a real, unholy melody. "Drake." She cocks her head like this is the dumbest question a male ever asked. "If I were any more certain, Apollo would lock me in his temple."

She says it with sass, with the kind of confidence only the truly unbreakable get to wield. I can't help it. I laugh too. It's rusty, out of use. Catches awkwardly.

Theia stares.

And snaps.

She pins my wrists to the bed with a stubborn set to her chin that says *I dare you to try and wriggle loose.* I don't. I wouldn't. Not if the ceiling collapsed. Not if every Keres in the Deep Realm banged down the door.

I'm at her mercy. For her pleasure.

She's stronger than she looks, and I'm more ruined than I've ever admitted. This—the pressure, the pin of her legs, the heat of her breath on my jaw—it's so desperately good I almost forget how to function.

My mouth works, but what comes out is, "You can say stop any time."

She shrugs at me. Confident. In control. "Not in my vocabulary."

I do try to hold back.

But my hands won't listen.

# 50

## Theia

### ALL THE REASONS ARE THE SAME. ORPHEUS LOOKED BACK BECAUSE HE WAS IN LOVE

Drake's groan vibrates through my bones.

The sound is spiked with desperation and I'm tuned to exactly the same frequency, body completely in sync with his.

I shudder, one of those full-body ripples you get right before an earthquake. He kisses me, hot and unyielding. All tongue, all hunger, like he's been starved for this—for me—since Chaos emerged. He's frantic, bruising. It's worship that could be construed as obsession if one were more negative than me.

His teeth skate over my lip. Bite. I lose it, clutching at the solid, unbreakable lines of muscle on his stomach. His shoulders, pecs, the glorious V.

He tastes like blood and crème de menthe. I want to drown in him.

He groans beneath me, hands where I set them at his sides, a bit of torture for him. Because I know he likes it.

He kisses me again, hotter, tongue caressing my fangs. He wants bite or be bitten—doesn't matter which, because I'm doing both.

"I love the way you feel," I whisper.

His mouth claims mine again, tongue shoving past my lips, so wonderful and deep I arch, rolling my hips down into his lap and rocking against the hard length trapped beneath his zipper.

Pleasure soaks into my soul, finding broken cracks and breaking them wider. I bite his tongue, kiss him again, take his hands and lock them on my waist.

He takes the direction like a trained hound, gripping me tight enough to bruise.

The idea thrills. Drake's mark on me. Not the brazen seal of our Nevro bond, or our mismatched brands, this is private, just for us.

He tears at the dress between us, thick velvet ripping easily in his strong hands, as if he's figured out how to break the laws of physics to get to me.

I tangle my fingers in his hair. He tears my sleeves, pushes the dress off. I drag his head back when I'm bare to watch the green turn unholy. Sea glass under moonlight.

I expect it. Crave the look of desire. What staggers me is the simple adoration beside it. My heart clenches. "See something you like?"

"Love," he corrects gravelly. "I see too much of what I love." The pads of his fingers trace the swell of my breasts.

"Are you going to do something with that love?" I grind down, until there's no space between us. "Don't make me beg."

He bares his teeth. "Let me handle the begging. You keep sitting there like a queen on her throne, and wait to be fucked."

Nyx, I want him.

His eyes flash heatedly before he dips his head to suck on my throat, the top curve of my breast, my nipple. Kissing, scraping blunt teeth. I writhe over him, shove and pull at him.

"I have never feared death," he rasps into my skin. "Never

in any of the tasks. I only feared living in a world where you were only a story I tell myself to survive."

Big hands cup my breasts, callused thumb teasing my nipple. He follows with his tongue. A sound punches out of me, so hungry I can't even pretend to be embarrassed. He keeps going, pressure perfect until I'm quaking, legs trembling around his hips, thighs glued to muscle.

He lets out a noise that's part growl and part prayer, then nips, sharp enough to make me moan, before soothing with heat and tongue and more of those obscene, exquisite sounds.

He's as wired as I am—heart, sick-quick, pounding against my ribs. He's hard beneath me, caged by nothing but the thin fabric and whatever's left of self-control. I could break it. I want to.

I grind down harder. The thick heat of him right there. He can't even breathe. Fingers dig into my hips, hold me steady, and then he flips us so I'm caged under him. He stays right over me, a plank of muscle as he undoes his pants, kicks them off and follows with his underwear. When he's naked, stretched out over me, he kisses me. Sweet.

I yank him down into me. Every ounce of him above, around, inside me. I want to purr, scream, and drink him down until there's nothing left in the three realms.

He rocks against me, slow at first, letting it build, letting me feel every inch, his cock thick and splendid rubbing over the messy-wet heat at my core. My thighs clamp around his waist. I tip my pelvis, craving friction, rhythm, anything.

He slides a hand under my thigh, hikes it high around his middle. "You okay?" he rasps, voice a gunshot in the dark, so careful beneath the violence.

"Don't you dare stop," I hiss. "I want your mark on me. I want it everywhere."

He groans, and it's a sin.

He nibbles my neck, chasing pleasure with a sting, as his other hand strips my underwear with a single, brutal yank. I arch into him, searching. Wet for him. He lines himself up with me, drags his heavy, weeping head over my clit. My vision blasts white at the edges.

"Now, Drake," I beg, low and mean and starving. "Do not make me wait."

He fills me in one long thrust. My body opens, takes him, and the burn is so intense I cry out into his mouth, nails scratching furrows into his back.

We inhale together. And when the pressure subsides, I wiggle and he moves.

Each thrust shatters me. Every slam is a promise, a brand, a vow that I'll never be alone again. My thighs shake, my hands anchor in his hair, his name is a spell punched out between panting breaths.

Every part of me is humming, pleasure coiling into ecstasy. My body is too many layers of sensation, red-hot firework at the hinge of every joint. Drake pounds into me, rougher, relentless, the headboard hits the wall. His whole body cages mine, black hair falls into his eyes and I shove it back, needing my favorite green.

I want to bite him. Tear out a chunk and keep it for a rainy day.

He gives me everything. Plunges relentlessly. A snarl rattles out of him. "Fuck, I want to split you apart."

"Yes," I beg, sloppily trying to meet his pounding rhythm. I'd wanted to make him mine at our wedding. I'd needed him to fuck me when I drank his blood. Now I want us to make scars on each other, reform together. "I want that. Give me that."

He shifts, one massive hand clutching my thigh, hiking my knee to my shoulder so I'm open, laid bare for him. He fucks me like it's an artform. A full-body, symphony-of-wreckage artform. Pulls out, watching our connection with darkened eyes. I might yelp or push and he thrusts back into me—deep, crushing. My Drake, Blackguard, destroyer, my Nevro.

I try to snarl a jumble of *more* and *godsyes*, but it tumbles out ecstatic, broken up by husky moans. He bites my breast, my ear.

The noise I make isn't legal in two realms.

He grins against my pulse. "You like that?"

I can't talk. Can't conjure language. Everywhere his mouth goes, heat riots. Every time his hips slam home, I'm knocked further off my axis. My head is noise. My heart is a journey to the sun—with detours through every pleasure spot the Gods ever invented.

*"Yes! Yes yesyesyes."* I might be yelling.

Each thrust shoves me higher up the bed, until he's dragging me back down, back to him, always coming back for me.

I'm off-balance, exposed, all nerves, all wet, dripping for him. And he loves it. Palms my ass, lifts me off the bed to fuck me.

I want to weep. Want to claw his name into my heart until it beats wonky.

He doesn't treat me like I'm weak or breakable or naive. He fucks me wild and desperate and world-ending. A male who'll ruin me so well I'll thank him for the pain.

"You're here. You're warm. You're mine—and I am yours. That's all I need."

My body clenches tightly around him, for him, like it's a religious imperative. "Drake."

He withdraws from me slow, letting me feel the drag, the ache, the stretch. His mouth eats my every whimper, every moan.

Scorching pleasure wrings around me. When I think I can't take any more, his fingers stroke my clit, mimicking the circle that makes me break—he memorized every touch when he watched me in my bed. "Oh, Gods, Drake, please, please."

He loves it. His mouth is a dark prayer at my ear. "You want me, Nevro? I'll give it to you. I'll give you everything, but you have to break first."

I climax, clenching until my vision spots. Pleasure scores viciously. I sob, maybe scream, shuddering as he fucks me through it and follows me over the edge—that's what it feels like, the ripcord snap. Annihilation.

He groans my name. The wrecked, euphoric look on his face absolutely going to my head. He stays inside me, deep, come leaking between us as he rasps how pleased he is with me, how I'm a fantasy, how he wants to do that again, now, but he also wants to hold me.

My lungs are pudding. My brain trapped on repeating: happy, happy, happy.

"Holy … wow."

He chuckles right at my neck, giving me goosebumps everywhere. "You're perfect." It's almost a growl. "You're unreal."

I am? I am.

He collapses half on top of me, half to the side, hand rising to my jaw. Not gentle. Thumb swiping my cheek, as if checking that I'm still real. Afraid I'm a dream he's having.

I wrap him up, every limb, every errant curl pressed to him.

"You're warm," he says, like he's discovering fire.

"So are you."

"I kept imagining this," he murmurs. "And every version felt like a lie."

I smile against him, happy to be squished together. "Then stop imagining."

A laugh—quiet, stunned. The sound of a male who expected ashes and found spring instead. "You gave up a crown for me."

"Of course I did." I kiss him. Wait for his eyes to open. "You came for me."

A longer beat.

"Of course I did."

The quiet settles—not heavy, not fragile. Just full.

He kisses me. It isn't desperate. Isn't frantic. Isn't a male clinging to a miracle.

It's steady.

Certain.

Like something that survived the worst and found itself unbroken.

# 51

## Theia

AND EURYDICE SMILED.

I want to say something worthy of a royal wedding, an immortal vow, and the realm's best post-bloodsucking snuggle. Instead, what comes out is, "Do you think the headboard's still intact?"

Drake's laugh vibrates through the mattress, low and rich and slightly smug, as if he knows he's just made me forget every other male's name, my birthday, the most delicious blood type. His arm rests heavy across my stomach. His hair is wonderful chaos. Beads of sweat cling in the strong line of his throat, and his chest rises and falls—a little too sharp, a little too fast, like maybe I stole more than his sense of shame and dignity.

I tangle my legs with his and gnaw playfully at his wrist. I could eat my way up his forearm and never stop. His pulse kicks under my tongue.

"You like that, Nevro?" His voice full sex-bruise, full possession. "You want it?"

I want everything. The promise of forever, the glorious mess, the way he cups my nape to keep me from spiraling off the bed, lets me bite, drink, take up space and hunger and love without flinching.

So, yes, I want it. And that's the problem. Because as soon as I taste him—I'll be on top of him again, demanding an encore.

And that's why we've been in bed the entire day.

He knows it. Barely able to stay awake, but ready. "Drink, sweetheart."

"Don't tempt me," I croak. "You're not a God. Another round and you'll be a husk. You need food and sleep."

"What's the point of being immortal if I can't please my wife?"

*His wife.* I'm melting.

"Stop trying to die in my arms, Nevro. Want me to scavenge for muffins?"

"No. Don't leave me." Full stop. Commandment, not plea. He tucks a curl behind my ear. "Don't. I'm still convincing myself this is real. Don't ever leave me."

I would inscribe it on the moon. I would tattoo it on my eyelids. I would say "never" until my throat bled.

Except the door flies open. Zeke appears, lugging a ripped plastic bag, looking like a raccoon expelled from a thrift store.

He eyes the destroyed sheets, the trail of murdered clothing.

"Are you using that shirt?" he asks, pouncing on Drake's balled-up black tee like it's Hermes' caduceus. "Not to be cute, but I think I'd like to smell like you. Might help with the blending in. You know. Sense of smell is very important to them."

Drake props up on his elbow, stares at Zeke. "I locked the door."

"I got the key from Rune's safe. His password is just a continuously revolving set of zip codes. Too easy." He sniffs my husband's shirt, cocks his head, and wipes a splatter of green goo off his plastic grocery sack.

"Really, Zeke?" Drake asks.

"What. You want it back? Sorry, hygiene is a social

construct and I'm about to Houdini the fuck out of here. This mission requires stealth. Camouflage. Scent-masking. Honestly, you should thank me. They'll think Drake Cosgrave is running around in underpants for, like, the next week." He eyes us both. "They'll smell you too, Princess."

I blush. Then laugh.

Because it's Zeke, and he's got that look: gravity-defiant hair, fuchsia scars, Katanas on his back and orange-painted toenails.

Drake pulls the covers higher over me, green eyes all kill switch. "What are you on about, Z?"

Zeke rolls his broad shoulders. "I just need to stop smelling like me for a while. Don't worry. Could be a hunt. Could be a desert mirage. Who knows?"

I melt again—not in a "let's get naked" way, but in a "please be my eccentric roommate forever" way. I sit up, dusting dried blood from my neck. "I always say thrift is the mother of—"

He points. "You don't say anything. You improvise clutch idioms and make Atlas's left eye twitch with the force of cosmic chaos."

"Zeke," Drake and I say together—his a reprimand, mine impressed.

"Look, do you want me to fix the curse or not?" Zeke asks. "Atlas gave us missions."

My husband rubs his temples, the same way he used to look at me. "You're supposed to monitor for Argos movement. You said that. I heard you."

Zeke half-salutes with the grocery bag. "That was the gig. Except it's been absurdly easy. No hounds, no pitchforks—nothing. Which, let's be honest, is suspicious as hell."

Drake's jaw clenches. "You think it's a trap? Are they coming for us?"

"Nah." Zeke tugs Drake's shirt overhead, sniffs the armpit, considers. "I think it's like the world's worst magic trick. Look over here, look over here, and meanwhile, the real show's happening in a windowless bunker fifty klicks east. By the time you notice, the star performer is gone."

I raise my brows, buzzed on all the sex and blood and Zeke's brand of apocalypse. There's nothing like this found family stuff, nothing at all. "You seem stressed, Zeke. Do you need help?"

He glances at me, the scars down his face seeming to flush pink. "You never have to worry about me. I just have, like, twenty minutes to cross a desert. Or I'm already too late."

Chills. My brain tries to get its shoes on, to catch up. "The desert? Too late for what?"

All humor drains from his face. "For Meda."

Drake sits up. "What happened to Meda?"

"She was attacked." A shrug. "That's not really the problem though. It's the kidnapping that's the real problem. No ransom note, no head. Not good."

My heart stops, starts, and hiccups. Meda is the lone female of the Blackguard, the expert thief, the only person to ever convince Nat to wear heels. "She was kidnapped?"

Drake's on his feet, completely naked and bristling. He opens his dresser, takes out a big silver gun. "Tell us where she is and how we get to her."

"No point," Zeke says, taking in Drake's bare ass. "You can't help. If you try, it'll make it worse. Atlas will do his thing, and it'll blow up. Only I can go."

"Why?" I ask, heart racing.

He grins. "Not why. *Where*. Don't tell Luke, okay? Don't even hint. If you do, I'll tell you the names of your children and you'll never sleep again. Trust me."

Then he's gone, taking Drake's shirt and three golden buttons from my coronation dress.

Drake turns to me, naked, runs a hand down his face. "What do we do now?"

I shrug. "I trust Zeke. If he says we stay quiet, then we should?"

"Half the stuff he says is insane."

"Yeah." I rub my chest where something burns. "Yeah, but he's always been right."

Drake drops his face in his hands. "So we leave her?"

"Zeke's going to help and Meda's tough as nails." I feel sure about this, Fate sure. We need to stay away. "Come back to bed, Drake. Don't leave me."

He doesn't.

Of course he doesn't.

The second my request hits the air, Drake is already moving. No argument, not even a token protest about Zeke being armed with half our wardrobe and a possible death curse. He just climbs back into bed and hauls me against him, sheets and all, one solid arm hard around my waist until I'm buried under six feet of *I-went-to-the-sunless kingdom-and-all-I-got-was-this-bloodthirsty-princess*. My head finds that sweet spot on his chest, the one with the ridge of muscle and my new favorite soundtrack.

I wrap myself in him like a snuggly cozy blanket and close my eyes. We'll never part. Never again.

Still. "If you do want to go … If you ever need to, I'll be right there. Following. Like a doomed little fangling, attached to your shadow."

He huffs. A chuckle. "Not behind. Never behind. By my side, Theia. Always. So I can see you."

Oh.

The universe tips, the planet doing a happy pirouette around the sun. I grab his jaw and kiss him slow, smiling against his mouth, the full-body I-can't-believe-I'm-really-married-to-you smile. "This is it, huh? We're married. There's no going back."

"Yes."

"You're mine."

"Forever."

"Did you think this through?"

He kisses me again. Deep, drugging. unapologetic. "I cannot stress how much I thought this through. I love you."

I kiss him. Because I can, because when you get the prize, you don't just hang it on the shelf. You show it off, you climb all over it, you leave little lipstick marks so the future archeologists know exactly who conquered what. And when.

Me. Now.

"I love you." I wrap my arms around his chest and drift, half-drunk on happiness, full-drunk on belonging.

I kiss him again.

Bite him again.

We're together again.

And when I wake, ribboned in sheets, staring at a patch of chest so firm it should get fan mail, my stomach drops.

Drake's awake, propped on his elbow, watching me. At my frown, he frowns. "What is it?"

There, beneath my ribs, turning and turning. A grit of sand trapped in the engine of hope.

"I have this feeling that Meda's not coming back. That we're going to lose her. Forever."

# Glossary

BROUGHT TO YOU BY SIN, MALE OF INFINITE, DEVIANT WISDOM

**The "Who's Who" of Creatures You Hope to Never Meet** (unless you crave a good dose of danger and drama in your life; mortals be grateful for your mundane existence)

**Anemoi** - Wind gods, each micromanaging their own direction. Great friends to have. Never a bad hair day.

**Argos** - Hera's all-seeing, flying creature cops who have nothing better to do than keep mortals ignorant while simultaneously inspiring widespread belief in angels. The multi-colored wings are cool though—fashion in a world of celestial surveillance.

**Asclepiades** - Snake loving spa enthusiasts now moonlighting as creature urgent care clinicians that don't accept insurance. Because I want a python near when I'm getting swabbed

**Blackguard** - Fearsome warriors cursed to be

BFFs forever, because nothing bonds a friendship like an ancient curse with no take-backs. Formerly known as Kingsguard.

**Boreads** - Children of Boreas, God of the north wind. Essentially walking tornadoes, what could go wrong?

**Charities** - AKA the Three Graces. Inherently sweet-natured, inexplicably beautiful, and basically the living embodiment of watching paint dry.

**Chimera** - A creature so confused with its mash-up of animal parts that it went blind when it tried to simplify. But hey, at least it can still breathe fire like a boss.

**Chire (Hecatonchires)** - Pointed ears, ruthless style. Some attain special glamours with maturity. Skills feared by both Titans and Olympians. Endangered.

**Cyclopes** - Basically Zeus's biggest fans. Master craftsman. Used to rock the one eye thing, but decided depth perception was worth sacrificing edginess.

**Demigod** - Forget distant relatives; these folks are direct descendants of the Gods, no second cousin removed bullshit here.

**Empusa** - *Shape-shifting menaces with a taste for cannibalism and a mysterious copper leg that they're touchy about.*

**The Fates -** AKA the Moirai. Decide the destiny of all creatures. Piss them off, and you'll be living in a rerun forever.

**Furies** - These terrifying females are Hades's loyal sidekicks, armed with whips and ready to give you your first wet nightmare. Also go by the charming name Erinyes.

**Gorgon** - Avoid these stone-cold babes with green blood that smells strangely alluring. One touch of their forked tongue and you're stuck as a statue forever. Avoid. Next.

**Hydra** - Loyal to Hades, they block the entrance of the Underworld. Can regenerate any part of their body. (Yes. Even that one)

**Keres** - Vile and barbaric. Bloodsuckers who can't handle a little sunlight. Endangered thanks to yours truly.

**King Kadmos** - One great male. Descendant of Elpis, God of Hope. Deceased.

**Lycaon** - Elitist and nasty, and thanks to Zeus's questionable judgment, able to transform into wolves

**Maenads** - Extreme worshippers of a damn good time. Just be prepared for the roller-coaster of fun to turn into godsdamn terrifying chaos at any moment.

**Minotaur** - Poseidon's beefy offspring, half man, half bull, full time arm wrestle champion. *Sure, they're strong, but let's be real, not exactly on the list for phone a friend in trivia.*

**Muses** - Highly intelligent and creative, and not into monogamy. Double jeopardy.

**Nymphs** - Mortals 2.0. Zeus's way of saying, "I can do better." Includes: Nereids, Oceanids, Hesperides, Dryads, Hamadryads, Oreads, Meliae

**Oracles** - Priestesses of Apollo, who live in prophetic ecstasy. Which sounds fun, but I've never met bigger bummers.

**Pegasus** - Poseidon's favorites, who don't even

need air to flaunt their track-star skills. We get it, you had wings and hooves, great. Now trot along.

**Queensguard** - A squad of badass warriors sworn to protect Queen Vinia—why she needs protection when her biggest threat seems to be boredom—the aesthetic?

**Queen Vinia** - Kadmos's worse half with twelve kids to feed. Descendant of Hecate, Goddess of Magic. Castle agoraphobe.

**Silenus** - Mortals call them satyrs. Males that used to be part horse but are now just incredible horndogs. Not known for their personalities. Plural: Sileni

**Siren** - Killer vocals. Got fame convincing pirates they wanted them and robbing them. Now they're mostly on scamming second cousins on Soundcloud

**Syclla** - Breathe underwater, permanent fish breath. Perform vindictive low level magic. Watch at a distance if you enjoy petty displays.

**The Blackguard** (Formerly the Kingsguard)

**Atlas Smith** – Chire commander of the Kingsguard, clawed his way from the palace kitchens to the right of Kadmos's throne before puberty. No known glamour.

**Calydon Ivanovich** – Better known as Vlad the Impaler. Immune to any magics and godly powers. Skewered by the Queensguard while in mourning for the King.

**Andromeda "Meda" Porter** – Smuggling

royalty, bestowed with gift of theft. Keeping the skill in the family with brother, Leto, thief of the Queensguard. Because nothing says "sibling bonding" like a good heist.

**Eleni "Leni" Amiace** – A literal firestarter with the memory of a goldfish. Make sure your home owners insurance includes Phoenix related damages.

**Sinis** – Most handsome and talented male to ever be born of ichor. Remarkable ability to taste and influence emotions. Not only does he look good, but he can mess with your feelings too. What a catch.

**Zeke Wildes** – Part time Witchhunter, full time crazy. Gift of sight, though he usually keeps it to himself.

**Cross** – Gentleman spy with the gift of shadows that make him impossible to remember - perfect for those times when you want to gather intel without feeling guilt to say thank you. Beloved by Leni

**Lev Mikhailov** – Inventor of organized crime, comes equipped with the Gift of Wrath that includes super strength, speed, and the elusive mega-punch. Prone to a bar fight? Lev's your guy.

**Rune Elison** – Viking invited to Olympus for acts of heroics. Gifted with animal transformation because why settle for just being a hero when you can also be a bear or squirrel? Helluva party trick.

**Drake Cosgrave** – Executioner of the Irish mob, invited into Kadmos's favor for his skill in torture. Can read a person's worst fear with only a touch of skin. Don't shake his hand unless you're ready for some deep-seated nightmares.

**Luke Donovan** – Mortal and former marine. Proving that even in a world of Gods and gifts, sometimes all you need is good old-fashioned mortal resilience. Or maybe he just got lost on his way to another story altogether.

**Natasa "Nat"** — The most beautiful, wonderful, bloodthirsty Fury to ever grace the mortal realm. Desperately, almost humiliatingly in love with Sinis, Lord of the Repeat Orgasm

**The Gods of the Dodekatheon**, AKA the Olympians

**Zeus** – King of Gods, God of the skies
**Hera** – Queen of Gods, Goddess of marriage and birth
**Poseidon** – God of the sea
**Demeter** – God of the harvest
**Hephaestus** – God of artisans
**Athena** – Goddess of warfare and wisdom
**Apollo** – God of prophecy and harmony
**Artemis** – Goddess of the wild
**Hermes** – God of trade
**Aphrodite** – Goddess of love
**Ares** – God of battle
**Hestia** – Goddess of the hearth

**Semi-honorable mentions**

**Achilles** — Look, he may be beautiful and skilled in battle, but all it took was an arrow to the heel to bring this mighty warrior down. Talk about a fatal flaw.

**Ambrosia** — Drink of the Gods. Get a brew directly from Olympus and attain immortality. (if you can survive it, which let's be honest, very few do—fine print).

**Caduceus** — Hermes's rod. Not like you're thinking. Fashion forward staff of intertwined serpents and wings. Looks cool, hurts like fuck when it whacks you.

**Calliope** — Chief of all muses, though epic poetry being higher ranked than music is a laugh. Mother to Orpheus, and it must be a pain to be the inspiration of every sonnet and have your kid cry in front of Hades.

**Cerberus** — Hades's three-headed hellhound. The head bitch, and mama to all. Slobbery kisser. Persephone's 'wittle baby'.

**Chaos** — The OG cosmic instigator who brought life and substance to the universe's void. The start of everything. And the end.

**Charon** — The very greedy ferryman of the dead, waits on the River Styx. Got in early on Silicon Valley, has never shut about it.

**Daedalus** — Mad scientist of ancient times who took "innovative engineering" to a whole new level. Made the labyrinth for the Minotaur, Asterion. Also made Icarus's highly successful wax wings

**Drachma** — Currency of the Greeks. went out of style for a while. But gold always comes back in style.

**Drakon** — Water dragons with hundreds of teeth. Super aggressive and sacred to Ares.

**Echidna** — Half-woman, half-snake. Full fucking monster. Mother to anything you've had a nightmare about.

**Elysian Fields** — Resting place for heroes who went above and beyond. Six gold stars. Eleven out of ten. Must have ichor to enter.

**Eros** — God of Love, son to Aphrodite and Ares

**Fated Bond** — A connection between only soulmates in which the Fates tie your life threads together. Lame.

**Fields of Punishment** – The ultimate bummer resting place where souls endure torment to reflect their specific crimes. Real party spot.

**Hades** — God of the Underworld, who's not antisocial—just really bad at making friends. Wears too much black. C'mon, this is the dude Zeus is most scared of?

**Hecate** — Goddess of witchcraft and enchantments. Has a major bone to pick with Hades. Who doesn't?

**Helios** — Titan God of the sun, legitimately has the best ride in the universe, a chariot led by Apollo's prized stallions that pulls the sun across the sky.

**Heracles** — Demigod hero who ascended to immortality after completing his twelve (fourteen) labors. Despised by Hera. The movie spelled his name wrong. Oh and he actually killed that hot chick Meg—oops.

**Hypnos** — The not-so-lively Chthonic God of Sleep.

**Icarus** — Uber aviation nerd. Built himself wings and flew too close to the sun. Literally. Deceased (obviously).

**Ichor** — Blood of the Gods. Silver and thick. Poisonous to mortals.

**Ilium** — Original name for the city of Troy, founded by Ilus.

**Menelaus** — Sensitive king of Sparta who

couldn't keep his queen happy and sparked an entire war over her wandering eye. If only he had invested in some relationship counseling instead of swords and shields.

**Moros** — Doom herself. The most feared entity in creation. No jokes. I'm not making Doom angry.

**Narcissus** — The epitome of vanity and self-absorption, this beautiful boy invented narcissism before it was the reason your parents never call. Legitimately fell head over heels for his own reflection

**Nemesis** — Embodiment of Retribution. The original karma queen. Do wrong and she'll hit you harder than a Greek tragedy plot twist.

**Nyx** — Primordial Goddess of Night. Direct descendant of Chaos—yeah that guy. So powerful, she gives Zeus the heebie-jeebies. Mother of death, specialist in eternal darkness, and because she's a badass, avid charioteer.

**Olympus** — The highest peak in the heavens. Home of the Olympians.

**Persephone** — Goddess of Spring and Vegetation and frilly little flowers. Also, the Dark Dread Queen of the Underworld. Besotted with Hades and very fucking terrifying when pissed off.

**Prometheus** — Good guy. Creator of mortals. Keeps getting punished for it. Classic case of creativity gone wrong. Titan. Gift of foresight. Brother of Atlas.

**River Lethe** — Underworld river that contains waters of forgetfulness, can wipe any mind clean.

**River Phlegethon** — Underworld river of Fire, flows straight into Tartarus

**River Styx** — Underworld river that contains waters of hate, so menacing and dark, none dare touch it. Charon's post.

**Tartarus** — The deepest part of the Underworld. A prison from which one never returns.

**Thanatos** — God of Dying. A henchman for Hades with killer sense of style

**Titans** — Those ruling prior to Zeus and his Olympians.

**Underworld** — The place of the dead, as deep in the earth as Olympus is high in the sky.

# Author's note

If that pesky parent is on you about what this book's about and you don't want to plunge into the details of a Sad Boy Mobster$^{TM}$ thirsting for a Fangy princess and their bloody bed play, tell them about the myth of Orpheus and Eurydice, which is a *classic* Greek myth and note, because you're so goddamned *informed* (and books with sex have lessons too) that it discusses:

i. how love requires absolute trust for it to survive
ii. Grief is an emotion that *must* be endured, avoiding it makes it twice as hard
iii. Men do not need to adhere to the masculine expectation of being a warrior. Orpheus was a lover, not a fighter and became a great Greek hero because he was secure enough to show his grief and share his feelings
iv. Hades is a big softy who appreciates a good fucking tune
v. Sneak in a mention of Virgil and Ovid, who both wrote their own versions of Orpheus's tale
vi. staying away from fucking snakes

Or tell them the truth.

You read a book about overcoming doubt and fear. And it fucked.

www.ingramcontent.com/pod-product-compliance
Lightning Source LLC
LaVergne TN
LVHW041102080826
845145LV00007B/1659

* 9 7 8 1 9 5 8 3 7 4 2 3 8 *